RUINED EARTH

Michael Gilwood

CACTUS RAIN
PUBLISHING

Arizona USA

RUINED EARTH

RUINED EARTH is a work of fiction. Names, characters, places, and incidents are fictitious or are used fictitiously. Any perceived resemblance to actual persons, living or dead, business establishments, events, or locales is false.

Published by Cactus Rain Publishing, LLC
San Tan Valley, Arizona, USA
www.CactusRainPublishing.com

ISBN: 978-1-947646-10-0

Cover Design by Cactus Rain Publishing, LLC.

Published date August 01, 2022.
Published in the United States of America

RUINED EARTH

Michael Gilwood

DEDICATION

To my friends and family.

The funny thing about life is that
we don't know when or how it's going to end.
We die wondering.
S.W.

PROLOGUE

Sooner or later, it was bound to happen. On 19 April 1918, the world escaped destruction by sheer luck - it was a margin immeasurably small by the standards of the universe. Again, on 12 February 1957 and again on 30 December 2019, the world had a narrower escape, when the second and third great epidemics began their assault. By the end of the twentieth century, there was no latitude left on Earth that could be safely used for viral target practice. The human race had spread from pole to pole. And so, inevitably at 09.17 GMT on the morning of 11 July, in the exceptionally beautiful summer of the year 2026, a fourth pandemic bequeathed us with its might. Most of the inhabitants of Europe had undergone some type of flu by then, but within days, the flu went virulent and claimed more victims than the Second World War. There was an endless list of the dead. As fast as it had come, it vanished within four weeks. In Austria, it began to disintegrate the tympanic membrane, producing a series of ear infections so terrible that more than a million people had their hearing permanently damaged.

They were the lucky ones.

December 2032

The woman's scream was distant and brief. Steve Gotlar looked up from his copy of *Time*. He cocked his head, listening. Motes of dust drifted lazily in a bright shaft of sunlight that pierced one of the mullioned windows. The thin, red second hand of the wall clock swept soundlessly around the dial. The only noise was the creaking of his office chair as he shifted his weight in it.

"What on earth?" he said, reaching the door.

Out in the street, people vacantly looked around, and then at each other. The still-audible TV in the lounge switched itself off. It was an overly cool, beautifully clear Saturday afternoon. Steve wasn't expecting anything unusual that day; it was just another winter's day as the air hung heavy, inspissated with ozone. Animals sensed it first. Dogs barked uncontrollably at an invisible intruder, while birds flew in all directions in a futile attempt at escape. There was another scream.

❋ ❋ ❋

Mara and Steve had moved to Zacatal in southern Mexico two years ago. They often drove to village in their Volkswagen minibus to take in a movie at the Renois Theatre, and had dinner at the restaurant on the corner. They picked up magazines and paperbacks at the cigar store across the street from the restaurant. That was the extent of their entertainment besides a rare phone call and the occasional letter they received in the weekly mail-drop at the post office. Their house had one telephone, the line had been run at no little expense by Creighton Development, the company that owned and sometimes rented the property down the road. Their house came with an old-style television set, which did away with conversation and the ever-important need for books. At the time it was a questionable luxury Steve should've done without.

The journey from their previous home in Panama City had been uneventful; arduous at times, and seeing this landscape was a relief. Even the air was cleaner. Steve wanted their retirement home in southern Mexico. To him, the region was still virgin territory with peace and tranquillity. Damn noise. Steve was tired of it all. Initially, Mara had wanted to move back to a city, she insisted it gave her a feeling of protection. The more Steve told her that city life meant gang wars and money-hungry super companies, the more persistent she became. In the end she succumbed to his insistent advice.

Steve bought a house he'd found on the internet on the outskirts of the village on the forgotten side of a hill. He made an offer for the Gonzalez house, which was less than half the size of the one Mr Gonzalez had recently built, but was a dream home to Steve. Though not a mansion, it was unquestionably a house that said the Gotlar family has done well, has made a fine place for itself. Steve's folks would have been proud of him, had they seen it.

Steve and Mara dickered a bit but finally agreed on terms, and the closing was achieved in ten days because Steve was paying in cash. The transfer of ownership was arranged without Mr Gonzalez and Steve coming face-to-face. This is not an unusual situation. Unlike some parts of the country, southern Mexico did not require a formal closing ceremony with seller, buyer, and their attorneys gathered in one room.

Steve's new home had a private road. He was ecologically in love again, for Zacatal was not only admired for its richness and variety of tropical plant life, it possessed the finest multi-hued contrasts anywhere on the American continent. To add zest to the already underrated setting, Zacatal's picturesque backdrop was placed on the slope of a twenty-five-metre, rocky hillside and made even the most bored tourist take out his camera and memorialise it.

As the house came into view, still more than four hundred metres away at the top of the narrow and badly paved macadam driveway, Steve stopped the car alongside the berm. He sat watching Mara. When she saw her new house for the first time, everything changed. The thoughts she had of losing her parents in the civil war seemed to dwindle into a distant smile.

Steve slowly realized what she was thinking as she peered through the dusty windshield against afternoon sun. This lovely house seemed too good to be true, and she was superstitious enough to wonder if such a great blessing could be enjoyed for long without fate throwing in a heavy weight of tragedy to balance the scales. Mara was worried about her overworked husband getting stressed, maybe afflicted by a small brain tumour. Steve knew Mara was always concerned about him, so he took the time to carefully examine the place where, perhaps, she could finally put her parents to rest.

Outside, the house was large, with ten rooms on two levels, spotted with railed porches and balconies. Its slate roof was precipitously steep and decorated with the blank eyes of attic windows which looked nothing like observation posts in a fortress. The house was painted in reversed colours that one sees along the Mexican seacoast: predominantly sky-blue, with a bright white trim rather than mostly white. This gave it a rich and a decidedly sinister look.

The driveway edged the cliff from the moment it turned off the public road eight hundred metres behind, and it fed directly into the loop before the house's large oak doors. On the right, as Mara faced the house, the lawn sloped down and came to the cliff where it stopped with a guard rail. She could see a set of steps complete with banister had been carved into the cliff to give the people in the house easy access to the beach, far below. To the left of the house, another property estate, thickly forested, ran out of sight.

Inside, the house had five large bedrooms, four baths, and a family room with a massive stone fireplace. It also had an "entertainer's kitchen," which didn't mean that Hollywood elite performed there, but referred instead to the high quality and number of appliances: double ovens, two microwaves, coffee machine, a warming oven for muffins and rolls, a JennAir cooking centre, two dishwashers and a pair of Sub-Zero refrigerators of sufficient size to serve a restaurant.

Immense windows let in the warm Mexican sun and framed views of the lush landscape, bougainvillea in shades of yellow and coral, red azaleas, impatiens, palms, two imposing Indian laurels, and the rolling hills beyond. In the distance, the sun-dappled water of the Gulf glimmered enticingly, like a great treasure of silver coins.

As fast as it had come, the strange phenomenon abruptly subsided. Seconds later as the first sparrows began chirping a gleeful feathery turn of events, the ocean began to rise. They could literally see it go up. In two hours it rose nineteen metres. Panic-stricken, the population scrabbled for higher ground, they thought the rising water would never stop. They thought it would climb until there was no more land to engulf.

As the days crept by, the electricity gradually returned from government-supplied portable generators situated on higher ground. A newssheet was handed out containing photographic information taken from Reuters' telegraphic imaging library. The detailed photographs explicitly spoke for themselves. It was breath-stopping to flip the pages and witness with total clarity their closeness to disaster; their escape from total oblivion. Astrophysicists called it a micronova.

The article read: "Head of the European Science Administration, Doctor Malcolm Wilkie, confirms that the micronova was caused by an imbalance of hydrogen-Tritium," he says, 'It's a perfectly normal growth process that puts our sun one rung farther up the ladder of evolution. As part of the sun's surface disintegrated, it triggered gravitational variations that caused the level of the seas and oceans to rise. The water, however, will begin to drop in the next few weeks as the solar surface slowly restores itself. Gamma radiations directly emitted from our damaged sun have stripped away a large part of our life-important exosphere. A hole, the size of the Asian continent, will slowly swing overhead in the next few weeks and the temperatures will begin to rise a few degrees. We urge you to remain calm as there is absolutely no reason for further panic.'"

Nobody could honestly believe that God's capabilities involved inflicting atrocities like this. Simultaneously, hardened sceptics believed that the micronova was sent by God to clean up the mess people had made of the planet. It was easy for man to point fingers at the wrong areas. Idealistic opinions, hypocritical chatter, it was all gibberish; maybe their background was to blame. But there again, one doesn't just change what had taken centuries to implant.

Two weeks after the flood, Pope Venerdicto made an emergency public appearance. He flatly stated: "Man has raped our world from the beginning. He has extracted its soul and has replaced it with waste products stemming from the very Alma itself. It was in man's nature to take what was not his. We are only boarders on this world."

Pope Venerdicto went on to say: "In comparison to what has taken place, it shows our true value and worth. In plain language, in God's vast universe we are nothing. Esteemed brothers and sisters, every one of us must consider this as a warning. If we do not heed these unspoken words and desist immediately with petty scrabbling for power, the price we will pay in the end will be the end of humanity itself." Fear, unsuccessfully camouflaged by his authoritative voice, gave the impression that not even the venerated head of Catholic hierarchy had the capacity or capability of concealing his human side.

Steve remembered the bodies floating downriver, dozens of them, hundreds of them. It was the survivors' duty to clean them up, so between all of the survivors, they dug mass graves in Palizada, forty kilometres to the south. Twenty gaping holes filled with the bodies of both man and animal, it was a horrendous task. They had to do it, as the smell of death was everywhere.

However, it wasn't only the water or the lack of it that had slaughtered the people, it was the tremendous heatwave that began its insurgency a month later. As the damaged exosphere gradually shifted and focussed onto the American continent, it took three hours for the temperature to rise twenty degrees. At first, they enjoyed its touch, its supernatural power. They were used to extremes such as this. This time, however, the mercury continued to rise until survivors of the recent disaster began passing out and dying on the street. Its stroke was everywhere and there was no escape.

After the incident, television commentaries appeared, soothing listener scepticism while commenting on the status of the planet.

"We are doing everything in our power to remedy the situation, please have patience and stay calm! NASA recently launched a high-altitude balloon filled with a powdery chemical substance. The results should become noticeable in the days ahead, hold out as long as you can," he said. Could a simple balloon save them? Could a simple balloon the size of a bus patch a gaping hole the size of Russia?

"The helium balloon, once it has reached a height of 145 kilometres, will explode and release its cargo of chemical powder onto the exosphere layer. It will bandage the hole caused by the solar eruption and prevent the damaging rays from penetrating it," said the NASA representative before looking down at a notepad on his lectern. "If it fails, we will keep on sending them up until such time as the temperature does begin to drop."

Optimistically, Steve looked towards Mara as she flicked the air conditioner to maximum. *Westinghouse wasn't only good for their fridges*, he thought as the breeze whisked against his back.

✳ ✳ ✳

Later that evening, Steve drove into the village for the local newspaper. *The Southern Tribune* was government subsidised, and on rare occasions, they received it daily. It was dedicated to local and international news. Almost a year later, memorable photographs of the event still haunted them. A whole page had been set aside for Zacatal victims and events. One whole page filled with names, sometimes a photograph of someone Steve once knew. It had been that way since the beginning. There were no advertisements or recipes, no sudokus or crossword puzzles. The pages were filled with death and heartbreaking images of pillage and struggle. Frustratingly, Steve threw the paper into a pile and went to bed.

At four the next morning, Steve lay awake and stared at the ceiling while listening to nocturnal desert crickets. The raucous chirruping, almost metronomic, soothed his agitation, as there was a noisy one right under the bedroom window. Mara, not conscious of his insomnia, lay by his side. She slept through almost anything, and it was only when she subconsciously snuggled closer, Steve began to realise something was out of place. At first, Steve thought it was the remnants of a dream, a vivid beginning to yet another day; but as he opened his eyes, forcing his unclear piece of world into focus, he felt his arm down by his side under the blanket and not outside, as it usually was. Steve took a deep breath.

"Mara, wake up," Steve said, leaning towards her.

"What's the matter, honey? What time is it?" She opened her eyes.

"Don't you feel it? Don't you feel different?"

Her eyes widened. "What on earth are you talking about?"
"Mara, the temperature; tell me you feel it, too. Please tell me you feel it!"

☀ ☀ ☀

Eleven months before as the mammoth heatwave struck, a massive evacuation process began. In all parts of the globe, people were making efforts to build themselves shelters; some used machinery, some dug by hand. In many cases, individuals were scooping out simple earth burrows in the hope that they would provide adequate protection from the heat.

By March 2033, the water levels had subsided, and the world's extensive underground rail networks were readied for human occupation. In London, tube station entrances were partially bricked up, and planking was hurriedly laid across the rails as the 409 kilometres of tunnels were converted to house up to five million people. It was announced that when this enormous shelter opened, places would be allocated on a first-come, first-served basis. Many people began to camp outside the entrances forming queues that stretched for several kilometres.

In some cities, communities were banding together in an attempt to try to convert mineshafts into makeshift shelters, and in a few countries, governments were making financial aid available for these efforts. People used everything below ground level to safeguard their future.

Public order first began to break down seriously when the heat declined to the mid-thirties. Even in the most advanced cities, mobs began roaming the streets; and governments, or what remained of them, were forced to put their carefully drafted emergency plans into action. Police and military units were immediately deployed to protect the remaining government installations and communications facilities, airports, and other sites considered vital to the continuance of the national administration. In less-developed nations, those strong enough to withstand the cauldron during the daytime then had to endure the panic-stricken mass violence that was unleashed in their communities at night.

NASA had not sent up one high-altitude balloon, they had sent up seventy. Not only had man successfully patched the hole, he had over-bandaged it, increasing the thickness of the exosphere layer and preventing the sun's life-giving rays from penetrating Earth's atmosphere.

That night a documentary appeared on the television.

"Honey, hey, did you know the Antarctic has been reduced to only 12 percent of its original size?"

The First Cases

The documentary was interrupted as the brown, creased face of Undersecretary Francisco Morales appeared on the screen. "Good evening, viewers. We apologize for the break in the program. Earlier this evening, seventy-three cases of Ragish-C were identified south of Veracruz in the Boca Del Rio area, one of our most important coastal fishing areas. The seventy-three victims have already been transferred to the Statesport Sanctuary in Xalapa, where they are under careful observation. Veracruz authorities are working to determine the origin of the disease and asked that we advise you to be on the lookout and report anything out of the ordinary."

A telephone number appeared on the lower half of the screen in big white numbers.

"If you have any information regarding this incident, please call the toll-free number you see on your screen." The shrivelled mug disappeared and the documentary continued.

"What the dickens is going on?" Steve asked as Mara walked into the kitchen.

Quickly peeking from behind the door, she asked, "What is Ragish-C anyway?"

"It's a brain bug," Steve said. "Not your ordinary everyday bug though. I read about it once in a *Time Life* magazine."

"Seventy-three victims, Jesus, it's scary." Mara's voice was strained with concern as she placed a bottle of water back into the fridge and closed the door. "Is it contagious?"

"Not sure. I do remember that *Time* said the project was abandoned after certain never-to-be-named people mysteriously disappeared."

"Until now," said Mara's sarcastic, droning voice. "I think someone just ripped open your *Time* article again."

"Why would anyone want to do that?"

"Your guess is as good as mine. What the heck, what do you want for supper? I'm starved."

The next day it was confirmed in bold, black front-page letters: 72 Victims on Veracruz Beaches Infected by Ragish-C Virus.

The article read: "Early yesterday evening, Veracruz police patrolling Playa Norte came across seventy-three local citizens wandering on the beach in what they collectively called an incoherent state. One of them was Gerard Callais, a French oceanographer who had vanished yesterday afternoon. Directly after his wife filed the missing persons report, leads given by locals immediately led the police to the beach to begin their search.

"Gerard Callais went into the Gulf early that morning on his boat, *Calypso Venture*, and was last seen docking it at four in the afternoon outside the estate. Soon afterwards, he disappeared. His wife immediately telephoned the police and explained her dilemma. Local police found him three hours later with six others wandering about the North Beach in a puzzled, lost state of mind. His sister has put up a reward for anyone who can offer more information on how he may have contracted the disease. Simultaneously, on three other beaches farther south, another sixty-five casualties were found.

"Gerard Callais will be remembered for his contributions to science, as he was the man responsible for the recent discovery of the world's deepest ocean trench 140 kilometres west of the Marianas. The area known as Saipan Island indeed has become a legend.

"Doctor Slaven Kolak says the symptoms and behavioural patterns of the seventy-two victims are definitely similar to those associated with Ragish-C, but he concurrently states that it is mere speculation at this time as the biological results won't become available until morning. The enigma of it all, Ragish-C was last reported eleven years ago in New Zealand and mystifies him as to how it might have gotten here."

✸ ✸ ✸

Mara switched on the television in time to see a sceptical Veracruz town council bickering about what had happened. After closely reading Doctor Kolak's morning testimony in the newspaper, all they could confirm was that the victims were near the sea when it happened. The next day amongst the trivial programmes, small waves of activist violence started making the headlines. Desecration and destruction began to stick its ugly head above the mould again and gradually creep its way into their lives. Steve's fears intensified.

Steve's firearm was tucked away in a wall safe in the study. An early retirement gift, they'd said. Five years of horrendous service in the Panama government was more like it. That was nine years ago. It had become just a dismal reminiscence of Steve's military and policing days, nothing more.

"You never know, you might need it one day," they said as they placed it into his hand and shook the other. God, Steve had thought of those words so often in the past. Yet he didn't, he couldn't go down that road again. Brushing bad memories to one side like he had done so many times before, he punched in the combination code and took out the box. Feeling the familiar weight in his hands, Steve flipped the lid, and the laser-sighted Walther Mk II .38 automatic, along with five sixteen-shot magazines, each fully loaded, came unforgettably into view.

✳ ✳ ✳

As days surged into weeks and the temperature dropped still further, they found themselves going from one extreme to the other. By mid-April it started to rain for the first time in more than a year, and by early May, it began to snow. That was when more cases of Ragish-C entered the headlines.

"Hey, I thought this Doctor Kolak said it could only be transmitted by blood," said Mara, ogling the front page.

"It's not Ragish-C, I tell you. It must be something else. I remember the article."

"Well, read it again, make sure."

Steve stored his old *Time* magazines under the bed in a sliding cupboard. Yanking them out, he started searching for the article he'd read all those years ago.

"Here it is." *Time* magazine, July 2029, the smiling, furrowed face of Wally Banks stupidly portrayed on the front cover. Wally was president of the Amalgamated Amerussian States and had funded the longest ocean road stretching across the Bering Strait, joining the Asian continent to America, only six years before. Steve had the unbearable pleasure of meeting him once. Wally was probably the most callous person ever conceived, yet Global Nations worshipped him, saying he was something of a god. Steve flipped the pages, intentionally skipping the Banks interview.

The article read: "Ragish-C, is it a genetic threat? Artificially spliced structural genes extracted during animal research were found to produce a variety of Ragish disease after their hereditary character was summed and replicated with the messenger gene. Scientists call it Ragish-C.

"Ragish disease, primarily designed for bacterial warfare, targets then shuts down the central nervous system, completely disabling its victim minutes after inhalation. Ragish-C is a ripened derivative. Apart from it being undetectable by conventional means, the gas that transports the virus is odourless. Donned with the ultimate weapon of war, Ragish-C victims indifferently wander about with the lust to maim or kill other similar species."

"Hey, maybe zombies do exist after all," said Mara.

"Don't be silly. Listen, here's more. 'As far as the medical specifics go, once the infection has begun its cycle, the disease can only be transmitted by direct contact.' Imagine this: soldiers infected with the Ragish virus, they just have to touch the enemy or vice versa. Mara, read between the lines. What they are saying is no bullets, no bombs, no expense, and most definitely no evidence."

"It'll be quite a reduction for the taxpayer's pocket linings, don't you think?"

"Yeah, jokes aside, it's the same damn thing what Doctor Kolak says; it doesn't even mention the water."

That evening, the television reported another nine cases in Champotón. Champotón was a poor man's fishing village. Like the victims in Veracruz, these revealed identical symptoms. The more Mara and Steve began to think about it, Champotón and Veracruz, separated by more than four hundred kilometres, had somehow shared cases of this new strain of virus. They looked towards the map again and gasped. Their eyes met painfully.

"It's spreading across the Gulf!"

✸ ✸ ✸

An ethereal panic struck the coastlines as more cases flowed from the television plasma screen to watching, impatient eyes. By mid-July, the entire northern Mexican coastline was suffering more than six hundred cases per week, augmenting as the non-existent winters brought with it ultralow temperatures. An international alert came into effect.

World Aid Special Programme, WASP, donated assistance for immediate distribution in all forms. A massive coastal evacuation was called upon, and special temporary housing units were set up inland to accommodate the human flood. The newspaper was full of it. The news began from as far south as La Ceiba in Honduras, or as far north as Tampico. No one really gave a damn about what was going on until it hit United States soil a week later.

Ninety sardine fishermen were picked up by Corpus Christi sea rescue teams and were immediately transported to Robstown Community Hospital, where they were individually treated. The CDC by this time was beginning to show particular interest in the virus.

Mike Branigan, chief bacteriological analyst, a microbiologist, opened the door and walked into one of the hospital rooms. The skewed, yellowed number on the door had obviously fallen off a couple of times before. Mike had been chief bacteriological analyst for the past ten years at the Houston-based Centre for Disease Control campus two hundred kilometres to the north.

"Good morning, nurse, how's he doing?"

"Good morning, Doctor Branigan, his temperature has come down, his body functions are reacting to nervous stimuli, his heart rhythm is fine, and his blood pressure has stabilised. This morning he even got out of bed to have a pee without wetting the floor. The weird part, I'm not getting any alpha or beta activity: It's as if his brain is switched off."

"How's that possible? Has he been eating?" asked Doctor Branigan, running his hand through his hair.

"No, he hasn't touched his food in two days, none of them have. Since they were brought here, they just sit on the bed biting their nails, mumbling."

Mike reached over and began to examine the patient. "What's his name? Did he have any identification on him when he was brought in?"

"Yes, his name is Alvaro Ramirez," said the nurse, fiddling her thumbs in an anti-clockwise motion.

"He's a Mexican-born American citizen. I checked his papers."

"Good. Hello, Alvaro, my name is Doctor Branigan. I am going to run some tests on you. Nod your head if you can hear or understand me."

The patient lay there, quiescent and motionless. The unregistering eyes didn't blink; the mouth didn't twitch on hearing Mike's words. He bent over with his stethoscope and unbuttoned Alvaro's shirt, placing the cold rubber concave cup onto his chest. The moment it touched the hairless frontal area, Alvaro gave a slight sound of discomfort and twitched his body to withdraw himself away from the rubbery menace.

"Look how he reacts to temperature change. Have you scanned him?"

"It was the first thing I did when they were brought in two days ago. They're all the same, every damn one of them."

"And the EEG, what did it tell you?"

"Absolutely nothing. The resident chief neurologist is going crazy. There's no sign of any tumour and there appears to be no cerebral damage."

Doctor Branigan listened attentively to the heart thumping a few centimetres away from the warmed-up rubber cup.

"It sounds perfectly normal."

Doctor Branigan opened his black briefcase, removed a crinkle bag containing a throwaway syringe. Noisily ripping it open, he removed the syringe and extracted ten millilitres of Alvaro's blood for examination.

"I'm going to take this back to Houston for examination."

Doctor Branigan placed a white sticker on the side of the test tube: Alvaro Ramirez, Room 21, and continued taking notes. Reaching once more into his black bag, he produced a penlight lantern.

"Haven't you noticed something odd? He hasn't blinked once since I've been here."

Doctor Branigan bent over, switching on the powerful xenon light and pointing it directly into Alvaro's left eye.

"GOOD GOD! Even his eyes contract normally. Nurse, get me his encephalogram results. Hurry, I need to see this for myself."

Scooting out of the room, the nurse disappeared down the hallway to the information desk thirty metres away. The information attendant quickly handed over a brown envelope to her. Grabbing it from the attendant's hands, she ran back to join the doctor.

"Here they are," she said, gasping for breath and watching as Doctor Branigan tapped Alvaro on the knee, checking his reflexes. She was just in time to see the left leg bounce itself high into the air. Doctor Branigan stood there flummoxed and began scratching the back of his neck.

"Let me have a look," he said as he opened the envelope, carefully flipping through the papers. Alpha and Beta activity—nil; electro-cerebral activity—nonexistent; thalamus regions—unstable; the diencephalon is non-functional.

"Is there nothing more?" said Doctor Branigan. "From the outside, this guy is dead. Obviously, from his point of view he is still very much alive."

"A zombie or alien from space?" the nurse said, half serious.

"Nurse, get me the patient's transfer papers. I'm going to take him to Houston with me."

Visitor

There was a knock at the door. Mara got up and went to answer it while pulling her angora sweater closer to her chin. As she twiddled with the doorknob, the mercury thermometer neatly positioned on the wall clearly marked minus-five degrees.

"Who's there?" she asked, giving the final jolt relinquishing the door of its closed position.

A feeble voice cleared its throat. "Hello, Mrs Gotlar. My name is Bernard Rand. I would like to talk to your husband, please. I have papers for him to sign. I'm afraid he has been called up for active duty in Villahermosa. We are building a safeguarded city to place uninfected people."

The door made a click as the latch released the heavy metallic mechanism. The man who had introduced himself as Bernard Rand stood in the doorway. He was over six feet tall and resembled a walking skeleton. He carried with him a well-worn brown briefcase that he immediately began to open as he stepped over the threshold.

Once inside, he officially introduced himself. "Stephen Gotlar, hello, my name is Bernard Rand." The towering man came to Steve and put out his hand.

"Hello, Mr Rand, how may I be of service?"

The lanky frame positioned himself into a chair with his briefcase neatly placed over his knees. "Mr Gotlar, I have draft papers awaiting your signature. I have to get them back to the construction site this afternoon, so if you don't mind, just a quick squiggle will do."

Bernard handed Steve a file with Steve's name neatly imprinted in black ink on the front page."We know about your past military history, Mr Gotlar. We would appreciate it if you came back with me to Villahermosa to fill in large gaps on our building plans. Mr Gotlar, it is not an ordinary city, it's bigger than you can imagine. We call them DOK cities, Detached Occidental Kingdoms. You and your wife will be given a place to live within its walls once we've built it. You will be responsible for the construction of the perimeter wall. When it's completed in the next few months, you'll be in charge of security."

"When do I go?" Steve asked.

"I'm afraid you'll have to come with me right away. The construction has already begun. Steve, your file says that you were responsible for the Northern Pacific Highway wall six years ago. Its astounding design was the main topic a fortnight ago at a human sciences conference. The DOK wall, your wall, is a frontline defence; it has to be resilient and top quality. Gregory Zimmerman, our Director General, sat down at this committee meeting and discussed your design in great detail. Twenty-five board members sat with him that day, and they not only agreed to incorporate your wall design into DOK 16, but into all of them."

Bernard laid out a plan of the future city on the table.

Mara emerged into the dining room carrying three mugs of steaming coffee.

"How many DOK cities are there?" Steve asked, taking a sip.

"Twenty, they're identical. Each of them will be built between three and eight hundred kilometres apart. Each one is going to be permanently linked by digital radio and television. All of a sudden the U.S. government has a bad feeling in its gut, and these cities started going up a few weeks ago. They obviously know something we don't."

"Where do they get their resources to assemble twenty such constructions?" Steve asked.

"That's a question you shouldn't ask. It's classified."

"Sorry, Bernard, if my husband is being literally forced to go, he has the right—sorry, we have the right to know what's going on, especially these classified bits. Go on, spit it out. What are you holding back?"

"Actually, I'm not holding anything back. The presidential DOK, or DOK 1, is made with all-American material. The other nineteen are made from Russian material, which is as we speak being transported over the Northern Pacific Highway en route to nineteen different locations. Russia made us a deal we couldn't refuse, so President Carnell signed the order without even twitching a hair. We need someone with your expertise to make the best of these lower-grade materials.

"Mister Gotlar, there is one clause, you will have to come alone. Your wife may join you in three to five months, depending on how the construction process goes. Until then she has to remain here. Do I make myself clear?"

"I don't see the point to all this," Steve said despondently.

Bernard interrupted Steve as his face began to redden. "Mr Gotlar, please. Where your wife is at the moment, she's safe. In Villahermosa and Tierra Colorada all sorts of problems have occurred; it's a death zone already. Hundreds of infected are wandering about the area. If she comes with us, we'll do nothing but endanger her life. Grijalva River is close by and we fear the disease may be related to the river as well. Whatever this thing is, it's getting out of hand."

Bernard paused. "Have you listened to the radio today?"

"No, why?"

"The virus reached Miami this morning. Half of New Orleans is contaminated. The U.S. is going nuts trying to figure out what is going on. They've got their best scientists and microbiologists working around the clock trying to find a cure. They are saying it doesn't even need the water currents to flow; it multiplies on a molecular level, so they've begun evacuating all major coastal cities."

Bernard stared at the already creased, detailed city plan and began showing them in detail the perimeter wall layout.

"There it is, what do you think? DOK's original design came from textbook drawings twenty years ago. Russell Norris initially designed it as a lunar outpost, but President Hussein didn't accept the exaggerated budget at the time. What did he say? 'It's a staggering idea, Russell, but with our limited lunar budget, I'm afraid it'll have to be put on standby. I will study the idea again in a few years.'

"Norris' design was perfect in every way. Every conceivable detail had been neatly explained and illustrated. Nine painstaking years of hard work and it took President Hussein nine seconds to send him away, back through the same door in which he had entered. Twenty years later, we are going to finally use Norris' idea as an Earth-based shelter, together with your wall design."

Steve looked at the plan—delicately adumbrating passages, doors, windows, control centres, ventilation: It omitted nothing.

Another similarly detailed layout revealed electrical cabling and internal generating equipment. Six explicit, superbly illustrated plans, individually specifying its area of engineering. The defence wall plan was the first, and by far the most important. Dubbed as the first line of defence, the twelve-kilometre-long wall had portions missing. In numerous spaces, the words AWAITING INSTRUCTIONS were in bold lettering.

"What's this?" Steve asked.

"The construction engineers are waiting for your instructions to fill in the gaps. Without you there, they're helpless. It seems you're quite the prize."

"How high are you going to build it?"

"It depends on the quantity of available material. With the existing order placed by President Carnell, it should reach eleven metres, but we're hoping for fifteen. Just remember, if this wall fails, if it's breached, whatever we have on the inside won't matter anymore. DOK would have been built in vain."

Steve walked to Mara and placed his arms around her.

"Why, of all the people on this planet, did I have to marry an engineer?" she asked. "If you were someone else, we could sit through this thing and fight it together."

"Sweet thing, don't start with your philosophical badgering. If I had been someone else, we would've probably been killed by now. You know it. I'll leave you the Walther; you'll be safer with it while you're on your own."

Bernard handed them a pair of palm-sized video transmitters. "Oh come on, it's not that bad. With these, you'll be able to contact each other whenever you want. You will not only hear each other's voice, Mara will see you, too."

"Gee thanks, I feel better already." Mara's sarcastic stare drilled into Bernard. "Bernard, if you don't mind, I would like to spend the last few minutes alone with my husband before you steal him away from me."

Without another word, Bernard walked out the front door and waited on the porch.

"I'll be alright, darling, don't worry about me. It's obvious they need me down there. I mean, he wouldn't come all this way to just have a chat and a cup of coffee, would he? I will keep you updated all the time on this video thing, OK?"

They kissed and Mara gave Steve another hug for good luck. "You just remember, Stephen Gotlar; I want to see your rear in one piece when I get there."

*** *** ***

At times during the drive, Bernard became agonizingly boring. "You know, my father lives in Chicago," he said with a toothy grin. "Do you know Chicago? Have you ever been there? Anyway, it doesn't really matter. He contacted me last week practically ordering me to move up there with him. He's so ruddy terrified of what's going on. My sister is, too. My mother died of cancer ten years ago: God, I miss her so much."

And so it went painfully on until Bernard's blabber was abruptly stopped by their first road sign. Most of the time during his yammering, all Steve could think of was Mara gaining distance on him.

The National Highway 633 road sign was bent. Someone had obviously reversed into the thing after taking the wrong turnoff. Bernard suggested that maybe it was someone who had driven off in a hurry without seeing it.

"What's the next town called?" Steve asked.

"Jonuta. Shortly afterwards we'll cross Rio Tora on the Old Tora Bridge. Just don't get a fright when you see it. It's got a nasty habit of scaring first-timers."

Twenty minutes later as they entered Jonuta, a windstorm blew down the main street, making the council building's doors bang against the frame. Leaves and garbage flew about in circular patterns as an empty shopping bag acted the role of a windsock. Creosote bushes were everywhere, neatly lining the road where badly laid tarmac ended. Most of the streets were dirt roads that facilitated all kinds of absurd growth patterns. Within the wind, a fine dust climbed into Steve's nose and eyes; it was a nauseating, choking sensation bringing with it an un-fresh, unhealthy smell. Steve wound up the window and switched on the air conditioner.

"Where the hell are the people?" asked Bernard as the car rocked slightly in a strong breeze. "There were people when I came through a few hours ago."

Flies were everywhere. They buzzed in vast numbers forming patchy clouds of black irregular shapes in the distance. As Steve and Bernard moved onwards, a cloud of flies blew over and encircled the car. Their numbers were so immense that a few of them got stuck in the venting system as the car went down the street. Eerie buzzes reverberated from beneath the plastic grilled outlet. As one came into the car, Steve watched it land on Bernard's hand, sticking its prehistoric teeth into whatever available flesh it could find.

"Ouch! Christ, these things are horrible," said Bernard as the other hand rapidly came down to squash it. It exploded beneath the sheer force of Bernard's clasping digits making a small blood blotch under his thumb. Bernard's left hand revealed a small bite mark that immediately began to swell.

"You better suck the poison from that wound!" Steve said with concern. "You never know what that thing was infected with. There might be animal remains around here somewhere. Damn it, Bernard, what are you waiting for? Bite and suck like you've never sucked before!"

Shocked by Steve's tone, Bernard nervously bit into his hand, producing a deep gash. His face reddened as powerful lungs inhaled body residues the best he could. As he spat onto the floor of the car, Steve gave him a handkerchief and he began wrapping it around his hand. Steve secured by tying two ends together.

"Thanks, I need that. Damn, it really hurts."

"Don't worry; it'll be OK in a moment. Next time, react faster."

"Hey, Steve, what's that noise? Can you hear something?"

Steve looked at Bernard's expression and focused his ears. "What is it? It sounds like whining, from over there."

On the right-hand side of the street, a badly parked caravan with an open side door came into view. Broken plates and a pot lay on the ground in front of the opened entrance.

Bernard drove closer. A body was inside; they could see it lying on the floor with one arm draping out onto the step.

From the security of the vehicle, Bernard flicked the headlamps to high beam and steered towards the vehicle to get a better look. Four or five metres away, the nearly fleshless cadaver crawled with life—flying life. Human leftovers were avidly being consumed. A low-pitched drone reached outwards as a million flies ate.

"We'd better get the hell out of here. It won't take them long to finish," said Bernard, reversing the car and heading once more back down the street. "God, whatever attacked this town, attacked it with malicious intentions. I suggest we stick to our original route without stopping." Bernard put his foot down on the accelerator and drove like the wind.

Old Tora Bridge was wide enough to accommodate only one vehicle with a maximum capacity of three tons. The information sign, firmly planted in the ground as they edged forward, made Steve look towards Bernard. The bridge was intact and luckily short, but from the confines of the car, the creaking joints and groaning supports made the hairs on Steve's arms stick up like static. Steve didn't look out his side window.

Tora River was raging only a few metres below, so they crossed at a snail's pace. The moment they reached the other side, Bernard complained of an acute headache. Bernard's temperature began to climb. Steve placed him on the back seat and turned down the heater to regulate his temperature the best he could.

Steve turned on his video transmitter, the Model Sonysubishi C-10 Bernard had given him, and contacted Mara.

"Honey, can you hear me?"

Mara's well-looked-after, thin face came onto the viewer. "Hello sweetheart. Blimey, these things are amazing. I read you loud and very clear! Are you there yet?"

"Not yet, we ran into some problems. We should get to Tierra Colorada in about an hour. We came across a real nasty swarm of hungry flies in Jonuta. Bernard's been bitten by one. I'll get him off to the local doctor once we reach DOK. In the meantime, I'm going to drive a bit, so he can rest. I'll contact you once we get there."

"OK, darling. You know I miss you lots already. Make sure you build that damn wall as fast as you possibly can."

"Don't worry, my love. I'll see to it myself. I miss you, too."

✳ ✳ ✳

Most of the drive towards Tierra Colorada was flat and arid, with a couple of distant, dried lakes and riverbeds resembling craters. Uprooted, desiccated trees scattered the terrain in every direction. They'd been blown about by the frequent windstorms that came out of nowhere. Yet life, as always, had found a way to reconstruct itself as a few, vague surviving roots began to rise above ground before being smothered by other, stronger forms. Creosote bushes and cacti thrived in their places. Vacant space was rapidly diminishing. This was a private war between cacti and bush as both species grew in their plight to dominate and procure the next available patch of ground. It was a survival of the fastest. The eleven months of forced evolutionary change due to the excessive heat had brought along with it a severe, unnatural transformation. The majority of species had died, leaving a few ultra-strong varieties. Not only flora, but strange, deformed species of fauna began to emerge. However, the heat had dissipated, leaving a small number of disfigured classes of life to roam in their hardened and newly adapted environment.

Creosote bushes and cacti were the only forms of life they had seen since leaving Jonuta. Seeing Tierra Colorada in the distance came as a welcomed sight. As if someone had placed an invisible stop sign, both bush and cactus had come to an abrupt halt two kilometres from the town's edge.

A smaller town than Jonuta, Tierra Colorada had one of its streets bordering a lake lined with ice. Steve inched onwards in the already failing light of day. Bernard painfully rose in the back seat and began staring through the rear window.

"I'll be damned," he said. "When I drove through earlier there were people here. Where the dickens could they have gone? It's the same as Jonuta. There's not a bloody soul anywhere!"

As they passed the shops, another lake that had naturally formed between two mountains came into view. Coffee plants were everywhere; but once again nature had lent a helping hand, and a few remaining water-seeking roots had won the battle as tiny growth patterns were emerging through the fine layer of snow and ice. They had to grow quickly, because the advancing wall of creosote bush and cacti were only two kilometres away.

"How far are we from DOK?" Steve asked.

"Not long now. We've got another twenty kilometres to go before we reach the outer limits of the valley."

Steve drove slowly as Bernard and he eagerly looked on both sides of the street in the hope of seeing someone, or at least something, move.

Steve saw a chemist's shop. "Bernard, look, a chemist. I'll go and fetch some antibiotics." Stopping the car in front of Colorada Farmacia, Steve opened the door.

"Steve, here, take this with you just in case," Bernard said, reaching over and opening the glove compartment. He handed Steve a Taurus-made 9mm Parabellum. "Be careful, they're explosive heads. Damn thing will stop an elephant."

The sun was already in its initial stages of setting and the temperature outside was close to freezing. Steve pulled the collar of his jacket closer to his chin. The sky was a dull blue. Steve felt uneasy. He was armed, but an uneasiness crawled over his body—bad thoughts, premonitions, disturbed emotions, he wasn't sure which.

Pacing forwards, thinking only of Bernard's hand, Steve came to the chemist entrance. A thin layer of icy sludge had irregularly curved its way upwards against the wall. As Steve opened the partially shut glass door, he noticed the sludge wasn't there. Scrape marks curved outwards 90 degrees in the hardened ice. Someone had been here not too long ago.

The inside of the chemist crawled with a rancid smell—a rotten, disgusting odour. Although there was nothing there to perish except pharmaceuticals, death had been a recent visitor. Steve was never any good at withstanding foul smells, so placing his right hand over his nose, he used the spaces between his fingers as a filter until he had accustomed himself. Steve went directly to the sales counter, lifted the side flap and began searching in the semi-darkness.

Alphabetically placed white drawers contained a wide variety of packing boxes. They were low-schedule drugs, the prescription drugs were under lock and key towards the back. The simple lock under normal circumstances would have been easy to break if he had a crowbar, but where would he find a crowbar in a chemist? He certainly wasn't going to go outside and search for one. Without further hesitation, Steve pointed the 9mm directly at the lock and looked away as he pulled the trigger. The lock shattered and fell to the floor.

Inside, there were forty or fifty brown bottles with dainty, barely discernible labels. Steve loaded them into a heavy bag he saw on the ground alongside a battered cash register and made his way back to the door. On the way out, Steve picked up some alcohol and bandages and stepped outside into the cool, fresh wind.

Confrontation

Suddenly Steve swung around. To this day, he would never know why he did. He put the blame on Bernard's frantic expression as Steve approached the car. As Steve turned and faced the chemist again in the direction of Bernard's pointing hand, he saw a thin man edging towards them. Instinctively, Steve ran the rest of the way to the car.

Bernard had opened the door for Steve by the time he got there, so he reached in and flicked the illuminated lights to high beam. Placing the drugs on the front seat, their presence was acknowledged by the man's waving hands and flapping lips uttering silent words. Ignoring Bernard's frenzy, Steve leapt out and returned to nervously face the stalker.

For an instant, they were face-to-face, eye to murderous eye. Steve imagined he could smell his fetid breath, inhaling the very air that it exhaled. It was a man yet not a man, and Steve guessed him to be about fifty. He was bald with patches of short hair on his forehead. As Steve drew nearer, the voice of Bernard screaming at the top of his lungs became discernible through Steve's numb, pounding ears as a faint whisper.

"Don't touch it!" His frantic tone made Steve back away with a jolt and he watched the pursuer gain ground.

"Stop where you are, damn it, stop! I won't hesitate to use this!" Steve shouted, pointing the weapon low. The figure continued, so before he could come any closer, Steve fired a warning shot into the ground just in front of the man, barely missing his right foot. Dust and granules of ice splashed into the man's face, but he continued unabatedly towards his reward. Steve had never killed an unarmed man before and his arms began to jitter. Thinking only of Bernard's hand and the threat before him, Steve lifted the gun, pointed it directly at the man's head, and pulled the trigger.

The man was only ten metres away as the dumdum bullet penetrated his brow. The head exploded. He hit the ground like a sack of potatoes. The body slid backwards for half a metre before a pool of crimson blood began eating into the ice. Bernard got out of the car and stood beside Steve, holding his injured hand tightly. Bernard's hand had swollen more, producing a large lump where he'd bitten into it. Bernard's lips were moving.

"Bernard, talk louder, speak up!" said Steve. "I can't hear you, the shot I fired in the chemist's has temporarily deafened me."

They climbed back into the car, and Steve opened the bag of pharmaceuticals.

"Here, take this. It'll help you fight whatever it is you've got."

Low, heavy clouds were beginning to form. Bernard's attention steered to the dashboard thermometer. His face twisted.

"Rats, I think we're in for a rough spell. The temperature is beginning to drop."

Bernard knew the climate in these parts better than Steve, and even before the remainder of Tierra Colorada had disappeared from view, a mixture of hail and rain began to fall heavily on the windscreen.

"Don't worry, I'm sure we'll get there in one piece," shouted a reassuring Bernard, returning a worried expression to the hand.

Steve saw the pain in Bernard's eyes as he began cleaning the wound with alcohol.

"DOK is on the other side of that hill just up ahead. Before we get there, I must radio them to announce our arrival. They already have sniper teams shooting infected vagrants," said Bernard loudly, inputting a number on his C-10.

"This is Bernard calling sixteen."

The crackle transformed into a husky voice. "Go ahead, Bernard, are you returning with the subject?"

"Yes, we'll be arriving shortly."

"Good, I'll notify the major."

The absence of hearing had affected Steve's sense of balance, making it difficult at times to keep the car stable. Just then, a sharp pain came from Steve's right ear, forcing his hand to rise. Steve clasped his ear and a tremendous hurting ping resounded, making both his ears throb. As it subsided, the first jumbled sounds in almost an hour modulated themselves into his brain. Steve heard the revving engine and Bernard's groaning as he continued grasping his swollen hand.

Halfway up the hill, the car's headlamps brought back to life a couple of dehydrated coffee plants. The higher part of the road, naturally carved between two hills, veered upwards between sandy curbs, forming vertical cliffs dozens of metres high. The road curved hazardously before it began its subtle descent towards the valley, where in the distance the first hazy lights of DOK lit up the basin. Even from their six- or seven-kilometre distance, its prominent circular shape overwhelmed the valley. During their descent, occasional subsisting species of trees that had survived the cauldron peered from their hardened life jackets, gloating at death. To the left of the road farther down the hill in the distance, an entire plantation of coffee plants and rubber trees were unscathed by the harsh climatic changes.

"In the valley, the temperature had only reached a maximum of thirty-five, even during the really hot months!" said Bernard, contorting his face.

"Bernard, no reason to shout. I can hear you now."

"Sorry. Some of the plants here managed to survive. It's one of the reasons why we decided to construct DOK cities in valleys similar to this one. Not only are we well protected from Mother Nature's bad moods, in this case, we have a seven-kilometre all-round view."

By the time they'd reached the bottom, the sleet had turned into blotches of rain often blurring DOK's distant lights. *At least there was life nearby,* Steve thought. *Hell, if it wasn't for these distant, wavering signals of humanity, the blackness would've been complete for sure.* Feeling better, Steve turned his attention once more to Bernard and watched him silently nursing his hand.

Farther along, one of the sharpshooters, having heard of their imminent arrival, swung his dull ray and smeared the car with a hint of light. A few hundred metres ahead, the road neatly separated the tropical plantation Steve had seen earlier. To the left, hundreds of coffee plants flourished in their cold, humid environment as the searchlight beam flickered through their toughened branches. Hypnotised by the anomaly, darkness came upon them once more, as the branches grew too thick for the guiding light to penetrate. Luckily, it was only a flash, as here in the middle of nowhere, it surely would make even the strongest mind lose control.

As their vehicle entered the plantation, the surreal darkness had gobbled up the guiding searchlight from DOK; and yet even as they ventured deeper and deeper into this factory of nightmares, the gloom seemed to dim still further. Hovering above the coffee plantation, the majority of the road, and breaching part of the rubber field to the right, an immense fog bank was waiting for them. This mixture of hot and cold humidity transformed into lingering, slow-motion grey waves across the man-made intersection. The visibility varied between five and ten metres, so Steve wound down the window to get a better view of the road. Tilting to the left, he popped his head out and sniffed the fresh air as it sponged him in the face. Suddenly the fog dissipated, and the thin shadows produced by dim spotlights in the distance once more revealed the way.

"Like I mentioned earlier," said Bernard, "sharpshooters patrol the existing walls with infrared during the dark hours. If something tries to approach DOK without our authorization, they have the green light to shoot it. As we speak, ten pairs of eyes are on us. Almost there. We've only got one more obstacle."

River Grijalva was in full torrential splendour. The only way for them to cross it was with the recently built Brook Bridge, but as the metallic structure came in sight, distant roving car lights distracted Steve's attention.

"Look, that must be another Russian supply!" said Bernard excitedly as one of their distant headlamps stroked the car with a gentle whisper. Thirty slow-moving vehicles were making their way, following their leader down the slopes on the far hillside towards DOK.

Bernard added, "Most of the supplies arriving in those trucks are electrical products: computers, radio receivers, electronic measurement gear, electrical cable, and a variety of electrical accessories. They are the basics, the start."

Before exiting Brook Bridge, Steve peered downwards through the driver's window towards the river menacingly flowing below. It was in flood. Grijalva River had risen to such an extreme that its banks were covered by a raging torrential current. A foul odour rose off the water. Evidently, the tide had washed a dead squid or a person in among the pilings. The rotting corpse must have been caught above the waterline on the jagged masses of barnacles that encrusted the concrete caissons. The stench was so ripe, that the humid air seemed to be not merely scented, but flavoured with it. It was as repulsive as broth from the devil's dinner table.

At the bridge exit, a suspended red light, reminding Steve of an old '60s Volksie indicator, tilted upwards in front of them.

"Stop," said Bernard, reaching into his jacket pocket.

As Steve pulled up, a gaudy horizontal bar lowered itself in front of the car and a synthesized voice emerged from a speaker inside the wooden post flanking the driver's window. Affixed to the top, a camera swung itself in Steve's direction.

"Authorization number, please," said a voice.

"J537BR," said Bernard, looking down at a piece of paper.

The camera hungrily scrutinized them like guests to a sovereign ball. Contented, it switched itself off.

"Code accepted," said the plastic voice as the colourful suspension bar lifted itself into the humid sky.

DOK

From the security exit of Brook Bridge, the remaining distance of four kilometres was barren flatland. Steve saw what Bernard meant when he said that DOK had been purposefully built on this site for its all-round clear view. Drawing closer, the spotlight that had previously swung in their direction continued guiding them towards what Barnard had described earlier as Gate-A. Distant, scurrying forms carried things walked back and forth from one unknown point to another. Bernard broke Steve's concentration.

"Most of the surviving inhabitants of Villahermosa and Tierra Colorada are here. We've kept them in their original trades, retaining their skills and levels of knowledge, but many of them are going to have to be trained as everyday workers. For the time being, as the construction process continues, the residents and workers will have to look after each other." A smile reached Bernard's face. "We have our own gardens, too. When you get the time, go and pay the greenhouses a visit. They are quite something."

Steve interrupted Barnard's enthusiasm. "What about water? It's not exactly high on the popularity list these days. What about the irrigation and the people?"

Bernard managed a grin. "Don't worry yourself. The two-hundred-hectare site has water that is artificially generated in what we call agua-genies. There are forty of them snuck in between the greenhouses. The agua-genies suck our water from the humidity and nighttime temperatures, effectively producing up to forty litres per minute. Of course, the water isn't only for human consumption. It's for agricultural purposes as well. There's a large water storage deposit being set up with a capacity you wouldn't believe."

Bernard's description was cut short by the pain in his hand. Steve continued the conversation in a vague attempt at diversion. "Two hundred hectares. Quite some chunk of dirt, don't you think?"

"Yeah, we are using sixty hectares for farm and agricultural. Meanwhile, ninety are going to be used for our living and recreation purposes. Remaining space is reserved for medical, scientific and administration, as well as affiliated requirements like military and security."

Bernard's obsidian stare met Steve's. "You know, we are going to rely on you and technology. DOK must be impenetrable. You saw the plans." He paused, taking a deep breath. "DOK 16, like all the others, has ten manned security posts evenly placed and close to the wall. They are our controlling points, auxiliary terminals. From them we can monitor all of DOK's functions. We call them Security Complexes. Anyway, it appears Major Gossard is quite anxious to meet you. He'll be in the Administration Building. I will show you where it is once we have gone through the front gate. I must tell you, before I left, he told me, 'Bernard, make sure you get him here in one piece. This guy's an integral part of our survival.'"

Bernard's voice didn't captivate Steve. Bernard glared at his hand again. His stare reflected pain.

Sympathetically, Steve offered comforting words. "We're almost there, don't worry. I am sure the doctor will have something to make the pain go away."

"Blast, I hope you're right. Ah, there it is. That's the hospital."

Steve didn't look in the direction Bernard pointed. Instead, he looked at the swollen purple lump. Pus had begun oozing onto the car seat. Even while Bernard was in agony, he took the time to explain in more detail the workings of DOK.

"In total, we are waiting for four consignments of Russian supplies. The trucks we saw earlier on the bridge were only the second. They come roughly once a fortnight, taking almost three weeks to get from their starting position in Habarovsk in eastern Russia. Their journey along the way is full of hazards. I mean, can you imagine driving across northern Russia, over the Northern Pacific Roadway into Alaska, and then all the way down the United States to eventually end up here in Southern Mexico? Some of the drivers are going to stay with us, and I can actually say, I don't blame them."

As they neared Gate-A, they could see that more than a million hollow bricks were neatly stacked into huge bundles.

"Fantastic, isn't it? We make them here," said Bernard with a smile. "I'm sure most of them are for your wall."

Steve couldn't help but notice the speed at which the gate had obviously been slapped together and erected. To call it flimsy would have been an understatement. Clumsily extending five or six metres above the ground, the wood-framed double-door gate supported by the adjoining wall was literally covered top to bottom by intertwining barbed wire like spaghetti on a fork. Hugging the gate on both sides, and mounted on separate telegraph poles, two remotely operated towering spotlights shed a penetrating brilliance towards the outer zone, often forming an out-of-focus blotch on the hillside. Steve watched as curious hands on the ground moved the mechanisms back and forth with incisive precision.

A brawny guard observed as the vehicle came to a standstill directly in front of the main gate, two or three metres from a wooden guard hut. Donning a raincoat, he quickly walked towards the car, firmly gripping his rifle. Steve wound down his window slightly, allowing a wisp of cool air to enter as bits of fine hail and splashes of rain entered through the slit. At the same time, it revealed a pair of inquisitive eyes.

The man switched on his flashlight, wiping the beam on the insides of the car. "Oh, Bernard, it's you. Sorry, I didn't recognize the car. This bloody storm has exhausted me. They've put me on a 16-hour shift: lack of personnel and all that bull. I'll notify the major of your return."

"Don't bother, Simon. He already knows, just open the gate. I must go and see Quaid. Something's bitten me on the hand."

Simon rushed over to the gate latch and flicked it upwards. On both sides of the gate, the existing wall constructed from long vertical planks of wood immersed into a clumsy cement brick wall was waving slightly in the wind. Behind the flimsy construction of wood and prayer, dug foundations lay in waiting for something else, something far bigger.

"We had it prepared for you, basing it on your previous specifications. They were still digging it when I left to come and fetch you this morning," Bernard said.

At first, Steve didn't know what to say. "Brilliant, this will save us at least three days."

Bernard said, "While we are busy transforming this fragile shell of ours into a city, the sharpshooters I told you about patrol the existing wall. It's their duty to protect us while we work. We call them wall-stalkers."

Even from his proximity, Steve had to look twice to see them. One greeted him as he forced his eyes toward a badly lit section of the wall.

"Have they actually shot anyone in the time they've been here?" Steve asked.

"Five vagrants in the last nine days. Three of them were shot only two days ago. Steve, this DOK complex is the most remote of them all. To the south of us there's nothing, and pretty soon they're going to start wandering northwards, passing us by in throngs searching for green cards."

Bernard raised his hand and pointed towards a two-storey building.

"There, you can see it a bit better now. That's the hospital. Leave me outside. Doctor Quaid is probably doing overtime. You, on the other hand, need to get to the Administration Building over there." Bernard swivelled his hand towards an illuminated box-shaped building.

Steve handed Barnard the bag of pharmaceuticals and wished him luck. "We'll meet again in a couple of hours. I don't know how long Major Gossard is going to keep me in there, but I'm sure he has plenty on his agenda."

Bernard climbed out of the car, closing the door behind him, and walked towards the hospital. In the meantime, Steve gazed towards the Admin Building in the distance and began to excitedly glance around at his new and unfamiliar surroundings with astonishment.

Steve's first unaccompanied impression of DOK was the enthusiasm and passion with which the workers performed their duties. Bulldozers and constantly shifting heavy machinery relentlessly repositioned themselves to-and-fro, lifting and digging. Frantic shadows were everywhere. Some buildings were skeletal frames, while others had already reached roof height. As four-wheeled persistency slotted in the pieces of the enormous jigsaw, Steve wound down the car window to get a better view. Quite a way off in the distance, two brick-making machines laden in light were labouring. Driving nearer, Steve watched personnel feeding the machines with precise quantities of sand, cement, and water, while others assisted the vibrating mechanisms ultimately creating the brick shape. Finished building products slid down a transporting gulley towards a conveyer belt whisking them off into neat piles a few hundred metres away.

To the right, a towering mound of sand reached the base of a heavy-duty mechanical grabbing arm suspended in the middle of a flimsy-looking triangular frame. There was a man sitting in the driver's seat high above, directing the grabber towards the pile of sand. Although it resembled a metallic hand complete with five hydraulic digits, the grabber's swooping arm picked up enormous quantities of sand and placed it besides the brick-makers before restoring itself back to its neutral position.

Steve parked the vehicle in a vacant spot between the Admin Building and the hospital. It was a flattened area thousands of metres square, with white lines revealed by the headlamps. He decided to walk the short distance to the Administration Building in order to get a better picture of what made this place tick. Getting out of the car, he put some Gotlar manuals into his back pocket and sniffed the air. It was a cold evening, but at least the rain had stopped. He zipped his jacket and put his hands in his pockets. The clouded night sky brought with it a nasty low temperature.

Although many of the first buildings lacked a coat of paint, the basic infrastructure was already up and in the final stages of completion. Bernard had explained earlier that eventually every amenity would become available to DOK residents. Even a church revealed its soft illuminated spire from behind the hospital's colourless frame.

Workers were busy with the finishing touches to the Administration Building. As Steve walked to the entrance, the scenario came complete with two posted security guards wearyingly waiting outside. One of them approached Steve as he eagerly walked up the narrow pathway. "Are you here on official business, or are you lost?"

Giving a slight grin, Steve looked up and asked him his name. The guard raised his weapon. "I'm the one asking the questions around here. Let's see some identification!"

Steve reached into his jacket pocket, brushing off a few water drops that had accumulated around the button, and handed the guard his orders.

"Oh, hell! Sorry, sir. I didn't know it was you. Go straight inside, the major is expecting you."

"That's all right, soldier. Lighten up a little. We're all good guys here; the enemy is on the outside."

The guard shrugged and offered to take Steve to the major's briefing room where he was waiting with two board members. Taking his offer, Steve followed him up the cement steps.

"It's the last door to the left, sir. Can I make you a cup of coffee to warm you up a bit?"

"Actually, soldier, that's a damn good idea. White with two sugars, if you please."

The soldier strutted down the well-illuminated hallway as Steve knocked on the wooden door.

A raspy voice shot out, "Who is it?"

Steve opened the door and walked inside, producing once again his orders given to him by Bernard.

"Major Gossard, my name is—"

"You don't have to tell me who you are. Thank goodness you made it. I was beginning to have my doubts."

Major Gossard held out his hand with anticipation. He was a short, stubby man on the other side of his fifties. Battle scars were plainly visible on his left cheek. "Let me introduce you. This is Rawling Stanford, our electrical genius. Rawling is cabling the entire city. The video hookups and audio links between DOKs are his baby, as well."

Rawling lifted from the chair and hurried to grab Steve's hand. His firm grip and lucid glance didn't come as a surprise.

"It's a real pleasure to meet you, Steve. We've heard so much about your work. I am here to incorporate security measures into the wall: video communications, hidden cameras, and all that. Nothing fancy, but I need to bounce certain ideas off you first."

"This is Matthew Gonzalez, our electronics genius and computer whiz."

Matthew's podgy form got up from the chair and lazily walked to Steve. His perspicacity made up for his size as his hand reached out, taking a sturdy grip on Steve's hand.

"Nice to finally make your acquaintance. The chaps back at the lab gave me superb recommendations about you. I'm sure we'll work well together." His brilliant white teeth and intellectual grin appealed to Steve.

Major Gossard continued. "Our agriculturalist, Arthur Payne, is out there somewhere tending to a problem. He told me he'll meet with you in the next couple of days. As of right now, you're in the limelight. Every available person is here to assist you. That wall has to go up as soon as possible."

"If I may ask, Major, what's the hurry?"

"You haven't heard, have you?"

"Heard what?"

The major looked at Steve for a second before diverting his look to the table top. "The virus reached Europe an hour ago; Lisbon reported the first cases. The official Reuters broadcast said the victims started appearing out of nowhere. Within thirty minutes, hundreds were walking around attacking anything that got in their way. They say they have no fear of weapons."

"I know, I've had a firsthand experience myself." Steve jumped slightly as a sharp knocking broke the rest of his thought with the realization of what Gossard had said.

"Come in," said Major Gossard in a relaxed tone. The security guard walked in carrying a blackening, silvered tray with four steaming cups of freshly made coffee. "That's just what we needed. Thanks, soldier. Leave them on the table."

The soldier, disconcerted by the major, nervously left the four cups on the table and walked out, closing the door behind him.

"Now where were we?" continued the major. "It appears the entire Northern Atlantic basin is infected, and it appears it's only a matter of weeks before all oceans, seas, and rivers go the same way."

Major Gossard placed in front of them a detailed layout of the wall. It was the same plan Steve had seen in Zacatal.

"Steve, I take it you saw the foundations have already been dug? The reinforcing rods you need for the base have been specially ordered and arrive in two days. Once the foundation is dry, more than ten million hollow bricks have to be accumulated and stacked ready for placement." Major Gossard took a long sip of coffee. "We have ten brick-making machines working double time, but the bad news is our resources are already running low, especially cement. Ten government helicopters are flying in daily loads from Mexico City, but I fear they won't be enough."

"How many bricks are there?" Steve asked.

"A little over six million. If you want the exact figure, it can be arranged."

"That won't be necessary. What about the labour? To build such a wall in this short period of time, we'll need a thousand bricklayers working 24-hour shifts, let alone the cement-mixing personnel and the carriers."

"Our qualified builders are training another two thousand uncategorized helpers. As their training concludes, we will mingle them with the rest of the qualified workforce. This, if I am not mistaken, will bring our total to around four thousand builders."

"It sounds perfect. Another point concerning the cabling for the outside spotlights, video surveillance, and intercommunications equipment, have you made the metallic protection tube to house the cables?"

"Yes, it's already been prepared to your specifications. Once the foundation is completed and begins to set, we'll place the twelve-kilometre metal cable protection tube on top of the drying cement. The engineers will drill exit holes every fifty metres to allow the four sets of cables to run their course up the inside of the wall to their final connection terminals a couple of metres above."

"Four sets of cables?" Steve questioned. "In my original drawing and in the drawings I am sure you have, I plainly demonstrate three."

"We do, of course, know this. It's one of the prime reasons for us having this preliminary meeting in the first place," said Rawling, breaking in before looking down at his notes. "We've used a pair of heavy-duty green earth cables for the illumination. They were the only ones available to support the current demand. Can you believe it? Our government ran out of brown and blue?"

"I wouldn't worry about that, Rawling. It's only colour. It's irrelevant," said Steve.

"Well, I'll tell you what isn't irrelevant. Some DOKs have dubbed us as the cesspool, not to mention other unmentionable criteria. Two days ago, I contacted DOK 18 to ask them about their video reference frequency. They answered by saying, 'Hey, it is those front-liners, I wonder what they want.' Swines, you'd think they'd have better things to do with their time. Between DOK 3 and us, we get all the verbal crap. What the hell." Irritated, Rawling picked up his notes again. "According to this, the spotlights are going to gyrate on double-axis motor controllers manipulated either from the wall or Security Centre."

"Yes, and?"

"Nothing, forget it. I took the liberty of sneaking through one of your manuals before you got here. You say you are going put each of the 700-watt lights 50 metres apart. Don't you think they are too close? Steve, according to my calculations, 700 watts exceeds our necessary requirements. Honestly, don't you think you've overdone it a bit? If we use 500-watt bulbs, they'll put a lot less strain on our generators."

"What are you suggesting?" Steve's adrenaline began to tilt.

"Like I was saying, I strongly recommend putting in 500-watt bulbs, there is no need for more light out there."

"Oh, really? Tell me, Rawling, have you taken bad weather into account? Fog, mist, or heavy rains? Five-hundred-watt bulbs will have the same penetrating power as a flea's dick. I went down that road years ago."

Rawling stopped and reviewed his notes once more. "Well, no. Truth is, I never took the weather into account."

"Tell me, Rawling, whose design is this wall anyway? Listen, 700 watts is the absolute minimum. Unlike you, I once played smart and opted for 1,000-watt lamps and we almost lost one of the generators. We cannot afford mishaps, especially out here. Have I made my point clear? How many generators are there?"

"Six, they are housed in the generator room next to the Security Centre. Sorry, Steve, I shouldn't have interfered. I should have known better."

"Don't worry about it, Rawling. I think it's best we know and understand who we are and why we are here. Each of us is a specialist in a specific area. For those present with professional doubt, I will explain my domain. I am a Grade-7 wall engineer and security technologist. I have maintained that title now for almost twenty years."

"Grade 7! I had no idea," said Rawling awkwardly.

Gossard gave Matthew a blank stare.

"Remember, I know what has to be done. I can expect, and only expect, mutual support from everyone, and that goes for the cleaning staff as well." Steve breathed deeply.

Gossard and Matthew during the entire scene never uttered a word.

"What about communications?" Steve asked, giving Rawling a one-lipped smile. He halted briefly for an extra second before continuing. It was during that second that Steve paused his anger. He had only just met the guy. *Calm down*, he thought.

Rawling answered, "The second set of yellow cables is to relay the inter-communication signals to the Security Centre and Security Complexes. Each simple wall-mounted bi-directional microphone-speaker system will be placed fifty metres apart for constant communication. The wall-stalkers are to warn us if they spot an enemy. It is one of their many duties.

"The third set of cables transmits video signals from the remotely controlled video cameras, both inside the complex and out. Security Centre will see and hear everything that goes on. From the control room, operators will be able to zoom and focus, even record images for future analysis. It is these video cables that will contain the digital controlling signals for the lights and communicators."

Steve was intrigued by Rawling's comeback.

Rawling continued. "Now let me explain what I am sure will fascinate you. We want to incorporate into your wall design a device we call a Light Shaper, or Light Super-Heated Active Plasma Radiation unit. It will produce an imperceptible, impenetrable shield on top of the entire complex, something like an invisible roof. It will allow in the heat from the sun, light from the moon; even fresh air will flow through its invisible shell. Once it's operational, a dim green phosphorescent glow, visible only during the nocturnal hours, will swim over our heads."

"What are these projectors like? Are they going to interfere with the structure?" asked Steve.

Rawling lifted a telephone. "Bring in the dummy, please."

He paused a second before taking a long gulp of warm coffee. "No, they won't interfere with your wall, not in the least. We need to make allowance for them on the upper-floor level of your wall design. The idea we have in mind is to mount them on separate reinforced, supporting posts above the wall-stalkers' heads. It won't obstruct their view, but would be fatal if one of them touched it. These fifty intelligent, all-spanning, all-protecting Light Shapers make our only exit-entrance through the three front gates. Luckily, your wall design has allowed us to make the entrances big enough to allow any land vehicle to enter with ease."

A man entered the room holding a large cardboard box. Placing it in front of Rawling, he rapidly ripped through the tape and produced a plastic oblong object. Rawling took it out of the man's hands and positioned it on the table in front of Steve.

"Here it is, the nonfunctional prototype of the Light Shaper. The real thing is six times larger than this plastic dummy. At least it'll give you an accurate idea of what I have in mind."

It looked like a video projector Steve had seen in the Tate Technological Museum in London, seven years before. It was a rectangular black box with a lens protruding from the front. It seemed antiquated.

"How does it work?" asked Steve.

"Each pair of Light Shapers will face one another from their four-kilometre distance. They project a beam of high-intensity ion plasma inclined at five degrees directly into the sky. The two beams will meet somewhere in the middle over our heads, forming a blanket of impenetrable bliss."

"Then, what about safety features? What if a light fails or if one goes kaput? Will rain get inside?"

"Steve, Steve, one question at a time, if you please. I admire your tenacity. Firstly, they are hermetically sealed, protecting the delicate electronics against moisture. Each Light Shaper has a battery backup system that enables it to last ten minutes longer while the auxiliary support generators come into action. DOK will be totally protected with just ten pairs of Light Shapers. We are putting up twenty-five pairs to overdo it, and in case some of them do fail. If, and I state if, under extreme circumstances a Light Shaper breaks down, the one alongside will automatically begin to work in its place, capturing the lost field." Rawling took a gulp and finished the cup of coffee. "What do you think?"

"Well, like you said earlier, it's Intriguing. I would like to see them in action. Tell me more about the DOK audio-video interlinks," said Steve.

"Each DOK city has six independent remotely operated cameras placed on twenty-metre poles. From here, or any DOK, we can manoeuvre, focus, and zoom them in any direction we choose. Norris' design originally had three in the main yard. We placed one outside the Security Centre. The other three are on the inside of each wall gate. We will be their eyes as they, in turn, will be ours. DOK 16 was the sixteenth city to begin construction and doesn't necessarily go by destination, which I am sure you previously thought."

Steve felt his C-10 vibrate. "Will you excuse me, gentlemen? My wife is trying to reach me. May I have a moment alone with her, please?"

"Of course," said Gossard as he and the others rose from their chairs. As they disappeared into what Steve presumed to be the kitchen, he pressed the receive button.

"Hi, sweet pea, how are you doing?" said Steve.

"Well, it's nice to see you are still in one piece. I thought you were going to give me a buzz once you got there. Thanks for making me wait!"

"Now don't you start. As soon as we arrived I dropped Bernard off at the hospital. The thing that stung him in the hand left some poison behind and it began to swell. Straight afterwards, I came here and started the meeting with Major Gossard. We begin construction of the wall in two days, once the remainder of the foundation reinforcement arrives. Are you all right?"

"Of course, I'm OK," replied Mara. "I just miss you like hell. You know, it's the first time we've been separated in our fourteen years of matrimonial bliss. The only thing I can think of doing is being there with you and helping."

"I know, baby. Just be strong and look after yourself. Don't worry. We'll be together before you can really start to miss me. Gossard told me the virus hit Europe a short while ago. This thing is spreading like crazy. Don't touch the water for anything. Use the water reserves I stacked in the shed. Make it stretch for as long as possible."

"When do I hear from you next? God, I hate this anticipation."

"I'll contact you at least once a day. I will call you when I have some free time on my hands. Right now, I have a wall to build. I'll contact you tomorrow, OK?"

"All right, husband. Love you and think of you all the time."

"Likewise, wife. Until tomorrow then."

Mara's face disappeared from the viewer, and Steve gently rubbed it with his fingertips, thinking of her alone in Zacatal. The major's excited voice and laughter of the others rushed from the kitchen door when Steve opened it.

"All done are we, Steve? How is Mara holding out?"

"As well as can be expected, I suppose."

"You must realise we did it for her own safety. If you want, I'll send someone to watch over her while you work. It might help you concentrate."

"Major, that's actually not a bad idea. I'll contact her tomorrow and tell her the good news."

"Excellent, I'll see to it right away then."

Steve sat down in the chair. Matthew wasn't far behind, with a grin that stretched all the way back to the kitchen door.

"Damn, at least someone can smile in all this. Where do you fit into the picture?" said Steve.

The grin disappeared. "I began the Light Shaper design over two years ago. I was grinning because I'm going to finally use them for everyone's benefit. One day, if you come down to the lab, I'll show you how they work. I'll even show you how they've evolved and the phases that went into their design. I am here to ensure that the video signals from our six external surveillance cameras are sent and received properly. I'm hoping the same enthusiasm exists in the other DOK cities. On the other side of the fence, I am programming a variety of plasma weapons for our soldiers, including, and may I keenly add, the only surviving helicopter in these parts. It's a Ka-58. She's a magnificent bit of machinery. Decoding telemetric and telegraphic transmissions, repairing computer systems, installing electrical equipment, undertaking regular maintenance checks of the agua-genies, and reserve tanks. That's roughly it."

A silence fell into the room.

"Who cooks and cleans around here? And where can I get my laundry done?" said Steve.

Gossard laughed. "Seven chefs work ten hours a day preparing our food. Yesterday, fresh peas appeared on the menu. We try to give everyone the best possible dietary intake, good quantities of artificial protein, vitamins, and nourishment. Arthur Payne is planting beans in the greenhouses, as the outside is still too cold for them to grow properly. A week ago, two farmers from Villahermosa brought with them their entire herd of forty cows and two bulls. Presently we are using them for milk, but once they settle down and their numbers increase, I am sure we will have meat every now and then. In relevance to your other question, unfortunately it's a two-week wait before you can do the laundry; the Council Building isn't finished yet. In the meantime, there's a multiuse, all-function, good old-fashioned plastic bucket and soap in the Administration Building toilet. Anyway, before I adjourn, tomorrow morning we are moving mounds of bricks close to the foundation as they come off the brick-making machines. Once the tubing arrives the day after, we can start filling in the hole. Steve, I think it's best you explain that part." Gossard steered his head in Steve's direction.

"Thanks, Major. Thanks to the low outside temperature, the cement will set slower. We'll have to pay extra attention to the drying foundation throughout the seven-day period."

Steve rose from his chair and handed out creased, simple two-paged brochures he had stashed in his rear pocket.

"If cracks do appear, they have to be corrected immediately. The entire surface is to be scrutinised. The foundation is the most important part of the wall. Before you are simplified copies of the Gotlar Foundation Guide, it explains cracks. It is a do's and don'ts manual. In there you will find how to deal with a crack, prevention, and remedying procedures. It explains where the little sods come from. Read it carefully and pass on its contents to the workers.

"Secondly, the order in which we insert the materials is of vital importance. In two days when the Russian consignment of metal tubes arrives, it has to go on top of a moist foundation base.

"Major, it's only a suggestion: We are going to need a lot of water. Can the agua-genies re-route their output directly into the foundation to keep it moist?"

"Yes, I will make the necessary arrangements right away."

"Good. It may be wise to leave it running directly into the foundation until the metal arrives. We can't afford any dry spots. Rule number one: Where there's a dry bit, there's a crack. I will not explain the consequences. Once the metal is in, it must be compacted. Another point, Major: I suggest we send out search parties to look for bits of scrap metal in the nearby villages. Metal rods will be particularly useful, as they expand and contract easier, making the foundation more flexible under strain. Once the rocks go in, after the metal has been compacted, we can start pouring in the cement mixed with fine stone. I have opted for a reasonably strong mixture in the base. So, Major, if you can organise more cement, it would be highly appreciated."

"I will see what I can do," said Gossard, scribbling notes.

"After that, we wait, and keep the cement as wet as possible. As the foundation begins to harden in four to five days, the workers can position the metallic tube on top of the cement in wait for the cables. Remember, we have to wait the full seven days before laying the bricks. It's the most critical time of all."

Gossard intervened. "Thanks, Steve, one more thing before you go: While the workers are building your house, you can stay here in one of the offices. I've had one furnished for you. It's a bit cold, but at least you'll be under cover and safe."

"Thank you, Major, that's kind of you."

✳ ✳ ✳

The same day the Russian consignment of scrap arrived, retrieval parties were sent to nearby Villahermosa to recover any scrap metal they found. Not only had they discovered almost sixty tons of useable metal, two hundred survivors came back with them. As soon as the metal went in, Steve gave the green light to throw in the rocks.

"This wall isn't going to move, even during an earthquake high on the Richter scale," said a passing worker, looking down at the work of art beneath his feet.

Almost seven million, double-sized hollow bricks were stacked into piles and awaited the day as more and more came off the fabrication line. Two of the brick-making machines had broken, and so another two were ordered from DOK 11 outside Mexico City.

"A month! We can't wait that long. I don't care if their stocks are low. Get Matthew over there to fix those bloody machines!" said Gossard angrily over the communicator.

As water flowed onto the foundation, the tens of thousands of litres they'd conserved in the reserve tanks for this purpose were depleted, and they started using the water from the main tank. More than two thousand mixing personnel waited on portable radios to receive their orders from Steve after his final inspection.

"Three, two, one. Pour."

Hundreds of mixing personnel around the perimeter of DOK 16 simultaneously poured the cement onto the rocks. It took four hours to fill the hole. Four hours of frantic, continuous mixing until the cement finally reached surface level. Prodders came and began sticking the wet cement with long rods to ensure the cement penetrated deep under the rocks. Then they began with the levelling out and the surface preparation for the first layer of bricks. The foundation was ready, but they still had to keep it as wet as possible. Every inch had to be continuously inspected for cracks. They put anything they could find that was long enough on top to protect it from the freezing nocturnal temperatures. This included old blankets, carpets, planks of wood. Facedown tables daintily dotted the surface. Someone had put military-grade cellophane across some sections. It was a crucial moment, and whatever protection anyone could offer was welcome.

✳ ✳ ✳

The seven-day wait had begun. It was a week that none of them would ever forget. In those scant seven days, the virus had completely breached the Atlantic and had initiated its unhurried path upwards into the Indian Ocean after brushing past the southern tip of Africa, leaving a trail of madness. People scoffed at the idea of a water virus circumnavigating the world. They thought it was a hoax, a bad joke. In Durban, South Africa, large groups of hoax-virus fans and admirers waited. Even a fake-virus welcoming party was held, complete with a beach braaivleis. Protestors lined the streets condemning further science investigations, while parades of angry people disregarded the fact that their lives were in danger. By early morning, infuriated banner holders continued chastising those responsible for initiating "rumours," but by then it was already too late. Anyone who had been near the beach that night was infected, and statistical numbers grew at a logarithmically, uncontrollable rate. After brushing past South Africa and heading eastwards towards the Seychelles, the eastern rim of Africa and India hopelessly waited as a mass swarm of people inclined for survival stampeded for higher ground. While all this was happening, the other wave had made its way south, passing the Falklands and eventually washing westwards towards a waiting, utterly immense and defenceless Pacific Basin. Scientists predicted it would take two months before they met somewhere in the middle: somewhere on the Australian coastline.

The two viral strains were subjected to different temperatures and dissimilar current conditions along their routes. Tropical waters had developed a less-virulent strain, whereas the colder water had metamorphosed itself into a malignant variety of the virus. Scientists named them Ragish-D and Ragish-E.

The South Africans had neither the time nor the resources to build DOK cities. Detected radio broadcasts revealed that South Africans infected by the bacteria reacted differently from people infected in Panama. Although medical specifics were never mentioned or made public, they just stated that the Americans infected seemed to walk quicker.

It was also during those seven unforgettable days that Quaid released Bernard from intensive isolation after a strict examination. Because of his strange condition, Quaid preferred keeping him under careful watch within the hospital walls for further scrutiny.

On the fifth morning, the twelve-kilometre metallic shielding pipe was neatly laid on top of the hardening cement floor, and one hundred kilometres of cables were fed into their permanent home to wait for their final connection in the forthcoming weeks.

It was during those seven days that another seven loads of cement arrived by helicopters from Mexico City. Most of it was stacked under moisture-free, temporary metal roofs for easy access when the time came. However, it was the next day that brought forth an orange dawn, a beginning in which four thousand bricklayers, builders and helpers would never forget. As the mounting sun marked the commencement of the eighth day, long, cold shadows emerged from the darkness like sinister reddish materializations unfolding and creeping upon the icy floor. Human apparitions were everywhere.

Tense bricklayers fighting the cold waited next to piles of bricks while rubbing their arms and legs. Their two equally frosted helpers, or mixing assistants, were there to slap together the ingredients before they handed it over in the correct proportions to a shaking trowel. They were to use three parts sand to one part cement, not an overly strong mixture, but they couldn't afford more. Steve had previously made calculations that, with the existing stocks, they would reach the eleven-metre mark with only a few bags of cement to spare.

Water collection points were situated every hundred metres, and it was the assistants' alternating job to collect it in buckets and painstakingly take it back to the mixing site. Later as the cement was ready to apply, waiting trowels everywhere were shuffling back and forth to load on the next podgy lump. As the bricks came to rest, the wall had begun, and the seemingly endless, impossible chore had begun to create its own shadow.

By the end of the first day of bricklaying, some bricklayers had reached knee height. Yet, even as the outside lights came on illuminating the periphery, their emotions overflowed with an inspired liveliness, and they continued working through the night in shifts of six to eight hours until once more the sun rose above the horizon. More than two hundred wall examiners patrolled the perimeter making sure no mistakes were made. Blunders were not on Steve's agenda, so he hung around just in case.

It was a dual, triple-brick wall with a hollow in the middle. Twenty teams were filling it in with whatever they could find, including leftovers of the temporary wall in front of the new one.

Every fifty metres in the base, Steve made allowance for a testing and inspection cover. In them, when the time came, they would perform the final connections before the cables twisted their way upwards. A brick square, twenty-by-twenty centimetres constructed on the inside of the wall, was to house the metallic tube and protect it against the elements both natural and otherwise.

Steve was called into a Security Complex. Gossard wanted him to explain a few details and give a progress report. "Steve, do come in. How's the wall going?"

"Better than I expected. The rain is keeping it moist, and the workers are in good shape."

"Great, how high is it?"

"It's rapidly approaching two metres. At this rate, we'll start levelling off in two weeks, give or take a day. Have you started the ladders?"

"They'll be ready by the time the wall is finished. I'll have them moved to the locations of your choice when you're ready. Where are you putting the exterior spotlights?" asked Gossard.

"Just to the left of the viewing port, so they'll be easy to mount or repair if problems arise. I've already made allowance for the cable tubes to extend up to the viewing portal. The Manually Operated Guidance System control panel is just behind it, affixed to the wall for easy access."

"Oh, you mean the MOGS. I see you mention them in your design as a multi-function, local or remotely controlled joystick. It's quite ingenious."

"Yeah, as the wall-stalkers search the outlands, they or Security Centre can manoeuvre the light anywhere they want."

Steve looked up from his notes. "Our three metal main gates are being prepared for installation onto the wall. The enormous aperture-opening motor is awaiting connection to Security Centre as soon as the gates are in place."

Suddenly, a shot reverberated nearby. The echoing sound was pursued by three successive shots following shortly afterwards. Gossard and Steve ran out of the office, trailed by two security guards, both brandishing firearms. As they neared the outer zone, another two shots rang through the vacant gate aperture.

Major Gossard reached the first sharpshooter. "What's going on?"

"It's vagrants, sir," said the augmenting voice as Steve drew nearer. "We fired a warning shot at their feet, but they just kept coming. It didn't scare them in the least. They left us with no alternative!"

"Were they infected?" asked Gossard.

"Most definitely, sir. They were advancing too slowly to be anything else. Normal human behaviour at these temperatures provokes a faster movement. It's what regulates our body heat.

Roger here was looking at them through the binoculars. He saw the foulness, ask him." The sharpshooter swung around and pointed towards Roger.

"How far out were they when you shot them, and how many were there?" asked the major.

"Three hundred metres," said the shooter, nervously revising his scanning device. "Three, sir, there were three of them. One got up again after we shot him, so we stuck another two bullets in him to make sure he stayed down."

Minutes later, two hazmat-suited workers returned in a Jeep and placed the three bodies on the ground a few metres away. The bodies seemed familiar. They wore that same insensitive, cold glare Steve had seen in Tierra Colorada.

Steve reached into his pocket and contacted Mara on the C-10. "Darling, are you there?"

"Hello, Steve. How's your bloody wall coming along?"

"That's a nice thing to say. Nice to see you, too. What's the matter, darling?"

"A few days ago a man came knocking at our door. And you know what?"

"What?"

"I nearly blew his head off with the Walther. You never told me anything about a guardian angel!"

"Damn, I forgot. Sorry, babe, I didn't have the time. We've had so much going on here. It's hard to concentrate sometimes. What am I saying? Hey, I'm not the only one with a transmit button, you know!"

"I know, husband. I wanted to see how long it took for you to contact me, that's all. I'm slowly going mad here. I even sleep with my video thing next to me on the bed in case your finger gets a twitch. Anyway, it doesn't matter. How's your wall going?"

"Oh, baby, you silly thing. Why didn't you contact me? We're just over two metres." Steve paused. "We've been receiving a couple of unfriendly visitors as well. I insist you come over. I'm going to talk to Gossard about your immediate transfer."

"Why, what's happening? What's going on out there?" said Mara with a worried tone.

"Let's just say unfriendly visitors are starting to appear more frequently." Steve swivelled the C-10 towards the three bodies lying on the ground and heard Mara's sharp voice of revulsion the half-metre distance from his ear. "These three were shot by the perimeter squad only moments ago. Their numbers are increasing."

"OK, but who, where do those bodies come from?"

"They are infected outsiders. They came wandering towards the complex looking for food."

"For food? I don't understand. If they came looking for food, why did you shoot them?"

"They were coming for us, darling. It appears we are the food. They come from the south and southeast, migrating in vast numbers, and occasionally some of them catch onto our scent. When I first arrived, one a day roamed outside. Now it's in threes. They move in herds, like wild animals, seven or eight kilometres out. If they come nearer, our smell overwhelms them. Thank God, they can only move at a snail's pace. They sniff and taste the air trying to locate us."

Mara caught Steve's meaning. "Stop it, I've heard enough."

"No, I need to tell you more. When you leave, close all the ventilators on the dashboard. Do you hear me? Don't stop for anything, even if it appears normal and healthy. Pour all the gasoline you can fit into the tank, fill it until it overflows. If you leave right away, you'll be here before dark." As Steve spoke to her, he looked towards the horizon. A fine mist had begun to settle on the upper slopes of the hills.

"Mara, it's starting to snow. Don't forget the chains."

"Don't worry, Steve, I won't. See you soon, I guess."

The Journey

In only twenty minutes Mara had prepared herself for the journey.

"Vicente, I'm ready to go. Have you packed in the water?"

"Yes, Mara. It's in the back behind the spare gas tank. It's almost 1:30, I suggest we get moving. Darkness comes early these days."

Mara had an old-model Jeep. Steve had it fixed up a couple of months ago and did minor alterations to pass the time.

Vicente's car was a black government-issued Nexus, real state-of-the art stuff. It came with all the trimmings, too.

"Mara, I'll drive ahead," said Vicente. "Between here and Palizada I'll keep to a steady sixty, and the moment we pass the Palizada turnoff, I'll increase to eighty."

"Alright, Vicente," said Mara as she climbed into the Jeep. She had calculated that their journey would last four hours, taking them onto the borderline of day-night, so their timely start was of the utmost importance.

Steve had been right, on the outskirts of Palizada oceans of flies swarmed the countryside. Resembling schools of fish out of their watery environment, millions of swirling, infected flies went in search of new breeding grounds: anything living or dead.

Mara's C-10 came alive with Vicente's concerned face. "Mara, remember what Steve told you, keep those ventilators closed. We can't allow even one of those things into the vehicle."

Flies were everywhere. At times, her vision was obscured as the fly-soup became so thick that she had difficulty seeing where she was going. As they hit the windscreen ending their pitiful lives, it sounded like heavy rain. Black waving, living fingers unsuccessfully attempted a way into the Jeep. As fast as they had come, they droned away to pursue less-difficult targets.

* * *

During the happenings of the past year, only one radio station had kept itself alive and continued transmitting. Mara turned on her Motorola radio and flicked the dial to 105.7 MHz. Mex-Radio gave continual news updates, prompt music reviews, and chat shows, maintaining spirit in the people in the non-alcoholic sense of the word. It was an advertisement: "For a better way of life and peace of mind, head for your nearest DOK city. There's one nearby waiting to receive you and your family. From there you can start over again, begin where you left off. Don't hesitate. Give yourselves another go. You deserve it. Life does exist in DOK. For more information come and see us at 55 Perfection Street, Mexico City. We'll give you a cup of hot coffee to warm you while you wait." The advertisement repeated itself twice before transpiring into melancholic, droning music.

Mara pushed the auto-search button in the hope of finding another station, but there was nothing. Local FM could only produce the usual white noise and sporadic crackle. Mex-Radio once more erupted into voice and music as the auto-search completed its cycle.

Steve's shortwave receiver, on the other hand, had revealed people from all over the globe. The airwaves were full of them, a nervous, panicky multilingual chatter of the Ragish viruses.

At 2:30, Steve contacted Mara on her C-10. "Darling, where are you?"

"We've already passed the Palizada turnoff and are heading for Jonuta. The landscape is full of cacti and creosote bushes. Did you see them when you came through?"

"Yes, they get denser the farther inland you go. You will notice between Jonuta and Tierra Colorada the terrain is full of them. Remember, darling, in Jonuta, don't stop for anything. Danger lurks around every corner."

"Don't worry, honey. I'll contact you once we leave."

✳ ✳ ✳

Before reaching Jonuta, the snowstorm that Steve warned Mara about began to abandon the clouds and settled on the ground. At first, it was a gentle wisp of whiteness, a thin white curtain falling before an invisible audience. As the outbuildings of Jonuta came into view, its true ardent might unleashed itself. In moments, their vision had deteriorated to metres.

Mara tried cutting the impenetrable barrier with the Jeep's powerful headlamps. The beams reflected back to her, and she lowered them again. It only uncovered nearby plants enclosed in a thin layer of snow. It was pretty, in a sordid sort of way, as she drove past, peering at infallible growth patterns attempting, even in sub-zero temperatures, to continue in their indefatigable raid upon the territory. Steve had explained their ravishing and groping behaviour, but at first Mara couldn't believe what she saw.

They entered Jonuta at 3:15, just as the snow began to make Mara's rear wheels skid. She contacted Vicente on the C-10 and told him to slow down to twenty. His rear brake lights shone through the white curtain, and her constantly battling windscreen wipers struggled to scrape the flurry from its sticky habitat.

"Don't worry, Mara. Keep your lights on and stay close."

Mara had been to Jonuta years ago when a friend of hers married a coffee bean refiner. His family, one of the wealthiest in the area, had built a palace for the two of them in Tierra Colorada. In the beginning of their married life, Mara frequently visited them. Fernando was a sweet and kind husband, her friend did well in selecting him. She deserved him, as he did her. The palace boasted six hundred square metres and over ninety hectares of terrain. Mara wondered if they were still married, as she hadn't heard a word from her friend in over a year. Had the heat killed them? Had the virus found them?

Mara did exactly what Steve told her and kept her eyes firmly on the road, watching for any form of danger. The snow had gained depth in some places, completely covering low objects. It fluttered downwards like white leaves from a silver birch. Mara imagined living figures out there. If there were any survivors, they would undoubtedly hear their engines and appear.

During their drive through Jonuta, they gave a good chance for anyone to make an appearance. If only Steve could see her now, he would definitely chew her head off. Nevertheless, what if there was someone healthy out there? Mara thought that she couldn't leave them in this frozen hell with nowhere to hide. As Vicente sounded his horn twice to advertise their arrival, they were welcomed only by phantasmal, snowy apparitions.

Mara's concentration came to an abrupt end as Vicente's gruff voice exited the C-10 speaker. "Mara, when we get to the edge of town, stop and put the chains on, the snow's getting heavier."

"Jesus, Vicente, you gave me the scare of my life. Yeah, good idea."

Mara's driving was becoming impossible, and it was only another two or three hundred metres to the end of the straight road marking the end of Jonuta. Vicente put his emergency lights into action and parked the Nexus close to the curb a short way ahead. Mara parked about four metres behind him. She ran to open the back section and remove the chains lying on top of the spare wheel. Mara had put them there for easy access when the time came. Steve had shown her how to put them on a few times, and she managed to place the four sets of heavy-duty chains around the tyres in ten minutes.

Vicente, on the other hand, had torn one of his gloves putting on his chains. With part of his wrist exposed, it began to freeze in the bitter air. Mara walked over and offered to help. The wind gained vigour, forming white rivulets that ran down the street before they disappeared from view not ten metres away. The snow had begun to fall with such vitality that Mara began fearing the remnants of their journey.

Both cars were left running to prevent problems of restarting if the engine cooled too rapidly, so while Vicente waited on the front seat with his sheepskin jacket warming his almost frozen wrist, Mara completed the task of putting the chains around his tyres. Vicente had parked too close to the curb. On all fours, Mara scrabbled through the snow, trying to get a sufficient depth, enabling her to enwrap the chains around his tyres. It took almost twenty minutes to complete the task. Every now and then, Mara turned towards him to see if he was OK.

"There, that should do it. Are you OK to drive?" asked Mara.

"Yeah, I'm much better. At least the blood seems to be circulating again. It would help if we could wait a few moments more before we move on."

The snow decreased in intensity just enough for Mara to peek towards the town. The end buildings came hazily into view: Ace Dry Cleaners then Ortega's Newspaper Stand. With them, two moving figures materialised through the mist, two unhurried moving forms. These were not illusions. They were real. Mara ran to the Jeep and took out the Walther that she had stashed in the glove compartment.

Vicente was by now aware of Mara's apprehension. "Mara, where on earth did you go?"

"Vicente, I'm afraid we've got company."

Barely feeling the Walther through her gloved hands, she clumsily raised it to chest height and aimed. But by this time the blizzard had returned, obscuring her vision. Maybe she was hallucinating. Vicente must have thought she was crazy. That was until a rock came hurtling through the air, barely missing her head. The two forms were not discernible through the dense snow, but they were there, inconspicuous and imperceptible behind a wall of white fear. They never advanced. Instead, the two individuals remained behind their cowardly protection, preparing the next missile, which came hurtling through the air scant seconds later. This time they hurled it towards Vicente sitting in the car. Barely missing him, the rock smashed against the side mirror.

Without wasting time, Mara moved forwards to face the two invisible attackers. At first they didn't see her appear from the side, surprising them. They turned and faced her with such torpor it must have taken them the half hour Mara needed to prepare the chains just to reach her from the outskirts of town. Thank God, the retreating snow had given her ample time for a sneak look. If not, she or Vicente would have been wounded by now.

As Mara steadily approached them, one stooped and began to search the icy smudge for another snow-hidden projectile. A distant smile reached his lips as success brought to the surface another rock. But before he could launch it in Mara's direction, she raised the shaking Walther. Pointing low, she pulled the trigger and watched as the bullet entered above his left knee, producing a loud crack as lead met bone. Mara cringed. Blood splattered in a semi-circle behind him as the bullet exited and ended in a snow pile.

Both man and rock collided against the snow. He didn't scream in pain as one would have expected, and by no means did he seem perturbed by his fractured knee or the presence of the firearm. Instead, he began crawling on all fours towards Mara, leaving a trail of blood behind him.

Vicente came running after hearing the shot. "Mara, are you alright? Oh God, just look at them. Be careful, they're infected and probably very hungry. Christ, whatever you do, don't touch them!"

The crawling one found an empty bottle and threw it at Vicente. The bottle hit him on the shoulder.

"These two are not going to stop at anything until they have us where they want us."

"And where's that?" Mara asked.

"Safely tucked away inside their stomachs. Where else?"

As Vicente spoke, a projectile hit him directly on the face, producing a loud crack. His talking had inadvertently distracted Mara away from their pursuers, so she lifted the Walther once more, this time aiming higher.

As the bullet entered his skull, the man fell with an empty thump and rolled slightly in the snow before coming to a standstill. The crawler, however, still intent on reaching them, uncaringly ferreted with sore-ridden hands amidst the snow. Mara shot him directly in the heart when he raised to throw a rock at them. Still perturbed, she turned around and looked at Vicente's face.

As she returned her vision to look at the two corpses, something caught her eye in the direction of the town. In the distance, about thirty metres away, a much larger group was coming. One of the nearer ones uttered unnatural sounds, almost a whimper.

"Vicente, for God's sakes, it's time to go! We've got more company. Come on, get up, and drive!"

Vicente, witless and woozy, struggled to his feet and climbed into the car.

"Wait for me a few hundred metres down the road. I'll pull up behind you."

As Vicente rushed off, a look of obvious pain creased his brow. Blood had been streaming from his facial wound and had fallen onto his chest and lap. Tearing her stare from Vicente's disappearing car, Mara looked once more towards the advancing column of Jonuta residents and hurriedly clambered into the Jeep.

Mara drove slowly, keeping an attentive eye out for the Nexus. It wasn't anywhere. Two or three kilometres farther down, she found the crumpled wreckage on the side of the road, billowing steam. It had veered off after hitting a snow-hidden boulder and landed against a wall of someone's abode.

As Mara pulled up behind him, she ran to the wrecked car and peered through the window while reaching for her communicator. Blood was everywhere. Vicente had passed out.

"Steve, are you there?"

"What's the matter, honey? Are you alright?" asked Steve with a concerned tone.

"We ran into problems coming out of Jonuta. Lord, everyone's been infected. Two of them started throwing rocks at us. I had no choice. I killed them both!" Mara gasped for air. "One of them threw a rock at Vicente and shattered his nose. Jesus, the poor guy is suffering. As he drove off towards Tierra Colorada, he passed out and trashed his car against a wall of someone's house. I'm going to have to drag him out somehow and put him on the front seat next to me."

"Calm down, calm down. Was there any blood on the rock?"

"I can't be sure, why?"

"Don't forget the *Time* article I showed you. Be very careful. DOK's resident medical specialist is spreading the news that if there's any trace of blood on an object, the transmission is positive. Be extra careful. Look for changes in his behaviour, it doesn't matter how small they are. Don't touch any blood and watch his body temperature. If it starts going up, you let me know immediately!"

"I'll do that, honey. I'd better get going. I'll see you before dark."

Steve's worried face flickered off, leaving Mara alone with Vicente. His unconscious body weighed a ton as she dragged it with all her strength from the front seat of the Nexus. She dragged him by his clothes, focusing on un-bloodied regions, but his nasal wound had made quite a mess. The body plopped onto the soft snow, and she pulled him like a sleigh towards the Jeep.

Struggling, she continued pulling him up and onto the front seat alongside her where she would be able to keep an eye on him and monitor his condition. Occasionally, he groaned, subconsciously holding both hands to his face. While Mara watched him, thinking of Steve's words, she began regarding the man who had confronted death from a different perspective. Had

Vicente been infected? Was he the enemy? Military-issue latex gloves came with them wherever they went. It was one of their few eccentric habits. But for once, she was glad to have had them stashed in the glove compartment. Mara put on a pair and checked Vicente's forehead temperature. He seemed OK.

It stopped snowing between Jonuta and Tierra Colorada around 5:30. The first wisp of orange sun broke through the clouds, provoking a roving patch of light that began patrolling the snow. Mara drove slowly at times, for the sea of white had transformed the road into a concave indentation. Occasionally she had to use her imagination to see where she was going. At least the nearer she got to Tierra Colorada, the blizzard hadn't been so callous. Surviving tendrils of green had come up for air. Mara turned and looked at Vicente. His augmenting groans had begun to outweigh the radio, so in the end, she switched it off and carefully put her foot down.

Driving into Tierra Colorada for the first time in two years, Mara anxiously waited for Ferguson Mansion to come into view. Ferguson Mansion, built in the late nineteenth century, was a well-known landmark. Even at her last visit, one of the family nephews had occupied it. Billy Ferguson had been an oil magnate, earning millions of dollars per week. Combining his egocentric attitude with fame and fortune, Billy allowed his majestic mansion to fall into wrack and ruin. As time went on, the mansion not only began falling apart by itself, hoodlums had entered, destroying the remnants of this wooden magnificence. Beautiful ebony window frames that were once the talk of the town gleamed like the toothless. Only one side of the mansion remained intact; the other, a scattered ancientness, lay in pieces on the ground.

Farther into town, someone had driven a truck through a worm fence encircling a group of security-enwrapped townhouses. Its voyage had ended against the wall of someone's dwelling. The more Mara looked around, she noticed dozens of derelict cars lining the streets. She started driving slower while making her way between the broken metal. Occasionally, Mara caught a glimpse of someone ducking and disappearing from view. At least here, there still existed a kind of normality, if indeed they were normal. Mara didn't stop and find out.

Farther up the street, Memorial Plaza, built to commemorate the war victims of the 2024 North Korean War, silently stood on its marble base with six hundred Mexican phantasmal citizens eternally resting their souls below in the mausoleum cenotaph. After the war, North Korea became the first Asian territory owned by America. Although the war only lasted five months, the list of the dead was endless.

An inscribed silver plaque bolted to the wall dominated the left of the vault entrance. Thieves had obviously tried to steal it on various occasions, as deep scratches and crowbar tears plainly demonstrated greed and the cruelty of man during these hard times. In the centre of the plaza, and with no one else around, Mara pulled onto the grass verge and felt Vicente's temperature.

He opened his eyes as Mara's hand stretched over. "My head hurts like hell. Where are we?"

"Tierra Colorada. How are you feeling?"

"Incredibly weak with an incredible headache. Can you give me some water, Mara? I have a thirst to end all thirsts."

The blood had stopped pumping from his nasal wound, and for the first time in quite a while, he sat up on his own. With one single gulp, Vicente emptied the plastic container and looked up. His left eye was completely black and had puffed up. He had congealed blood hanging in strands from his nostril.

Mara reached for her C-10. "Honey, are you there?"

"Hi, babe. Where are you?"

"We've reached Tierra Colorada. Vicente has come around and seems to be okay. There's no sign of a temperature and he's just drunk a litre of water."

"Good, you're not far now. I'll inform the sharpshooters of your arrival. If you leave right away, you'll be here in twenty minutes. Remember, keep to the road, and when you see the hill, go over the top. DOK's on the other side in the valley."

"Alright, honey."

Steve's face disappeared and Mara placed the C-10 back on the dashboard.

"Well, Vicente, are we ready to go?"

"Ready and waiting."

Mara put the Jeep into first gear and slowly edged forward. The snow had already begun melting in places, forming slippery patches, and at one point, the Jeep frenetically swung around twenty or thirty degrees, giving them quite a fright. As Vicente told Mara to drive slower, a dull ping followed by a shard of glass landing on the floor to her left made Mara look around. It appeared out of nowhere. Mara caught a glimpse of someone running away in the distance before managing to duck behind a large rubbish container. His white clothing blended in perfectly with the surroundings. Mara turned to ask Vicente if he'd seen the fleeting figure disappear behind the container. As her eyes met his, Vicente's inanimate gaze met her astonishment. His unmoving eyes were silently fixating on nothing. Mara looked down to see he'd been shot in the chest. One clean shot through the windscreen had taken his life, with sanctuary only around the corner. Why would someone shoot a wounded, defenceless man?

Suddenly three white-clad figures ran towards the vehicle. One of them brandished a sniper rifle. Mara slammed on the brakes, skidding on the icy surface before coming to a halt. She grabbed the Walther and C-10 from the dashboard. Mara jumped out and pointed it towards her assailants. A stifling silence cut the air.

"Stop where you are! Don't bloody move!"

The three of them stopped dead in their tracks as they noticed the Walther's laser pointer jitter nervously on each of them. Slowly backing off, they began to inch back the way they'd come. One managed to disappear behind a parked caravan before crouching and slinking his way toward an open door of a building. The other two unthreateningly melted back into the nothingness.

Mara climbed into the back of the Jeep to put on her winterwear. She decided to go on foot. In the Jeep, she was too vulnerable. Anxiously climbing out from the Jeep, she looked down one last time at the silent corpse of Vicente on the front seat.

She made slow progress in her baggy winterwear, inching her way towards Steve. The snow reached to her knees, and at times she battled to move on. But it was the thought of Steve safely waiting for her at the shelter that was making her do this; he was her life.

As she turned the corner to enter Perrier Avenue, Mara nearly collided with the three white-clad rough-looking individuals as they ran around the corner. Mara nervously ripped her glove from her right hand and thrust it into her side pocket. But even before she could draw her Walther 38, the leading figure made a lunge for her. She wasn't sure in the end if it was the same figure she saw back at the Jeep, or even if it was the one who had shot Vicente.

A knife appeared, so she moved sharply to the right just in time to see her attacker slip on the ice. Flicking the safety catch on the Walther with her thumb, she levelled its laser-guidance beam at the two remaining figures standing in front of her. The Walther was the only thing between her safety and a certain death as both of them had their eyes fixated on her.

"Stop where you are or I will shoot!" Although she had the gun, she was more afraid than they were.

The two of them were bundled so close against the cold that Mara couldn't make out if they were male or female. As they separated and broke formation, she swung round to see the one who had slipped on the ice. He was definitely a male, scrabbling to his knees and searching in the snow for his fallen weapon. One of the other two began to lurch forward, grunting and advancing towards her.

Mara was a competent markswoman. Steve had trained her on weekends, honing her weapons skills and showing her how to hold the gun and most certainly when to fire it.

She fired a shot directly in front of him, but it ricocheted off the hard tarmac below. The bullet scathed his right kneecap. Mara watched as both hands rushed downwards and groped the knee before the man crashed into the snow. The other attacker was crouching only a few metres away. Then she swung back to face the one who had slipped. He had not moved. Neither had he made any attempt to assist his fallen comrade, who was moaning in pain just to the side of him.

Swivelling her body back and forth like a stuck second hand, Mara kept the gun trained on both sources of danger without taking her eye off the one lying on the ground bleeding. Stepping carefully backwards through the deep snow, she went between two abandoned cars. She put the glove of her left hand into her mouth and pulled it off. The bare hand reached down into the supplementary provisions pocket of her thermal survival suit and extracted a high-energy protein bar in a colourful wrapper. Throwing it onto the snow, she stood back to watch. There was no movement towards the bar.

"Oh God, it wasn't food they wanted."

She ran back to the middle of the road and began to run as fast as the suit would allow. Making it to a crossroads, Mara wondered if she should have shot and killed all three of them, but she knew herself to be incapable of such a cold-blooded act. Moving into a large open space, she saw many vehicles. Knowing the risk of someone hiding behind one, she walked backwards, continuing her vigilant journey in the direction of DOK. Never once letting the slowly advancing figures get out of sight, Mara gripped the gun tightly. The excruciating cold in her right hand made her transfer the weapon to the left. Thrusting her right hand into her suit's woolly pouch, her eyes followed them, stalking from a few hundred metres behind. What did they want? Every so often, she would spin around, keeping her gaze on the tiny, darkened pursuers that flitted behind deserted cars and snowdrifts as they trailed her.

The one who had slipped in the ice suddenly leaped out from behind a car, pushing through knee-deep snow like a wounded bull in the ring, brandishing a knife. Before getting to her, he stopped and stood in the middle of the street only six metres away.

Nervously, Mara aimed and quickly squeezed off two shots with her left hand. One was a warning shot and the other was aimed at his foot. As she fired, the man fell down screaming. Mara resumed her careful backwards walk, her weapon's trembling laser beam swept from left to right across the street as she tried to keep her pursuers at bay.

At the next intersection, she crossed to a ransacked apartment block behind the old plaza hotel and hid behind a corner. Crouching, she saw the three figures still following her, having fallen back slightly. The one she had shot in the foot was upright again, leaning on the shoulder of another. Mara used this opportunity and switched her gun from her freezing left hand back to her warmed right.

Without wasting any more time, she switched on the C-10. "Honey, are you there?"

"What's up? I can hear something's wrong just by the tone of your voice."

"I am still in Tierra Colorada. They've shot Vicente, he's dead. Now they're coming after me!"

"Honey, don't move from where you are. Use the ammo reserves, shoot to kill! Where are you? I'll be there in a jiffy."

"I'm on Constitution near the old Ferguson Mansion."

Without another word, Steve disappeared and the C-10 flickered off. From where Mara was hiding, the three oncoming ruffians couldn't see her, but she could hear them scuffling close by. As one incautiously came close to her hiding place, Mara's sense of fear had already vanished. Steve was on his way.

"Her footprints lead over here," said the man in Spanish. Mara rushed out from behind the alcove and faced them five metres away, pointing the Walther directly at the leader's face. Sensing the laser dot on his nose, his face immediately turned curtain-white and he stopped dead in his tracks. He studied Mara briefly, quickly feeling unhindered by her obviously bad feminine technique of intimidation. The other two, one propping up the other, hobbled closer. The newcomers, lacking animosity, looked upon Mara with dubiousness and insecurity. Their rifle, empty of rounds, drooped downwards and their only weapon was the knife.

"Don't even think of it," warned Mara. "I'll kill you before you can get within two metres! Who the heck are you, and why did you shoot my friend in the Jeep?"

"He was infected," said the man convincingly.

"Why in the name of—why didn't you tell me before? And how in God's name could you tell from that distance?"

The man, unhindered by Mara's brash tone, began to speak again. "When the body is exposed to a severe blow or extreme shock, blood normally leaves in a darkened state, almost black. His blood, the blood of your friend was pale, too thin. I saw it through the telescopic lens. But you, of course, wouldn't know because you've never seen it before. Here, it is becoming part of our daily routine. Over these last few days, I have shot and killed six of them. We tried approaching you when you first parked the

Jeep, but you scampered in fright." He moved away and stood directly in Mara's line of vision.

"The blood changes that quickly?" Mara asked.

"It does."

"But you tried to attack me!"

"We wouldn't have hurt you. The knife was a precaution."

"Who are you, and who gave you the right to shoot a man without explanation? Who the hell made you judge and jury?"

"In the real world I am a sergeant in the local police force in Tierra Colorada. I had retained that title for sixteen years. I think I earned the right to preserve the privileges of human dignity where I see fit, including putting a man down because he is about to inflict an end worse than death upon another without her knowing it."

Mara stared at him, finally understanding the gravity of the situation. This sergeant was emotionless. Did a man's life mean so little?

"Did he touch you in any way?" asked the man.

"No, not at all." Mara's voice stumbled, thinking of Vicente next to her, alive and infected. She would be dead now if he had touched her. This guy wouldn't blink an eye to kill her, either.

"What are you doing here? Tourist season is over." His lucid, calm stare and soothing tone made Mara feel a bit easier.

"I am here to meet my husband."

"Then why is he coming to collect you? And who was that guy in the Jeep?" His tone changed again.

"He was my bodyguard. My husband sent him to look after me while he works on a project the government has him doing."

"And what project might that be?" said the man, squinting.

"He's building the wall for the DOK city in the valley."

The man relaxed, while the two alongside struggled to maintain their posture. "Keep still. You're heavy," one said.

"I've heard rumours about this DOK place. Isn't it a refuge?"

"Yes, it's a refuge for people like us. Like I told you, my husband is in charge of the wall. He has something to do with the security as well."

There was an excited pause in the conversation as he began churning around ideas. "Listen, there's nothing for us here anymore. Do you think he could use some help?"

"Well, whatever your name is, I am sure he could use all the help he can find."

The opportunity-seeking man gave a smile. "I'm sorry, I haven't introduced myself, I'm Tino. The one with the injured knee and doing the propping is Nathan. The one you shot in the toe is Jose." He extended his hand towards Mara and the other two hobbled closer and did the same.

"My name is Mara Gotlar."

"My apologies, I didn't mean to frighten you back there. I just did what had to be done. I did it for your protection. You must believe me. I've seen many dangers around here lately. I know what they're capable of, and it seems to be getting worse." He turned towards Nathan and Jose, giving them a smile.

"Tell me more about this DOK city."

"It's more a fortress than anything else. The government is putting up twenty of them to keep the survivors safe from the infected. The wall is the first line of defence. It's very important to the inhabitants."

As Mara finished her sentence, Steve's snowmobile came skidding to a halt a couple of metres away.

"Get the hell away from her!" shouted Steve as he opened the side door. Jumping onto the snow like a rabid dog, Steve rushed over, holding a military-issue 9mm and pointed it directly at Tino's head. Two other security officers followed closely behind.

"Honey, wait!" Mara cried. "Don't hurt them. They're here to help. He's a police officer. His name is Tino."

Mara's soothing words didn't calm Steve's acid glare and true aim towards the three figures.

Mara tried again. "They shot Vicente because he was infected. They saved my life!"

Steve grumbled something before finally lowering his weapon and placing it into the holster.

The two security officers came and thoroughly frisked the three of them head to foot.

"They're clean, sir," said the guard, holding the knife and turning towards Steve.

"All right then, let's go. We don't have much time," said Steve.

"Honey, we can't just leave them here. Tino can help you with whatever it is you are doing in DOK."

"So you want to come with us, do you?" Steve paused. "Well, we'd better get a move on. It's already getting dark. They come out during the dark hours. Honey, where's the Jeep?"

"Two hundred metres down the road. Vicente's body is still on the front seat." Mara handed the keys to Steve, who in turn gave them to one of the security guards and told him to fetch the Jeep. The young athletic figure rushed down the road in the direction of Mara's pointing hand.

"So, you're a police officer, eh?" asked Steve.

"Yes, sixteen years of it," said Tino.

"Has my wife explained what I am doing?"

"Not much. Something about a wall. Tell me more."

"In due course. You know, if I was to leave you here you wouldn't last a week. The rate at which these things are mutating, I'd be surprised if you see the light of day tomorrow."

Tino gave Steve a stare and immediately changed the topic. "Over the last couple of days we've been hearing rumours about a city in the valley."

"Oh yes, it's quite a project. What the heck, you can put your experience back into action, can't you?" said Steve as the security officer returned with the Jeep.

"Sir, there was no body inside," said the officer. "It must have been dragged out. The snow outside the passenger door was washed with blood. Two sets of footprints and drag marks led up to an old shed on Fisk Street."

"Oh, God! I knew it," said Tino worriedly. "That's the Menendez residence. I found Pete's half-eaten body cut to shreds a few days ago on the front lawn. Poor man, he was in a real mess. Since that day, the infected use his property as a meeting place. They gather themselves in small groups going out for the hunt during the gloomy weather. I watch them from time to time with infrared. They don't talk to each other, but they still manage to communicate somehow."

"They use a subsonic frequency, somewhere around three hertz," offered Steve. "I haven't a clue how they do it. All I can tell you is they are all interactively linked with invisible wires, every damn one of them."

"Mark my words, when they raise their left hand close to the nose, the communication begins. It never fails," said Tino.

The cloud layer had risen, revealing patches of purple starry sky.

"It's time we were going, it's almost dark," said Mara, hardly containing her anxiety, opening the side door of the snowmobile to be with Steve. As the last strands of sun succumbed to darkness, Mara began the final part of her journey.

Tino and one of the officers climbed in the Jeep with the rest.

✹ ✹ ✹

Nearing the hillside, the first signs of DOK were lights visible as murky patches of whitish haze reflected from low, dense nimbostratus clouds gathering on the horizon. This implicit signal of light guided them to their salvation. However, they were not alone. There was another nocturnal sound as they left the outskirts of Tierra Colorada. It was desert crickets, one of the other few survivors of this world. Their thritting blended in delicately with an occasional distant crash from an infected, who frustratingly knew the circumstances of his irreversible illness. Tino said that their reactions always ended in violence, either towards themselves or towards others who were near. Objects were thrown about, as it temporarily alleviated their exasperation and insatiable appetites for flesh.

Tino was a smoker. The two officers could hear his lungs were heaving with bearable tolerance as the cold air flowed into them. Squinting eyes revealed accustomed pain. One security officer was medically trained and was in the back of the Jeep with Jose attending to his wounds.

"Sit still. It's not so bad. The bullet went straight through!" The officer bandaged the wound the best he could in the moving Jeep.

"I'll get Quaid to take a look at it when we get to DOK. In the meantime, put your hand on the gauze. It'll help stop the bleeding," said the officer.

Ahead, the snowmobile's lights were opening up the road on both sides. Steve's snowmobile was better adapted than the Jeep was to the extreme conditions. Turning his head from the front, he lovingly examined Mara's face. He was concerned for her safety. Even having her next to him in the snowmobile didn't calm him. Until she was safely within DOK beside him, he would worry.

As the road began levelling out, a floating mist had taken over the valley, completely obscuring Brook Bridge and part of the northern wall. From Steve's perspective behind the steering wheel, he began glimpsing upon his fortification with an excited animation. It encouraged him to watch its illuminated round structure gently lift, slowly filling the horizon from left to right. Steve was looking at DOK with the very same eyes an infected would. He even felt apprehension as he peered at it with a similar hunger and ferociousness, that same want and desire.

Days before, the builders' sights were set on the infinite desert and its unlimited supply of sand because their stocks were already getting low. Two battered lorry scoops excavating the nearby terrain dipped their shovels into the sand and removed tons at a time. Cranes, lorries, and people were zipping about in all directions. A short way outside the entrance, some trusses and scaffolding formed neat piles on the ground.

Seeing it this way brought back memories of the protecting wall Steve had designed and constructed six years before. It formed the end of the eighty-five-kilometre-long Northern Pacific Road that linked the Asian continent to America. The original wall design was six kilometres long and took Steve almost eight months to complete. Not only was the wall surrounding DOK 16 going up in record time, it measured twice that of Steve's original design.

Steve contacted Gossard on his C-10. "Major, we're two kilometres from the gate. Mara is with me. We picked up a few strays in Tierra Colorada, will bring them in for interrogation when we arrive. Mara wants to meet you quite badly, it seems. Where do you want us to settle down?"

Gossard's voice was chirpy. "So glad she's OK. Come directly to the Admin Building. I'll have sleeping quarters arranged for you both. Tell the other vehicle to go to the Security Complex. I'll get our security guys over there right away. I'll welcome Mara later."

"OK, Major, I will tell them right away." The C-10 blinked off.

The condition of the road made the twenty-kilometre distance arduous, and if it wasn't for DOK in the distance, Steve and Mara might have thought they were alone in the world. Mara felt at ease with her hand on Steve's leg. With one hand on the wheel,

69

Steve's right hand came down and held on tightly, rubbing his thumb over her fingers. Smiling, she watched his searching eyes roam the landscape and foliage for danger, protecting the two of them. She was home.

October 2033

The next day, as the third week of construction began, they breached the seven-metre mark. It was Monday, October 16. That day, Steve decided to walk the entire length of the wall to see it for himself. Not from the car window, or from the back seat of the Jeep, he wanted to walk along its base taking only a notebook and pen. Steve wanted to meet the workers, the ones responsible for transforming his design into reality. Steve wanted to experience their enthusiasm.

In Sector Four, a scrawled message written on a drying patch of wall caught his eye. From a distance, it seemed like scribble.

In the beginning, there was DOK.

In the end, there was nothing.

Steve quickly rubbed it off, thinking it must have been someone's bad idea of a joke. The rest of the day was uneventful in graffiti terms. It also seemed to pass by quickly. Steve's only goal that day was to meet as many workers as possible. He wanted to show off the old mug a bit around the place and have an occasional joke thrown at him. He wanted to let them know who he was. The vibe these workers possessed, the keenness, left him dumbfounded. This wasn't just work, it was an orderly devotion. Their unleashed frustrations blazed forth like an unstoppable energy that ended in the construction work they were doing, and by Thursday, one of the teams had already reached eight metres.

"Ah, there you are. Team Nine in Sector Five has reached eight metres," said Gossard excitedly as Steve walked into the Security Centre.

"Excellent! Tell them to go help the others. I'll go congratulate them."

As more worker teams reached first-floor height, they relocated their tools to remaining sections of the wall to help their co-workers. By late Friday afternoon, the first and most difficult section was completed.

"It's perfect!" Steve exclaimed to himself as he opened the door to the Security Centre after completing his perimeter check. "It's absolutely perfect."

* * *

Early the next morning, the workers began affixing the ladders onto previously marked locations, while others were busy assisting in the erection of the three front entrance points. The gate's four-ton mass was to be slotted into place on the waiting, strong pivoting hinges mounted on the side of the wall. Rawling's team was there wiring the enormous geared electrical motor, but it would be Rawling himself who would test each gate aperture, assuring its stability, opening speed, closing speed, and bounce.

Gossard didn't want gaps. "When it's shut, I don't want to see even a desert ant crawl under it."

Those were Gossard's exact words, and it was Rawling's painstaking obligation to keep him happy, notwithstanding the long list of safety parameters each gate aperture included. Rawling was to check them all, one at a time.

As an addition to the security, Matthew was going to install what he called Slim Shapers (miniature versions of the Light Shapers) onto the top of each gate. As soon as the ladders were secured to the wall, the workers started with the second section. Long metallic rods, deeply embedded in the new floor eight metres up, waited to pierce the bricks, marking the beginning of the second level and adding to its strength and support. The second level, a single, double-layered three-metre-high wall, was going to be built onto the outer rim of the new roof facing the landscape. The inner side would eventually become a fully prepared walkway for hundreds of wall-stalkers.

As per Steve's design, spaced every five metres at one metre sixty from the floor, a one-metre by thirty-centimetre rectangular lookout hole was going to be carved into the bricks. They were the vantage points and observation holes. Wire guide tubes were in position, pointing their dangly hollowness in random and occasionally whistling directions while MOGS, camera, and communication units waited neatly in their boxes on the ground for installation.

Before the roof of the first section had dried, they put beams of wood between the two triple brick walls, enabling them to walk the two-metre span without injuring the drying cement at their feet.

Gossard approached Steve with a concerned look. "Steve, our cement supplies are running low. The hills outside DOK are rich in alumina, lime, and silica. We have a couple of tons of pre-bagged iron oxide stashed away in the warehouse. I'm thinking, with another hundred tons of cement in stock, we wouldn't have to worry about future deliveries from Mexico City."

Gossard opened a file and reviewed the geological reports handed in by Matthew two months before, when they first selected the site for edification.

"Just look at these hills," he said, looking over the file. "Tens of thousands of years ago all of this was once part of the Gulf. When the water retreated, it left behind infinite deposits of coral and shells. This fossilised accumulation of limestone is ours for the taking." Gossard's look intensified. "Extraction in those hills would be suicide."

Gossard mumbled something as Rawling walked over. "Rawling, I've got a better idea. Round up some of those foundry chaps, they are familiar with the process of cement manufacture. It has recently come to my attention they have some free time on their hands. Tell them to dig up samples. I'll put together a small protection force to accompany them."

✳ ✳ ✳

During the making of cement, twenty of the forty agua-genies permanently routed to the wall dried up the reserves, producing panic among the inhabitants. They found themselves without water on two occasions, nocturnal temperatures froze the water supply hoses and caused blockages in the feed tubes. They dug furrows and placed the tubes below ground to protect them.

In the distance, workers started running towards the gate. "It's another Russian consignment!" shouted one worker as he disappeared behind a wall of a Security Complex in the direction of the gate. Even before the monstrous gate had time to open fully for the first time, thirty Mercedes supply trucks and two depleted refuelling wagons stormed in.

Major Gossard quietly came beside Steve in amongst the rumble of the engines, giving Steve a fright as his husky voice broke the continuous drone. "How's Mara? Has she settled down?"

"She's still a bit jittery after her journey. I've given her a couple of pills to calm her down."

"She'll be OK. Don't worry. Steve, I'm afraid this was the last Russian delivery."

"What are you talking about, Major? Wasn't there supposed to be four?"

"Yes. General Slavinavitch contacted me this morning. As the fourth consignment started on its journey, it was ambushed. We lost the whole cargo, everything. The bad news is, it had our seeds in five of the trucks."

"Seeds? What do you mean?"

"Herbs, vegetable, and medicinal plants, not to mention the tree saplings and shrubs. Hell, Arthur needed them urgently for his greenhouses. He doesn't know about it yet." Gossard's stare intensified, making Steve look downwards.

"Steve, I want you to put together a scouting party," said Gossard, attracting his attention again.

"And go find seeds?"

"Yeah. I'm positive a nursery exists somewhere in Tierra Colorada. Get out there and bring back whatever you can find." Gossard reached into his top pocket, producing a list. "This is roughly what we lost."

"Don't worry, Major. Arthur will have his greenhouses up and running one way or the other. I'll see to it," said Steve.

"Good. These plants are of the utmost importance. Without them, we'll eventually starve." Gossard gave a smile.

✳ ✳ ✳

As the humongous gamma wave emitted from the micronova hit all those months ago, artificial satellites orbiting the Earth at the time were vaporised. Their metallic outer skins, exposed to temperatures in excess of 2,000 degrees and levels of radiations beyond human comprehension, innocently faded from view. Their disappearance left Earth without communication and weather-forecasting abilities. Months later, as they gradually returned to shortwave, reborn telegraphic signals and Morse code started filling the airwaves with their constant babble. Ham radio returned like a fashion rave and became a nightmare every time they switched on. Thousands of surviving groups worldwide had ruptured the ethereal silence with their antiquated, but still functional transceiver sets. Of course, the only problem was to decipher the signals. No one had used, let alone heard, Morse code signals for more than three decades. Matthew rigged up a computer with software to decode the airborne noise.

Steve picked up his C-10. "Matthew, I need you in the Security Centre."

"What's up, Steve? I'm cabling one of the heaters at the school. Can't it wait?"

"No, I am picking up International Morse. I need you to detangle it. You're the only one who knows the software."

"Hold your horses. I'll be there in ten minutes!"

✳ ✳ ✳

A strong, damp sensation lurked in the air as recent cement and still-drying plaster hadn't abated this place of sophistication. Steve began to think it couldn't be good for sensitive electronics. Although tiny ventilators were constantly working against the threat of component oxidation, Steve wondered about their success rate. Waiting for Matthew to arrive, Steve began fiddling with a radio dial. A harmonizing melody immediately caught his attention.

"Radio Seven-Oh-Two. "Hello everyone, you got Pete the Meat, and this is Radio 702 coming direct from the Dutchman capital, Pretoria, South Africa. Anguish and sorrow reach our ears on a daily basis. For months now this wretchedness, this global suffering has had one name. Dear listener, I refer to the Ragish-C virus. All remaining television and radio stations around the world have predominantly overwhelmed us with its presence. My dear radio listener, whoever you are, wherever you are, the dreaded virus has reached India. Bombay is in chaos. The first reports came in only moments ago from the Reuters hotline, as they have journalists worldwide still with the means to circulate news as it happens. Our working telephone lines in the meantime haven't stopped ringing.

"From what I have gathered and the atrocities I have been hearing about, it is a pity this virus isn't lethal. If we could conceptualize, even imagine for just a moment, if this, whatever the hell it is, was fatal, we wouldn't be in this predicament. Radio listener, we know perfectly well by now that once the infected begin to get the grumbles in their bowels, there is no safe haven and no place to hide. Wherever we go, they will hunt us down like vermin.

"Our best scientists are onto the problem, but foresee no breakthrough in the next couple of weeks. There is also speculation that this is not even a virus at all, that it is, in fact, something molecular, something totally new. All I can say to you at this time is stay away from the water and move inland. Forget your belongings, they don't have importance anymore. Save yourselves and your families, and maybe when this is all over, just maybe, I will play some of that nice music I once played."

As his well-trained, firm voice faded into gentle classical music, a single drop of sweat slowly ran down Steve's brow. The reality of the situation had tightened in those scant moments he was in the Security Centre. To hell with International Morse. Steve suddenly had an urge to run out and find Mara to tell her the news. Steve needed to tell her. He would go find these damn seeds if it was the last thing he did.

Just then, Matthew stormed in. "Sorry, Steve. I came as soon as I could. Heck, what's up? You look pale."

At first, Steve didn't know what to say. "Have you listened to any radio broadcasts recently?"

"No, why?"

"You're lucky. I've just had the scariest radio encounter of my life."

Deliberately, Steve paused himself. That voice, that crackly static was fresh in his mind. He didn't know where to begin, so he ran out of the Security Centre and went to find Mara, leaving Matthew watch him disappear.

Mara was busy adjusting herself in the Admin Building as Steve ran in.

"Christ, why don't you knock? I almost wet myself!"

"Sorry, honey. I turned on one of the radio receivers in the Security Centre. I suppose I was being nosy. I needed to know if there were others suffering like us. While I was waiting for Matthew to come unscramble an unusually fast Morse code, I started fiddling with one of the radio's frequency dials. That was when I heard it."

"What? Heard what!"

"A radio broadcast coming from Pretoria, South Africa." Steve paused. "This thing, this thing is getting worse, far worse!" Steve paused again.

"And what? Tell me what you heard."

Steve related the entire scary scene, word by word. Her face twisted parallel to Steve's own sentiments.

"India, oh my word! It isn't stopping. It's going to contaminate everything. When will the Pacific and Indian ocean strains collide?"

"At the rate it's going, we have seven weeks. In the meantime, Gossard wants me to go find seeds in Tierra Colorada. The last Russian consignment was ambushed, and part of Payne's payload was on it. Without these seeds we won't survive six months, or at least that's what Gossard seems to think."

"When does he want you to go?" asked Mara worriedly.

"Within the hour," Steve said.

"And what do you want me to do while you're away?" asked Mara with a concerned look.

"Just do what you know best," Steve said with a smile.

"What's that?" Mara's look turned into a smile.

"Everything you do," Steve turned and faced the door.

"Now don't you try and soften me up, you old man. You take care of yourself while you're out there. You hear?"

"I will, darling, don't worry. Bernard is coming with me. Quaid discharged him from the hospital this morning. It appears he's fully recovered from his fly bite."

"Good, I know when he's with you, you're in better hands than you should be."

"Do me a favour, love, while I'm away. Contact Arthur Payne. Tell him I'll catch up with him on my return."

"Don't worry, you just make sure you look after Bernard this time and stay away from stray flies! Who else is going with you?"

"That new cop fellow, Tino, and his companion Nathan. Tino knows the town better than anyone. Gossard is also bunching together a couple of volunteers to go with us. He told me that one of them gave him the cold shivers."

"Sounds dandy. Looks like you've got quite a bit of activity on your plate."

As Steve closed the door, Mara gave off a look of concern. Although she was a solid woman, she couldn't hide her inner fears from him. Hell, he'd been married to her for fourteen years. Steve didn't particularly want to go back out there. Just the thought of it brought on goose bumps. But as Gossard had plainly lain out, the journey was important.

Back in the Security Centre, Tino began to draw a rough sketch outlining Tierra Colorada on a piece of A4 paper he'd dug up from the reception desk in the Admin Building. "We'll access Tierra Colorada from the south. It's the best way for us to get in without being seen by infected. Here's what's left of the rainforest. We will go directly through the middle of it to reach the hills separating us from Tierra Colorada. These are the hills. Directly over the top of them is Tierra Colorada."

Steve followed Tino's hand to some squiggles and blotches he'd jotted down.

Tino continued. "The moment we enter, TC Garden Store is on the left-hand side of Constitution Avenue." Tino marked the paper with an X. "Five hundred metres down the same street, on the same side, we will come across Dedos Verdes commodity store." Another X appeared on the surprisingly well-sketched map.

"Thanks, Tino," said Steve. "Four sharpshooters in a battle tank are going to eliminate any strays we encounter. They will be using silenced weapons. We don't want to attract any attention. Remember, people, everything we find in Tierra Colorada has to be stored in the truck. It's been fitted with temperature-regulated shelves. Each of you has a full list of Arthur's requirements. Study them before we get there. Another thing: Most of the trees will be dead, so we'll have to concentrate on bulbs and seeds in packet form."

Steve handed around a small bag of dahlia bulbs he'd nicked from the Admin Building storeroom. "As you can see, the label clearly shows what's in it. Remember, quantity is important. I want it all, everything."

As chattering swirled around the room, Steve silently turned towards the man who spooked Gossard. Steve ignored his maniacal exterior and studied the unobvious characteristics, the invisible, the thing most people were afraid of. His inquisitive scan was greeted with an equally intrusive cold lucidity. It penetrated Steve's skull. Disinterested by Steve's impertinence, his trenchant eyes flicked around the room from person-to-person.

"You there, soldier, what's your name?" asked Steve.

The huge man redirected his stare towards Steve. "Anthony Bismark, sir." The reply was spontaneous.

Steve stared into his intimidation. "Anthony, can you tell us why you've volunteered to come with us on this little crusade?"

Mara always said if something henpecks the brain and scares the living daylights out of you, look at it in the face and never back down, not for anything. Steve looked at Anthony straight in the eyes. Despite Anthony's tremendous size, it was obvious; people only saw the man's hardened exterior and not the soft, humane warmth that emanated from his inner self.

"I thought you might need an extra pair of hands," replied Anthony. "I've got good experience in night shooting. I was Vice-President Gomez's bodyguard for three years. I helped him out of some really shitty situations. Sir, if you feel uncomfortable, I'll stay behind."

"Anthony, your presence here is the bulldozer we need, so don't even think about staying behind."

Anthony disconnected his look with a snappy smile. Steve added, "Arthur Payne is expecting the full list on our return, let's not disappoint him."

Before they left the complex, Steve spun around and faced his side gunner. "You there, soldier, what's your name?"

The young infantryman turned his head. "Dimitri, sir." Glad at finally being noticed, his frown changed into a distant, half-hearted smile.

"Do you know what's out there? Do you know why you're here?"

"Sir, Major Gossard told me I was here to protect you."

"Yes, you are, but danger lurks around every corner. You see anything out of the ordinary, you make sure you let us know, got it?"

Silently, without a word, Dimitri tore himself away and continued with his blank stare out and beyond the minigun.

Just then, the whine of the engines altered, and seconds later the radio erupted with a gruff commotion from Lieutenant White. "It's all clear, let's move!"

Nursery

Snow hadn't accumulated on the ground; it had been ravished by the hungry desert. Mother Nature, in an attempt at restoring her politics, had absorbed liquid in whatever form it came. Victorious in their methodical dominion, tiny green shoots appeared above the hardened surface in sparse patches, triumphant over the icy drought. Desert grass, although short and stubby, was taking the first unaccustomed gasps of cold air.

Bernard pointed towards one of the denser patches of green.

"Look, those are rubber trees, I'd recognise them anywhere."

Resembling fattened grass, a huge area of apple-green strands covered the ground. They stretched for hundreds of metres in every direction.

Ignoring his interest, Steve asked, "How's the hand? Is it still hurting?"

"Only when I bend the middle finger. I think it's muscular, surely nothing serious. Getting better by the day."

The driver suddenly swung around and announced their closeness to the hillside. In compliance, the ATV started to grumble a bit as loose soil made it skid. The sharp, sudden movements made them feel uneasy, especially with the side gunner who sporadically looked in Steve's direction for comfort. Steve could see he was scared. His directionless thoughts were plain even in the red illuminated interior of the cabin. His unfocused eyes penetratingly peered at Steve.

"What are they like?" he asked innocently. "These infected. I've never seen one."

"They look exactly like you and me. Infected move slowly. Never go near one, and more importantly, never touch one, not even a dead one. Before the night's finished, you'll know what they are like."

Dimitri gave Steve a half-hearted nod before screwing his body to face him. The look of fear was written all over him.

"Remember, we are here to help each other," said Steve.

Dimitri's trembling facade conveyed the mental connection Steve was looking for. Suddenly their vehicle began to rise.

"The battle tank's found an old road. I think he's going to use it. Hold on tight. It's going to get rough," shouted the driver as the ATV started bouncing around like a child's toy. They levelled out ten minutes later with a strong, acrid smell coming in through the air vent. In the distance, a raging fire was eating its way through a square, multicoloured building.

Moving towards the town and down the slope, Steve began to recognise the smell of PVC. "It must be an electrical fire," he said, noticing the driver's nose twitch, analysing the uninvited air.

"That's not cabling, Steve. It smells like the Union Liberty Chlorine Company on Perrier Street. If that place goes up, we're going to have quite a cleanup on our hands," said Tino.

On the outskirts of Tierra Colorada, creosote bushes had made an appearance amongst the desperate cacti. One-on-one they fought for available space in these lower-than-normal temperatures. The cacti were sticking their needles onto the sides of the bushes in a vain attempt at stopping further growth, while the creosote bushes intertwined their spikes in an equally vain attempt at choking the cacti. There was no conqueror. It wasn't the time. Each species was looking for the other's weak point, adapting itself to the changes in the other.

As the sun disappeared behind the thick, light-brown veil of smoke, the smell of chlorine got stronger. Their throats began to hurt. The driver reached under the chair and handed out gas masks.

"Here, put these on quickly."

Taking one from the driver, Steve handed it to Dimitri. Dimitri hadn't seen one before and revealed an impatient fascination for the device as Steve held it towards him. Dimitri's rough, harsh breathing concerned Steve, but it returned to normal once the white filter covered his nose. Steve, on the other hand, was quite used to them, as he had used them during his military days.

During the ascent, Bernard didn't say a word. He sat there as white as snow, scratching the sore on his hand.

Then the chlorine plant exploded. They were only a few hundred metres away when a dull, abrupt shudder made one of the side windows fall in.

"Stop, it's too dangerous! Not even our breathing gear will help us!" said Steve.

As the chlorine company exploded, the three vehicles were shifted sideways a metre from the shockwave that brought bits of buildings and debris flying through the air to their remote position, landing close.

Moments later, a green prowling mist scanned the barren landscape. Ultra-poisonous, ultra-corrosive fingered tendrils inquisitively searched beneath outcropped rocks, scanning the insides of abandoned vehicles and derelict houses with delicate precision. A slight breeze whisked the green death typical of chlorine higher into the air. They waited ten minutes within the safety of their vehicles until the voice of Lieutenant White blurted through the speaker. It made them all jump.

"Let's proceed. Remember, people, once you are outside, you still have to wear your respiratory apparatus. Don't let the wind fool you. Chlorine likes to hide itself in forgotten areas. It is a heavy gas, it'll be where you least expect it to be."

As they moved closer, the visible damage from the blast was so immense that the buildings closest to the Union Liberty Chlorine Company no longer existed. Mess and charred remains were everywhere.

"Let's not waste time looking at what has no remedy. We have a job to do," said Lieutenant White.

They drove to the beginning of Constitution Avenue, then down towards the first target, TC Garden Store. Stopping directly in front of the store, they got out and frantically looked around. They hadn't seen a single living soul since their departure. Solitude and desolation, accompanied by the sound of a rustling wind dancing between roof struts and telephone wires produced an eerie, empty whistle. They were alone. The emptiness magnified the concept that the world had finally gone mad.

"OK, I want three teams," barked the lieutenant. "Two up the road, two down the road, and two to remain here in the tank. Remember, not far, fifty metres. If something goes wrong, I want to know I can still save your sorry butts! Anthony, you to stay in the battle tank. If you see anything you damn well let me know immediately; your eyes are better trained. The rest of you, we've got work to do."

TC Garden Store was bigger than Steve had imagined. On both sides of the building, dozens of vacant parking places with trees forming aisles had been set up for clients. A restaurant aptly known as TC's Diner governed the side entrance, and a row of wooden telephone booths lined a wall in front of the WC. The front entrance had four pried-open and empty tills.

Farther inside, colourful propaganda adorned a wall. Another wall contained ten shelves filled with simple garden products like jars, vases, and decorative paraphernalia. Two wide shelves on the third wall had a couple of disorganised garden products like shears, root-cutters, plastic tubes, insecticides, and books.

The state of the plants in the entranceway didn't come as a surprise, seeing as they had died of dehydration some time ago. The next section, however, was different. Water had been applied on a timer system, five drops per hour, enough to sustain life before a client bought it and took it home to a waiting hole in the garden.

"Load all of it, don't miss anything. Load these books, too, and that plastic irrigation hose," Steve said as he looked around at the wealth of plant life, both cultivated and artificial.

Some trees still had their roots individually wrapped in black plastic bags to preserve their freshness. Some of them exposed their heredity as they frantically went in search of soil and water, attempting to escape from their enforced and forgotten habitats. No one had been there to cut and tend the excess stems or remove unwanted weeds. It was horticultural havoc. Despite the mayhem, Steve breathed deeply and sampled the wonderfully fresh air that drifted throughout the nursery.

In the far corner, magnolias swayed in a breeze offered from an undiscovered entrance. It was a long tear in the rubbery plastic walling. Dirty, whitish translucent flexible flaps fluttered wildly inwards, demonstrating nature's authority to the voiceless examples on the other side. Steve peered through the hole.

Fifty metres to the back amongst a disorderly waving of plants, Steve saw an office with a single window. He made his way through the undergrowth and walked to the office. Threatening stone and small cement statues stood to the right, guarding the entrance alongside piles of treated wood. Neatly placed cement fountains formed a semi-circle to the left.

Stepping over the planks, Steve entered the open doorway. On the wall to his left, reels of twine in fifty-metre lengths offered a variety of colours. In front, six wooden shelves contained alphabetically placed packet seeds and bulbs. The light was beginning to fade, so Steve contacted Lieutenant White on the C-10 and quickly told him the news.

"Fantastic, I'll send someone over right away to pick them up."

Two or three minutes later, two of White's team appeared and recklessly began packing whatever came to hand. It took four trips to empty the office. By that time, anything green and healthy on the outside, including the shrubs and bushes, had been crammed into the truck. Steve returned to the front reception and told them to fill up whatever available space there was in the ATV with pots, books, and insecticides.

By 7:30, the nursery was empty, and the last of the sun's rays entered through the translucent plastic ceiling above the cafeteria entrance. Although the cafeteria's floor was in turmoil, Steve looked around and thought it must have been exciting to sit down at these tables. He imagined people with shopping baskets filled with plants while taking sips out of dainty coffee cups and eating freshly made tortillas.

A couple of plants came in the ATV, as the truck was full. On the outside, Lieutenant White was once more giving orders. "Lookout team, change to infrared. I'm not in the mood for surprises. Anthony, talk to me. What's the view like from up there?"

"It's quiet, sir. Not a god-damn thing."

"Good, it's time to go. Drivers, get those engines turning. Let's get the hell out of here."

Lieutenant White climbed into the battle tank. The rest crawled between plants and pots. To Steve's right, close to Dimitri, an oversized prickly rosebush was in full bloom. The scent wafted through the air, arousing wonderful memories. Yellowy-pink flowers delicately enriched the sordid cabin with vibrancy. It smelt like heaven. Arthur would be pleased with this specimen.

Dimitri reached into his pocket. "Sir, I've something to show you. While we were waiting down the road, I found a coin lying in the street. Here." As Dimitri reached over, his arm bumped against a rose thorn. The coin fell to the floor.

"Shit! Sorry, sir," he hollered before quickly retracting his arm.

"What's the matter, Dimitri?"

"This damn rose thorn scratched me. Don't worry, sir. I'll be alright in a minute."

As Dimitri rubbed his arm, Steve saw it immediately begin to swell. "Let me take a look at that."

Dimitri nervously moved his arm over, and in the brief second that had passed, the tiny scratch had puffed up into a small, reddened lump.

"Christ, a rose wouldn't do that, it couldn't." Suddenly it hit Steve like a sack of potatoes. "Our consignment must be infected, a truck full of contaminated plants. The water used to irrigate them must have been infected. Oh my God!"

Steve saw one of the loaders drinking from a fountain in the middle of the nursery. Without hesitation, Steve contacted Lieutenant White on the communicator.

"Lieutenant, get a move on. The cargo is infected!"

"Steve, what are you babbling about?"

The response was abruptly cut in two as a stressful silence sliced his sentence with surgical precision. His reply to the others reverberated through the ATV as it came through the speaker.

"The plants are infected. No one touch anything!"

The tank and truck accelerated. By the time they reached the base of the cliff and began their ascent, the last breath of sun disappeared behind the hill. Steve began to sweat as an eerie melancholy crept into the vehicle. They silently stared at one another. Their solitude had suddenly taken on a different perspective. Dimitri was scared. He sat trembling in his new painful world, aware of his infectious state.

Steve reached for his C-10. "Gossard, we've got a problem."

"What's up? What's going on?"

"The plants at the nursery were being irrigated with infected water. Not all of them, I hope. Some of the crew members have fallen ill."

"What! Are you trying to say that all you've managed to do is fill up the truck with infected plants?"

"It would appear that way, Major. We are on our way back. I think I warned them in time."

"I'll have quarantine quarters set up by the time you arrive."

The C-10 blinked off as Major Gossard's infuriated face disappeared.

The moon shone through the roof of the ATV. This evening, the Sea of Tranquillity had taken on a duller aspect. It was but a nose in amongst two eyes formed by other craters. It was laughing at them, ridiculing their superior intellect.

"Dimitri, damn it, put the scratch in your mouth. Suck out the poison!" hollered Steve.

Bernard, watching the scene, began to tremble as he relived his own experience. The Bernard who Steve once knew wasn't there. His garrulous manner had gone. Maybe he wasn't cured after all. Maybe his infection had a side effect, something not yet understood. Steve shuddered, changing the topic of his thoughts.

In the thirty minutes it took for them to reach the outskirts of DOK, no one had said a word. Even the driver had stopped whistling "Nights in White Satin." Steve was glad. It was becoming a clot in his jugular. Stuck in the ATV with the others, Steve found himself thinking about their failure and what Gossard would say. Breaking his concentration, he looked up and peered through the window. Far in the distance, the first breaths of light from the searchlights began illuminating the lower cloud layer, and an ease surged through him.

"Not far now." The driver's unnatural tone broke the silence. "You know, it could have been a lot worse if we were inside Tierra Colorada when that chlorine company exploded," he said, failing in his attempt at reassurance.

Steve occasionally looked at Bernard and Dimitri without turning his head, just his eyes. They, too, glanced at Steve. The silence continued until they finally approached the front gate. A special security containment team was waiting for them the moment they entered.

"Everybody out!" said a voice carrying a megaphone. Steve couldn't tell who it was. All he knew was, it wasn't Gossard. Six separate makefast quarantine tents had been set up at the front entrance, each with two well-armed security guards posted in the front.

"Hurry, please. It's for your own benefit!"

Several teams came towards them donning anti-bacterial protection suits. "Name?" barked one of them.

"I beg your pardon," Steve said, cringing at his lack of warmth. "What's your name, please?" he repeated with full eye contact.

"Steve Gotlar."

The man looked down at a list and said, "Go to tent six, if you will. It's over there." The man pointed with his hand and walked to the next person behind Steve, repeating the same question.

Inside the tent was a table and chair. Behind the table, a medical examiner fidgeted with a laptop.

"Ah, come inside. Steve Gotlar?"

Steve nodded.

"Tell me, Steve, what happened out there?"

Steve related the entire story of the nursery, the chlorine factory, the scratch on Dimitri's arm, Bernard and the fly.

"Steve, you were exposed to infectious material. Did you mistakenly touch anything?"

"No, I can assure you I never touched anything."

The medical examiner began to squint at Steve, who found his stare drilling into his skull, extracting whatever it was he was looking for. A drop of sweat maybe, a skewed word, or an odd look? Who knew?

"Are you quite sure? Think for a moment. It's important. Everyone is undergoing the same examination, so don't worry. Relax and tell me, did you touch anything out of the ordinary? Do you feel numb? Does your head hurt in any way?" The medical examiner adjusted the recording volume on his laptop.

"No, I'm positive. I never touched anything. I feel fine."

"Good. Then, just a warning though, we are going to have someone watching you for the next twenty-four hours. We're going to watch your ass, get my drift? You want some free advice? If I hear any negative chatter, they're going to haul your butt back here and it won't be for a chat. Do I make myself clear?"

"Crystal. May I go now?"

"Not yet, I need a sample of your blood. Roll up your sleeve."

Taking off his jacket, Steve exposed a bulbous vein on his arm. The medic got out of his chair and walked towards a small cabinet alongside the table. Opening one of the drawers, he produced a disposable syringe.

"Keep still. It won't hurt. I only want fifty millilitres, nothing more." Seconds later, it was over. "You can go now. Oh, one more thing, Mara is waiting for you in your new quarters. We had her transferred there while you were out. I'll have someone accompany you and show you where it is." The medic scribbled Steve's name on the side of the test tube before placing it into the cooler.

Bernard was waiting outside. "Where's Tino and Nathan? They should be here by now," said Steve.

"Nathan's infected. He was carted off by medical security two minutes ago. Idiot drank water from a fountain. Tino's OK, though. I think he's gone home to rest," said Bernard.

"And Dimitri. What happened to him?"

"He's still inside. He went in after Tino came out." Bernard hardly had time to complete his sentence.

Dimitri's hysterical voice spurted from one of the tents. "I'm not infected, I tell you. I'm not infected!"

Poor Dimitri was frantic. Two security guards with anti-bacterial suits ran into the tent and dragged out his squiggling body before placing him onto the back of a truck.

Steve walked back inside tent six. "Can you tell me where they are taking Dimitri?"

"Why all the concern, Steve? Quaid is going to examine him in the hospital. We have to find out sooner or later what this thing is. Don't you agree?"

"Yes, it's just that he's a friend of mine."

"Don't worry about him. He's in good hands. Quaid's the best."

Infuriated, Steve stepped outside again.

"Well?" asked Bernard.

"All he said was that Quaid is going to study them in the hospital."

"I don't know, Steve, something doesn't smell right. How the hell can they tell with only a few questions?"

Just then, Steve heard footsteps and turned around. A security guard walked up.

"Excuse me, sir, I'm to show you to your new residence."

"Thank you, soldier. Lead the way."

"Steve, they're hiding something, I tell you. They are playing the fool with us," whispered Bernard as they walked off. Anxious, hungry eyes tagged behind like stray dogs as they approached the temporary quarantine exit.

"See you tomorrow, Bernard. It's going to be a long day. With some luck we'll finish more of the wall. Rawling's team is anxious to begin with the cabling."

Bernard's disappearing form made Steve think about his condition. Steve was sure he was still infected with something, but Quaid obviously thought otherwise. Why hadn't he been carted off with the rest? What the hell was this virus, anyway?

The guard spoke as they neared a group of houses. "It's the second house from the corner. We helped Mara move your things inside this afternoon. Sorry, as you can see, it's not much."

"Hell, anything is better than living in the Admin Building. The bloody floor was always too cold. Thank you."

The unfinished house was white and had been constructed on an incline. Its discernible shadowy, neutral colour became noticeable, thanks to well positioned lights placed throughout DOK. Although DOK's interior was flat, the incline supporting their house was definitely man-made. A simple, unpainted brick wall encircled the grounds, and from the empty back garden, Steve could see over his wall. On the other side of the wall, an incessant, sweeping spotlight brushed over land and hillside. Guards and workers had already accumulated on the first level, and Steve fascinatingly watched their tiny forms as they scuttled back and forth.

Looking towards the house, Steve counted five windows. One of them gleamed onto a porch overlooking the south, directly towards the main wall. Their Jeep was in a makefast garage adjoining the house with an unfinished door. As Steve walked into the front entrance, there was a smell of burning wood.

Mara was asleep on a sofa in front of the fireplace. The already-dying fire crackled and popped lustfully as low flames went in search of more fuel. Smiling, Steve walked by the sofa and placed two large chunks of wood into the fireplace.

"Honey, wake up. It's me."

Faintly grunting, she opened her eyes. "Hi, darling. What was all that commotion? I heard you had some problems." Mara raised herself from the sofa and tuned her eyes into Steve's.

"Some of us got infected. One of the three chaps we picked up in Tierra Colorada has fallen victim, not to mention the man in charge of the operation. Stupid really. The plants in the nursery were being irrigated with infected water."

"Oh my God! What's going to happen to them?"

"The quarantine examiner told me they've been carted off to the hospital for observation. Quaid's going to do some research on them and stick in his scalpel. Damn shame. Dimitri, our side gunner, only wanted to show me a coin he'd found in the street. He's only a boy, for God's sakes. As he passed it over, he scratched his arm on a rose thorn. Ironic, don't you think?"

"Yeah. Just remember, if it wasn't for Dimitri's untimely movement, it could've been worse."

Steve looked towards her and thought, *Thank goodness she is here.* He wouldn't have known what he would have done without her. Steve moved closer and gave her a kiss.

"What was that for?" she asked.

"I promise, I will never leave you alone again. I don't want to relive this experience without you."

Returning the affection, she placed her arms around his neck. "Now don't you be silly. It wasn't your fault. I was there when you received the orders, remember?"

"I know. I just think I should have been more insistent on you coming with me in the first place."

"Well, I'm here now. I'm safe with you."

Steve breathed deeply. "Hey, come on. Show me around a bit. I've already seen the garden. I saw there is a good view of my wall from there. When did they finish the place?"

"Yesterday. They built it on this incline so you can see the wall. The creation has to be observed by the creator, or something like that."

"Yeah, creator of the wall, true. DOK is Norris' design. I am the one putting it together for him. Too bad he isn't here to see it for himself."

After the short tour, they returned to the sofa. The only word that came to mind about their hypnotic, crackling fireplace was miraculous. As the flames painted fantasy figures on the walls, Steve excitedly and curiously turned his head once more to look at the surroundings of the empty living room. Their silhouettes shimmered and bobbed on the bare walls. It comforted Steve to see them that way. A smile left his mouth.

"As soon as you left for Tierra Colorada, the workers helped me move our stuff here. Sorry, darling, I didn't have time to go see Arthur," said Mara, lightly running her fingers up and down Steve's arm. Her darkened eyes glimmered in the hypnotic light of the fireplace. They held hands and reminisced on the sofa, their only piece of lounge furniture. The yellow stroboscopic light, blending in with the warmth and proximity of Mara at Steve's side, encouraged them to tell their individual stories of their journeys from Zacatal. Eventually, they fell asleep in each other's arms.

✻ ✻ ✻

At 6:00 in the morning, there were sounds of gunfire ricocheting through the complex. Mara gently shook Steve's shoulder.

"Honey, wake up."

"What's up?" Steve said as five more shots echoed through the empty room. His eyes immediately began to focus.

"Something's going on," said Mara nervously as Steve lifted himself from the sofa. Putting on his trousers and shoes, he headed towards the door.

Mara moved over and put more wood on the fire.

"Stay here and keep warm. I'll be back in a jiffy."

"OK, love. Hey, there's still a couple of those irradiated pork sausages stashed away. I'll go and fry us a couple. They'll be ready by the time you get back."

Steve's stomach gave a groan in compliance. "That's a wonderful idea," he said putting on his jacket.

✻ ✻ ✻

Outside, all hell had broken loose. Anthony Bismark watched as Steve approached the wall. His acuteness had followed Steve from the moment he'd left the Security Centre until his hand reached the top of the ladder.

"Jesus, Anthony, you gave me a start. What the dickens is going on? What were they firing at?"

"There's a small group of infected moving towards us and some of the stalkers got frightened and ran off. The stalkers think there are more of them over the hill."

"Where are they?" Anthony handed Steve a pair of military binoculars and pointed towards the dim reddish horizon.

"They're about three kilometres away. It's going to take awhile before we can pick them off. These buggers move slowly, and the wall-stalkers can't shoot them until they get closer."

As Steve climbed down the ladder and walked to an assembly of workers two hundred metres away, Gossard drove up in an Army Jeep.

"What's going on here? Who was firing?"

"Major, we've got company. The stalkers are scared. They think if we kill them, others are going to come looking for them."

"What!" Furiously, Gossard walked out in front of the gathering of people and called out names on his C-10. They were head wall-stalkers.

"Sanchez, Gomez, Hartley, Wishton. In my office, on the double!" On saying this, he immediately got back in his Jeep and drove to the Administration Building.

The workers were trembling, so Steve turned and faced a large group. "Look, you are responsible for the construction of the wall. You're constructing it for everyone's benefit, yours included. When it's completed, no one will be able to enter. Not even God will trespass here without our permission. I promise you, you have nothing to fear."

The workers began to mumble and fidget. "Sir, there's a hundred coming. What if five thousand come?" said one of them.

"What about fifty thousand?" said another voice.

"Look, the faster you build the wall, the quicker we can put the defence mechanisms in place. Once you have done your job and our defence devices are operational, DOK will be impenetrable. Your own lives are in your hands. Wall-stalkers are there to look after you and protect you while you work, so leave the worries of protection to them. You concentrate on what you are doing and what you've been trained for."

A hand rose in the air. "Sir, tell us something about their communication abilities. We've heard rumours they can talk to each other over great distances."

"We think it's a subsonic communication of some kind. We're not entirely sure at this stage. Remember, only when that wall is completed, will we be ready. If they attack us while the wall is still under construction, our vulnerability will become everyone's reality. The choice is yours."

Mumbling became movement, movement became alliance. Steve couldn't lie to them. These people deserved the truth.

In the distance, Steve saw the four head wall-stalkers walk out of Gossard's office. Sanchez was a competent man. Steve had seen him many times patrolling the wall, observing the outlands. As he returned to his post, Steve walked up to him. "Sanchez, what happened?"

"We panicked, it's that simple. We could see their tiny forms ambling through the telescopic sights, but the swines were too far away for us to do anything. Damn rifles are useless."

"Sanchez, you, of all people, should know you have to wait until they come into range. The infected can't hurt us behind this fortress. Hell, why do you think we are building the wall in the first place? If it's one hundred or one hundred thousand, what's the difference? It's you holding the gun. Their only weapon is their illness or an odd occasional rock if they venture too close."

"Gossard wants more wall-stalkers up there," said Sanchez. "What about bigger weapons?"

"Don't worry, Matthew is working on a plasma rifle and a rocket-propelled grenade. Right now you have to make do with what you have."

Steve accompanied Sanchez to the first level and joined with Anthony lingering motionless and patient a short way down the wall. "How far are they?" asked Steve.

"Just over two kilometres. We've got maybe half an hour."

By this time, all onsite construction had halted, and all the building was re-routed to the wall. By ten o'clock, thousands of workers of every category were completing what they'd started two months before.

While this was going on, Anthony selected a crew of twenty sharpshooters and went outside to meet the oncoming threat. Unable to contain their anxiety anymore, this super army of DOK soldiers voluntarily started their own task force of anti-infected called the DOK Protection Force, or DPF. The DPF was gaining volunteers by the hour. By nightfall it had gathered forty war-trained veterans, all ready, willing, and able to protect their civilian counterparts in its helm.

That cold November evening as Steve entered his home tired and hungry, Mara was once again sleeping on the sofa.

"Darling, why don't you wait for me in bed?"

"Hello sweet thing. Truth is, I enjoyed last night so much, I fancied a bit of a re-match on the sofa. I waited until eleven for you to come home and have breakfast. You never arrived."

"Are you trying to tell me you were worried about me? Did you miss me?" said Steve while trying to contain his smile.

Without saying a word Mara jumped up, ran over, and gave him a big hug. "You know, I had a visit today from someone. He's told me all about you," said Mara.

"Oh really, a visit from whom? What do you mean?"

Mara grinned, walked to the bedroom and opened the door.

He was light brown and probably two years old. His fur, shiny and well-kept, reflected snippets of light offered from the wall lamp.

"He just wandered in. I couldn't say no. Darling, please let us keep him. I was all alone. I want to call him Orson. He'll keep me company while you're out working."

The Labrador was a wonderful specimen. His intelligent eyes were striking. His tail began to wag when Steve called him. He immediately put his front paw onto Steve's lap.

"It's probably the best thing that could have happened. Of course, we can keep him. I don't know what we are going to feed him. These things are meat-eaters, and that stuff is scarce around here. Speaking of which, what did you do with my breakfast?"

Mara looked at Orson just as Orson looked at Mara. The tail gained velocity.

"You didn't."

"Sorry, honey, he looked so hungry. I just couldn't resist. Don't worry, I've made supper."

Orson looked up, pretending to understand them as his tongue changed sides. In front of Steve, the table containing a collection of tasteless gifts was under scrutiny. Orson strolled over and picked up a roll of toilet paper, and gently placed it between his jaws, before returning and placing it into Steve's hands. Steve tried to look impressed by the dog's feat.

"Thank you, Orson," he said looking into the dog's gentle eyes. The tail stopped wagging and he was off to the bedroom, and could be heard jumping onto the bed.

"Oh no you don't, anchovy breath. If you want to live here, you sleep on the floor like all other decent dogs."

Orson, interpreted the tone of Steve's voice, turned his head and crawled to the floor. He lay there and went to sleep.

"Poor thing was so tired when he wandered in," said Mara, putting two plates on the table. "Don't worry, I only gave him one of your sausages. I saved the other two before his eyes could focus on them."

Accompanying the two bangers was an artificial mashed potato mix made with wheat and dried potato, complete with vegetable gravy. It was filling and actually quite tasty.

✳ ✳ ✳

At 7:00 the next morning, Major Gossard came and knocked on Steve's front door. "Steve, open up, it's me."

"Major, this is a surprise."

"I thought I would come and tell you personally that the last brick has just been put into place. The wall is finished. Matthew's teams are out there right now putting in the final touches. I think it's time I demonstrated how the Light Shapers work."

"Come inside, Major. While I get dressed, Mara will make you something to drink."

Mara opened a sideboard and revealed their irradiated stocks. As tea bags came into view, Major Gossard gave a sigh. "What the—say, do you mind if I have a cup of tea? I haven't tasted the stuff in almost a year."

"Of course, Major. You know, we bought these in Zed's Hyper Store a week before the sun split sides. We don't drink much tea now, as the thought of getting used to it again somewhat frightens us. Old habits do die hard, I'm afraid."

As Major Gossard placed his cold hands around the cup, he inhaled the unmistakable aroma. "It smells wonderful. I'd almost forgotten."

Mara smiled. "All the general food stores were emptied after the water surge and heatwave. What you see is what we have."

At that moment, Orson waddled over and began sniffing the major's shoes. "What's this? When did you get a dog?"

"He roamed in yesterday. He's a dream come true, a real help when Steve's not around. Orson, this is Major Gossard."

Orson's tail began to wag and he moved towards the major, looking for free affection.

"He's so friendly," said Mara.

"Alright, Major, ready to go?" Steve stood at the front door. The major hurriedly finished his cup of tea and made his way to the door. "Thanks, Mara, it was great."

Fifty metres from the house, Mara ran out with Orson beside her. "Darling, come back. It's official. The virus has reached Bangladesh! It's all over the news!"

"Sorry, Major. I'll join you in a short while. I need to see this."

"Not without me, you don't," said the major. "I have to relay this news to everyone else. Truth is, I hardly ever miss these broadcasts."

They retraced their steps and went inside.

"Sorry, honey. As you left, I turned on the television. You know how these campy soap operas boost my morale."

They received the television signals from the only working repeater station in Southern Mexico. The picture quality wasn't that good, but the important matter was, and they were able to understand what was going on elsewhere.

The commentator was halfway through his speech as they walked in. "After materialising in Colombo ten days ago, the virus drifted northward towards Pondicherry and made its deadly appearance in Calcutta eleven hours ago. Reuters says Calcutta is in turmoil. Here is a scene that was recorded on CCTV only moments ago."

The snowy reporter's face disappeared, and a video clip gripped the plasma tube.

Mara held on to Steve's arm. "Oh God, look at those poor people!"

The silent image was the inside of a large provisions store. Judging by the short shadows, Steve figured it to be around midday. As a video camera swung in the direction of the front door, a slow-moving band of people walked in and passed by two security guards. The small group slowly broke rank and walked up to others nearby. One-on-one, they touched them, biting them. One spat at a person crouching on the floor, crying and begging for mercy. The security officers didn't know what to do, and before one of them could draw his weapon to defend himself, he was bitten by his companion. The invisible enemy spread through the provisions store in less than two minutes. They were speechless. No one could leave and no one was immune.

"Holy moly, just look at the speed at which that damn virus spreads, it's so fast! The first cases in Vera Cruz took at least an hour," said Steve.

The reporter's face reappeared. "Some more reports have just come in. Boiling the infected water does not make it safe to drink, neither does adding any chemical product. Scientists claim it's a virus so minute that it appears as a molecular deformation, an inflammation of the atom. Atomic sores. The other half of the virus circumnavigating the Pacific Basin reached Hawaii and Tahiti four days ago. I will not disclose the occurrences and likewise will not reveal what happened in those locations. The only word that could possibly come to mind is atrocity. I assure you, our Reuters' sources are quite reliable."

Mara and Gossard looked at Steve, hardly believing what they had just heard.

Steve spoke. "Major, it's time we get those Light Shapers up and running. Show me how they work."

The virus was sweeping across the world with unprecedented demise; and it had begun to evolve within itself in its watery environment. Scientists were trying to solve the puzzle of how it jumped or how it caused this wild mental change within the victims.

Orson, however, had intuition as he stretched himself on the bed. This time Steve left him there. In a way, he deserved that bed as much as they did.

December 2033

"Light Shapers need high voltage, lots of it. In order to give them exactly that, I have installed six high-power generators. They await the final connection to the Light Shapers on the wall towards the end of the month. Come, I've set up two working examples over here for you to see," said Matthew.

The testing site was full of electronic equipment. Truth was, it was a wall-to-wall technological carpet, full of flickering numbers and continuous blinking lights. A tinge of ozone delicately floated across the room, while two duteous technicians continuously read information from displays. Their fingers were typing data onto palm-sized computers, while small arrays of blue and red lights danced against a wall to their left.

Faint mechanical sounds that reminded Steve of a milling machine or a lathe sounded from behind an office door. Steve's eyes quietly frisked shelves, looking for something vaguely familiar. He recognised nothing.

There were white-clad designers, printed circuit board-creators, component-mounting, component-soldering, and finally the quality controllers and testers were busy with their work. Even the quality controllers had their own quality control of sorts. There were no errors. It was a super-laboratory, where no expense had been spared. On two worktables in a corner of the laboratory, two familiar, but larger, video projector cases had been set up about ten metres apart.

Major Gossard reached over and dimmed the lights. "These are our working dummies. They do everything the real thing does."

Gossard flicked a switch on an aluminium box, producing a low, susceptible hum.

"It looks eerie," Steve said, glancing at the flat, hypnotic, green membrane swimming from one projector to the other.

"As single units they have a five-kilometre effective range. This efficiency reduces the farther away from the plasma source they are. For this reason we have opted for pairs. As multiple, or paired units, the adjoining beams will complement one another, adding extra support."

"Do you think DOK could be protected using single units?"

"Yes, if our enemy were dust and leaves. In our case, if an intruder manages to climb the wall, the Light Shaper protecting an area from four kilometres will not have sufficient power to vaporise him. DOK is so big that we are forced to use pairs. The width of the plasma beam auto-regulates with adjacent Light Shapers alongside, ensuring there are no gaps or way to breach the wall."

A note of diversion touched Gossard's face. "Here, throw something at it."

Steve reached down and picked up a pen. "Is this alright?"

"Throw anything you want. Go on. What are you waiting for?"

Steve didn't throw it hard. He was thinking of what would happen if Gossard's half-sized experiment failed. These were not even the real things. They were still prototypes. If this green hallucinatory film botched up, Steve would be the one subject to his mood change.

After Steve's intentionally feeble attempt, the pen landed on the green wavy film about five metres in. The instant the pen touched the green skin it vanished: no smoke, no sparks, no flames. It simply disappeared.

"Damn, that's impressive," Steve said as it reanimated his interest.

"As you already know, it's our roof. It's the only protection we have from above. We are one of three DOK cities using this technology. The others have opted for fresh air. They feel they have enough protection with sharpshooters. I told them they were crazy. One of them threw down the phone in my ear."

"Are the video links up yet?" Steve asked.

"Hell, thanks for the reminder. Matthew wanted a word with me. Apparently, DOK 3 hasn't finished their first level. I must get hold of Kalakov and find out what's going on."

"Hello, Major, Steve." Matthew strode into the room. "Major, I can't get any sense out of them. They insist on saying it is a strike."

"What are you talking about? That's absurd. Don't they understand what's going on or what's going to happen?" asked the major.

"They say they can't build the wall in the time necessary like the other DOK cities. Something about the temperature being too low."

"Has he put the additives into the water?"

Matthew didn't know the answer.

"Give me that damn video phone!" Gossard reached over while Matthew patched him through.

For the first time, Steve got a crystal image of what was going on inside another DOK city. Like their own, there were workers busily scampering about eagerly trying to finish the wall; but there, instead of thousands, there were fifty.

Matthew pressed a button. "You're on, sir."

Gossard caressed his chin. "Kalakov, can you hear me?" The speaker hissed.

"Who's that? Oh, good Lord, Gossard, it's nice to see you."

"Don't you give me that Russian bull. What the hell are you trying to do, commit mass suicide? My guy here says you're on strike. Is it true?"

"Yes, once these damn video phones became operational, our workers started getting nosy and began sniffing around other DOK cities. They think being here on the northwestern part of Alaska is the same as being in California or in Mexico. I can't get it into them. They don't realise the climate is different. They won't move until I can resolve the problem."

"Listen, Kalakov, I don't know how to say this, so I'll let it climb out of my mouth naturally. If you don't complete that wall, you're going to get infected or eaten. Five kilometres to the west of you is the Northern Pacific Road, linking the entire American continent to the Asian continent. If your wall doesn't go up soon, you are going to get visitors, infected visitors. Not ten or twenty—twenty thousand, and that is if you are lucky. They will be hungry and won't stop at anything until they have climbed over your non-existent wall or through your non-existent gate apertures and eaten all of you alive. Your bodies will give them the strength and stamina they need to move on to the next DOK city. DO I MAKE MYSELF CLEAR?"

There was silence as Kalakov looked away one or two seconds before making eye contact again. "Gossard, we know the dangers. We also know what'll be coming down that road. It's a matter of convincing them, that's all," said Kalakov in his Russian-English accent.

"No, you stupid moron. It's about giving a direct order to a man. If he doesn't comply, he must be punished. That is what it is all about, Kalakov. Now get that blasted wall up! DO YOU HEAR ME?"

The screen flickered off and Gossard furiously marched out of the Security Centre towards the Administrative Centre across the parking lot.

Matthew trembled. "Ho-lee Mo-see, I've never seen Gossard in a mood like that before."

"Yeah, but we know he's right," said Steve. "The similarity between DOK 3 and us is clear. We are both front-liners. These infected enjoy the cold temperatures, and I think Kalakov's going to start getting guests sooner rather than later."

✳ ✳ ✳

Mara took Orson with her to the agricultural area. "Hello there, can you tell me where I can find Arthur Payne?"

"You got him looking at you. Who might you be, young lass?"

Mara blushed at the remark. "My name is Mara Gotlar. Sorry my husband Stephen didn't come himself. He's been dying to meet you, though. I'm here on his behalf."

They shook hands.

"Hello, Mara, this is a wonderful surprise. God, you're prettier than the rumours I've been hearing."

Mara briefly broke eye contact and went red again.

"I love his work," said Arthur. "I've been admiring it these last couple of weeks. I personally think he's a genius."

"Thank you. I'll be sure to pass on your message. My husband told me about what happened in Tierra Colorada."

Arthur's grin turned sour. "Yeah, they were such good specimens, too. I had most of them removed and destroyed."

Noticing Arthur's uneasiness, Mara broke the atmosphere. "It's quite a place you got here. Why don't you show me around? I want to know what an agriculturist does when he's faced with restrictions. What sleeved secrets he might have stashed away.

What I'm trying to say is, how do you manage to keep this city alive despite the limitations you're faced with?"

"How easily you twist my arm. Come, I'd be delighted to show you around. Prepare yourself, valiant lass, for first in line we have the greenhouses."

Arthur, adopting a childlike expression, led Mara outside through the main door where tall cylindrical metallic shapes were facing the sun, collecting the rays. Arthur watched as her gaze moved up and down each of them. Copper tubes running vertically from top to bottom joined at their bases before disappearing underground. They reminded her of gigantic spoons.

"Those are the agua-genies. It's where our water comes from. Those copper tubes you see end up in one of two deposit tanks behind the second greenhouse."

Mara could plainly see that their gastronomic requirements were in Arthur's hands. He, of course, knew this and started explaining the operation with added enthusiasm.

"The first greenhouse is totally vegetarian. Peas, carrots, potatoes, cabbages, onions, celery, tomatoes, beans, beets, and all that stuff. A few of them are still in the early stages, but with a bit of branch-twisting, they will be ready in the next couple of weeks. The second greenhouse is slightly smaller than the rest. I've used it for the herbs and spices."

On the outside of each greenhouse, a squared signboard revealing type and species was bar-graphed in three colours, indicating quantity and time availability.

"The yellow line denotes the amount in kilograms or quantity available. The blue/red stripe means if it is blue, as in this case, there is none on hand, but will be available in two weeks. Alternatively, this red stripe here means they have been ready and ripe for picking for the past week. It is a freshness scale, if you like."

"Well, Arthur, it's certainly a wonderful collection."

There were many familiar names written on the tri-coloured graph paper. Oregano, marjoram, thyme, mint, parsley, turmeric, and dill were among a few. They walked inside.

"A lot of these herbs have medicinal qualities. This is dittany. It originated from Crete. It is also credited with many medicinal virtues," said Arthur, excitedly picking a leaf and rubbing it between his fingers.

"Come, the next greenhouse is the fruit and citrus section. It's not much at the moment, but with careful grafting, I expect to see results in six to eight weeks."

He was right. It was quite bare, with the exception of frail, infrequent examples growing in dedicated areas.

"Don't say anything. I know it's not much to look at. I have never done so much grafting in all my years as a horticulturalist."

As Mara walked down the aisle, she passed lemon, apple, and peach. Suddenly her attention was drawn to a few bushes furiously growing next to a plum.

"What's that? They're not fruiting trees."

Arthur gave a smile. "It's Nicotiana tabacum, a tobacco plant. I grow it for the workers."

As Arthur spoke, Mara watched the gentle manner he moved his hands. The guy was a humanitarian, a plant psychologist.

"Despite what's going on, there are still smokers here?"

"Oh yes. It tranquilises them, just like it did when I smoked as a young man. I still smoke occasionally."

"You can't be more than forty."

"Thanks for that. Actually, I'm fifty-eight. I put it down to my good living." Arthur was probably one of the only well-fed people in DOK. His slightly paunchy appearance and lax attitude all pointed fingers to a laid-back, stress-free way of life.

They walked back outside. "You know, before the world went crazy," said Arthur, "I spent most of my years in Mexico City. My brother died the day the sun went mad, so I travelled down here to bury him in Jonuta. Of course, once I got here, the return trip was impossible, so in the end I moved into his house."

"You went to Jonuta?" Mara asked. "I got myself into problems there. Apparently, after the infection started, the inhabitants disappeared. My husband drove through on his way over without seeing a single living soul. It's as if God put his hand down and scooped them up overnight."

"They're still there, Mara, mark my words. No one just ups and vanishes, especially people. Hunger is one of the greatest forces within us. Although you didn't see them, they saw you. You can count on it."

Mara shivered at the thought.

Arthur continued. "I arrived a week before Steve. One day, the military came knocking at my door, practically dragging me out by my short and curlies. My reason for living had died when my family succumbed to the heat. What had I to lose?"

"I'm sorry, Arthur, real sorry. Truth is, I do not know anyone who hasn't lost a family member or a loved one. If it wasn't the water or the heat, it's this bug thing. The human race isn't really having a very good time, is it?"

"You're right. You know, Steve's a very lucky man to have you by his side."

"As I am lucky to have him. He's pulled us through some sticky situations. I'm convinced if he wasn't around to back me up, I wouldn't be having this little chat."

"Don't be so melodramatic. You have the strength to look after yourself, with or without him. I can see the trait."

Mara had only just met the man, but she found herself speaking to Arthur as if she had known him for years. The thought of the population subsisting their way forward made her feel quite comfortable. Together they were obligatory inhabitants of DOK. Orson, on the other hand, didn't share her sentiments.

"What's your dog's name? He's a lovely specimen."

Orson having heard the word "dog" looked up, unmotivated. Orson stood motionless. His unflinching tail, unruffled by the obvious need of free attention, lay dormant. It was completely unlike him.

"This is Orson. Now don't you be rude to a friend. Sorry, I can't explain why he's acting this way."

"He could be ill. I can put you in contact with a good vet. A few of the workers here are vets."

Orson steered his vision away at the mere sound of the unfamiliar word. His altering glance flicked in Mara's direction.

"What's the matter? Have you eaten too much irradiated sausage again?" she asked.

"Don't worry, Mara, introduce him another day. Right now, I have a date with a couple of castor oil plants, it's castor bean day."

Without further ado, Mara bid farewell. "I'll come and see you again soon. It was a pleasure to have met you."

"You do that, and likewise. Send my regards to your husband. I think he's doing a grand job out there."

As they walked back home, Orson began cheering up a little. "What's the matter, boy?"

Orson glanced up at her with his usual warmth. Mara trusted Orson's sixth sense more than her own. *If only he could speak*, she thought. But there again, sometimes a dog doesn't have to speak to make himself heard. Orson's message was coming through loud and clear.

Steve arrived home that afternoon in a bit of a mood, so Mara cheered him up with a cup of tomato soup and some homemade bread.

"What a day! Some of the lights on the far west side were out of order. I've been digging up and fixing cables the whole bloody afternoon. Someone had cut them, hacked clean through they were."

Orson went and sniffed Steve's shoes.

"Hello, boy. I suppose you've had a better day than I've had."

"Actually, darling, he's had a wonderful day. We went to visit Arthur Payne today."

"About time. What's he like?"

"A nice chap, very likeable. Orson didn't share the same idea, though. Truth was, I thought he was a bit scared of Arthur."

"Strange, Orson's not like that."

"Yeah. Anyway, how's the wall, apart from the cut cables?"

"Fine, the workers are concentrating themselves on the inside for a change. Gossard told them there are two schools that must go up before the end of the month. He's put six squads out there. I've got a meeting with him tomorrow. I think he wants to discuss the building security."

"Oh, that'll be fun. What did he say about your cut cables?"

"Not much. What could he say? If I catch the person responsible, I'll hang him facedown outside the walls for all to see. Gossard's one of the good guys, but he has a bit of a temper at times. You should've seen him this morning when he spoke to Kalakov. Smoke came out his ears. Anyway, he means well."

"And now tell me: When's Gossard going to put you in your post as head of security?"

"I'm sure once everything is up and running on the wall, I'll be in the security office."

"What are my responsibilities in all this?" asked Mara.

"You are my wife and you are free to help wherever you want."

Mara opened the gas oven. "What about Lieutenant White, Nathan, and Dimitri? What's he done with them?" she asked, slipping on the kitchen gloves.

"The funniest thing. A week after their admittance, they were discharged, the same as Bernard. I know they have something, I can feel it."

Mara produced two steaming browned loaves of bread from the lower shelf of the oven and placed them onto a cement workspace, then turned off the bubbling soup.

"Hon, if these guys are infected, they're a health risk. Surely Gossard knows it."

"Of course he does. The man's no fool."

That night Steve went to bed with questions swimming about in his head. *To hell with premonitions*, he thought. They were only two days away from a non-existent Christmas. So what? They'd celebrate it all the same. They celebrated it every year. Last year Mara said she wanted a mountain bike, so Steve made up a big empty cardboard box, wrapped it in colourful wrapping, and perched it against the wall in the lounge. Steve thought of all the millions of presents that would normally have been opened by this time of year. Not anymore, there were no present-bearers left. The spirit of Christmas had died along with the world population more than a year ago. Where was Christmas when the world went to hell?

✷ ✷ ✷

The next day, Steve was awakened by a knock at the front door.

"Who is it?"

"Anthony, sir. Are you ready to go?"

"Give me five minutes! Sorry, honey. I have to go. I forgot Anthony was coming to pick me up. He wants to review the communication links to the Security Centre from the wall."

"Don't be silly. If you can promise me to be back in a couple of hours, I'll make breakfast. You know what happens if you don't show, don't you?"

Orson lifted an ear. Steve hurried outside.

"Sorry about that. Did I catch you at a bad moment?" asked the bass voice of Anthony.

"No, Mara and I were up chatting last night. Before we knew it, it was already three in the morning. Where shall we start?"

"In the Security Centre before coming out to pick you up this morning, I ran a diagnostic check on the communication boxes on the wall. Twenty-six of them are out of order, I want to go and take a look."

"In what sector?"

Anthony paused. "Seven. It's the same area where you found those cut MOGS cables yesterday. You don't think it's sabotage again, sir?" Anthony's heavy frame had a definite threatening look about it as the words surged out.

Steve sternly looked towards him. "Tell me the video cameras were working."

"Not only are they working, they've been recording data for the past eight hours except between nine and eleven o'clock, the cameras pointing towards Sector Seven only recorded static. Someone must've switched them off early last night. I checked them myself this morning."

"What! But why Sector Seven? What's so special out there?"

"Nothing. Sector Seven is the most western part of the complex. It's just desert. Reconnaissance teams rarely go there, skeleton watch only. If you want, I'll put together a surveillance team and have them poke around the entire area brick-by-brick. If there's something out there behind the curtain, we'll find it."

"Yes, do that. I can feel it. This is not going to be an easy search. Get some metal detectors on the job as well."

Anthony dropped Steve alongside the Security Complex and drove off. Inside, Steve switched on the single monitor display panel directly linking him to all the Security Complexes and Security Centre two kilometres away. As the display shimmered to life, Steve logged in and pinpointed the fault within minutes. Whoever this person was, he not only knew where the cables were, he knew where to cut them. Steve's fingers went to work. Rhythmically caressing the keyboard, the option to change the user password beckoned him to the centre of the screen. *To hell with this*, he thought as he tapped in a new code and turned off the computer. Steve heard the sound of an approaching car engine. Anthony had returned with company.

"Let me introduce you. Steve, this is Bruce and Gregory. This is Security Chief, Steve Gotlar." They shook hands.

"Bruce and Gregory are specialists in terrorism techniques," said Anthony. "They are members of the DPF." Bruce smirked. Gregory opened a black satchel and produced a metal pole with an electronic panel protruding from one end. Emotionlessly switching it on, both of them disappeared through the door and walked towards the wall a hundred metres away.

"We'll find it, whatever it is," said Gregory's fading voice.

"Those two are good. I've seen them work," said Anthony as he walked out the door after them. Grabbing the repair bag and palm-sized computer, Steve followed him into the morning sun. The air was cold, so he pulled his jersey to his chin. Glancing around at the surroundings, debris was everywhere. With the cleanup crew only due to arrive in a week, the dusty surface, revealing empty bags of cement and broken bricks, still managed to restore the pandemonium of recent memories. Bruce and Gregory, ignoring the scatter, climbed a ladder in the distance and stepped onto the first level, scanning the surface and scatterings for any irregularities in all directions.

During the wall construction, Steve had placed service inspection panels every fifty metres to alleviate painstaking measurements if a fault appeared in an inaccessible region of the wall. Extracting an opening tool from a repair bag, he knelt down, gently flipped the lid and exposed the cables. Reaching into the service bag, his fingers fumbled for the multimeter. Placing the two probes onto the yellow cables, Steve turned the knob to the voltage scale and watched as the needle rose to 12 volts. Here, everything seemed normal, and the cables were in the same state they were when he'd put them in place weeks ago. Feeling satisfied, Steve closed the lid and walked towards the next service panel fifty metres away.

Kneeling down, Steve noticed deep pry marks had peeled away part of the metallic conservation paint, then he contacted Anthony.

"Anthony, I think I've found it."

"Wait, sir—don't touch it, Let me take a look first."

In less than two, Anthony's enormous frame ran towards Steve, lifting dust particles into the air.

"Hmm, I see what you mean. Yeah, it's definitely been forced."

Revealing a microfibre camera from his side bag, Anthony introduced the flexible optical wire behind the lid and switched on a monitor device placed on the ground. "Jesus, what bedlam. I think he's done them with a pair of scissors!" said Anthony.

Dozens of mutilated wires filled the viewer. "I'll have to get Matthew's guys over here to fix it. There's just too much damage. It would take me hours. Wait! What's this?" Anthony moved closer to the viewer. Attached to the inspection lid, a very fine strand of wire led off to a small rounded plastic capsule hidden behind broken cobwebs of cut cable.

"It's an explosive device! Thank the stars for small miracles. Just one tiny movement of that inspection cover and—" Anthony never finished his sentence.

Steve looked toward the image. "It's got our trademarks written all over it. It's our own military explosive, for God's sake. This guy must have walked into the armoury and helped himself." Steve sat back on his haunches, speechless. He never would have suspected their own weaponry to be used against them. His heart pounded, then missed a beat.

Producing a pair of fine cutters, Anthony delicately snipped the almost-imperceptible wire joined to the explosive device and held it out in his cupped hands.

"There it is. A Ferguson-McCray anti-personnel micro-mine. What a beauty. Don't worry, without the interlinking cable, it's as harmless as a baby toy. Steve, if you want a bit of advice, you'd better watch yourself from now on, at least until I can find out what's going on."

Anthony contacted Bruce and Gregory. "How are you two doing out there? Have you found anything?"

"Nothing, boss," replied Bruce. "There's nothing out here, but bare wall and scrap."

Steve contacted Matthew and requested a repair team. "While you're at it, put together a surveillance squad. I want this area closely watched."

Fifteen minutes later Matthew arrived with three men. "What's up, Steve? Where's the damage?"

Steve pointed to the opened service panel spewed on the ground.

"Oh my, who could have done this?" exclaimed Matthew. "What on earth happened in there?"

Matthew's authenticity emitted a panic and made Steve stare towards the unobstructed inspection cover. Someone had really tried to end his life by assassination. Steve began to tremble and without hesitation solemnly walked away.

"Remember," he called over his shoulder, "we need to get those communicators up and running before midday. I am going home to put my head down. I want to check them all before we switch on the wall this evening."

"Don't worry, Steve, they'll be ready."

✳ ✳ ✳

At home, Mara was in the dining room cleaning a shelf. "You made it just in time. I was beginning to tell Orson today was his lucky day."

"Not now, honey, someone tried to kill me."

Mara's look turned to stone. "What—what happened? Is it connected with what happened yesterday?"

"Yeah, it came in the shape of an anti-personnel mine. Same sloppy style of cut cables, too. This time our wire cutter turned off some of the communicators. Matthew's out there fixing them now."

Steve's thoughts returned to Anthony and he grabbed his communicator. "Get your guys to check the outside of Sector Seven. Maybe what we are looking for is outside."

Anthony's face erupted over the communicator twenty minutes later. "Sir, they've spotted something in the sand wrapped in a plastic bag. Bruce has climbed down to fetch it."

Minutes later Anthony's voice surged through the C-10. "It looks like a badly made remote control unit. What's this all about? What's going on?"

"Get some stalkers out there on the double!" ordered Steve. "I want that whole damned area watched like a friggin' bank!"

"I'm on it."

Anthony's fading voice brought a fleeting smile to Steve's face for the first time all day. They'd found something unexpected, something extraordinary. Thoughts began to rattle through his brain. Steve's mind was uneasy. Infected don't think rationally. They probably wouldn't even know how to press a button. Did they have someone on the inside, someone who they could contact, give orders to, even trust in? Steve's thoughts returned to Nathan, Dimitri, and Bernard. They had been exposed. They were carriers and they were released on doctor's orders. Who was this doctor, anyway? Was he normal like us? Were they all in it together? Someone had to know what was going on. Steve decided to pay the doctor a visit.

"Sorry, honey, have to go. Anthony has found something outside the wall in Sector Seven. I'm going to check out a few things at the hospital."

As Steve pulled up to the hospital and got out of the Jeep, the two administration security guards waved from a distance.

One of them broke away from his post to meet Steve. "I see you're headed for the hospital. Planning on going in?"

"Yes, why?"

"We see people going in without coming out. We stand here, day in and day out, bored out of our soddin' minds. We watch people with our binoculars. There's not much more to do here, really. It's just these last two days, though. You know, I'm glad they made you security chief. I like you."

"Thanks. Let's get back to the missing people. Did you recognise anyone?"

"Only Doctor Quaid. It's the same ugly face twice a day," said the security guard.

"Maybe they sleep overnight and leave in the morning. Maybe there's another exit door," Steve said, scrutinising the guard's eye movements.

"You're joking. At the moment the hospital has only six beds, and there's no emergency exit," said the guard, waving his hands high in the air.

"Are you sure of this?" Steve's eyes followed his hands.

"Absolutely. We've been doing guard duty since it went up. Hell, we even helped them build the place."

"Tell me about the ones who disappeared."

"Not much to say, really. They were all men. Ten of them in the last two days."

"Why didn't you let me know sooner?"

"No one gave us your C-10 code. We couldn't contact you even if we wanted to."

"Who did you ask?" Steve questioned.

The guard frowned. "Why, I asked Doctor Quaid himself. I didn't tell him the reason for my enquiry. He just looked at me and said he didn't have it."

"He lied. All DOK superiors have my dial number. I'm sure this Doctor Quaid even has it pinned up on the wall next to the photo of his aunt. Who is he, anyway?"

"Some of us refer to him as Doctor Death. He was the medical intern at the Villahermosa University before they shipped him here. Two years ago, six patients died because Doctor Quaid administered a lethal gas instead of oxygen. The victims died immediately. At the public hearing a week later, he denied everything, mentioning the word "framed" repeatedly. He blamed two nurses for the screw-up, and was duly acquitted on charges with insufficient evidence. The two nurses were not so lucky. He's not the most popular doctor around. I know that Major Gossard was trying to get him transferred to another DOK, but no one wants him."

"Well, what would you say if I told you that I'm going to pay this Doctor Death a visit?"

The guard's eyes widened. "It's an inviting thought. Just be careful. He's quite a handful. Hey, fancy a cup of coffee?"

"Now that's an inviting thought. When I come out we'll talk about it. Right now I have an urge, and besides, you better get back to your post before someone misses you."

"We'll be waiting."

Doctor Quaid was responsible for treating Bernard, Dimitri, and the others. That part Steve knew. What he didn't know was the doctor's side of the story. Steve was intrigued. Fortunately, he didn't need search warrants. Steve was the law in the eyes of DOK. His compensation for the successful completion of the wall was not only a place within the secure boundary of DOK, but he was DOK's second-in-command. Steve was free to practice the law, his unrestricted law of good and evil. Nearing the hospital door, Steve could feel the closeness between them. Good and evil didn't exist here, they were one fetid body.

As Steve entered the main door, he naturally presumed the only person who came in sight to be Doctor Quaid. The scraggly man, unconscious of Steve's interest in him, traipsed around the floor like a lost, misguided spirit. He was uneasy, deep in thought and obviously somewhere else. Steve wouldn't introduce himself as Steve Gotlar. To him, Steve would be Officer Gotlar, Chief of Security.

"Doctor Quaid, I am Officer Gotlar, Chief of Security." Quaid went white as the smattering of words accentuating Steve's lack of humour revealed his unsubtle manner at meeting new friends. His frame wiggled slightly. Steve was glad he began their little meeting that way. Quaid was short, stocky, and clumsily dressed. His unbrushed hair and thick neck revealed his persona in unspoken words. His nose began to twitch at Steve's glance. Although he didn't know why Steve had come, Steve was sure he had a good idea as to what rattled around in Steve's brain.

"You know why I'm here, Doctor Quaid, so let's dispense with the shilly-shally. In September when I arrived, you treated a patient for a fly bite on his hand and another for a thorn prick. I saw the release forms you signed. Bernard and Dimitri have both shown them to me." Steve lied about Dimitri, he had seen only Bernard's. "What do you know about this virus? What can you honestly tell me that I don't already know?"

Quaid slowly regained confidence. "It's spreading so fast that when the two strains meet next week, it's going to cause unprecedented effects on this planet. What we've seen to date is nothing. The virus hasn't even begun to live."

"What are you babbling about, begun to live?"

Quaid's true inner self abruptly came to the surface. "Just as I thought, you're nothing more than another nosy po-lice-man with a badge pretending to do good for the citizens of somewhere. Well listen up, mister po-lice-man, it has already arrived on Australia's east and west coast. It reached them simultaneously just over an hour ago. My job here is to prepare an antibody, a contra-reactive virus. All I can tell you is I am close. In the thirteen patients I have received so far, it has proven effective."

"You're delving into the unknown, Quaid. Truth is, I think you're nuts. How can you prepare an antibody without the proper knowledge of what it is you are really dealing with? You are basing supposititious ideas on sick patients with no proper medical histories."

"You still don't get it, do you? The virus is still inactive. It will remain that way in its dormant phase until next week. When the strain from the East collides and associates with the strain from the West, billions overnight will hear its shout. This pandemic goes much further than someone's medical history. Am I getting through your thick skull?"

Angrily, Steve drew his pistol from its holster and pointed it directly toward Quaid. "Don't you dare intimidate me with that crap, you simple man! Let me tell you something. Possibly, the development of our cerebral cortex has been the greatest achievement of our evolutionary process. It allows us the thrills of intellect and the pangs of self-consciousness. It is all too often overruled by our inner instinctive brain, the one that tells us to react, not reflect."

Quaid briefly gave Steve a dirty look and said, "The brain tells us to run rather than ruminate. I have often thought that maybe we have gone as far as we can go. Maybe the next advance in our evolution, whatever that may be, will be made by beings we create ourselves. Perhaps that step forward has already been achieved somewhere else by organisms that had a billion years' head start on us. I consider the possibility. It is somehow connected to our present-day dilemma. Think for a bit: If these beings ever visited us by walking up to our front door, would we recognise what we were seeing? And by catching sight of us, would they react in anything but horror at seeing such mindless, primitive creatures?"

A brief silence dominated the laboratory as Steve looked down at the gun. "Quaid, I haven't come here to listen to your overactive mind. I need answers. I've got someone out there threatening me. He's also cutting cables. You talk about dead viruses and next week. What about us?"

"Oh please, Gotlar, you're boring me," said Quaid, unthreatened by the revolver. "Consider this, the man that engineered the virus was brilliant, absolutely brilliant. I've never seen atom-hacking like this before. There are probably only two men on Earth who could do it."

"Are you saying someone made it, and then set it free?"

"Without a doubt. If only I could tap into its signature." Quaid scratched his head. "You know, Bernard is a good guinea pig. I am using his particular illness to stimulate a molecule I call molecule-H. It treats and pushes down the inflamed atom, reducing the redness. His body is full of it. I am monitoring his condition daily. I am monitoring all their conditions, and I have only one more week to do it. In relevance to your last statement, I have no idea what you're talking about, and I have far better things to think about than breaking cables. Now, if you don't mind, I am extremely busy."

Bells began to clang in Steve's head so he placed the gun back in the holster. "Doctor, if what you say you're doing is beginning to show results, why not get someone to help? I mean, there must be someone suitable out there."

"Because who I need is an atom scientist, not a plumber. Now, good day, mister po-lice-man!"

Steve stomped outside.

"Here, I hope it's not too cold," said one of the two guards, handing Steve a cup of coffee. "How did it go in there?"

Feeling inadequate, Steve said, "I want you two to look after our good doctor like he was your father, you hear me?"

"You're joking."

"Do I look like I'm joking?" Steve drank the coffee, dismissed himself and drove towards the Admin Building.

"It's reached Australia," Steve said as he walked into Gossard's office.

"Yes, I heard the news as it happened, almost two hours ago. Close the door, Steve, and sit down. Quaid just told me you paid him a visit and started pointing guns. You know, there's really no need. Not only are we fortunate to have him with us, I leave him be to do whatever he has to."

"That's not what I heard from those two security guards propping up the outside wall. They said he's a walking health hazard, not to mention your determination to send him away to another DOK." Steve annoyingly picked up a staple gun and moved it furiously to one side.

"Steve, the stories you heard were only scandal blown out of proportion. It was never proven. Anyway, even if it were true, in the medical profession no one is immune to mistake. I guess it's what makes us human. I have protected the work of Strabovich Quaid since we began here in August. He's eccentric, brilliant and, may I add, tireless. Not only have his efforts so far brought new scope and ideas on this menace, his vaccines are proving to be effective. He shows me the results on a weekly basis. What was the reason for you wanting to see him anyway?"

"Someone's been cutting our cables, and I thought he had something to do with it. Early this morning, Anthony and I drove to Sector Seven to find out why a couple of communicators had gone on the blink. When I removed one of the inspection covers, Anthony found a fine wire joined to an anti-personnel micro-mine. It had been put there to explode as the cover was removed. It scared the living hell out of me."

Gossard interrupted Steve with a smile. "Anthony had that explosive analysed for both fingerprints and DNA. The results have just come in. Do you want to know what they were?"

"Surprise me."

"The explosive was a dud, a fake, a sand-filled casing put there to scare you. I can see whoever put it there succeeded in their plan."

"And the fingerprints, the DNA—what do you know about them?"

"As we suspected, the only fingerprints on the device were Anthony's and a partial part of another. Apart from that it was clean. We sent the partial print to Mexico City's central computer, which is luckily still operational. The operator told me the results would take awhile, so we'll all get updated in the next couple of hours. Until then, I suggest you go home and get some rest. I'll catch you once we have what you're looking for. Remember, tomorrow's Christmas. We don't want to screw it up any more than it already is."

"Yeah, speaking of which, is everything ready for the Light Shapers tomorrow?"

"Yes, both Rawling and Matthew are ready. By the way, did you finally meet Arthur Payne?"

"Not personally. Mara's met him though."

"What did she think of him?" enquired Gossard.

"A very likeable chap. She said he knew what he was doing."

"DOK 16 has to be that way. In here, we are fighting two wars. One is the continuing battle of a self-sustaining survival entirely within these walls, which I am happy to say we are winning. The other is on the way. We are not entirely sure of its capabilities, not even Doctor Quaid can give me specifics on the matter at this stage, but we expect the worst. You must give him your full support. He needs you as much as you need him."

"Thanks, Gossard. Apologies for my earlier performance."

"Forget it. His actions are for the good of everyone. He's doing everything in his power to cure this, whatever it is. Your job tomorrow is to finalise our wall defences and see to the needs of the wall-stalkers. We have to be prepared."

On the way home, Steve contacted Matthew. "How are the cable repairs coming on?"

"All done. I couldn't check them, the computer didn't give me access."

"Blast! I changed the password. Sorry." Steve turned the Jeep around and headed back to the Security Centre.

In the Security Centre, after restoring the code, Steve looked towards the twenty control monitors, each depicting another DOK city. These live and direct images were demands for help from the other workers. To the right of Steve, a detailed map of the Central and North American continents hung on the wall with numbered drawing pins representing the locations of the other DOK cities. On the central wall, two complicated control panels, together with a large number of unidentifiable gizmos, displayed life in the form of pulsating red and green lights.

Even DOK 3 had made significant progress in the lifting of its wall. It was amazing the power of human persuasion. Gossard had definitely left his impression. Steve stood for ten minutes gazing at sequenced images fluctuating every two seconds from Patio South, to Gate-A, to Gate-B, to Gate-C, to Security Centre, to Patio North, and then back to Patio South to begin the cycle over again.

Christmas Spirit

As Steve entered the front door, to his surprise Mara had put up a Christmas tree. It wasn't lit with flickering lights and fancy little balls of colours, neither did it have any dainty Father Christmas dressed in red hanging on its branches. Those things were not available. Neither did they have the means to make them. Instead, she had stripped a hungry creosote bush of its needles and decorated it the best she could. Handmade paper figures adorned branches. Next to the tree was one of Steve's old winter socks adequately covered in cotton hung over the fireplace. Inside was a surprise.

"I remember as a child," Mara was ecstatic, "we would normally see these socks hanging over the fireplace. Of course they weren't grey and stinky like yours. They were red with a fine snowy topping. They were filled with sweets with noisy wrappers and money to go and buy the present of your dreams. Don't worry, I did wash it first."

"This is wonderful. What's in it?" Steve asked.

"Ah, you'll just have to go and take a little peek, won't you?"

Steve felt like a kid, forgetting all his problems. The world could wait a few minutes while he encountered the source of his childish ecstasy. Whatever it was, it was big, like a book or books. *How did she squeeze it in there?* he wondered. Mara knew his likes and dislikes even better than he did, so he unhooked the stocking from the mantle and fiddled about the inside. Not only was it a book, it was in good condition, too.

The familiar blackened frontal, the white lettering and the stale book smell symphonically reopened wonderful memories. It was poetry. Steve loved poetry. It had been an affiliation of his since childhood until his insertion into the police force. His personal favourite, without any doubt, was Charles Bukowski.

Bukowski's interpretations of hardship were more than enlightening. Steve had always found each poetic analysis, each page, a perfectly pictured description, even autobiographic in the sense that it revealed in his own life's struggle, authentically reanimating his pain. Steve had read it hundreds of times; that was, of course, until book and he parted company twelve years before. His socked present was the very book he had lost.

"I don't believe it. Where did you find it?" he said with a smile.

"The day I left our house in Zacatal to frantically come here, I opened some of the boxes under the stairs and found it there. I never told you about it, because I wanted to give it to you for Christmas."

"Oh baby, I thought it had been lost for all these years. Thank you, darling. It means so much to me," Steve said, as he opened it for the first time in more than a decade.

"I will give you yours tomorrow morning at twelve. It's the tradition, remember?"

Mara acknowledged with a shrug.

Peering happily once more towards the Christmas tree, Steve got up and contacted Anthony. "Any news on the fingerprint?"

"Oh yes, the results came back from the central computer, all right."

"Well?" Steve was biting his lip.

"It's one of those three you brought back from Tierra Colorada when you rescued Mara. It's Nathan."

"Get someone out there to collect him. It's time we had a little chat."

"Already done. They should be arriving at his place shortly. I'll let you know once we have him back at the Security Centre for interrogation."

Steve turned to Mara. "Darling, I have to go. Anthony has identified the wire hacker and would-be assassin."

"Who was it?" asked Mara.

"Nathan. He was infected during our last trip out. I think this infection has something to do with his condition."

The Security Centre Building was a little over a kilometre from their house. The drive everyday was becoming more difficult, as the ever-increasing number of houses was hurriedly swallowing up vacant land. Infuriating heaps of rubble, debris, and bricks strewn in disorderly piles aggravatingly seemed to pounce up in front of the Jeep. Workers continuously got in the way. It annoyed Steve to go around them. The houses were built in lines that stretched from DOK's northern wall to the southeastern tip. In only four months, more than a thousand homes had appeared in varying stages of construction. Steve and Mara's house was in the middle of the housing development.

Steve arrived at the Security Centre twenty minutes later and started checking the communicators, lights and video cameras while he waited for Anthony's call.

After repairing the cable in Sector Seven, Matthew began reconfiguring the armament hardware. For him, it was easy to prepare the remaining plasma rifles, rocket-propelled grenades, and helicopter for the wall-stalkers when the time came. But where the dickens was Nathan, and why hadn't Anthony contacted Steve?

"Anthony, what's going on? Where's Nathan?"

"I've just got here. We had a bit of a problem dragging him out. One of the DPF got hurt. Quaid's heard about it and wants to see you down at the Admin Building right away."

"I'll be right over."

The view of the Admin Building from across the parking lot conveyed turmoil. Even from a distance, Steve could see the riotous mood Gossard was in. As Steve approached, various pairs of eyes focused on him.

"Steve, for the love of God, why has this man been arrested?" asked Gossard. His face creased momentarily.

"He's the one responsible for putting the dummy explosive into the inspection cover. He also cut the cables. I bet he made the remote control as well."

"What proof have you, po-lice-man?" asked Quaid cynically.

"We have his fingerprints, atom brain!"

"Calm down, both of you!" shouted Gossard, forcing himself between them. Steve moved to one side, quickly facing Quaid again, but Quaid beat him to the punch.

"Steve, look," said the doctor, "I'm sorry we got started off on the wrong foot. Nathan is a patient of mine. He has been since you brought him back from your little plant charade."

"Your patient, Quaid, and thanks for calling me Steve, is a menace, a hazard. He's under some kind of spell. They have control of him—shit, why don't you see it?" Steve inhaled deeply. "Listen, if you cannot keep Experiment X here under control, I'm going to lock him away for our own safety. Right now, my only concern is to find out what is going on. When I am satisfied with my findings and I have what I believe to be an appropriate answer, I'll let you all know what I am going to do. Is that clear? Anthony, take him downstairs to the interrogation room!"

"Will do, sir," said Anthony, shoving Nathan down the concrete steps.

Without saying another word to either Gossard or Quaid, Steve followed not far behind. At the foot of the stairs, a large, square and scantily furnished room with a cubicle came into view. Lit with fluorescent lights, it reminded Steve of a small garage with lots of squared columns. The air was fusty and emanated an undesirable coldness.

Anthony was closing the heavy metallic cubicle door and taking off his gloves as Steve appeared. "He's all yours."

Nathan sat in an uncomfortable-looking chair opposite a metallic table two metres away. Separating them was a thick glass protection window that stretched to the ceiling.

"Do you know where you are?" Steve asked as Nathan looked towards the wall. A few seconds passed, so he repeated the question.

"Nathan, do you know where you are?" Pulling his eyes away from the wall, Nathan looked at Steve. "What did you say?"

"I asked if you knew where you were."

"I'm in a basement of some kind. Who are you?"

"Don't you remember? I'm the one who rescued you in Tierra Colorada."

"Oh yes, I remember now. Why am I in a basement?"

"You are here because I had you brought here."

"And why did you bring me here?"

"You tell us. Why do you think you're here?"

Anthony produced the remote control his chaps had uncovered from the outsides of the wall and placed it on the table in front of Steve. "Nathan, do you know what this is?" he asked.

Evading the small elongated box, Nathan wordlessly steered his head.

"I asked if you knew what this was!" Anthony banged his hammer fist against the glass, making Nathan almost bite his tongue in fright.

"A small black box," said Nathan nervously.

"Good. Did you make it?"

"No, I didn't, they told me what to do. They made it."

Steve asked, "What do you mean, "they" told you what to do? How did "they" tell you how to make it?"

"They entered my mind and told me what to do."

"Did they tell you to cut the cables, as well?"

"Yes, they told me everything."

"Did you put the anti-personnel mine in the inspection cover?"

"Yes, they told me to put it in there to scare you. They feed on your fear whilst they roam the outside. When they get inside, they will feed on your flesh."

Anthony gave Steve a look that wasn't normal, even for him.

"Who are they?" demanded Steve. "How can they feed on my fear?"

Nathan gazed once more towards the wall.

"Steve, try a different approach," whispered Anthony.

"Do you know Doctor Quaid?"

Nathan's seemingly unfocused mind once more tuned into Steve's voice. "Yes, he's doing tests on me. I hate it when he does that. Every time he sticks me with his needles, it interrupts our communication, the communication between them and me. I don't like to break our communication. They don't like to break our communication."

"When do they communicate with you?" Steve asked.

"All the time. I can feel them now. They tell me what to say. They tell me they can hear you. They tell me they can sense your fear. They love sensing your fear. They tell me to say 'Thank you.'"

"Anthony, go upstairs and get Doctor Quaid. Bring his butt down here."

Steve was afraid, all right. The words coming from this simple man's mouth made them both afraid. There were things in this world that no man could run from, and one of them was fear, fear of the unknown.

As Doctor Quaid entered, Steve looked at him furiously. "Like I told you previously, Quaid, you haven't a clue what you're dealing with. This man here sitting before you claims to be able to talk to them, as they in turn talk to him, they give him orders."

Suddenly, Nathan placed his left hand to his nose. "We can see you with these eyes. I can hear you with these ears. I can smell your stench. I can taste your fear. And I can communicate with this mouth. We have many mouths to talk from."

At that moment, Nathan folded up, holding his head, and fell to the floor, dead.

"What the hell? What's going on?" Anthony rushed over and unlocked the door.

Doctor Quaid was behind him. Bending down he moved to Nathan lying limp on the ground. "Don't touch him!" Quaid shouted. "Even though he's dead, they can still see you through his unmoving eyes."

Anthony unemotionally rolled on a latex glove and patted the flaccid eyelids shut. "Not any more they can't," he said.

"Care to comment on what has just happened?" Steve asked.

Doctor Quaid walked over and perched himself against a wall opposite the cadaver on the floor. "What lies before you is human because it has human shape. It could talk like one, think, and see like one. Its five senses were operational until they came and took them over, all five of them." Quaid breathed deeply. "Scientifically, the virus is known as ABC or All Bodily Control. During its transition, ABC shows an interest in our cerebral functions. It attacks our minds in a variety of different ways. This, of course, varies from patient to patient. We found ABC-positive European patients reacted differently from American patients. Two years ago, a Doctor Morcel from the Mexico City University discovered a way to fine-tune the virus, legitimately putting him in control of his sick patients. Although he never told me where these patients of his came from, I made a guess they were the residues of inglorious wars or government projects gone wrong and the like. Doctor Morcel had been studying molecular-link physics and atom science for more than twenty years. Soon after his shattering discovery, the project did a screw turn. What had started with a simple way for him to wedge his way into the patients' disease had also become a way for others to gain control of an enemy without them knowing it. While man's technology went smaller, better and faster, Morcel's went a lot smaller. And you don't go smaller than an atom, or so we thought.

"Morcel announced that the virus—please note he called it a virus because it shared the same physical imperfections—caused you to become ill, you vomited with a sharp rise in temperature, the headaches, the muscular pains, and so on. However, the disease came with a difference. His patients shared a particularly interesting quality, one of which even he wasn't prepared for. While one of them faced the back wall, Morcel wrote a sentence on a piece of paper. The patient had written the very same sentence and in the same style.

"As his findings matured, telepathically Morcel asked the patient a question. The subject would then duly answer for everyone to hear. Like a gold rush, he started gaining so much popularity in his experiments that the United States Army started showing renewed interest in their leftovers. However, as fate would have it, that same week the sun almost went nova, killing a billion people, including his family. Morcel honestly believed that the governments somehow were responsible for this inhumane act and was never heard from again. That was when the complications arose: the hunger, the maliciousness, their unity, the viral transference, and so on.

"The virus spreads on a molecular level. Morcel knew this, but he honestly thought it would dilute in a large quantity of liquid. The idea was surpassed when he administered one micro-litre of ABC to one litre of distilled water. In an hour, the litre of water had acquired the same potency as the original batch. The manner in which the virus mutated astounded him. He dubbed it 'molecular alliance growth principle,' or the 'magpie dominance.' His formulas proved that water was indeed a solid mass conductor, and not liquid. Up until the time of his disappearance, he had naturally captured the attention of the most prolific and sophisticated minds on the planet."

"Do you think Morcel was responsible for this?" Steve asked.

"Oh yes, I do. I'm convinced of it."

"How can you be so sure?"

"Because he was my brother. We shared many things in the laboratory." Silence once again ruled the basement.

At that moment, Gossard came down the steps. "What's going on down here?"

Quaid began first. "I was just explaining some of the finer details to our little dilemma."

Gossard looked at Nathan on the floor. "Good Lord, is he dead? What happened?"

"He's physically dead, if that's what you want to know. Tell us, Major, can you explain why the North American government was already planning the construction of DOK cities before the real crisis began? Carnell had already signed up the consignment contract agreement with the Russians weeks beforehand. Did they suspect something?"

Gossard's null look didn't slip by Steve. He was as blind as the rest of them.

Steve faced Quaid. "Quaid, we are going to have to put the rest of them into one area, a holding den. If they want something to look at during their stay, I'll hang up a television on the wall. I'm going to have one built right away. And get this body out of here!"

Quaid wasn't stirred by Steve's sense of humour. "I'll get to it right away," said Quaid as he reached for his C-10 and called for a cleanup team to come down and remove the body.

"What else did Morcel tell you before he vanished? He must've told you more," Steve asked as the body removers departed.

"Not much, most of our conversations were scientific. I'm afraid you wouldn't understand half of what he had to say. I will say this, when ABC bridges itself on Australian territory next week, all hell is going to break loose."

"What do you mean?" Steve asked sharply.

"Before Morcel's disappearance he was ranting on about a blue virus. He didn't tell me much about it either. I just know that when ABC East meets ABC West next week somewhere on Australian territory, it will become the Blue virus."

❋ ❋ ❋

That afternoon, Steve began the final wall check. Anthony and Tino from Security Centre contacted Steve with the C-10 while he walked the entire length of the wall, inspecting every communicator, MOGS, lighting controller, video camera, and support, ready to mount the awaiting Light Shapers tomorrow. Not only did he inspect the electronics, he checked the portholes.

This would take time, so Anthony insisted on helping him. Steve was glad, because he trusted Anthony's scrutinising eye. He walked south while Steve went north; that meant they could finish in half the time.

Steve pressed each communicator's touch pad as he walked along the walkway and recited the station number corresponding to that unit. Tino then repeated the station number as he logged it into the notes. The same process was used for the video cameras as Steve stepped in front of them. As Steve's face appeared on Tino's screen, he adjusted the focus and zoom, provoking a barely susceptible whizzing of the stepper motors originating from the inside of the plastic housing.

Then it was time for the MOGS controller units. They were white boxes with two buttons and a gyratory lever. One button switched it on or off, while the other worked in conjunction with the lever adjusting the beam intensity and direction. The afternoon sun withholding, the MOGS' effectiveness revealed a faint beam wiping the ground nearby as Steve swivelled it around. Cameras hanging on DOK's exterior awaited checking by a special unit after the Light Shapers were up and operational.

Attached to the second section of wall every 250 metres, the 3-metre-high column Rawling had described months ago marked the spot where each Light Shaper would be placed. Steve glanced upon his creation. Its superb O structure stretched towards the horizon, gently curving. Even as the sun began to set in a bath of reds and oranges, they continued until the lights from the upper section immersed them in silvery luminescence. It was 11:00 when Steve shook Anthony's cold hand.

"Hey, I was thinking," said Anthony, "did you have time to go to the Recreation Centre to find a present for Mara?" he asked.

"I was there yesterday. Of all the possibilities in the world, she is least expecting what I found for her. She'll be euphoric." The Recreation Centre had accumulated all kinds of junk; yet, in amongst the mounds of paraphernalia and riffraff, Steve had found Mara the perfect gift.

"Anthony, how are you coming on with that lady you met last month? You know, you haven't even told me her name."

"Ingmar. She's German. She lost her family in the heatwave, but managed to stow away in a boat destined for Vera Cruz last year. At least she seems happier than she was when I first met her. Anyway, I'll pick you up at 7:00. Remember, tomorrow is not only Christmas Day, it's Light Shaper Day. You know, I have been wondering if the wait in the end is going to be worth it. These things, these Light Shapers, do you honestly think they'll protect us?" asked Anthony.

"Gossard demonstrated them to me in the lab. They seem quite efficient. That is, of course, if our enemy were pens. I threw a pen at it and watched it vaporise."

"You should've thrown in a chair, or a filing cabinet, or better still, you should have thrown him in." They laughed.

"Now then, you erase those thoughts. Tomorrow they go up. At least it's a start."

"Well then, until tomorrow." Anthony climbed down the ladder and called somebody on his C-10. Five minutes later a car pulled up and he climbed in. Mara's hidden present was in a box in the back of Steve's Jeep. Steve had stashed it underneath a dirty old oilcan. He knew she wouldn't look there, because she never fiddled about in the back of the Jeep. It was too dirty, or so she said. Nevertheless, this was a curious time of year, and Mara was a curious woman.

Steve always left a mark or scratch somewhere to reveal if someone had moved an object or gained entrance to a room. Once Steve discreetly slid a small piece of wedged paper between the doorframe and the door. If someone opened it, the piece of paper fell down, becoming just another piece of paper lying on the ground.

In this case, Steve put the dirty oilcan inclined at a 45-degree angle. If Mara had been overly nosy, she would have moved the can. Steve would've seen the difference. When Tino collected him and left him outside the Security Centre in front of the Jeep, Steve opened the back section and looked inside. Everything was exactly as it had been left. Carefully picking up the present, Steve put it on the passenger seat and drove off.

Mara and Orson were waiting for him when Steve walked in the front door. Orson wasn't a normal dog. To start with, his dog intelligence ran off the dog scale, if such existed. If Steve had believed in reincarnation, he would've said that in his previous life, Orson had been a banker. A curious nose came wondering over and immediately went behind Steve's back to sniff what he held in his hands. It was only a dirty old box, how could he know? How could Orson possibly know that what was in that box wasn't for him? Maybe he thought it was. His tail bobbed about, sensing the happiness and the bond between these two people. Mara knew something was up and purposefully withheld her usual enthusiasm.

"Hello, darling. How's your cable? Did things work out?"

Steve looked at Mara and immediately began to laugh. "Yes, honey, everything's fine. How was your day?" Steve said with a smile on his face. They looked at one another and broke out into roaring laughter.

"Orson helped me sow some seeds. And look, Arthur gave us a houseplant."

Mara pointed towards a superb example of a mother-in-law's tongue. The long reddish-green filament reached upwards a half a metre. It was a magnificent specimen.

"Why don't you put it next to the front entrance, it'll look better there," Steve said.

"What could you possibly know about interior decorating and plants? You're an engineer. They are not supposed to know anything about anything, except of course, when it comes to Christmas. You do remember that today is Christmas?"

"Well, wife, unfortunately Zed's hyper store was closed for the afternoon, so I had to especially order your Christmas card." Steve reached into his top pocket, still holding the box behind his back and produced a piece of white paper. On the inside, he had written:

For those who wait,
Time is merely a splinter in thy eye.
All the memories, the trees, and snow,
The eternal wait, as angels reincarnated
Gently sway on branches
Stirred by the winds of memories past.
You are my history,
My uncertain future,
And yet,
Without your love, I am the unguided soul
Drifting the night.

The remnants of a shell once filled with an essence,
Your essence of Christmas.
Outside, as once silent Night Thrush's sing
In their December voices.
Our love passes by
As time buries itself deeper into our minds.
Your presence is my direction
And my eternal gift,
Merry Christmas, my love.

Mara read the card three times before looking at Steve. "That's the nicest thing ever. Thank you. You know. I haven't told you recently, I love you. And thank you for being who you are."

"Now don't you start getting soppy on me. I've got something else for you."

Mara couldn't contain herself any longer. The excited little girl deep within erupted outwards. "Tell me what it is!"

Stepping backwards, Steve produced the stained box from behind his back.

"Sorry about the grimy bit, I had it hidden in a place you wouldn't think of looking."

"I can see that," said Mara, gently taking it from his hands.

"Zed's was closed and the Christmas wrapping was used up."

"Don't worry about that," said Mara concentrating on the box. "Now what could possibly be inside?" she asked as she placed the box close to her ear and rattled it about like a child's shaker before carefully lifting up one of the flaps to peer inside.

"No, it can't be. Where did you find it? It's beautiful."

"In the Recreation Centre. They have all sorts of bits and pieces out there for the taking. It is more of a collection of useless rubble that's used and exchanged by others. I found it lying on the table in amongst the debris."

Mara had forgotten her carefulness. She wrenched off the lid and produced the baby doll. Her red miniskirt and pink blouse and pretty, smiley face, together with a long flush of blonde hair, came bundled together with a baby smell that somehow still adhered to it. It also came complete with brown sports shoes. Although one was missing, Mara picked it up and hugged it with almost as much passion as she hugged Steve.

"Careful now, I might get jealous."

"Now, I have something else to love."

"You wouldn't dare."

Mara carefully put her baby doll down on the couch in front of Orson's watchful eye. "Don't you even think about it, Orson. If you go near it, you'll do twenty years hard labour in the worst dog prison."

Orson identified the tone and moved to his corner near the kitchen.

Mara came over and kissed Steve. "Thank you, sweetheart. It's the nicest gift ever. Let's go to bed."

"Those are the best words I've heard all day."

✳ ✳ ✳

At 7:00 the next morning, Anthony came knocking at the front door. This time Steve was ready for him.

"Morning, Anthony. Here, Mara gave me two vegetable scones for the two of us."

"Thanks. Oh, I see Mara liked the present all right."

"You mind your own business. Are the Shapers ready for mounting?"

Anthony smiled. "Yes, Gossard has already put them in front of the wall close to where each one is to be mounted."

Workers normally began with their daytime responsibilities at 6:00 in the morning. As Steve and Anthony set off down the road, it was amok with bustle. Persistent forms were everywhere fulfilling their duties. Today was a special day, and this day they were going to work especially hard.

"Quaid has a good part of the workforce building the holding den," said Anthony. You think these guys are fast, you should see that holding den already. In only a day, they've almost completed it. I admire their drive, their stamina. These guys don't stop for anything."

A week ago the entire street of houses was at foundation level, and now they were at roof height. "There must be over sixty houses in this street alone," Steve said as they passed a group of workers with headlamps.

Farther still, the horizon bobbed about with light that reminded Steve of the glowworm he had as a kid. As Gate-A loomed nearer, they saw the entire working area was enshrouded by an artificial whiteness provided by six manoeuvrable spotlamps on wheels. Forklifts carrying boxes deposited them on the ground, while a generator churned with a constant din. They had to begin while it was still dark. The deadline was strict, and Gossard wanted to check the Light Shapers before the end of the day.

As they drove up, Gossard was standing between two of the illuminating towers with some of Rawling's men.

"Morning, Steve, Anthony. There it is. What do you think?"

"Bigger than I expected. Where's Matthew?" said Steve.

"He and his team are already on the other side of DOK. He got an early start."

"What's this?" Steve said, walking to the Shaper, pointing to something attached to the side.

"Those are the plasma rifles' recharging points. I'll explain in more detail later." Gossard walked off towards a group of workers as a crane dipped and took hold of the waiting Light Shaper nearby.

"There are still many preparations ahead of us," noted the major. "At 6:00, I want to switch them on and run diagnostic checks. Between you, Anthony, and Tino, the wall-stalkers must be aware of the imminent dangers proposed by the Light Shapers. Matthew will give you assistance with the finer detail. Right now, tell them what to do, when to do it, and what it is we are waiting for. They have faith in your wall, they must have faith in you."

As the sixth Light Shaper went up, graffiti caught Steve's attention.

Believe in the mercy of Christ
soon they cometh.

"Hey, what's this?"

Gossard spoke first. "Damn scary stuff. Must be someone's idea of a prank. Idiots. Don't forget, half these workers are Catholic fanatics. Religion is their way of life. Apart from building, it's the only thing they know." The infernal words on the wall left a bad taste in Steve's mouth. It certainly captured his attention.

A worker passed them by, eight metres above. "Hey, you!" shouted Steve. "Who wrote this? What does it mean?" Steve's hand pointed to the phrase on the wall. The worker climbed down to talk quietly to Steve.

"Morning, sir. The goings-on around here are beginning to scare us. Some of us believe that Satan is going to unleash his almighty wrath on the world. They work hard because they feel the harder and faster they work, the farther Satan moves away from us. It's their strongest motive for survival."

"Do you know who could have written this?"

"It could have been any one of them, sir. It could have been any one of them." The worker scuttled back to his chores.

✹ ✹ ✹

At 4:00 in the afternoon, the massive operation had concluded. Rawling, Anthony, Matthew, and Steve were in the Admin Building when Gossard entered.

"Good, we are ahead of schedule. Let's take this meeting to the Security Centre. With the exception of Matthew, it's time I showed you the operation in more detail."

Steve was the last one to enter. "Anthony, come closer," ordered the major. "I want you in on this as well. Apart from the uninterrupted power source, Light Shapers require a digital signal coming from the Security Centre to operate. The absence of this signal means failure. We are responsible for its constant running, so I have put into operation a preventative security operations code. Only Steve, Matthew, Rawling, and I will be able to modify the life-supporting parameters. Your security codes are on these papers."

Gossard handed papers with their personal access codes to the three of them. "Steve, you have Priority Two. Rawling's and Matthew's are Priority Three. My code is Priority One. I am going to let its inventor demonstrate how the system works. Matthew, enter your code, if you will."

They inched closer as Matthew's well-accustomed fingers glided over the keyboard. The plasma display screen revealed twelve X shapes representing inputted numbers. Suddenly, the control panel lit up in an eerie yellow glow.

"There, it's activated," said Matthew. "The screen is divided into two segments, power input and power output. It's really quite simple. The left side, or power input, shows a steady flow of current exiting the generators and entering the Light Shapers. As you can see, voltage and current are steady at 3,000 amperes. When we switch them on later this evening, each Light Shaper will consume no less than 100 amperes. The other half of the display shows to us the beam direction, width, and intensity. At the bottom, you can see the digital control signals coming from the Security Centre."

"Thanks, Matthew," said Major Gossard. "Later, when I switch them on, you will see a lot of activity on that internal video oscillogram. Remember, people, the first test begins in a little over an hour. If one goes faulty or if a failure occurs, an alert signal appears on this console. It not only tells where the fault is, it tells what it is. The units are also self-checking twice per day, relaying the results to this console. One of our duties will be to review these results as they appear. In addition, Steve, the recharge points you noticed earlier on the lower supporting section of the Light Shaper are indeed the same as those we added later under the window ports. It is in these recharging points where wall-stalkers plug in their plasma rifles to recharge the battery. Matthew, you take over."

"OK, Major." Matthew pushed a button on the side of the plasma rifle and a yellow cable zipped out. "The recharging process takes eleven seconds. It is plugged into these spaces on each Light Shaper, or window socket, and the metal-cadmium cells will do the rest."

They watched as Matthew introduced the cable into a dummy yet functioning Light Shaper close by. "The moment it's inserted, a red light appears on the side of the plasma rifle. When it turns green the yellow spring cable will automatically return to the rifle, allowing you to continue firing. Light Shapers are fundamentally wide-span, short-distance laser beams. Dust, leaves, bits of anything—nothing is going to get in here. From above we are impenetrable. It is of the utmost importance we explain to the wall-stalkers and civilians alike the dangers of the beam. If one of them inadvertently touched it, he would lose his finger or hand. I won't explain the extreme possibilities."

"Does the beam cauterize? Is it hot?" asked Tino.

"No, the beam itself doesn't have physical temperature. On certain alloys and metals the beam has been known to reach 10,000 degrees. It's quick and efficient, and painless."

"Will the Slim Shapers be as effective as the Light Shapers?" asked Anthony.

"Yes, it's the same plasmic beam, Anthony. Soon you'll witness their potential. Remember, Super-Heated Active Plasma Radiation, or Shaper, is not only manipulable, it's flexible like a fluid. It can be controlled in every way from this control panel." Enthusiastically, Steve typed in Mara's number. "Honey, the Light Shapers are being switched on at 6:00. Fancy watching it?"

"That'll be interesting. I'll be right over."

Mara arrived ten minutes later. "Whew, that control panel looks complicated. You sure you know what's going on?"

"More or less," replied Steve. "We got a crash course from Gossard and Matthew before you arrived."

Mara looked away. "Hey look, that's Payne over there. The one in the black trousers." She pointed to a man perched against the wall of the Security Centre. She called him and he came over to her.

"Hello, Mara. Oh and let me guess: This must be Steve. It's a pleasure to finally meet you." They shook hands.

"Arthur Payne at last. I must apologize, we've both been so busy it was impossible—"

Arthur Payne broke in. "Don't be silly. I see your work. Truth is, I've been admiring it. You're a genius."

"Thanks for your kindness, Arthur, and belated apologies for the infected plants."

"There was no way you could have known. Besides, I'm making good progress without them. I'm using the growth accelerators on the seeds you bought back. The results are quite extraordinary. You must come and see them sometime."

"I will. You can count on it."

Payne's piercing look traversed Steve's skull. "You were right, Mara. He's wonderful. You make an astonishing pair."

Gossard's stern voice called to Payne.

"What was that wonderful stuff all about?" Steve asked Mara.

"He was just finishing off one of the conversations we had when I first met him."

"Nice guy. Bit direct. I like him. Hey, where's Orson?" Orson had crept up behind Steve and was waiting for a belly rub with his four feet in the air.

"Funny, he does the strangest things when Payne's around. Who knows what goes on in his brain?"

As Payne reached Gossard, they exchanged a few words and immediately started walking back. "Hello, Mara," greeted the major. "Ready, Steve? It's time."

They returned to the control panel display where Gossard and Matthew made last-minute checks. After satisfying themselves, Gossard pushed buttons on his C-10. "Security complex teams one through ten, is everyone ready and away from the wall?"

Ten different voices answered. "Complex One all clear, Complex Two all clear," and on it went until all ten had reported.

"Alright, Steve, you can do the honours."

Steve walked to the console and pressed a button adequately named "Function." The code keypad swivelling on a horizontal arm surfed towards him and came to a halt centimetres from his stomach. A small yellow lamp placed inside the keyboard flicked on, elucidating the alphanumeric touch pad in which Steve entered the twelve digits before pressing a square, green illuminated button. The moment he pressed it, the monitor came to life displaying its vital signs.

Matthew came over. "Now you have to connect the power from the generators to the Light Shapers. You see that pulsating red button?"

"Yes."

"Press it."

The moment everybody had been waiting for arrived. Even as the red light stopped blinking, Steve's attention was averted back to the monitor. Numbers, once zeros, had transformed into large quantities. Everyone was staring, Steve was sure of it. Then another light blinked on.

The screen went frantic. "Don't even ask. You know what to do. Look, those are the oscillograms I told you about earlier. Watch how they guide and control the beam flow."

Matthew's voice almost reached crescendo. Simultaneously from the outside, shouts of apprehension and joy altered into sounds of accomplishment.

"It's on!" they shouted. "The Light Shapers are working!" Some clapped hands, some came into the Security Centre to tell them the lights were working.

Gossard cleared his throat. "Yes, we know!" he shouted reassuringly, trudging outside to view the spectacle. Everyone followed him out where thousands of curious faces had gathered to witness the spectacle. Steve's first impression of it was a light-green blanket. Of course, against the daytime light it was barely perceptible, but it was there all right, a faint bluish-green layer of deadly impenetrable mist offering the sky a different tinge. One of the workers picked up a rock and hurled it upwards with all his might. As if someone had turned off gravity, the rock never returned. It never made any sparks, obviously unlike the worker had expected. Feeling disillusioned by the lack of fireworks, the worker threw another rock, this time heavier than the first. His actions were rewarded with the same results.

Gossard grabbed a megaphone. "May I have everyone's attention, please?"

Faces pulled themselves away from the heavens.

"That green barrier above our heads is our roof. It effectively separates us from the outside and the perils from above. While this protection barrier is operational, our only three points of access will be protected in a similar manner. Please allow me to demonstrate. You there, the one who threw the rocks."

The worker gyrated and looked dumbfounded at Gossard, who told him, "I believe the desired effect you're looking for you'll find on the front gate."

As they walked with hundreds of curious stalkers and workers towards Gate-A, the worker bent down and picked up a rock the size of a fist before looking towards Gossard for confirmation.

"Go on, throw it, don't be afraid."

The rock left the worker's hand with the enthusiasm of a cricket ball towards the stump. As rock met gate, sparks flew in all directions and a brief yellow flame surged outwards before being sucked in and consumed by the force field. The obviously chuffed worker bent down and picked up another rock.

"I think that's enough for one day, don't you?" Gossard said as the worker dropped the rock in fright. "I want you to spread the word to the rest who haven't seen it today. We are one of three DOK cities using Light Shapers as a primary defence system. We are now safe within this world in a world. Remember, people, we are here to keep the human race alive. If this DOK city fails, we, the human race, will fail along with it. Tomorrow morning we begin with training exercises on the wall. Steve, Anthony, and Tino will be your training officers. I know that some of you will not need it, but most of you will. It will be for your own benefit that you go through that training. Tomorrow is a long day. Lastly, as of this day, my security chief Steve Gotlar will officially become Head of Security. This makes him second-in-command. Now, I want all of you to go home and enjoy what is left of Christmas."

Without another word, Gossard walked back to the Security Centre.

When the hundreds of workers dispersed, Steve thought about what they would do when there were no more building chores. Would they become full-time husbands? Would they become gardeners or plumbers? There was always something that needed fixing, especially in a city.

✳ ✳ ✳

At home later that night, Steve retired to the kitchen and ate a bowl of minestrone soup with Mara's homemade bread. After their meal, they walked outside and looked towards the night sky. It was an unusually dark and cold night, and the sky, a radiant phosphorescent green, became the new stellar constellation. Lethargic yellowy tendrils swam in amongst the green blanket over them. It seemed alive. Was it a psychological barrier? Could this green film really protect them in their hour of need? Their enemy wasn't psychological. Mara crept closer to Steve's side to keep warm, so pulling her nearer, they went back inside.

Anthony came earlier than normal the next day. Steve cursed at the customary knocking in the usual rhythmical pattern: three short toks, followed by his unceremonious, "Sir, we have to go, they're waiting."

Luckily, Mara had been sleeping. She slept through almost anything. Steve left her in her world of slumber with Orson stretched out beside her.

Wall-stalkers were specially prepared volunteers. All they needed was spirit, drive, and a will to learn. They were trained both physically and mentally, giving them the opportunity to use a weapon. Wall-stalkers had to be ready at any time during the day or night, sometimes both. They were the ones who walked the wall. They were the eyes, the early-warning detectors. Every fifty metres, two wall-stalkers took it in turns to parade back and forth watching the outer regions. Anything unusual had to be reported.

❋ ❋ ❋

During the first three months, since the beginning of DOK, an average of one infected per day had been shot. This average, by the time they reached late November, had increased to five. By late December, their daily count had risen to eleven. All other DOK cities were experiencing the same increment, all with the exception of DOK 3. One of Major Kalakov's last transmissions indicated that he had a daily average of fifty settling onto vacant space. Due to the ambient temperatures, his wall in places hadn't reached two metres, and he reported that moral fatigue amongst his men was returning. Gossard had done what he could.

At home, 480 wall-stalkers patrolled in 6-hour shifts while another 480 replacements waited. Head wall-stalkers constantly mingled with wall-stalkers and possessed a C-10 link directly to Gossard. They were the mentors. The wall had become the mentors' life. Wall-stalkers needed them there. They were the situation analysers, guiding and assisting the wall-stalkers in predicaments. Their presence on the wall made everyone feel more at ease.

Since the beginning of December, wall-stalkers had begun using plasma weapons, thinking that the normal un-silenced weapons would attract the infected with the sound it made. It became one of the duties to give them advanced training using the plasma weapon. Anthony showed them how to climb and get off the ladder efficiently. What to do in a crisis and how to deal with panic.

The question arose: "Sir, what if one of us gets infected while we are doing our duty on the wall?"

"He would have to be dealt with in exactly the same manner as you deal with the rest. Do you want details?" The worker melted back to his place.

Another question followed: "Sir, what are we waiting for?"

"We are waiting for hordes of infected that are likely to move north in their search for food. At first, we believed this food to be protein based; now, we are under suspicion that they feed on our fear, or both. Remember, they know by now there is nothing down south of us, and we can expect them to arrive shortly. Many will die before they reach here, especially those who come from far southern countries. But those coming from Guatemala, Honduras, Panama, and many of the northern territories will pass by us. It won't be a social visit or an invitation to a garden party. Like I told you previously, they'll be hungry."

A silence governed the foyer as wall-stalkers whispered and mumbled amongst themselves. The whispering in no time at all gained in intensity and became shouting as fists started waving in the air.

"Please, people! Please settle down. I haven't finished!" Twenty or more angered wall-stalkers calmed themselves as Gossard continued. "The infected are armed only with the disease they carry and will try to gain access into this facility. The manner in which they will is still unknown at this stage. It is a possibility they will throw rocks at us supposing they do get close enough. First, they will spit upon them, rubbing it all over the rock before they hurtle it at a human target. It won't matter if he misses, someone at some stage will touch it, picking it up to hurtle it back whence it came. By then it will be too late. The moment his hand touches the rock the infection will spread through him like electricity. If this happens, the infection will eat its way through DOK fast. It would take only an hour to get an irreversible grip on us, eliminating what you and the next man have created and maintained so well over these last few months."

A hand rose. "How do they find us? How do they know we are here?"

"We anticipate they hone in on our fear. Quaid is still trying to work that one out."

* * *

They started the last few days of December with exercise. Fifty push-ups followed by leg-ups, a couple of abdominal exercises and a brief two-kilometre run. At 8:00, they would run up the ladder, along the walkway, down the next, and so on.

At 9:00, Matthew began the advanced training programme. "This, as you already know, is the Plasmox Five, Model One plasma rifle. The telescopic sight has been altered to obtain the maximum range to give the weapon an effective range of over two kilometres."

He showed the wall-stalkers how to hold the weapon properly, allowing it to fit into them instead of them fitting into it.

"How many shots do we have before the plasma rifle needs to be recharged?" a wall-stalker asked.

"Normally seventy. Some batteries are better quality, allowing eighty or even ninety shots before you're forced to recharge."

Matthew walked to a curious wooden crate on the ground besides Gossard. He flicked his fingers and a worker strolled over and unfastened a flap. Inside were plasma rifles. Matthew handed them out to wall-stalkers and began explaining the principle of the plasma ion.

"Model Ones don't leave body parts behind like our conventional rifles do. They disintegrate the body. Their practicality, superior efficiency, and greater range have allowed us to venture into this war with an ace card. But this also means they are immensely more dangerous, and care should be taken while using them."

Selected wall-stalkers held the rifles and opened fire on creosote bushes almost two kilometres away. The valley had succumbed to their spines, needles, and devastation for so long, but now the bushes had a new competitor apart from the encroaching cacti not far behind.

At 12:00, they had an hour's break. While everyone was eating out in the fresh air, Steve went home. Mara prepared the nicest meals, even though they remained vegetarian. Meat was only going to be hopefully à la carte as of mid-January. Steve preferred looking at her instead of staring as others swallowed or silently filled their mugs. If the workers did talk, all they could speak about were infected people crossing the desert in search of the uninfected. It got tiring at times pretending to enjoy someone's company. Steve had endured three months of it, and so now he just went home, where he should have gone all those months before.

At 1:00, wall-stalkers performed exercises working off excess calories before adjourning to the hospital where they learnt first aid, and basic medical backup. The first day they learnt how to deal with burns, cuts, and bruises. Whereas the second day they learnt cardiopulmonary resuscitation, taking blood pressure, body temperature, heart rhythm, and so on. As a result of this basic training, on the fifth day after the medical lesson, the wall-stalkers and DPF were carted off to another site. It was the holding den. Quaid wanted to show them firsthand what the infected were like.

They climbed down a flight of stairs and reached the freshly positioned security doors at the base. As they opened, Steve noticed Bernard and Dimitri next to Lieutenant White. They were three of thirteen infected sitting motionless on plastic chairs, staring at the floor. As the area slowly began to fill with people, they gently turned their heads and raised their glance towards Steve and the rest. Tearing away from Bernard's emotionless stare, Steve looked assuredly at the security division separating him from the infected. It was a glass barrier, like the one he'd seen in the Admin Building.

Quaid interrupted Steve's thoughts. "The infected go into this stasis, a mental lapse. Once we've been here a few minutes they'll begin to wake." A soldier moved an arm. Lieutenant White grunted while others were chewing their nails.

"We believe it to be a nervous reaction of some kind, forming part of their supplementary diet or self-preservation. Although their nails and hair grow at an astounding rate complementing this strange menu, we put it down to desolation. In most cases, I have recorded five millimetres of growth per day. All their body's vitamin requirements and needs for this strange diet are there. Don't worry; down here, they cannot harm us or alert the others."

Dimitri swivelled his head towards Steve. Obviously the minimal basic memory function still worked. His lips began to open, emitting a groan. He whimpered. His snivelling lips started uttering words. They were hazy at first, but his incoherency began to make sense. "Soon we come. When we come, you die. Prepare yourselves, we come."

Dimitri repeated the simple words over and over until they'd reached a perfect pitch and clarity. Wall-stalkers, hearing the absurdity, panicked and ran out of the holding den.

Quaid gasped. "Shit, what's this? They weren't like this yesterday."

Steve looked back only to see Dimitri laughing. His face was contorted, creased, and seemingly old. His retracted eye sockets were those of a cancer victim. Dark-red rims outlined once healthy cells, and blackness now lived where healthy eyes once saw. His hair lay on the floor in clumps.

Steve closed the door, unable to witness more. What in the name of Jesus had happened to him? Dimitri couldn't have been more than twenty-two years old.

January 2034

Matthew had constructed a tree in the middle of DOK to commemorate the coming New Year. A handful of people had gathered to watch the switch-on as he unemotionally put a plug into an extension lead. The majority of the workers had become true believers in non-deity, as this was a new year with little sentiment. Matthew had revived what little there was into a couple of light bulbs placed onto a tree-on-loan from Payne.

January had started cold as a biting wind coming down from the north clung on to them with all its might without letting go. The New Year's commemorative tree swayed in the rash breeze, bulbs were clinking and switched off. On rooftops, a thin layer of ice had gathered.

Quaid came running, faster than the wind itself towards Gossard's office. The two heavily dressed security guards moved to one side, making way for this charging rhinoceros. As he disappeared through the door, he left it open. Remorse for the cold-stricken wasn't on his agenda. Without knocking, he entered. Gossard was talking to Colonel Blake in DOK 9.

"That's right, Colonel, you have my full support in the matter." He glared at Quaid. "What the hell is going on?" asked Gossard angrily. "Colonel, I'll call you back in a moment."

Furiously hanging up the communication device, Gossard went red and exploded. "Quaid, what the hell do you think you're up to, barging in like that? Damn it, man, even you should know!"

Un-apologetically Quaid moved closer. "Go to hell, you imbecilic moron. Now you damn well listen to me! Yesterday, I started noticing big changes in our infected in the holding den. Apart from threatening words, they had blackened eyes, receding hair and all that stuff. You know I listen to Reuters' secure broadcasts at least three times a day."

"Yes, so?"

"The two strains bridged this morning at 10 minutes past 2:00 Greenwich Mean Time. That was an hour ago. After the Reuters report, I went and had a peek at our little shop of horrors. What do you think I saw? Thirteen bald men who could have easily passed themselves for old men. They were perched against the reinforced glass barrier, looking at me as I opened the door. It scared me to see them like that, waiting for me even before I opened the door."

"I think you've lost it. I saw them two days ago. Of course they were infected, but they were physically fine. What could've possibly happened in two days?"

Gossard called back to Colonel Blake. "Blake, have you noticed any strange behaviour in your infected?"

"As of late, no. Give me thirty, I'll call you back." The C-10 flicked off.

"Don't listen to him," said Quaid, sneering. "He doesn't know the difference between a stamp and a coin. Come, let me show you."

Following an excited Quaid, Gossard went outside. The wind rustled and whistled discordantly through a blackness filled with make-believe shadows. The main lights were switched off, as even the workers didn't work tonight. It was New Year's Eve, and only a couple of emergency beacons were sporadically switched on, provoking eerie imaginative patterns. The workers were in their homes, hoping and praying to their gods that some good would eventually come of all this.

As Gossard and Quaid moved on, fog had materialized from around the corner of an unfinished building and curled its way in the cold air, forming monsters and evil transformations. Gossard, taking note of this phantasmal iniquity, buttoned his jacket. The absence of the moon amplified the deficiency of artificial light as the emergency lights spaced twenty metres apart provided little or no help. Eventually in all the gloom, Quaid and Gossard reached the holding den. A furious, heavy bashing ruptured the nightly silence.

"There, what did I tell you?" snapped Quaid.

"What the hell are they doing? It sounds like they are bashing up against the reinforced glass barrier trying to get out." Gossard reached for his C-10 and contacted Steve. "Sorry about this, we've got a problem at the holding den. The infected are trying to get out. It sounds like they are succeeding."

"I'll be there in ten minutes," replied Steve. "I'll contact Anthony and Tino and tell them to meet me there with some of the DPF." He turned to a worried-looking Mara. "Sorry, honey, have to go. Gossard's got problems at the holding den."

"But darling, it's ten o'clock!"

"Now, don't you start worrying yourself. I'll be back as soon as I can, I promise."

All along the route, Steve saw ghostly forms of wall-stalkers patrolling the wall. It was strange to be driving that late at night. As he pulled in front of the building, Anthony was already there.

"Are the DPF on the way?" Steve asked.

"They should be here any moment." As he spoke, the armoured vehicle screeched to a steady halt next to the front entrance.

Tino wasn't far behind. "Christ! What the blazes are they up to? Have they gone completely nuts?"

They cupped their hands over their ears to shield the noise.

Anthony and Tino moved closer together and began reviewing a notepad Tino had produced from his top pocket before walking to the armoured vehicle to face four men perfectly lined up and awaiting orders.

"Don't look so relaxed," said Steve, "two of you are going down there."

At precisely that moment, the din stopped and an obscure silence fell as desert crickets regained confidence. The men looked around and at each other, dumbfounded.

"What the hell? How odd," said Tino, nervously activating his plasma rifle.

"Manuel, Joseph, get in there," Steve ordered. "Do a recon. Go!"

Manuel, reaching the holding den first, began to fiddle with the latch securing the door. Sliding the deadbolt up and back to its neutral position, it clinked metallically before the door opened.

Gossard activated his C-10. "Manuel, talk to me. Get that radio up and working."

"Yes, sir. Sorry, sir. We're halfway down the steps and nearing the door at the base. It is as if we are alone. There's nothing, not a sound."

"I can assure you, you're not alone. Keep on talking to me, soldier, and keep that rifle up high!"

As Manuel and Joseph descended towards the entrance of the holding den, their slinking shadows visible to those on the surface revealed their true nervousness. "We are five steps from the bottom. It's still quiet." Ten seconds passed. "We've reached the base, sir. I'm going to open the inner containment door."

"Is it damaged in any way?" asked Gossard.

"No, sir, not a scratch."

"Remember your training. One of you is to stand back while the other opens the door, and don't fire unless you absolutely have to."

"Yes, sir."

Manuel nervously turned the silent knob, revealing the vast lower holding section. The prisoners had smashed the armoured glass separation plate and were sitting on the floor like an audience waiting at an open-air concert. The moment one of them noticed Manuel nervously peering behind the opened door, they got up and started moving slowly towards the two petrified law enforcers waiting only scarce metres away.

"Oh hell, they've seen us," said Manuel on his radio. "The place is a mess down here. Shit, and it looks like they want out."

"Both of you get your butts back here on the double."

Seconds later, Manuel and Joseph ran through the exit door on the surface and fell in line with their companions.

Gossard quickly walked toward Anthony and Tino. "Tino, I want you to finish this. Shoot to kill!" The hard words came with confidence.

Anthony and Tino entered the surface doors looming side-by-side at the top of the stairs, and waited for the infected to appear through the opened door at the base. The moment the infected stepped through, a single burst of energy instantly reduced them to a grey stain on the floor.

"That's twelve," muttered Tino. "One must still be inside!"

"Sod it," said Anthony, "get down there and find him. He's probably playing hide-and-seek!"

Stirring ashes, Anthony and Tino diligently moved closer to the opened door and peered inside. In the far corner, a single man sat on the floor with his hands clenched in fury.

"It looks like Dimitri, I think," said Anthony. "Shit, what's happened to him?"

Anthony and Tino walked over to the incarnate form looking towards the floor with his head on his knees. Dimitri slowly turned his head sideways to look in their direction. Spiritless eyes drilled into them. "We are coming for all of you. I'm going to enjoy watching you as you suffer."

Dimitri never finished his speech. The ray from Tino's plasma gun disintegrated him where he sat. Without warning, a voice came from someone running down the stairs.

"Who was it?" The voice belonged to Doctor Quaid.

"Dimitri, he wanted to have a little chat," said Tino as Quaid rushed beside him.

"What did he say?"

"They are coming for all of us, and he's going to enjoy watching us as we suffer. That was when I pulled his plug."

"Did you notice anything else, anything strange?"

Tino and Anthony redirected their glance toward Quaid. "What do you mean?" asked Tino.

"Something physical," Quaid turned and faced them both.

"Well, he was bald, and now that you mention it, yes, he did have dark eyes," replied Tino.

"Could they have been blue?" asked Quaid.

Steve joined them.

Tino replied, "It's possible, why?"

"Think, Tino, think! It's important. Were his eyes blue when he died?"

"Yes, they were blue."

"Oh God, it's already happening!" Quaid began to explain in gruesome detail what Morcel had revealed months ago. "If Tino's observation is correct, the virus has already mutated."

"Into what?" asked Steve.

"What is not the problem. The thing is alive and it's still looking for water; and in case you didn't realise, it's just run out of the stuff!" Quaid had a hard look.

"It seeks, it finds, and it corrupts. It is during this atom-snatching process when it joins the two molecules together, intellectually fusing them as one. What I am trying to say is, as this thing travels and grows, it gets smarter. Each water molecule forms a part of its ever-growing brain. It has grown well out of proportion. You could even say the two hemispheres of the brain on the Australian coastline are now complete, and it is beginning to think and function as a brain normally would. This is exactly what the infected were waiting for, this collision of the two hemispheres! Hell, it is using us to search for other uncorrupted water molecules. I fear there is no stopping it. It's attacking our minds because our minds are our weakness. As we are absorbed, we feed its immense being with our own knowledge. After nearly four months of exhaustive study, I have to say I'm no nearer the answer than I was when I started." Quaid's worried glance steered towards the opened door.

"ABC uses the water as a vehicle in the same way metal conducts electricity. Where there's a water molecule, they can spot us, even from the remotest of places. Hell, think of it how you want." Quaid's look turned sour. "With all the Earth's water contaminated, where could it possibly find more?" Quaid abruptly stopped talking, making the others look around and at each other, dumbfounded, waiting for him to continue.

"Just before my brother disappeared," continued Quaid, "he said if ABC reaches Blue Phase, it will undoubtedly appear in the rain. Yes, I know what you are thinking, will it alter the colour or texture of the rain like it does our blood? It's not likely, but we will have to wait and see. The virus was genetically designed to put the world population out of action. Not just scratch the surface."

A long silence filled the open-air space.

"Can this ABC Blue be reversed?" asked Steve.

"Steve, I haven't found a cure for ABC yet. To be truthful, I don't foresee a positive ending to all this."

Without saying another word Quaid got into his car and left.

* * *

At home Mara waited by the door. "Hello, darling. What's with all the rush, was there a problem?"

"Depends on what's your definition of the word problem," replied Steve. "To start with, our infected prisoners in the holding den turned the place upside down. Gossard gave orders to Anthony and Tino to destroy them to prevent the infection from spreading. The scary part was, at the end one of them didn't come out with the rest. According to Anthony, it was Dimitri. He

Michael Gilwood

said as they walked in, Dimitri was sitting on the floor clenching his hands; moving nearer, he started speaking."

"What did the poor thing have to say?" Mara had a distinct tone of worry.

"Poor thing my butt! He said, 'We are going to infect all of you and we'll enjoy watching you suffer.' That was when Tino, what he termed, zapped him."

Mara looked expressionlessly at Steve.

Truth was, as Steve stared at her, unwilling and unable to tell her more, the reborn vacant stare began to worry him. He had never seen anything like it, not once in their fourteen years of marriage.

Just as odd, at first light New Year's Day, Anthony didn't come and fetch Steve as was his usual tendency. While waiting for his familiar rhythmical announcement of arrival, Steve pranced about the kitchen floor, wondering if last night's occurrences had affected him in some way. Becoming worried about Anthony's absence, Steve went outside into the cold morning air and called him on the C-10.

"Anthony, what's up?"

"I'll be there in five minutes. Sorry sir, I got hung up on the wall. It appears there was a bit of late-night activity outside. I'll explain when I get there."

Steve switched off the C-10 and fleetingly glanced at Matthew's tree in the distance. Its twisted zenith, barely perceptible from above the neighbour's wall, revealed that it hadn't been commemoratively switched on during the night as it should've been. Improbable that someone had already switched it off, it was too early. Instead, Steve began toying with the idea that maybe the spirit of New Year and Christmas had finally died, along with the souls of those thirteen men the night before.

The sound of Anthony's car coming down the street broke Steve's concentration.

"Climb in. I'll take us to the wall." Before Steve could close his door, Anthony had already begun to accelerate.

"Christ, what's the hurry?"

"After you went home last night, Tino and I drove around the wall. Suddenly, Tino said he'd seen something scuffling about on the first level. I didn't have time to ask him what, because he got

150

out of the car so fast. One moment he was there and the next he was gone. When I walked out behind him I realised we were in Sector Two—you know the area closest to the holding den. Dozens of fully armed wall-stalkers had amassed on the wall's first level, peering through the observation holes. Do you want to know what they were staring at?"

"What?"

"No less than two hundred infected sitting just out of range of the plasma rifles. Tino turned up the volume on his audio tracker. They were groaning and whimpering, a bit like a bear or dog in pain. They sat there in the same pose for more than two hours before they got up and walked off toward the horizon."

"Anthony, damn it! Why didn't you contact me?" demanded Steve.

"Honestly, I thought you'd seen enough action for one night."

"So much for my being your head of security. Show me where this happened!"

From Sector Two, the holding den was two hundred metres. As they arrived a couple of curious wall-stalker faces were still looking through the portholes towards the barren landscape.

"There's no one, sir. We haven't seen movement out there for a couple of hours. None of the sectors have reported anything."

Anthony picked up his binoculars and began sweeping the entire area. "He's right, there's not a damn soul anywhere."

"Anthony," said Steve, "the next time this happens, for God's sakes, let me know. Our armoured Jeeps are more than capable of wiping these small groups out. Damn it, they've probably gone for reinforcements!"

Anthony, astonished by Steve's words, could only manage one of his own. "OK."

Steve asked, "Where are the rest of the stalkers?"

"After last night's episode in the holding den, most of them climbed off the wall and went home. They're scared stiff."

"Idiots, don't they understand what's going on? If they don't fight and face these fears, they won't have a tomorrow! Christ, what's happened to self-preservation?"

"Steve, we have to understand that before they came here, most of these wall-stalkers were plumbers, painters, carpenters, or electricians. Many of them have never even held a gun before. That is where we come in. Think of them as unqualified, untrained volunteers whose hearts are in the right place."

"And it is up to us and the DPF to make lion tamers out of encyclopaedia salesmen, right?"

"Yeah, something like that," said Anthony.

"Anthony, get Gossard to summon a meeting. I think it's time we all had a little chat."

As Anthony disappeared towards the Admin Building, Steve stood with his hand propped against the wall and looked at the holding den plainly visible in the distance. Infuriated, he walked to the Jeep and took out a crude battery-operated megaphone.

At first, the wall-stalkers and workers arrived in dribs and drabs, but inquisitiveness and enthusiasm got the better of them. They had questions written all over their faces. Steve had never imagined what it would be like, seeing everyone in DOK standing in front of him. Although they had a small population in comparison to other DOK cities, it gave him quite a stir to see them standing there, waiting for his soothing words. Thousands of faces were all concentrating and focusing on Steve. He raised the megaphone.

"Can I have everyone's attention, please?" The shuffling stopped. "I am trying to put myself in your situation, as I know what you–" Steve didn't have time to finish as a hand rose.

"Sir, I had family living in Spain," said a voice from the crowd. "I contacted them twice a week on a portable transceiver my dad gave me when all this nonsense started. He told me I would be safer in America and paid a small fortune for me to board an airplane and come here. From the day I landed, I continued talking with him and my family. One day he told me that the infection had reached the Mediterranean and begun eating its way into all the rivers around the Iberian Peninsula and European continent.

"Luckily, my family had access to large amounts of money, so my dad and the rest of them moved south to North Africa into a drought area where there was no water. They only had the reserves they took with them, thinking that by the time they'd dried up the scientists would have found a cure for all this crap. They moved south because in Spain, everyone was falling ill and it was only a question of time before my family succumbed to its deadliness. They thought the Sahara was safer. Truth is, it was safer, until their water reserves ran out. I last heard from him a week ago. Since then, I only get static and hiss." The worker began to cry, he was so worried about his family.

Another hand rose. "What guarantees can you give us we won't get infected?"

"Impossible, I can't," replied Steve. "All our available water comes from agua-genies. If we use them without outside contact, theoretically we'll be safe. As a city, we have to defend and maintain that position however possible. That brings me to last night. The infected imprisoned in the holding den were not only there for our studying purposes, we retained them for your own safety and protection. A few days ago, as some of you witnessed firsthand, one of them threatened us in a way not even I could imagine. They were behaving oddly. They'd changed, both physically and behaviourally."

Gossard intervened. "Steve, they don't need to know about that!"

"Sorry, Major, with all due respect, don't you think it's time we let them know what's really going on?" Steve paused a few seconds, averting Gossard's dirty look.

"The infected down in the holding den were different, they'd changed physically. They moved and reacted with precise, calculated actions. Even Doctor Quaid said they seemed to be responding as one. Accompanying this new appearance and improved intellect were the blue eyes they possessed. They appear to form part of this new physical aspect. This horror combination we call the Blue Virus, and we feel the crossing of the two strains in Australia has something to do with it. I will finalise by saying that no one wants to fall victim to this damned infection, so if we stick to the rules, we can win this battle. We have the weapons necessary to destroy these beasts."

"They are not beasts, they're human beings." The voice surged from somewhere in the throng.

"Who said that?" Steve demanded, but the anonymous voice held its tongue. "It doesn't matter. Whoever it was, you're right. They are human beings only because they look like us. Remember, because they have our human form doesn't mean to say that they can think like us. Millions of people out there were caught catnapping. Their minds have been taken over and altered, giving them a totally different perspective of survival. To them, we are their survival. Without us, they cannot exist. They need you, they need me, they need all of us in order to continue in their way. Are there any more questions?"

Another hand rose. "Rumours say that it isn't a virus at all. Some say it's greed that's unable to contain itself in the frail human body." Some of the others broke into laughter.

"I have no idea where you heard that insipid remark. I assure you, you have been wrongly informed. Some of those walking out there once were millionaires, corporate buffs, family men and women. People like you. Some of them were even famous."

A worker raised his hand. "What happened last night after the holding den incident? Wall-stalkers told us there were hundreds of them out there on the horizon. What did they want? It scared us to bits."

"The virally infected attract others with the same or similar dysfunction. They communicate with each other, bringing others from many kilometres away, sometimes hundreds, or even thousands of kilometres. We believe the ones some of you saw last night were only curious. It is possible that they had received calls for help from those we were holding in the den. We also believe that others will come and that the ones you saw last night indeed went to bring others here. We are not sure. They wanted to scare us, which provokes an intense fear that they appear to feed on.

"While we are on this point, I must add one very important factor concerning the water. During the heatwave, I am sure you can remember scrabbling for its very existence. You ran just to get a swig of its neutral taste and life-giving properties. You did anything just to touch it and feel it between your fingers. Well, I am afraid to say that in an undetermined period, the virus will begin to fall in the rain as well. If a drop does come through the barrier, under no circumstances are you to touch it. Are there any more questions?"

The morning air had stilled, and only a tang of distant hope lingered. People thought absurdities as they walked away. Steve was sure of it, yet he didn't care. At least they knew the truth.

Brushing off their senseless sentiments, Steve went to see Arthur Payne in his wondrous world of seclusion. From the outskirts of the greenhouses, a forgotten odour crawled in through the side windows.

"Nice of you to come," said Payne. "I liked your speech. I especially loved the way you handled Gossard when he butted in. Your respect comes with a firm hand. We need that around here, especially now. You're a natural guide to the unguided."

"Oh come now, Arthur."

"No, I mean it. Mara tells me you are quite the poet, too. She came around the other day bragging of your Christmas card. When we get out of this nonsense, I'd love to see some of your work."

"That's kind of you. I would be only too happy to show it to you. Did any of the paraphernalia we brought back from Tierra Colorada help in the end?"

Payne's face creased. "Oh yes. Thanks to that little episode, I permanently borrowed one of Quaid's electron microscopes from the hospital. You want to know something else? I looked at every one of those plants. Quaid showed me what to look for, so I hooked it up myself. Nine of the plants you brought back were fine. They obviously got their water from a different sprinkler. Speaking of which, I'm checking the water for abnormalities. At least here in the agricultural centre, I seem to have things under control. Come, I'll show you where it is."

Steve walked with Arthur, passing by dozens of healthy plants in a variety of stages of growth and alphabetically placed into rows. In a separate room to one side of the second greenhouse was a cold room where the jointly manufactured Zeiss, Bausch and Lomb high-energy electron microscope sat on top of a metal table. The viewing monitor placed to the left was blinking.

"It's a real beauty," boasted Arthur. "It shows us what we're up against. Hey, have you ever seen an infected molecule?"

"No, never. I'm curious, though."

"Real ugly little critters, they are." Steve followed Arthur to the white box at the left of the microscope. "This button supplies the juice."

When Arthur flicked the switch, a gentle perceptible hum increased in intensity and a red light appeared. "Now we have to wait a couple of minutes as the liquid helium flows through the tubes, cooling the delicate innards. When it's ready, the red light will turn green."

Arthur excused himself and disappeared into a cubicle. A short while later, he reappeared donning an anti-viral protection suit and holding a glass receptacle in his left hand.

"This little sod I picked off one of your prize lemon trees," said Arthur's muffled voice. Opening a porthole on the side of the microscope, Steve watched as Arthur placed the receptacle inside and closed a flap.

"The electron microscope allows us to analyse any part of the leaf we select. You see, electron technology doesn't need light like a conventional microscope. It uses a storm of electrons bombarding the surface. The result is revealed on the monitor before you."

Arthur twiddled a few knobs. "Ah, there it is. This is two hundred thousand magnification. As you can see, it appears normal." Arthur mumbled something about amino acids. "Let's go a little deeper inside." Arthur twiddled more. "At 1.5 million times magnification, the picture takes on a more hairy aspect."

Steve inclined himself towards the monitor. He looked at an image that resembled an apple or a plum with a bruise. It was rounded, but definitely had a fruity aspect. It was everywhere.

As Arthur rotated the specimen, the same damaged images came into view. Not a single atom was spared. "Pretty, isn't it?" Arthur's sarcastic tone ruptured Steve's fascination. "Now you can see for yourself what we are up against. No one understands how the molecular virus affects living tissue the way it does."

"Maybe it's a software virus that got bored of its microchip environment and escaped into the sea," said Steve.

"I doubt it. This thing's man-made," said Arthur.

"And computer viruses aren't?" Steve said sarcastically.

"Of course they are. ABC doesn't have the signature of a computer virus. Not even close. It doesn't add up, none of it. I'm sure someone with a big forehead knows the answer. You know, one of those unheard-of government scientist types, the ones who've had their names erased from the Yellow Pages."

Steve said, "What do you think happens when scientists with big foreheads form friendships with snoopy bureaucrats? Wham!

Bureaucrats are a menace to society at the best of times. Do you think this is some government project gone wrong?"

"Or gone right. Maybe the people who made it incriminated Quaid's brother before setting it free." Arthur paused a moment. "You want to know something, Steve?" said Arthur's muffled voice. "The world was a mess, alright. It's always been that way. The point is we just made it messier. What was the purpose of this man-made molecular virus, anyway? What the hell was he going to achieve by it? I believe this is going to be a storm we are going to have to ride out, whichever way we look at it."

Steve continued looking at the magnified image. In reality, it was 1.5 million times smaller than what was portrayed on the screen: something so small, and yet not insignificant.

"Arthur, got any ideas as to how this thing spreads? Look how it crossed and infected the entire Pacific in only two months."

"Quaid didn't tell me much, but what I could make out from his jargon, one single molecule wasn't harmful, so it had to survive by a process he called molecule bouncing. As it bounced from molecule to molecule, infecting and growing, it began to collect information, much like a foetus growing inside a womb taking the full nine months to reach maturity. A molecule that forms a perfect imprint of the next as it attacks and overwhelms, ultimately becoming intellectually stronger. The molecule you see before you appears damaged, but in reality it is not, it's only been modified. As its form began spreading across our oceans, its only goal was to survive, grow, and conquer. It needed to escape from the laboratory domain and now it is free, out there, everywhere."

Arthur scuttled back to the adjoining room and reappeared a few minutes later in casual attire. "The more I learn about this thing," he said, "this virus, or whatever you want to call it, the scarier it sounds. Returning back to my original question, what was the purpose of this man-made virus anyway, and what was man going to achieve by using it?"

"World domination. What else?" Steve said firmly.

"Feasible, but I doubt it. If it were world domination, he's just made his own world useless. Man's not that stupid. Then maybe an antidote did exist in someone's bathroom cupboard. Maybe as we speak, someone was having that braaivleis after all, or that midday merienda drinking Five Roses tea; maybe he was sitting back and watching a movie."

"What did Quaid tell you about his brother?" Steve asked.

"Not much. Why?"

"Quaid told me quite a bit about him during our little chats. He's adamant it was Morcel. I think he would even bet his reputation on it. A brilliant scientist with a grudge doesn't wipe out an entire planet, especially one with innocent people on it. This molecular infection comes from a much higher source."

"Oh, you mean the bureaucrat-scientist principle."

"Yes, it's a possibility. The more we talk about it, the more it begins to make sense. God, how could I have been so naïve?"

"Well, I won't argue with that."

"Which part? The higher source bit or the naïve bit?"

"The higher source bit." Payne smiled.

"Arthur, thank you. You've been a real help. One more thing, why do you think my dog doesn't like you? My wife mentioned Orson had a positive dislike to you. You wouldn't perhaps know why?"

Arthur laughed. "Ultrasonic seed cleaners, they operate at 40,000 hertz. Poor thing probably went mad. Sorry, I never even thought of it. Give her my apologies, will you?"

✳ ✳ ✳

One of the things Steve liked most about being head of security was the time it gave him to attend to non-work tasks like helping Mara around the house. Quaid had given them ten litres of a limestone extract the foundry workers asked him to analyse. It was a by-product taken during cement formation. Steve used it to paint two of the rooms. It was also during one of those days when he repaired and fixed the old sofa.

By early January, the DPF had already instated more than two hundred veterans into its flanks, and they had started to integrate themselves in among the wall-stalkers.

Death of a DOK

As DOK strengthened itself against the outside dangers, the emergency signal arrived from DOK 3. Steve was inspecting a faulty MOGS controller on the wall in Sector Five, explaining the procedure to a worker, when suddenly his C-10 erupted with Gossard's anxious face.

"Steve, Kalakov's got problems. I'm in the Security Centre!"

"What's up?"

"The infected are walking through the unfinished gate apertures."

Steve dropped the MOGS control. It fell and broke into pieces on the ground. "Tell Matthew to give you another," said Steve to the worker as he slid down the ladder.

By the time Steve reached the Security Centre, Kalakov had already shut himself into a solid steel containment room with a remote camera. All DOK cities had them. Kalakov's bloodied face was talking to Gossard on the monitor as Steve walked to his side.

"Sorry, Gossard," groaned Kalakov. "I've stuffed it up, haven't I?"

"Yes, you have," replied the major. "Jesus, why didn't you listen when you had the chance? Now it's too late."

"I'll leave it to you to fill out the report. Don't make it all bad."

"Don't worry, Kalakov, I won't. I'll put good words in there for you, I promise."

"Hey, do you remember the time we went surfing together in Starlight Bay?"

"Yes, of course I do. I won't ever forget those days."

"What happened to that charming girl you met?" asked Kalakov. "What was her name?"

"Sandra. I married her. Remember, you came to the wedding the next year as best man."

"Oh yes, how is she?"

"She was killed in the heatwave fifteen months ago."

"Oh I'm sorry, Gossard, really sorry."

"Don't worry about it, old friend, it's all behind me now."

Kalakov paused, putting his left hand to his head. "I feel so strange, my head is so numb. Shit, what's happening to me?" Kalakov rubbed the back of his neck. "I'm scared, all the men, women and those children out there. Damn it! What have I done?"

Gossard looked away from the screen for two or three seconds. In that brief instant, Kalakov began to cry like a baby as his inner self was wrenched outwards in a raging fist of fury. It was his last desperate cry for help, and there was nothing anyone could do.

"I'm sorry, old friend," said the major, "if only you'd listened to me in the beginning."

Kalakov, lowering his face towards the floor, embarrassed and unable to meet Gossard's stare any longer, cupped his hands against his face.

Seeing this, Gossard moved closer to the monitor and with a tender voice, he asked, "Kalakov, how can I contact your brother? I'll notify him."

Kalakov, undisturbed by Gossard's larger image on the screen, continued to peer towards the floor through his fingers. The question of obvious importance was not even being processed by his brain.

"Kalakov, do you hear me?"

In the split of a second, Kalakov glimpsed up towards the video scanner like a jack-in-the-box.

Gossard shrieked in fear at what he saw. Steve's stomach tightened.

Kalakov's creased face, highlighted and accentuated by two iridescent blue eyes, almost made them heave. He grinned. A sickly bleeding, toothy-gum smile exuded complete madness. Close to his nose, a lump began to appear. A slow-moving finger beneath the skin was pushing its way outwards. It was an irregular, inflamed lump.

Steve watched it slothfully beckoning its way before eventually dwarfing the nose alongside. They watched as his moustache fell off, leaving vestigial traces intact under his nose.

Kalakov's bloody, fixating stare vacuously gazed towards the camera. Five of the other DOK cities by this time were watching the horrendous spectacle as it happened, but as the word began to spread and more DOK cities came online, his lips began to part. A gurgling, spitting babble became a distorted whisper. The murmur slowly transformed itself into comprehensible words. At first, they were out of order, but as reminiscent leftovers of his once-intelligent brain battled against the virus within, they started to form intelligible words.

"We are coming for you, all of you."

There was a second of silence as mouths, unable to pronounce even the smallest guttural sound, did nothing but gape. By this time, many DOK cities had turned off their viewers in sheer disgust or fear, or both.

Gossard followed suit. "Poor bastard, I knew that man almost fifteen years before we went our separate ways."

"That may be true, Major," said Steve, "but that wasn't Kalakov. Jesus, you saw it. It was his body—nothing more."

Gossard's attentiveness turned once more toward the monitor display. "Colonel Blake, were you watching that?"

"Unfortunately, I was, Gossard. Such a tragedy to see men suffer that way, especially when there's nothing you can do for them. May God take pity upon their souls."

Gossard spoke: "This unspeakable incident will put everyone on maximum alert. We are making preparations against this damn rain. Several DOK cities have reported rain. Luckily, it's not infectious yet. It has the remaining sixteen unprotected DOKs in an uproar, us included. Although we have begun construction of gigantic platforms to hide under when it rains, we feel they won't be ready in time. Some of us don't have enough supplies. DOK 11, just west of you, hasn't a single grain of cement to its name, and there's no way for anyone to get supplies to them. Even if they could, there's not enough to go around in the first place. It's almost as scarce as uncontaminated water."

"Colonel, who's next in line after DOK 3? Who'll receive the wave of infected as they go east and southwards?" asked Gossard.

"DOK 2 and DOK 5 in northern Canada," answered Blake. "Why?"

"It'll take a few days before they can reach them, so in the meantime we'll put together whatever we can and airlift supplies to DOK 11."

"I'll notify them and make the preparations," said Colonel Blake.

As the monitor blinked off, Gossard turned towards Tino. "Tino, your dossier says you're licensed to fly the Ka-58. Is that correct?"

"Yes, sir, I am. I know it inside and out. Hell, I know the thing better than my own backyard."

"Good, select two men to go with you. You've a drop-off to make at DOK 11."

DOK 16, amongst other DOK cities, continued watching the spectacle at DOK 3 through the video cameras. As each scene flicked onto the viewing monitor, it revealed havoc. A wave of infected had simply walked through the open gate apertures and completely ransacked the place. Wooden planks were speckled about the icy terrain, and many buildings were on fire. Some vehicles were outside the walls billowing huge columns of black smoke. In the middle of it all, hundreds of corpses in various stages of consumption lay on the thick whiteness for all to see.

Steve looked away from the vile content. It was mayhem. Kalakov, however, remained in the sealed-off containment unit, unable to escape. He was frantically smashing anything and ranting like a wild animal. He furiously wanted out, and yet all he had to do was flick a switch behind a panel. Thousands like him were now moving south. Likewise, thousands more were moving in a northerly direction, and some of them would cross the path to DOK 16.

Blake's face filled the monitor again. "Gossard, both Mexico City and DOK 11 await your chopper. They'll have your reserve fuel ready by the time you get there. Mexico City will call the attention of your pilot with green smoke at the landing pad. Tell him to keep an eye out for it. I've sent a list of requirements that DOK 11 needs. I hope your helicopter can handle all the weight."

"I'll have it off the ground within an hour. Our pilot is Tino. He's taking two others with him."

Hearing this, Tino walked out of the Security Centre and began issuing orders through the communicator.

As he disappeared towards the Admin Building, Steve followed him, reaching for his C-10. "Sanchez, what's going on out there?"

"Little movement, sir. There are small groups wandering about. I think they are too far away to see us. They seem to have their sights set on something else farther west. I suggest you talk to Gomez or Hartley. Maybe they can tell you more."

Steve switched off his C-10 and moved towards Tino, wearing a look of stone. "Sanchez says there's some action west of here. When you're up there send us all the video you can. I want to know what the dickens they're up to."

Tino's two compatriots were fully trained guerrilla combat soldiers with scars that bragged of years of experience in either hand-to-hand combat or open conflict. Tino was certainly taking a pair of suitable men with him.

One introduced himself to Steve as Bill. He was six feet tall with a neck like a tree trunk. Coherent eyes revealed an obvious disconnection from the wants of others, yet compassion and concern manifested itself in the way he moved.

From Steve's first impression, the other soldier seemed more human. He was a thin and agile man, and clearly the oldest of the three. An opinionated, pretentious stride brought him to present himself with folded arms. His name was Rod. A beard stubble smeared his chin, giving him an intimidating presence. Beneath his well-travelled jacket, two revolvers popped into view. By the time Steve's first impression had terminated, he realised this man's sense of humour was as lifeless as he was.

Tino's short list predominantly had cement as the most urgent, all five tons of it. They also needed a variety of citrus fruit, and some medicines.

Steve paid Arthur a visit.

"That was quick. Did you miss me already?" said Arthur.

"Don't get your hopes up. Arthur, I need citrus fruit for DOK 11. Whatever you have to spare and ready for immediate delivery. Did you get what happened to DOK 3?"

"Yep, poor bastards. And Kalakov, damn. I'll never forget that face."

Arthur silently and expressionlessly took Steve to the fruiting section. "We don't have much ourselves. I can maybe squeeze in three hundred kilos of mixed citrus without endangering our own stocks. Hell, I'll even throw in some apples and pears if I knew it would save them."

"Get it bagged and have it sent to the landing site. The helicopter is waiting to take off. Arthur, thanks for your help. They'll really appreciate it."

At the landing site, the medication had been prepared and waited in small green bags while Tino's two companions and ten workers busily loaded the last of the cement onto the chopper.

As the last pallet disappeared, Gossard walked to Tino. "These guys are expecting you in five hours. Contact us once you're in the air and before you reach Mexico City."

"OK, sir," Tino walked off, only to appear moments later in the cockpit, giving the thumbs-up sign.

As the fruit and medication went into the enormous belly, Gossard turned on his C-10 and issued an order to Rawling in the Security Centre. "Alright, turn it off."

The barrier quietly fizzled off and the helicopter slothfully rose and made its way towards the horizon. Before the chopper disappeared from sight, Steve punched in Tino's dial number on the C-10 and his concentrating face appeared on the display. "Tino, are they going west? Was Sanchez's description correct?"

"Not only can I confirm what Sanchez saw," answered Tino, "the whole damn country seems to be making its way west. Christ, some are even crawling on all fours to get there. It must be one hell of a party." Tino swung the external heli-camera downwards and pointed its macro lens towards immense queues of marching infected.

"They're headed for Mexico City, alright. It's as if they know where it is, or there's an invisible radio beacon directing them and pushing them forward."

"How long will it take for you to reach Mexico City?" asked Steve.

"About two hours. Bill's in the back throwing hand grenades into large groups of infected."

"Contact me once you get closer," said Steve.

"Will do, sir."

The C-10 made a peep and went off. Suddenly it hit Steve: moving west, what the hell? Of course, it was obvious. Mexico

City was the Central American nerve centre. They must be going there to disable the communications. Steve had to warn Gossard.

Gossard was in the Security Centre when Steve entered. On a screen before him, Major Vermeer, head of DOK 11, had an intense look about him. He was worried.

"Vermeer, calm down for God's sakes," said Gossard. "Our chaps will be there in a few hours. We've sent everything you needed. Our agriculturalist has put in some additional fruit."

"Thank you. That's kind of him. We have an epidemic here of a more natural nature. Our medic thinks its scurvy. He has not found a single trace of Vitamin C in their bodies, and it's progressing so fast we fear we may lose some of them before your guys get here."

"Just sit tight, they'll be there." Vermeer's profile disappeared off the screen.

"Scurvy, how odd," said Steve.

"Yes, obviously we can expect anything now. We are vulnerable to attack from all angles."

"Major, I came to talk to you about Mexico City," said Steve.

"What about Mexico City?"

"Tino has confirmed the infected have diverted themselves towards Mexico City. Sir, I think their plan is to cripple our communications."

Gossard grunted and switched on a monitor display. "Harris, how the devil are you?" said Gossard.

"Gossard, it's good to see you. Your chopper should be here soon. They've forwarded to us reports of heavy activity around the perimeter. I have positioned more than two thousand men on the city limits. These infected are in for a big surprise."

"I hope so, Harris. Listen, Stephen Gotlar, my head of security, thinks the infected are on their way to disable your communications. What's your opinion?"

"Gossard, we are well armed and ready for a full-on attack. Anyway, I wouldn't go worrying yourself, these blasted things move slowly. When they do make an appearance, I'll notify you. Tell me, how's DOK 16 doing?"

"Actually, under the circumstances, very well. We've reached a good level of existence. Our population last week increased by eleven. What more can I tell you? I suppose you saw what happened to DOK 3?"

"Of course I did. I reviewed the images a few times. Then I shared it with my officers, and they, in turn, showed it to the troops a few hours ago. It served as a good wake-up call. Truth is, it scared them shitless. Excuse me, Gossard, my secretary has called."

There was a brief silence as Harris momentarily left the screen. He returned to say, "Your helicopter has arrived into MC airspace, and will be here in fifteen minutes." Harris broke contact.

Steve contacted Tino. "Tino, Harris has just informed us you're almost there. What's the situation outside the city?"

"Well, sir, tell Harris there's a mass coming from the east headed directly for him. I would say with their present heading and speed they will breach the outer boundaries in two hours."

"How many are there?"

Tino hesitated. "About half a million at least, sir."

"Thanks, Tino, I'll tell Harris." As Tino's face disappeared, Steve began thinking about two thousand fully armed men against half a million infected. What were the odds of their survival? Mexico City only had a population of three million. It was a drastically reduced number after the heatwave had slaughtered many of them a year ago.

"Harris," said Steve, "our pilot tells me that you have more than half a million infected due east of you, only hours away."

"Half a million? Holy crabnuts!" Without uttering another word, Harris disappeared like a scared rabbit off the screen.

✳ ✳ ✳

"There's the green smoke!" said Tino's voice erupting from the speaker.

"How far away are you?" asked Steve.

"Two or three kilometres. There's a couple of shooters down there having a whale of a time. Hope to God they know what's coming."

"They do, thanks to you. I've just given the news to Harris."

"Sir, have to go, the landing pad is just ahead," Tino disengaged the transmission.

"Put her down on the yellow line," said Bill's rough voice. Two armed guards awaited alongside a kerosene truck. One of them had a fuel hose in his hand. As Tino settled onto the landing pad, Rod and Bill climbed out. The other security guard who stood alongside the refill truck jumped back a few paces as Bill's giant frame moved onto the landing area.

"Qué demonios es eso?" said the guard. Bill, overhearing the phrase, walked over.

"I'll tell you what the devil I am. I am the one risking my life going up to DOK 11 with supplies. Do you want to come along for the ride? My friend here would love to play with you. He gets bored on these long trips." Rod spasmodically turned his head towards the alarmed guard.

"Sorry, sir. I didn't mean to offend you," said the guard in bad English. He didn't disconnect his eyes off Rod for a second.

"Don't worry, soldier, I don't offend easily," said Bill intensely.

Rod grabbed the fuel hose from the guard, almost knocking him to the ground. Rod's piercing stare was accompanied with sprightly movements. The guard visibly shook as Rod moved closer. "He's lucky I am in a good mood today. Excusez-moi, do you speak English like your friend here?" The guard, giving off a blank, drifting expression, exuded fear. Rod added, "I thought so, the lights are on, but there's nobody at home. It's like talking to a fish. This guy hasn't understood a bloody word I've said."

Tino butted in. "Leave him alone, Rod. Get that tank filled. You want to play the smart one, why don't you talk to him in Spanish? We've got people to save up north, remember?"

Rod gyrated on one foot, releasing a short animal cry as the metallic fuel hose disappeared into the helicopter's tank. Bill had opened the engine compartment door and checked the water and oils while ensuring nothing was loose. The moment the tank was full, both guards dropped whatever they had in their hands and ran for dear life.

"Come back and fight, you weeds." Rod's imitating, almost feminine voice made them run even faster.

"I see you two make friends easily," said Tino.

"Yeah, we do tend to leave good impressions wherever we go," answered Bill.

"Hey, don't criticize. I just wanted to play," said Rod.

"I know, Rod, I know," said Bill as he climbed back into the helicopter.

Five minutes outside Mexico City, Bill's startled voice expressed alarm. "Good God, look, there's more of them!"

Tino steered his glance Earthwards. "Christ, there must be over a million of the sods down there, and they're going straight for Harris."

Tino reached for his C-10 and called Steve. "Sir, we've refuelled and are on our way to DOK 11, but I'm afraid I have bad news."

"What's the matter, Tino?"

Tino switched on the external camera. "This is what's coming down from the north. Harris had better start saying his prayers and kiss his—"

"Now you hold that tongue, soldier," said Gossard overhearing the conversation. "What's going on, Tino?"

"Major, like I was explaining, there's more coming down from the north, a lot more." The audio channel switched over to video again.

Gossard leaned towards the monitor. "Tino, continue that video feed, I'm going to patch it directly onto Harris' desk." Gossard pressed the touch-sensitive button under the monitor. "Harris, are you there?" On the second attempt, Harris' wrinkled face appeared on the monitor.

"Gossard, heck, I'm glad it's you," answered Harris. "Our foot patrols have already spotted the mass coming from the east, crawling over the hills. With a bit of luck we may be able to stop them from entering the city. I've got grenade launchers and snipers on the outskirts wiping them out as they come into range."

"Harris, listen. Our chopper took off from your launch pad five minutes ago and has sent me firsthand video images of what's about to enter Mexico City from the north. Look." Gossard flicked a button on the console and fed the video directly from the helicopter onto Harris' monitor.

While Harris watched in horror, Gossard spoke. "There are more than a million of them. There's nothing you can do against these numbers. The odds are against you."

There was silence.

"Before we give ourselves up, we will kill as many of them as possible," said Harris.

"You still don't get it, do you? There are no prisoners. You don't give up, YOU GET INFECTED! Once you are infected, you join them and move on to contaminate the rest of us. After they have dealt with you, they will accumulate what is left of the population and move north and west again towards DOK 11, DOK 4, and eventually to us. If you come here, I'll shoot you myself. You hear?! You shoot those bastards. You shoot every one of them until there are no more. When the last one goes down, you contact me. Until then, I don't want to see your face!"

Switching off the link to Mexico City, Gossard contacted Tino.

"Tino, how far are you from DOK 11?"

"About two hours, sir," replied Tino.

"Have you enough fuel to make it home?" asked Gossard.

"Yes sir, why?"

"I want you to take as much video as you possibly can and head back here. I am afraid there is nothing we can do for DOK 11. It is every man for himself from now on. If DOK 11 didn't have the foresight to plant fruiting trees in its gardens, it's their problem. Don't worry, I'll take full responsibility."

"Yes, sir, on my way," said Tino.

"Major, you know they'll die without those supplies that you promised," said Steve.

"You think I don't know that, Steve? It's better for them to die; they'll be better off," said Gossard as he approached the door.

❋ ❋ ❋

While they waited for Tino to arrive or more news from Mexico City, Steve decided to go home. Mara was in the garden with Orson, so dissimulating the occurrences in Mexico City and forcing a smile, he walked over.

"Hi, babe, what are you planting?" Orson ran up to Steve.

"Thyme," she said, moving over and giving him a peck.

"Nice to see you, too. What's to eat? I'm starved."

"Cabbage stew."

"Again? My hair is starting to go green."

"Hey, I've got an idea. Why don't we club one of Arthur's rabbits on the head and find a big pot?" Mara said.

"Good idea, but Arthur said the genetic experiment failed. He won't risk us eating them until he's satisfied with the results."

"Failed. We don't need prime rabbit on the table, just anything that's not a vegetable. I think it's time we had a chat with him," Mara said and went inside, ignoring Steve's remark.

Mara was a handy person, she could do anything. Once their dishwasher broke and Steve found it neatly disassembled on the floor before she laboriously put it together again.

"Steve, I put up some shelves in our bedroom while you were out today."

"Brilliant. How did you manage to put those lines in the wood like that?"

"Now that's a trade secret. If you want to know my secrets, you'll have to marry me first."

"Hmm, I would have to think about that one."

Hartley's face appeared on Steve's C-10. "Sir, we've got movement near Sector Three."

"How many are there?"

"Can't really tell. Maybe a hundred."

"I'll be there in ten minutes." Steve turned back to Mara. "Sorry, love, I have to go. Go talk to Arthur, convince him to part with one of those darn rabbits. We could do with a bit of cholesterol around here."

"I'll try," she said as Steve closed the door.

✳ ✳ ✳

Hartley was waiting at the top of the ladder for Steve as the Jeep pulled alongside.

"There they are." His hand pointed through one of the window apertures. "You can barely make them out with the binoculars."

"Hartley, before the wall-stalkers do their stuff, let them get a little closer. Let them feel that they have achievement in the palm of their hands. It's time I knew what happens. Just concentrate on keeping one of them alive. I'm curious to know what it's going do when it reaches the wall."

Hartley turned and faced the waiting wall-stalkers. "Listen, everyone. No one is to fire a shot until I tell you. I want one alive. Steve wants to know what it does when it reaches the wall."

Three wall-stalkers could place their weapons through the wall portals at a time. Steve squeezed himself between two of them.

One wall-stalker took an interest in Steve's presence. "Sir, do you think we'll make it out of here alive? Look at what happened to DOK 3."

"Of course we will. We are better equipped and better prepared than DOK 3 was. Major Gossard not only blames Kalakov for the disaster, the ultra-low temperatures lent a hand, as well. Relax, both of you. Here, those errors don't exist. You have to bear in mind those poor men lost a lot of time, and it was only when they saw the construction results taking longer than anticipated, they began sinking in their proper mire."

The wall-stalker, pleased by Steve's interest in him, turned once again and faced the oncoming threat.

Slightly later, Hartley's voice broke Steve's thoughts. "Three hundred metres, sir. Shall we fire?"

"Not yet, a bit more." The infected were hunching towards them, probably thinking they hadn't been seen. "Remember, Hartley, I want one of them alive!"

"Two hundred and eighty metres, shall we open fire?"

Steve looked through the inspection hole. "Go on, get to it, and wipe them out!"

Hartley had lifted his hand high in the air. Upon Steve's order Hartley dropped his hand swiftly in a downward motion. A flurry of white energy needles bombarded the outland. The skirmish lasted seconds. The brief encounter, accompanied by a strong smell of ozone, drifted through the air as the plasma rifle released its deadly charge.

"Leave that one, the one on the left," Steve shouted. Hartley looked towards Steve for confirmation.

Gossard climbed the ladder. "Where is it?" he asked, grabbing Steve's shoulder.

"There, down below." Steve's hand pointed towards the terrain.

"What do you want to do with him?"

"I want to know what he's going to do when he encounters a solid object like our wall. Will he try to climb it, will he walk around it until he finds an entrance, or will he try to go under it? Secondly, if our uninvited guest tries to climb, I think it's time we tested the Light Shapers. Until now, I've not had any volunteers."

Gossard managed a dry smile.

"Not long now, sir," said an excited wall-stalker breathing over Steve's neck.

Faint trudging was followed by a dragging sound. As each foot came down, it brought him just that little bit closer to triumph. It was probably thinking I can smell them, they must be close. Suddenly the infected disappeared from view and the perturbed wall-stalkers looked towards Steve.

"Calm down, relax," said Steve. "He's too close to the wall for us to see. I thought you would have realised this was going to happen. The outside cameras will be our eyes from now on. They were installed for that purpose."

Gossard raised his C-10. "Ivanakov, give me camera 91."

As the image appeared on their LCD displays, they watched as the infected arrived at the base of the wall and placed his hands palm-down against the brickwork.

At first, Steve thought his intention was to push it over. Withdrawing his hands with an agonizing slowness, he looked around, dazed and confused, before stepping backwards a metre. A few seconds later, he lethargically steered his head to the left and looked briefly towards the horizon before repeating the process to the right. Once he saw there was nothing in either direction, he glanced upwards. Somehow comprehending the impossibility of the climb, he looked downwards and started digging with his bare hands like a dog burying a bone. Sand and dirt flew in every direction.

"All right, I've seen enough," said Gossard. "Get a team out there right away to vaporise it."

The infected continued digging. Down and down he went, until a ray of light from someone's rifle ended his victory in a glorious surge of yellow flame.

"So they are diggers. Charming," said Steve.

Gossard looked at Steve. "What makes that so interesting? It's a nightmare."

Steve said, "I was thinking if I ever build a wall like this again, I should make it double-reinforced at the base. As we are, they can enter undetected."

"Are you saying that these things can dig under the wall and get in?"

"Yes. I never figured on them being diggers. I honestly thought he would try to climb."

"God, that's reassuring," said Gossard sarcastically. "So if one of these two-legged terrors attacks us at night, there's a chance it'll get in?"

"If the wall-stalkers don't see it, yes, most certainly."

Acknowledging Steve's statement, Gossard silently went down the ladder towards his car and drove off.

✳ ✳ ✳

In the Security Centre, Steve was familiarising himself with the faces that appeared every now and then on the monitors. He looked up, thinking about DOK 3. The surly look of Kalakov was gone. Where DOK 3 normally had his face filling the viewer, video static had taken its place. Steve imagined the monitor to be faulty, or un-tuned, but deep within he knew this not to be the case. Kalakov had smashed it, doomed to an eternity of confinement by his own hand.

Steve returned his thoughts to Mexico City and lowered his glare to the monitor. It had been over two hours since they had heard anything.

"Harris, this is DOK 16. Are you there?"

A woman's face jumped on the screen. "Who the hell are you? You're not Gossard."

"Good afternoon' normally comes before the insult. I am Gossard's second-in-command, Steve Gotlar. Who are you?"

"Harris' secretary. He's gone to fight off these things, these beasts. They're attacking us from all sides. You should have seen what came from the south." A silence glued her lips together. It was then that Steve realised that Tino hadn't flown south. There was no way Harris, or anyone for that matter, could've known what was coming.

"He's got the army, the navy, the marines, the anything out there," said the secretary. "Anyone capable of holding a rifle is fighting for their lives." Her voice deepened. "You go to Eleventh Avenue, you go to Pristine Street, you go to Tourmaline Avenue, well, find a place to set it up!"

Steve thought her acting was pretty good for a secretary.

"It's been like that for the last hour. Twenty minutes ago, Harris just disappeared into thin air and I haven't seen him since.

He's not responding to internal communications either. As he ran out, he was ranting on about something. He said those that took too long to transform from their normal bodies into the infected state were eaten alive. What that means, I will never understand. Do you know what it means?"

"I haven't the foggiest idea." Although Steve hadn't heard it before, he made a pretty good guess.

"W—what did you say your name was?" she asked.

"Steve Gotlar."

"Well, Steve Gotlar, do you think we're going to die? I mean, all of us?"

As the last bit of sentence left her mouth, Steve jerked his head back and blinked. What the dickens was this? She was physically changing in front of Steve's eyes. Her left eye, little by little began to turn black. It darkened and started puffing up like a tiny balloon. The process took ten seconds. When the ring had accomplished the task of encircling the eye, it remorselessly began on her right. Throughout the short transformation, Steve didn't say a word or breathe. He was agape with horror. Steve paused a second longer before speaking.

"No, I think we are destined to live long and prosperous lives, especially you. I can see it." Steve stalled her, as he was sure that not even she knew what was happening to her.

"Tell me more," she said.

"It's the tone of your voice, it tells me so much." Steve fixated on her ugliness.

"Come on, Steve, tell me more."

Steve began stretching his imagination. He was stalling the process of change. Kalakov was still fresh in his mind. "A voice is like a physical aspect," said Steve. "It's a signature, a description of what that person is all about. I can see you and I can hear you. This means, I have the best of you right in front of me. By the way, what's your name? You know mine."

"Geraldine, Geraldine Moraz."

"Well, Geraldine, I don't think it's our time to die, not yet anyway. Looking at you I'd say you are destined to live a long life."

"Go on," she said inquisitively as the words fell out of her creasing mouth. Geraldine gripped her side in pain as infected molecules forced their way onwards through her body, taking over her will. She buckled over, holding her hands over her face before rubbing her eyes in the same eerie manner Kalakov had. Without watching more, Steve switched off the monitor. He couldn't force himself to watch the transformation. Not again. Once in a lifetime was enough.

Mexico City, like DOK 3, was gone. Who could be next? On the Mexican side, there was DOK 11 and DOK 4. After them, it would be DOK 16, seven hundred kilometres to the east. On the American side after DOK 2 and DOK 5, it was an open party.

Steve began to think that if humankind had really progressed, then what good were these achievements and these breakthroughs in the first place? What stopped them from opening the front gates? Come on, infect all of us; we are at your mercy. Nothing stopped us, we were human. We are humans with a mind, a subconscious, and a never-ending curriculum of greed. What we didn't understand we ran from, and what we did possess, we took it over, until it had but one owner. Could man have really been responsible for all this?

Tino's metallic voice interrupted Steve's fury. "Steve, I'm approaching the city, prepare the barrier."

Steve leaned forward and entered his code. Pressing the red button, the console made a blip before deactivating the power source to the Light Shapers. The two active monitors blinked off.

"You're clear to land, Tino."

Tino was tired. He told Steve that after Bill had run out of hand grenades, he slept the entire journey and, of course, climbed out as fresh as a rose.

"Here, I think you and Gossard might want to see this." He placed a video disk in Steve's hand.

"What is it?"

"Video information on the two groups that came from the north and east. Get Gossard over and I'll explain."

"Did you see what happened to Mexico City?"

"Yes, as we were leaving Mexico City airspace to return home, guards were fighting amongst themselves. Bloodshed was everywhere. It was chaos."

Steve switched on his C-10. "Gossard, Tino's back. We are in the Security Centre. He has something to show you."

"I'll be there in five minutes."

"Gossard's on his way over. Care to enlighten me a bit?"

"Have patience, sir, patience." Tino inserted the video disk and started inspecting certain scenes. Gossard anxiously opened the door.

"Look at this, Major." Tino pressed the playback button on the video player. "If my eyes are not deceiving me, what we are looking at are huge divisions, thinking and behaving like an army. After we left Mexico City to return home, this is what we saw."

Gossard moved closer to the screen just in time to see massive gatherings of advancing infected, forming perfect lines hundreds of people long and dozens thick, making their way towards strategic targets in Mexico City.

Steve counted at least fifty of them.

Gossard continued gluing himself to the display, watching people fighting amongst themselves, often to the death.

"I knew they wouldn't make it with more coming down from the north. There were just too many of them."

"But Tino, it wasn't only those that came from the north, another huge army came from the south. They attacked Mexico City from all sides. No one could have prevented it. I spoke with Harris' secretary before she metamorphosed into one, the same as Kalakov did," Steve said.

Gossard swivelled his head. "Steve, get more wall-stalkers on that wall, we've got be ready. Are our communications still up?"

"Yes, it wasn't their intention to cripple them like I thought. They want to cripple us."

"And Vermeer, has anyone spoken to him since Tino got back?"

"No, sir, not a word."

"Then get him on the viewer. He's going to want to hear my story, and chew my head off. I'm sure of it."

Steve tried Vermeer and his secretary a few times and then buzzed the main reception, but there was no reply.

"Switch on the exterior cams," ordered the major.

The camera inside the Security Centre revealed nothing. When the automatic sequencer flicked to the outside gates, they realised what had happened. It was snowing and the all-too-familiar chaos was everywhere.

"Oh God, not DOK 11 too!"

Steve looked towards Tino and he returned the look with a glum nod of his head. "Sir, Mexico City had more than two thousand sharpshooters. What chance do you think we have?"

"Tino, we have open terrain: Mexico City is like the Austrian Alps. They wouldn't have seen a bloody zeppelin if it fell on top of them. Here, we have a seven-kilometre visibility all round. I think they know this."

An orange flashing console light suddenly drew Tino's attention towards the barrier display monitor. "Something is happening—the barrier current is increasing!"

"It's probably a dust storm," said Gossard, nonchalantly looking away. However, their attention once more was called to the control panel, as the console light went red.

"It's raining!" shouted a voice from outside, near to the front entrance. Tino, switching off the video player, shoved past and opened the door. Workers, wall-stalkers and officers alike were standing in the middle of DOK Plaza, staring upwards.

Above their heads, the blackness was already competing with a darkening sky of evening. The accumulation, unleashing its full torrential power on top of them, made them cup their ears from the racket it made as it disintegrated on the barrier above. Both Arthur and Quaid went to an extreme end of DOK, in Sector Twelve, to extract a drop of rainwater for analysis.

After rushing the water specimen to the electron microscope, Arthur confirmed its infectious state within minutes.

Unmoving, uneasy and quiescent, they waited for the storm to finish while everyone looked around nervously for confirmation that no one had converted or changed into some demonic thing. As the minutes passed and no one seemed odd, or mad, they realised they had survived their first rainstorm. The months of hard work had paid off. They had won this mini-battle against nature with a man-made fortress of brainpower and muscle. A scream of triumph ping-ponged through the complex. Their accomplishment this day had brought them closer together. DOK 16 became their own commemorative stone statue, a mental sculpture, invisibly inscribed with the residents' names.

Tomorrow was the anniversary of five months. Deep inside, Steve had believed it would have been more suitable if each day they continued their existence was an anniversary. This day had been unforgettably long, maybe too long. At home in his own DOK of sorts, Steve drew the curtain aside in the lounge and surveyed the night. Their tiny garden moved as small fragile trees swayed and stirred. The wind had returned, and Steve saw a darkness travel over his head that came from the north, from the Gulf. The moon was on the shift again. Worn clouds flung themselves across the face of the moon's silvery radiance like ripples in a soured sea. Their garden had transformed itself into a winter stream, and the light purled like water moving over ice.

In bed, Mara leaned over and gave Steve a kiss. "Good night, honey," she said as Steve rolled over and immediately went to sleep.

Dream State

Steve saw the illuminated wall come alive with scampering forms running to and from their security points. It was dark, unnaturally dark, and supernatural, almost ghostly. The wall lights formed irregular yellowed V-shapes elucidating wall-stalkers on their nightly patrols as they guarded DOK. Various emergency beacons had been switched off, ensuring power to the protective barrier overhead, so Steve's side of town was obscure and shadowy. The house consisted of a large dining room with many windows. There was an office and two bedrooms, a kitchen, and one bath. The walls were a darkened mahogany, giving a flavourful contrast to the wooden floors.

Looking out of the dining room windows, Steve could see them, thousands of them in the distance like blue lanterns, blue light-emitting diodes, slowly repositioning themselves on the other side of the wall. They were concocting a way to get in. Steve could hear them growling, frustratingly trying to evade the wall defences. In the one corner of his eye, he saw them digging below the wall after having discovered a weak point in their defences, an area where they weren't watching at the time. The wall-stalker wasn't there.

Using the opportunity at hand, they dug down and under until the absent wall-stalker discovered them. Soon, others would come and continue where they had left off, digging farther down until eventually the lights of DOK became visible on the other side of the wall through their infected eyes.

If they did manage to slip by the observant wall-stalkers and enter, they went directly towards Steve's house, slipping in a glass patio door on the side. Steve didn't intervene, he was disarmed. His only weapon was how his dream ended, or how he wanted it to end. Once inside, they started searching the rooms one at a time before finally coming out of the kitchen door on the other side. Suddenly he imagined he could see through their eyes and he could think what they thought. Steve imagined their roles had changed for just a moment and that they had become the hunted. But even as Steve slept, he knew this to be nothing more than a fallacious illusion. Instead, while still in his dream state, Steve hid in a cupboard and waited.

Their appearance was that of Kalakov, indistinguishable. Body lumps surfaced in different places, some appeared on their arms, on their legs, one was on the neck. One outside had two lumps on his face. Steve heard them scuffling up the passageway towards the bedroom. Frustratingly, they began to search under beds before ripping them into pieces. Steve began to sweat, he had to get out of the cupboard before they found him. When three of them, seemingly hearing his desperate thoughts of flight disappeared behind a door, Steve opened the cupboard and ran for dear life.

They didn't see him, but they continued searching all the same until one of them discovered the cupboard he'd escaped from moments before. Victoriously, the thing began sniffing the air and started to groan. On reaching the dining room, Steve looked once more towards the outside wall. Blue eyes on the other side of the wall were making their way towards the entrance hole to join those already inside. The creeping blue fear was the water itself, an ambling, swaying sea gently making itself towards Steve's house.

In Steve's dream, his house was constructed twenty metres away from the wall, and at one stage his attention was on those who had recently gone inside and not on the one that had sneaked out the kitchen door. The monster raised his head and looked directly towards Steve, groaning and alerting the others. Moments later, as one large group, five of them exited the door, bent down and lifted rocks. That was when Steve woke with a jerk in a sea of sweat.

Mara was still asleep. At least he didn't wake her. Orson, on the other hand, was aware of Steve's conscious state. He knew of his nightmarish dilemma. He came to comfort him in doggy fashion. Orson's way of comfort was a lick on the face and thirty kilos of weight plopping itself on one's lap. Steve didn't mind his now mostly vegetarian body on his. Quaid had given them a substance to pour onto his vegetable diet every day. It disguised it, giving a meaty smell. Steve knew Orson wasn't an average dog, somehow he knew and loved them all the same. He loved them for giving him a home in the first place.

As Steve lay on the bed with Orson spread over his chest, his thoughts returned to Arthur and his rabbits. Maybe tomorrow would be a stew day. Just the thought of it kept Steve awake a few minutes longer than necessary, but finally he dozed into a peaceful slumber as he felt Orson's body heat creep to his side.

The next morning, Orson's limp body was still there. His mouth was wide open and revealed a large pink tongue laden with pale taste buds. His breath stank like anchovy. As Steve moved to stretch, Orson's eyes regained their conscious brown state and opened.

"Morning, boy. Ready to face the world again, are we?" The tongue bobbed about playfully. Drool oozed onto the sheets.

"What, hungry again?" Steve picked up his watch. "There's still three hours before your feeding time, you know that. It's the same time every day, that's the rule."

Orson moved his head close and licked Steve on the face, so he began to fight Orson back. It woke Mara.

"Sorry, honey, I was telling Orson he had to wait for his food, but he told me he wanted it now and started to lick me to death."

Mara laughed. "Fancy a cup of tea?"

"I'd love one."

Four thousand litres of milk were available on a weekly basis. Each household was allowed half a litre per week. Everyone was one and the same, irrespective of who or what you were.

Steve had become an expert teabag squeezer. Their diminishing stocks had made them teabag-aware. The seventy bags they had on arrival had already dwindled to thirty. Sometimes one single teabag would last three days in a row. Sometimes they left it in water overnight to catch the last bits of flavour. When these options had run dry, it was time for a new one. Their sugar was artificial—it tasted artificial, but at least it resembled sweetness. They had become accustomed to it. They had no choice.

Arthur was proud of his invention, his "sugar cane," and the truth was it was not so bad. Once mixed together, the overly squeezed teabag, the artificial sugar, the limited quantity of milk, and the artificially made water, it really wasn't so bad.

After the teabags were completely used up, Mara normally dried them out and used the leaves in the garden. Sometimes she mixed them with Orson's meal he received once per day. At least the plants loved it. However, Orson knew there was nothing else. He accepted whatever he was given, and in return, he gave them more love than any person was capable of giving.

✳ ✳ ✳

During the night, wall-stalkers and DPF eliminated twenty-six infected wanderers. It was the highest number recorded so far. Steve received the news that morning as he walked into the Administration Building to collect the results of the previous night. Result collection was a perfectly normal procedure for any officer or higher military ranking personnel to do. These informants kept them fully up to date with the happenings during their absence. Also during the night, there had been no further transformations and no reported cases of strange behaviour from contact with the infected water. His real surprise, though, came as Steve walked into the Security Centre. To his horror and disgust, five DOK monitors displayed static. Steve called Tino on the C-10.

"What's this? When did this happen?"

"Six hours ago," replied Tino. "It appears there was another wave sweeping west from the eastern seaboard of the United States. It just came out of nowhere. Anthony was doing a bit of night work when he called me to see exactly what you have just seen. It took them two hours to wipe out three DOK cities. I checked the inter-DOK video monitors at first light. The results are the same. It's identical destruction everywhere."

"How did they get in?" Steve asked.

Tino paused.

"Tino, how did they get in?"

"I think we showed them what to do. They dug under the walls." Tino paused again. "They must have been watching the DOK cities from a distance, patiently waiting for the right time to strike. The results are displayed on the monitors before you. Check them if you want to."

Linda

Before Steve had time to review anything, Quaid ran into the Security Centre.

"Have you seen what's coming?" ask Quaid.

"Quaid, what are you talking about?"

"Come outside and see it for yourself."

Quickly following Quaid, Steve looked where his hand pointed southwards. Clouds were coming, black vengeful clouds. An ever-expanding wall of wrath had them neatly lined up in its sights. A floating, blackened taxman was coming to receive "full payment due."

Of all the natural forces on Earth, Mother Nature was by far the most powerful, most relentless, far exceeding their present predicament. Steve had seen her devastation many times before. She was angry, all right, but nothing Steve had seen even came close to what was happening to them today, and it wasn't even Mother Nature's doing. Mother Nature always won in the end with her small, focused battles dotted here and there. Right now, it looked as if she was coming to clean up the mess mankind had made.

The darkness wasn't natural. Looking at it made Steve quiver. Its unknown fury was bringing something deadly along with it as it travelled northwards, consuming the warmer air of the Mexican Gulf.

Security Centre later diagnosed the blackness as a hurricane force bringing lightning, hail, rain, and winds exceeding 200 kilometres per hour. It was still in its young stage. The security computer quickly plotted its path.

"Just look at those clouds!" exclaimed Steve. "I haven't seen anything like them since Mara and I were living in Texas."

The storm's formidable twirling form brought back sour memories. Four years before, Steve was offered contract work, so they moved to Baytown, just outside Houston. In the beginning, they enjoyed it, a few hours of work per day, ending in a fat salary cheque at the end of the month. It was an easy six-month contract of security work. Mara went with him as his secretary.

During their stay, one day there was sun, the next it rained. It was Texan weather, and they got used to it. Then one early October morning, the workers began to frantically run around finding shelter, fastening down anything that could be clamped. The experience was new to Steve and Mara, and they honestly had no idea what the urgency was. Workers seemingly ran faster than the wind itself. Papers and bags were flying about in all directions like stringless kites. And the noise, that damned incessant noise the wind made as it gained strength, howling through the metallic structures.

A worker stopped in front of the sleeping quarters and banged on the door. "Steve, Mara!" he shouted. "For God's sakes, find cover. Rita's coming!"

At first, Steve thought Rita might have been the big boss, el gran jefe, or even the boss of the big boss. Mara came to his side and told him to look out the side window in the bedroom. She'd been alerted to the window as a cardboard box had whacked against the side of the house.

"Come and look," she said.

Closing the front door with difficulty, Steve followed her to the side window. The blackness in the sky had snuck upon them like a thief in the night, an explosion of rapidly moving bad weather. Steve told her it was normal. When Mara pointed towards an even blacker-than-black patch, Steve saw it threateningly sucking its way towards them, wreaking disaster. They were insignificant against it, this roving building a thousand stories high that was about to descend upon them.

Its funnel was noticeably rotating, spinning like a liquidiser. Powerful blue flashes of lightning struck everywhere. Then the hail came. They were small stones at first, but they got bigger and bigger as the smaller, lighter ones were sucked up, and then pulled back into the cold, swirling void of the hurricane. In the centre of its remarkable mass, they gathered more water before re-freezing. As the hailstones became too heavy, they fell below, larger in size. The hailstones were like missiles. Suddenly, a roof tile came through the roof and their little piece of world became turmoil. Remaining workers were directing themselves into a cellar, through a flap in the ground. Down and down they went, disappearing through the rain into safety. It was through the rain that Steve distinguished a human form running towards their prefab. His labouring, staggering movements disclosed his obvious difficulty to move in the wind.

He began banging on their door so hard, Steve thought the door was going to fall off. "Steve, Mara, for God's sakes! Get the out of there and into the storm shelter! What are you waiting for?"

The house shook as if they were experiencing an earthquake. Leaving the door open, they crossed the road to the shelter with only the things they held in their hands. Mara held on to Steve with such force that his arm began to bleed.

They were in the shelter for hours, enduring crashing wind, solemn faces. As the reinforced metal cover was finally unbolted and laid back, and they emerged, trees were down and houses were gone. They were astonished at the destruction.

In the next few days Rita travelled north. She had barely missed Dallas, and totally destroyed Oklahoma City. Where many prefabs had once been, their concrete foundations lay like tombstones. Force Five winds had plucked them off the ground like they were made of paper. Their prefab had disappeared, with Mara's comb lying on their concrete slab like a memorial. The experience happened fast. They weren't warned of its approach because the inhabitants were so used to that kind of natural battering it never occurred to them to educate Steve and Mara.

In the next few days, lists of names were pasted everywhere throughout the refinery. Rita's insurgency left nine hundred people dead and tens of thousands homeless. They eventually found Steve and Mara's house two kilometres down the road with another fourteen prefabricated shacks scattered alongside. One of them had a body inside. They never learned who it was.

※ ※ ※

"That, gentlemen," said Steve, "is a good replica of what we saw four years ago."

Quaid was dissecting the storm like a beetle, thinking. Steve was sure of his subsistence in the hands of its obvious power. He watched its distant twirling form slowly gather size and shape. Sporadic lightning flashes tainted the blackened cotton swab with dazzle and glitter. Steve began worrying about all this dazzle and glitter hitting the Light Shapers, or the generator room. Electricity attracts electricity. Steve had thoughts of hailstones repeatedly hitting the Light Shapers. What about the shield above the greenhouses and their food supply? One thing for sure, they were completely reliant on the Light Shapers, and if something happened to them, they were doomed.

The DPF were itchy about what was coming on the horizon. Patrolling in twos was not their style.

Nearing the wall, Steve's eyes met the same graffiti as before, "Believe in the mercy of Christ." He rubbed off the chalked message with his handkerchief. He wasn't about to let this idiosyncrasy inseminate them with its insanity. This was DOK 16. They had the resources and the facilities to win this onslaught. Steve was sure if the time came, they would be able to hold out in their fortress against these infected. What frightened him was the water. It could enter undetected. A single dewdrop could end their existence. A dewdrop couldn't be shot with a plasma rifle, although it was an interesting thought. The infected were only carriers, the results of what the water contained.

Steve needed clarity, so he paid Rawling a visit. Steve found him with his crew, making last-minute adjustments and security checks to the Light Shapers. Rawling's men were working against the clock; they all were.

Gossard came over and began dishing out orders. "Rawling, get a squad over to Arthur Payne. Those greenhouse roofs are a disgrace, even I could blow them off. Imagine what a hurricane can do. You've got only four hours to make that place like a vault. I want to hear those roofs laughing at that hurricane."

"Yes, sir."

Five laden vehicles disappeared as Gossard focused on Rawling. "How are those supports? Did you find enough steel in the end to make all of them?"

"Seven are a bit shorter than the rest."

Gossard's glance intensified. "What do you mean, a bit shorter?"

"Forty centimetres shorter. There just isn't any more steel."

Gossard's look turned to worry. "Did you look behind the school? There's a pile of heavy plate I put there for safekeeping."

"We've already used it. We searched everywhere. There's nothing left."

"Then use the doors from the underground storage cubicle. Rip them off and weld them on. I don't care what it looks like. Just get those Light Shapers protected."

Rawling, without hesitation, issued orders to ten men. "Well, you heard the major. Go get me those doors!"

As Gossard directed himself to other chores, Steve looked up at Rawling on the first level. "Getting ourselves into trouble, are we?"

"No, not at all." Rawling gave a smile. "Come on up."

A group of workers were welding a small metallic plate onto the front of a Light Shaper as Steve climbed onto the ladder.

Rawlings told him, "These plates we're putting on will help protect the electronics on the inside against hail and rain."

"What about lightning?" asked Steve. "This beast is going to bring the whole family along for the ride, mark my words."

"Steve, if a stray lightning bolt or hailstone does hit the wrong spot, there is a chance the Light Shaper will go off. If that happens, it will temporarily expose a small area to open air. Some rain will penetrate. It'll be only a few drops, but it's those few drops we can do without."

"Aren't these things overlapping?" Steve asked.

"No, they are paralleled. If one goes off naturally or otherwise, the Shaper next to it automatically begins to work in its place. Our teams are doing everything possible to make sure the fixtures and clamps holding them in place are doubly secured."

As the workers arrived with doors, Steve climbed down the ladder and made his way to the school. A wooden door led him downwards towards another similar wooden door at the base. All the way down, opaque lighting produced shadows that gave him the feeling that someone was following. The sound of intensifying chattering came from behind the door leading to the underground chamber. He placed his ear on the door. This was one of DOK's four underground storage sites. Thousands of litres of water were stacked on shelves for a rainy day.

"Psst, careful, it's the head of security," someone whispered as Steve walked in. A man smoking a cigarette got off a crate, stood up, and offered him one.

"This must be Arthur's brand," commented Steve. "What the hell. Let me try one. What are you doing down here? Why aren't you up on top helping the others?"

"I came down to make sure my wife was safely tucked in. Sorry," he said, extending his hand. "I'm Ted and this is my wife Sarah."

"I'm Steve Gotlar. And hey, this doesn't taste so bad after all."

"We know who you are. We've seen you many times. We think that what you are doing is marvellous. We have spoken about it, between ourselves, I mean. Workers do tend to talk amongst themselves, you know. The other guy in charge is mean. If he caught me down here, he would have shouted at me. He would have told me to go and help the others."

"Oh, you mean Gossard. He means well. He might be meaner than the rest, as you put it, but he's good at what he does."

"Mr Gotlar, do you think we're going to die down here?" Ted and Sarah clung tightly together.

Seeing fear in their eyes, Steve managed a thin smile. "Don't be silly, we're more than ready for this hurricane. You've got nothing to worry about. Anyway, it's going to miss us by quite a distance."

Ted and Sarah listened attentively.

"Tell me, Ted, what do you do? What's your job?"

"I'm a cleaner, sir. I clean the floors. I make them shiny."

"Well, I tell you what, Ted, during the storm stay here and look after your wife and any others that might come down. OK?"

"Thank you, sir, thank you," Ted came over and shook Steve's hand again. Sarah was just behind him.

"You're a saint, Mr Gotlar," she said. "I appreciate what you've done for my husband." She leaned forward and pecked Steve on the cheek.

As they walked away, Steve looked around as more people started taking up their places. In one far corner the bottled water reserves were stacked on the ground. A toilet was to the right, and a crude kitchen, complete with a big ventilation duct, occupied a large part of the wall.

Outside, the sun had reappeared, but the wall of blackness was definitely drifting closer. Steve decided to make his way towards the greenhouses.

"Hey, you've smoked one of my cigarettes," said Arthur as Steve walked over. "I can smell it on your clothes. What do you think of them?"

"Nice. The last time I smoked anything was over two years ago. I see the workers have already left."

"Yeah, they've fitted big bolts through the rafters. I feel better knowing they're there."

"If Arthur's happy, I'm happy. Tell me, your tobacco isn't addictive, is it?"

"What do you mean? Of course it is. Here, take a packet. When we get out of this nonsense, I must go into business. By the way, how is Mara? Is she going down to the shelters before the storm hits?"

"No, she wants to stay with me, we discussed it earlier." Steve paused, placing the packet of cigarettes into his jacket. "Mara feels her talents would be wasted down in the shelters. She wants part of the action."

"A woman who kills not only with her looks is a danger to society."

"Not this one, Arthur. Mara firmly believes in us, she'll die to protect the world."

Arthur's look intensified. "You're a lucky man, Steve Gotlar, a lucky man. Come, I'll show you the roofs if you want to see them."

"I'll pop in before the storm. I must make sure the church underground storage areas are ready."

"Alright, then. I have to move all the exterior plants into the sealed greenhouses. The wind will tear them to shreds if I don't."

"Well, and thanks for the pack of cigarettes."

"It's a pleasure."

House of Worship

The church, the only holy place to have a variety of conflicting philosophies within the same walls, was built on limited space and with limited supplies. This unique temple of optimism and hope had miraculously risen from the wasteland. Over the months believers had flocked into its walls with artefacts and relics donating optimism and prayer. This 24-hour sanctuary born of sorrow and confusion had successfully separated reality from love. It was their last refuge of God. The hypnotic flickering of candle flames blended themselves with a sickly fragrance of burning incense.

Steve sighed, thinking of his own faded Anglicanism. Its significance had died along with the world more than a year ago. His wife was his belief. Apart from her, he believed in nothing.

Against a wall, multilingual, neatly placed hymnals donated their versions of the same idea. Some were tatty or just loose pages, but their inspiration was where it belonged. This legacy of bricks and faith standing on the verge of doom and bequeathed by God, was saviour in the eyes of many.

Entering the church, Steve's eyes caught sight of the entrances into the two subterranean storage rooms. Unlike the school, the church had constructed storage areas inside its venerable mass, having been the duty of the faithful to complete its construction. Outside, many spoke of the hurricane's arrival. Although Steve believed they didn't really know what was coming or where it came from, they just knew the threat existed.

"Excuse me, aren't you the head of security? Have you come to say a prayer?" said a short, stubby man.

"Yes, I am. And no, I haven't. I came to make sure you were all settled in and if there was anything you needed. Linda is due to arrive in two hours." Steve paused a bit as the man moved closer.

"You know, my son, I sense your concern. Did you know the conquest of our fear lies in the moment of its acceptance? Firstly, we have to understand what frightens us. Those beings out there, extraordinary only in their ordinariness, are our spawn. Fear of the unknown is an irrational response to an excessive imagination. I say, it is our fear of the lurking stranger, the sound of footfalls on the stairs, the fear of violent death, and the primitive impulse to survive is as frightening as the acceptance of knowing that they are coming for us," he paused, breathing deeply and changed his thought. "How strong is Linda?"

"She's at Force Three."

The man, noticing Steve's agitation, moved closer. "You want to know something else? We've thrown all our beliefs into one cooking pot. Not much choice, really. We call it Pragmatism. Over the months we have reached an equilibrium we all respect and live by. We are proud of what we have become." With those words the man wandered off and attended to others nearby.

In the few months since its construction, the church had begun to produce its own waxy spiritual etherealness. A battered organ rested against a wall. Steve never asked how they got it here or where it came from. Instead, he looked at it and smiled. Steve felt strangely attracted and hypnotized by the churchgoers, enchanted by their devotion. As people walked past, Steve thought of this blend of beliefs. Maybe something good would come out of this after all. Here, in their honest and capable world, they would look after each other. Although the thought of what lay below in their subterranean store produced an uncertainty of a sort, Steve didn't enter.

On the surface, the wind had picked up strength. The same historic nightmare he'd shared with Mara four years before was coming back in vivid detail. Steve called Mara on his C-10 and told her he was approaching the Security Centre.

"Well, that's nice of you to think of me at this late hour. Orson and I have been waiting for you for the past half hour. Where have you been?"

"In the church. I went to see if they needed anything before the storm hits. I'm nipping over to see Arthur Payne. I'll be back in twenty minutes."

"Not without me, you're not. In case you've forgotten, we've always shared nature's good humour together. Come and collect me. I'll be waiting just inside the door. Hoot when you get here."

Mara told Orson to go lay in a safe, out of the way spot. She knew that he didn't like it, but he would stay there until her return.

Driving from the church to the Security Centre only took two minutes, during which time occasional gusts of wind slammed against Steve's vehicle, making it difficult to keep it steady. By the time he came to a halt in front of the Security Centre and hooted, it began raining like nothing imaginable.

"Why on earth do you have to see Arthur now? Can't it wait until after the storm?" asked Mara as she climbed in.

"Because I told him I would go and see him."

As they drove off, sensing the low level of light, the emergency lights flickered on. Steve contacted Rawling. "Rawling, switch off the emergency lights, the Light Shapers are going to need every bit of current. Is everyone set?"

"Yes, Steve, everyone is set and waiting."

"Good. And the repair backup teams?"

"Yes, everything's ready. Don't worry yourself." Rawling sounded irritated, so Steve returned his attention to Mara.

"Where's Gossard?" Steve asked.

"In the Admin Building seeing to last-minute transmissions in case we don't make it. He said other DOKs have to be aware of what we've done in case we don't pull through."

Steve faced Mara. "We'll pull through. Linda is still at Force Three. She'll dissipate before entering the Gulf. I'm sure of it."

The car was suddenly slapped on the side by a gust of wind.

Mara jumped in fright and said, "I wish that statement was true. According to Matthew, Linda's getting stronger. When she crosses the Gulf and hits Texas tomorrow night, it'll be at Force Five. Matthew's worked out the trajectory. You know, DOK 9 and DOK 19 are unprotected, and they lie directly in its path. Colonel Blake and Major Lawrence are going nuts trying to figure out what to do, so Gossard's lending a hand."

"Yeah, that sounds like Gossard, all right." Steve's C-10 lit up and Blake's voice came through the speaker. Steve said, "Hey, Gossard must have patched him through for us to hear."

Blake was ranting on about a gigantic metallic roof housing that had just been finalised.

"It's open from the sides! For the love of God, man, you need to be protected from all sides, not just the top!" said Gossard.

Frustrated, Steve switched off the C-10 just as a flash of intense bluish light broke the nightly day. Two seconds later the light was followed by an immense thunderclap. The storm was nearing. Mara looked at Steve's uncomprehending stare.

"Honey, what's the matter? You've gone pale."

"Sorry, sweetheart. Turn on the C-10 again, will you? I need to talk to Gossard." Mara complied.

"Gossard," said Steve, "Mara told me about DOK 9 and 19. Is there anything I can do?"

"Forget them, Steve. No one can help them now. I was talking to General Graham in DOK 15 moments ago. In mid-sentence, his image vanished, the transmission stopped. It was as if someone pulled the plug. I checked all the remote cameras. It is the same turmoil on all cameras. With DOK 15 gone, that's more than half the American continent already under their spell."

"What are you talking about, Major? With DOK 15, I count six."

"My dear friend, in the last two hours fourteen rain storms were recorded on American soil. Five of the fourteen storms affected DOK cities, and as fate would have it, they were unprotected. Now we've got this bloody thing on top of us. I'm not sure if we are even going to last that long either."

"What about the DPF, are they standing by?" asked Steve.

"Oh yes, they're waiting, all right. You know what they're like."

The DPF's prime objective was the security of DOK: Deaf to any order, foreseeing the total safety of the DOK residence. DPF assisted others, even saving lives from time to time, their training saw to those kinds of needs. Apart from these humane details, DPF had the authorisation to liquidate anyone under suspicion of infection. The workers and wall-stalkers called them cleaners, sanitary enforcers. They said it was for the good of everyone.

"Mara and I are going to see Arthur. We'll be back in fifteen minutes." The C-10 went off. Steve caught a glimpse of Mara's face as a lightning strike discharged nearby. To the right of him through the passenger window, he saw a tornado in amongst the cloud and torrential rain that ended just above their heads. The blackened gyrating, remorseless funnel was coming.

Parking as near to the greenhouses as Steve could, Mara climbed out behind him and clung to his arm for dear life. "Does that look familiar?" Steve shouted. Mara trembled.

"It brings back memories, all right," shouted Mara. "I thought I had forgotten them."

"We will never forget them, my dear, never. God will see to that," Steve said.

"Hey, what's with this faith and God stuff? You been hanging around that church too long, haven't you?"

"Not now, honey, we can have this discussion later."

Before they reached the entrance, Steve looked upwards, conclusively comprehending the importance of the green phosphorescent barrier gorging itself only pitiful metres above their heads. He also comprehended the five-metre distance between the front entrance and the car door. It was eternal.

The wind picked up force and felt like they were swimming against a torrent of water. They pushed their way through the double doors to find Arthur standing in the shadow of two DPF officials next to a table covered with empty pots. Stunned by their entrance, the three flinched slightly. The rain's constant din often forced Steve to repeat his words, and even from close up, Arthur couldn't hear what he was saying.

"Arthur, hide in the microscope room, it's got an extra door. You can lock it from the inside!"

"We'll help him over there," one of the DPF shouted. "Don't worry, he'll be safe with us!"

The doubt never crossed Steve's mind. The DPF were here to protect Arthur. He was a major chess piece on this board.

"Do you want one of us to go back with you to the Security Centre?" asked a DPF.

"Don't worry, we'll be OK."

The inner doors shook as the wind went completely out of control. Arthur walked over. "Steve, why did you come? You could have waited until after the storm."

Mara, catching glimpses of the conversation, gave Steve a glance.

"I came to see if you're okay," explained Steve.

"I'm fine. Now get the hell back to Security Centre. I'll contact you when the storm's passed."

Mara brashly grabbed Steve's arm and they doubled back towards the trembling doors. Through the darkness of daytime, their attention was caught by the hurricane's immensity.

"Oh my God! Just look at the size of it. Damn, it's as big as the one we saw in Baytown, if not bigger!"

Lightning was striking every three to four seconds, and it seemed to be striking everywhere. From the north to the south, then came two flashes east. Then the terrible noise widened Steve's attention. At first, he thought it to be multiple claps of thunder, but it was too drawn out and too high-pitched. A continual crashing broke even the sound of the vaporising rainfall. A constant crash from a cymbal in perpetual batter meant it had begun to hail.

Their nightmare had started. Even inside the car, it became impossible to hear. Steve's shouting became useless. He could see the funnel move, rotating its enormous swirl. It hoovered its way over the land. No one was safe from it. Steve realised that if that funnel came directly on top of them, they would be crushed like a paper cup.

Gossard was already inside as Steve and Mara stepped through the door. Orson stood and waited for Mara to join him. "Amazing," said Gossard, "they are holding out better than expected. If they can absorb this, they can absorb anything."

Security computers revealed that over forty tons of water and hail reached the barrier every second, and not one single drop had penetrated so far. As the funnel passed them by a mere two hundred metres to the east, the humungous otherworldly form dislodged Light Shaper Number 41 from its holding. The welding that Rawling's team had vigilantly put onto the wall crumbled under tons of pressure. As the Shaper switched off, Number 42, alongside, automatically began to work in its place, offering as before a green life-preserving blockade.

"Where's Number 41 situated?"

"It's a housing area, close to where you live."

Steve quickly looked at the electrical layout on the table and saw that Number 41 was only three houses down from theirs.

"Damn it, get a cleanup team over there right away and cordon off the area. Watch for puddles!" said Gossard excitedly.

Rawling told Steve that in those sparse fifty milliseconds, forty litres of water had entered DOK soil, contaminating Area 41.

Within ten minutes, Tino and fourteen other DPF were standing by, ready to put into effect their maximum law.

"Tino, use the megaphone, tell them not to come out of their homes unless they are assisted by an official. Got it?"

Suddenly, Bill's voice came through the C-10 speaker. "Sir, we've got quite a mess here." His words were distorted in the communicator by wind. It sounded like, "Wet gardens, wet roofs and wet vehicles."

Through the rustle, Steve couldn't make out any more. "Bill, are you still there?"

"Sorry, sir, it caught fifteen civilians as well. We had to, you know. I didn't—I couldn't do it. I knew those people. Tino came and did that part. The man's a freak, a bloody ice cube."

Bill's voice disappeared into the drowning wind. Mara noticed Steve's worried look and grabbed his arm, holding tightly. Steve looked at her. Gossard could do nothing but bite his lip in aggravation. A wall-stalker stormed into the Security Centre.

"DPF spotted a small group of infected residents making their way across the street. Jesus, you should have seen them putting the infected down. No one could stop them."

"How many?" Steve asked.

"Not sure, maybe forty or fifty."

Steve looked away from the man's reply. As Bill had said, he knew some of them; they all did. Gossard, speechless, looked at the wall-stalker as he rushed out again. They had never given the streets names. Gossard decided that once the storm had passed, he would make it a priority.

The opportunity came sooner than they expected. Within an hour, just as Matthew had predicted, the storm began its journey northwards. It disappeared, leaving them with a lowering sun and a lot of cleanup. As Matthew and Rawling directed the cleanup crews, Arthur and Quaid received hundreds of plant and soil samples to check. DPF were everywhere, observing people's behaviour. If a person looked a bit weird or suspicious, Quaid was there to take blood samples.

By the end of the day, sixty-six civilians had been cleaned. Sixty-six innocent lives, spent in the blink of an eye, spent to preserve the rest for a possible future.

Gossard named Steve and Mara's street Pine Street. He wanted to give all the streets names of flora to commemorate their survival and progress.

"Sometimes people have to die to preserve the masses from extinction," said Gossard. "Wars have proven that point again and again."

"True," said Steve, "but we're not exactly a mass, are we?"

Gossard shrugged off the comment and looked at the monitor console. Eleven monitors displayed static. Gossard pressed DOK 9's communications button below the screen.

"Colonel Blake, are you there?"

Blake's not-so-smiley face appeared. "Gossard, thank the stars. I see you managed to pull through in the end. I've been busy surveying your video monitors. I see you lost one of your Light Shapers. Was there much damage?"

"Not too much. Blake, look, I didn't contact you to discuss our situation. How are your shelters coming along, are they ready?"

"Tell me you're joking," said Blake in a desperate tone. "We ran out of cement six hours ago. It disappeared along with the morale. Like you, like the rest of us, there's thousands of infected just sitting outside our walls, six kilometres away. Bastards are too far away to kill and they damn well know it. They just sit there waiting for Linda to arrive. I spoke to President Carnell an hour ago, begging for help, and all he could say was, 'Don't worry, my boy, God is with you.' I personally think he is a bloody moron. God knows how the hell he made it into politics in the first place!"

Steve moved closer to the monitor. "Speaking of which, how's he holding out in all this? I haven't seen his face recently. He's keeping a low profile, isn't he?"

"He's the president, he's entitled to keep his mug low when things get a bit sticky and rough."

"Why do you say that?"

"The sharp drop in the ballot, why else? Infected don't vote."

Gossard laughed. "Blake, at least you still have your sense of humour."

"I don't have anything else, Gossard. I'm scared shitless. My whole camp is scared shitless. You should see what is waiting on the horizon out there. Switch on your surveillance cams and have a look." Without another word Blake disappeared.

But it wasn't only Blake, it was Lawrence, too. Both DOKs 9 and 19 had infected waiting on the outskirts of the cities, tens of thousands of them, patiently waiting for feeding time.

Turning away from the monitor, Steve told Mara to go home with Orson. "I have to go see Quaid. He's been working so hard, maybe he knows something."

* * *

Steve soon came to realise that Quaid hadn't an answer. Quaid still thought the virus was a giant brain circumnavigating the Earth. What he called it was a sea of invasive molecules unstoppably seeking them out with malignant intention.

Quaid said, "We are human targets, and they know our weak points in every mathematical detail."

At first it sounded absurd, but the more Steve listened to him, the more it began to make sense.

Quaid spoke softer. "Infected troops, incalculable trillions of molecules, thinking and acting as one giant body. Their joint intelligence is staggering. They appear slow and ignorant, but accumulating them on a massive scale like this, they are not. They read us like a book." Quaid looked downwards. "As far as a vaccine goes, I've given up. I've never seen a molecular structure so damn complicated. I've not scratched the surface."

"What are you suggesting, Quaid?" Steve asked.

"I'm not suggesting anything, Steve. The longer we can sit through this nonsense the better. Our only defence is to annihilate them as they come closer. Damn it, Steve, I just don't have answers. I wish I did." Quaid walked heavily back to his research lab.

Steve left the building with an equally heavy conscience. Their last hope had backed down like a flustered bull. Steve had a bad feeling in his gut. Before going home, he collected two vehicles and five able workers and took them to Sector Seven. It gave him the chills to see it again. With the exception of an unfinished Security Complex, it was nothing more than a walled existence of dust and vacancy. It was the reason why he had chosen the site for his next project.

"I want the five of you to hollow out part of the wall. I'm making a crypt, a storage place where I am going to put the knowledge we have accumulated during our stay. I want it to be ten metres long, one metre wide and two metres high. I also want a concealed door with a viewing hole. One more thing: No one is to know about this. How long will it take?"

"About a week, sir," said the worker.

"I give you that week."

Steve got into his car and went home.

* * *

At home, Mara had a disconcerted look. "We knew some of those people," she said. "What did Quaid tell you? How's his vaccine coming along?"

Steve paused and took a breath. "Quaid's given up. He says the virus is too complex. He said, and I quote, he's not even scratched the surface. He thinks the infected form part of a much larger, super-intelligent organism."

Mara looked at Steve sideways. "Are we talking about the same bug that attacked our coastlines months ago?"

"That was only the start of it. Since then it's changed, mutated into this bloody nightmare."

Walking away, Mara said, "How many more innocent people have to die before we can find a solution to this?"

Steve didn't know the answer to that one. Orson, on the other hand, didn't know anything about anything and just sat there with play in his eyes. They ignored him for probably the first time ever, so he strolled off to the bedroom.

Following Mara, Steve took her by the shoulders. "Quaid told me our only solution is to outshoot the enemy. Hell, we do have the capabilities."

Mara, looking away from the statement, didn't respond. Instead, she grabbed Steve's hand and led him off to the kitchen.

"Fancy a cup of tea?"

"I'd love one."

Tea refuelled the tiny splinter of hope Steve had piercing him on the side.

* * *

The next day, driving down Pine Street towards the Security Centre, Steve saw Rawling and his men busily replacing Light Shaper 41. His thoughts returned to the sixty-six victims. He drove to Sector One to begin checking the instrumentation for himself. Walking along the first level, Steve came across Sanchez with his head on his knees. He wore a glum look.

"I've seen better-looking hamsters in my time." Steve gave a smile as wide as a slice of lemon.

"It's the other DOK cities, sir, they're being systematically wiped out. People like us, people with families. The same is going to happen to us, isn't it?"

"Sanchez, that's speculation. They were infected by rain, not by those who roam the land. They were defenceless, and I'm afraid to say they felt they could defend their DOK with guns and plasma rifles. No one expected an aerial attack; the warning was too late. What's happening outside these last few hours?"

Sanchez stared at Steve with the same glum look he had before. "One question, sir. Do you know Sheri?"

"No, why?" replied Steve.

"Sheri was the wife of one of those that got cleaned yesterday. Earlier this morning she went to the gate controller and shot him dead. She took his remote control, opened the gate, went outside, and walked towards the hillside where they are still sitting. An hour later, some of us heard distant shots. One of the wall-stalkers said there were eight shots. Sheri never came back. This happened three hours ago. She's become one of those walking freaks, hasn't she?"

"Calm down, Sanchez, calm down. If it is true, she has also killed eight of them. I think it evens the score a bit. Now tell me about these groups up on the hillside."

Sanchez was stunned by Steve's lack of humanism. "They are big groups, sir. Could be about ten thousand in each." Sanchez's words hit home like a whack from a professional boxer.

"Ten thousand. Give me those binoculars." As Steve focused on the mammoth gatherings, itchy trigger fingers on both sides of him anxiously petted their weapons.

"Remember, they are no match against these weapons," said Steve. "You point and shoot, nothing more. When you get a break, recharge it, have it ready at all times. Never forget, this rifle means your life, and ours. So look after it."

The wall-stalkers looked ready. At least in a better shape than Sanchez. With Steve's presence on the wall, even Sanchez seemed perkier than before.

Steve's C-10 vibrated. "Steve, I need you in the Security Centre!" said the disoriented voice of Gossard through the C-10.

"What's the emergency?" Steve asked, but the C-10 had already gone dead.

As Steve walked in, Gossard didn't speak. Steve followed the direction of Gossard's hand. "I've checked them all, it's real. Look!" The monitor displays were blank except five images.

Gossard's glare deepened. "Later tonight, both 9 and 19 will go the same way. That leaves DOK 1, DOK 6 and us. DOK 6 has almost two million people living behind its walls. It's a prime target. The presidential DOK is just a mega-fortress housing the super-rich and powerful. Their influence doesn't count anymore. And then, of course, there's us, a well-protected nothing, in the middle of nothing, with nothing to go home to after the show."

Steve lowered his voice in the hope of consolation. Then he thought, *Who am I trying to fool*? So he perked up his finesse. "Have you contacted DOK 9 and 19? How are they taking it?"

"There's a good chance they die of fear first. They know their survival is balancing on a decomposed thread of cotton. Adding salt to the wound, the president is going to make an appearance later this afternoon on the monitor. Can you believe it? He wants to give us a speech."

"Bit late, don't you think? But yeah, it does kind of provoke hope, doesn't it? Tell me what time, I'll need to rig up my video recorder."

Gossard laughed. "At seven."

"I'll be here."

During the early afternoon, Steve prepared one of their battle tanks to go out and do a bit of cleaning up. Anthony, Bill and Tino had tried antagonising the infected into coming closer to DOK, so the wall-stalkers could pick them off more easily from their vantage points. Instead, they just sat there waiting. Tino said they were easy prey. It's even as if some of them wanted to die. By 5:00 they had moved a little closer, but by then, Steve realised their numbers had increased. It wasn't ten thousand any more, it seemed more like fifty thousand. What the hell were they up to? Steve began rattling around the idea that they probably had a night raid in store, so he positioned another 480 wall-stalkers on the wall.

By 7:00, the officers and anyone interested in what the president had to say gathered into the Security Centre. Rawling had patched the video feed into all of the surrounding Security

Michael Gilwood

Complexes for all those interested. At precisely 7:00, the DOL 1 monitor flickered on.

"My fellow Americans, and all those watching this live broadcast, I wish to convey a message of hope and optimism. Our best scientists within the walls of what is known as DOK 1 have been frantically working on a way to reverse the unethical madness that has gripped our world for months. Regret comes to my lips as I have to declare there is no way we can unravel this mystery in time for it to be a benefit for those who still exist as human beings. We have combined our efforts with other surviving scientific research laboratories with no success. The results were the same everywhere. The viral code is so advanced and so sophisticated that our limited progress has reached the extent our technology can permit."

Quaid's voice reached out, "He never asked me for any help!"

"Be quiet, Quaid!" said a voice.

"We will continue on our quest to solve the world's dilemma until such time we are either successful or no more. We have no idea how or why this started, or by whom. My prayers go out to all those who have suffered and especially to those now under attack. It has come to my attention that hurricane Linda is about to enter American soil in the next hour. DOKs 9 and 19 are in its path. May God have mercy on their souls." The monitor blinked off, as everyone looked at one another.

"Bloody great. Where's his message of hope and optimism? He doesn't boost morale like he used to."

Sanchez's voice came over the C-10. "Sir, they're up to something all right. They're spreading out and surrounding us."

"Thanks, Sanchez."

By 8:00, Steve had positioned more than two thousand individual shooters on the wall. By 9:00, all twelve sectors reported movement on a massive scale at distances varying between three and five kilometres.

"These critters want in, all right," said Anthony as Steve walked up beside him. "Just look at those numbers." Anthony handed over his infrared binoculars.

Even before they came into focus, Steve saw them like army ants exiting a gigantic anthill. With their prey in sight, hungry eyes were looking for a way into the fridge, or that jar of forgotten marmalade on the second shelf below the biscuits. They edged forwards, moving over terrain, and they seemed unstoppable.

"Sanchez, double-check the rifles are charged and don't fire until I give you the order, you hear?"

"Yes, sir!"

Steve relayed his message on to the emergency channel to all those in charge of groups of wall-stalkers. The reports he heard were scary—in every sector there was movement. Implausible numbers made him look twice through the binoculars. He was sure the spectacle before them was being received in the same manner as DOK 9 and 19 were receiving: Linda was twenty-two hundred kilometres to the north. Gossard liked to share with his friends in need, but right now Gossard's only friends were within his DOK. There was nothing they could do for Blake or Lawrence. They were on their own.

Anthony checked his distance with the plasma rifle, but even adjusting the telescopic sight didn't make any difference. At this distance, he wouldn't hit anything with enough impact to kill it. Although the plasma rifle disintegrates the targets at short or medium distances, they were primarily short-range weapons. They had been proven in medium-range situations up to two kilometres.

"We can do nothing but wait," he said as Mara ran to Steve's side.

"You didn't think I was going to miss all the fun, did you?" she said. Anthony gave a grin.

"Heck, sweet pea, what are you doing here? It's dangerous!" Steve snapped.

"And you think I don't know that? I prefer to spend this time with you. At least if you're not going to come home, I want to see it for myself, not read about it on a piece of paper."

Rushing forward, Steve gave her a kiss and quickly explained to her the workings of the plasma rifle and how to hold it.

"Is everyone ready?" he asked. "They are still two hundred metres from minimum damage distance. Five minutes, people, five minutes. Remember, get those rifles charged. If you're not sure how, ask the man next to you."

While they waited, the security computer worked out their numbers.

"These must be some of the leftovers from Mexico City," Steve said to Anthony as he checked the distance again.

The plain became silvery white as light from the MOGS lit up their adversary with a wonderful precision. There again, Steve thought, *Maybe we were showing them the way into the larder. Almost there, just a little more.*

Steve's C-10 sounded. It was the temporary helper in the Security Centre. "Sir, I've got those results you asked for."

"Go ahead," Steve said over the nearby chatter.

"One million three hundred thousand, sir."

"Anthony, how's that distance? We have got to start firing soon. Come on, talk to me!"

"Wait, sir, just a bit more. Come on, come on now, just another metre. That's it, sir. It's a go!"

Steve hollered into the C-10 microphone, "Fire!"

The single word announced a release of accumulated frustrations and anxiety as wall-stalkers and DPF unleashed hundreds of randomly directed flashes of white towards the oncoming threat.

"Death to those who have taken our land!" someone shouted.

"You came here without our authorization!" yelled another.

"You'll pay for this, you bastards!" another said furiously as white needle-bursts of plasma energy lit the landscape with radiance and fury.

Their hatred towards their adversary had become their strength and obsession. Their need to defeat this enemy on the move planning on them as the main course increased their determination. Although their sentiments were mostly detestation and hate, there was talk between the wall-stalkers and DPF about what it would be like to be infected.

"Are they in pain? Are they suffering?" one asked.

Their combined conclusion was they were suffering, and the sooner they could put them out of their misery, the better it was for them. Above all the commotion and uproar, Steve heard another comment from a wall-stalker. He was asking a head wall-stalker just to the right of Steve. It was Wishton.

"Sir, do you think they have feelings?"

Wishton laughed at the stalker's question. "Definitely not, soldier. Neither will you if you don't pull that damn trigger."

Infected appeared out of nowhere, and they moved in straight lines as a surgeon's scalpel toward a wound. DPF recharged and continued. The DOK's immense number and firepower had little effect on these walking remnants of a world once sane. Gossard shouted into his communicator. "We need more wall-stalkers up here, NOW!"

The infected's fortitude and resilience was born of their frustration as they were unable to locate an entrance or a weak point in DOK's defences. Nevertheless, they continued with persistence. Columns of ashen ionised smoke lifted into the air, and Steve watched as it was silently disintegrated by the defence barrier over their heads. More wall-stalkers and DPF came up the ladders and pushed their way in between the officers to find gaps in the windows.

Anthony handed Steve the pair of binoculars while he fiddled with a MOGS controller on the wall.

"Don't you notice anything strange about them?" asked Steve, peering through the binoculars.

"What do you mean?"

"Take another look, they are closer now."

The differences were remarkable. Their predecessors were hairy, but not like this. These examples were covered in hair from head-to-foot. The only details Steve could make out were the scalp and chin. He didn't see a mouth or a nose. It was definitely apelike, an evolution within an evolution, a sea of primordial mistakes accompanied by a horrendous smell they emitted into the air. Steve and Anthony were sick at the sight of dying people. After two hours, their numbers finally began to dwindle enough to see the hillside lit up by the searchlights, just as it was before.

"Death to those who come to destroy us!" said a harsh voice to Steve's left before pulling the trigger. The firing continued until another wall-stalker shouted.

"We've almost done it, damn rabid dogs!" But they weren't rabid dogs, they were once sane, healthy human beings whose choice at life had been snatched away from them.

Plasma blasts gradually reduced to sporadic flashes. Steve watched as the bustle of wall-stalkers moving in every direction eventually began to direct themselves to their homes. Two came to relieve Steve and Anthony from active duty. They would stand there till morning. Mara was shaking as she climbed down the ladder. She dropped her plasma rifle on the ground and broke the handle.

"Don't worry, honey, Matthew's chaps will fix it. That's what they're trained for." As Steve reached the bottom, she grabbed on to him. He could feel her trembling.

"I thought we weren't going to make it," she whispered.

"I know, babe. I am sure many felt the same way. I did."

As Steve walked with her towards the vehicle, sadder news reached his ears. It was Gossard on the C-10.

"Steve, I'm in the Security Centre. DOK 9 and 19 are gone!"

"I'll be right over. Mara, go home. I'm going to see Gossard. DOKs 9 and 19 have been destroyed!"

"Oh no, you don't. I stick with you. I don't want to go home thinking what might be out there."

"There's nothing more out there. Orson will protect you. Come on, go home. I must go see Gossard."

As Mara climbed into the Jeep and drove off, Steve ran like the wind towards the Security Centre, only to find Gossard gawking at the flickering monitors.

"They're gone," he said. "Linda swallowed them whole. They just disappeared. It's as if they were never there to begin with. They didn't stand a bloody chance!"

"Where did they construct DOK 6?"

Gossard's hand pointed towards the Rand McNally map. "In California, Kings Canyon National Park, close to Mt Williamson. The place is surrounded by water."

"Who's in charge?"

"Major Pedro Moralis. He's a real nasty piece of work. Tough as they come. There was rumour that once a brick fell on his head and the guy never even battered an eye."

"He's not a relation of yours by any chance, is he?" asked Steve.

Gossard didn't answer. He pressed the button under the DOK 6 console. A rounded, moustached, and pitted face came onto the screen.

"Ah, Gossard, I knew you'd be contacting me sooner or later. I thought it might have been the president again. Heard the news about Blake?"

"Of course, Pedro. He was unprepared for what hit him."

"Unprepared! Don't give me that crap. He knew the risks like all of us, damn fool. I didn't really have a high regard for the man. Now he's gone and killed them all. Every damn one of them."

"And you, Pedro, how are you holding out? Any major battles recently?"

"Two hours ago. More than a million of them tried creeping up on us. We wiped them up like dirt off the floor. They sit out there in the mountains watching us from a safe distance. Don't come near unless it's dark."

"Yeah, it's the same here," said Gossard.

"I just spoke to one of our wall-stalkers. He tells me they're out there again," Moralis said coldly.

"Oh really, how many?" asked Gossard.

"A couple of thousand, no big deal."

Gossard moved away from the monitor. "Excuse me, Pedro, I have to contact one of our head wall-stalkers. I'll get back to you in five minutes."

"That's fine Gossard. By the way, who's that standing beside you? I know that man."

"Steve Gotlar, he's the one responsible for the wall design."

"Of course, that's it. The Northern Pacific Road, Wally Banks, I remember now. Damn good job, Steve. Damn good job."

As Pedro disappeared off the screen, Gossard immediately contacted Sanchez.

"I don't recognise Moralis, and my memory never fails me,"

"It's not you, Steve. Moralis had facial surgery done two years ago, not even his own wife was able to recognise him. One moment, Steve. Sanchez, are the infected out there again?"

"Yes, sir, they've just shown up."

"Thanks, Sanchez, that'll be all."

"There's the proof," said Gossard, pausing. Without another word, his hand pressed the button below the DOK 1 monitor.

Carnell's secretary came online. "What's up, Gossard?"

"Peter, a quick question: Do you have infected sitting outside the walls?"

"As a matter of fact, we do. They have been sitting there for a couple of minutes. How did you know? The cameras aren't even pointing in that direction."

"They're here, too, and in DOK 6. We're being systematically watched. Any encounters recently?"

"A couple of hours ago we exterminated more than a million of them."

"Interesting, we did, too, and so did DOK 6."

"Is that so? I'll pass this on to the president. Thanks for the call, Gossard." The screen flickered off, leaving Gossard with one of his looks.

His hand pressed the DOK 6 monitor switch again. "Pedro, I was right. All three of us are being watched. The sods have synchronized themselves somehow. They're up to something, all right."

"Quite peculiar, don't you think? You're three thousand kilometres away. How could they know?"

"I don't know, Pedro, I really don't know. I'll go and see our resident bag of neurons and see if he can come up with some answers. I'll be in touch."

"They are observing us, all right, preparing an attack," Steve said irritatingly.

"It's possible," said Gossard. "Go see Quaid. I've a couple of things I have to take care of. Dig up whatever you can about their intercommunication skills."

* * *

When Steve walked in the hospital entrance, Quaid enthusiastically met him at the door. "Steve, damn fine job we did tonight, don't you think? I've got a little surprise for everyone to celebrate our victory." Quaid held out a bottle of brown liquid.

"It's pretty potent, but it has a nice flavour. This one's artificial raspberry, almost 60 percent proof. Come on, try some."

"Later, Quaid," said Steve.

"I've sent a few bottles to the workers. I hope they like it."

"Don't worry, I'm sure they will. Quaid, something important has come up. I've just come from the Security Centre. It appears that all of the remaining DOK cities are being simultaneously watched. The three remaining DOK cities are being analysed in the same way."

"What do you mean?"

"I'm saying we are being systematically studied. DOK 6 and DOK 1 had their confrontation at the same time we did. All three

DOK cities have infected around on the hillside. Gossard thinks they are communicating together as one."

"But they are. We know they can communicate one to the other over long distances."

"Quaid, we are talking about California and Philadelphia? Damn, do you know what kind of distances we are talking about here?"

"Of course, they use the water as a medium to communicate between themselves."

Steve's C-10 sounded. It was Sanchez. "Sir, they're on the move again, they're going west."

"Thanks, Sanchez. Keep me informed."

"Will do, sir."

"Sorry, Quaid, I must contact Gossard." Steve pulled out his C-10. "Major, our walkers are on the move west. I suggest you contact Pedro and Peter, and find out what's happening with them." Without a word, Gossard's face disappeared.

"Sorry, Quaid, you were saying?"

"It's the water, I tell you. That's how they do it. It's their medium of long-distance communication. The water controls them, giving orders and strategy. There are no breaks in the water; it's one continuous being that stretches everywhere on the planet, into every home. All three DOKs have water around us. Truth is, it's one long clear line of communication and it's never disengaged."

The C-10 sounded again. "Major, what have you got?"

"Pedro's hill dwellers are on the move east. Apparently, they just upped and left five minutes ago."

"And DOK 1?"

"Nothing, they haven't moved. Everything is as it was before."

"That's interesting."

"Has Quaid told you anything useful?" asked Gossard.

"Only that the water is their medium of communication, nothing else, but Quaid's not sure how."

"Well, suck him dry. I want to know how they do it."

Quaid steered his irritated stare in Steve's direction after hearing Gossard's tone through the speaker.

"Well, you heard the man," Steve said, turning to Quaid.

"He's got a bloody cheek. I don't know anything else. I was working on them at a molecular level, not studying their nattering capabilities. Maybe it will shed a different light, something we haven't thought of."

Steve walked out of Quaid's research lab into the fresh air.

April 2034

The fear of invasion over the past weeks had spread through DOK like a continuous Sunday tranquillity. Although they'd regained equanimity of a kind, the wall defences remained on full alert. It had been eighty days since the last sighting. In those eighty days their re-established, although constrained, way of life had reanimated their hope. Pedro hadn't seen a single infected for the same duration of time. Unfortunately, that couldn't be said for DOK 1. The presidential city, the abode of the rich and important, was receiving thousands on a daily basis. They were stockpiling themselves into immense groups six kilometres outside the city walls.

It was April 20th when Steve's C-10 vibrated. He was with Quaid in the lab, who was filling Steve in with the latest advances.

"Major, what's up?" Steve wasn't expecting anything bad that day. He thought those days were behind them. They had mentally forced them into the past. Just last week, Gossard had invited Mara and Steve to his house to celebrate Mara's pregnancy. With her at home with Orson, Steve was with Quaid, enthusiastically stuck in his welcomed routine of untroubled life and sampling his raspberry brandy after weeks of arm twisting.

"You haven't forgotten about the infected, have you?" asked Gossard ironically.

"Of course not, why?" asked Steve.

"I've got them on-screen again." His words made Steve's stomach drop like a cement column on the breakfast table. He looked at Quaid, holding the C-10 even closer to his ear.

"Damn it! Where the hell are they?"

"DOK 1, every blasted one of them. Peter told me the world is sitting out there. The place is chaos gone wrong."

"Good God, they won't survive an onslaught of those proportions!" Steve said.

"I know and I'm sure they know it, too."

"What's he going to do?" asked Steve.

"Probably fight them until the last man is dead or converted." The voice of Gossard sharply changed. "Holy mother of Jesus. Steve, get over here. There are enormous explosions right in the middle of infected people. It's a bloody massacre. Carnell is blowing them up!" The C-10 abruptly switched off.

"Sorry, Quaid," said Steve," something's come up. DOK 1 has problems. I must go. Thanks for the sample, it was really good."

Running out of the research lab, Steve got into the Jeep and drove to the Security Centre. Since the communication from Gossard, it had only taken moments for invisible premonitions to spread the word to the civilian population that something was wrong. Their tranquillity was in the grip of an absurd mental change once again. Steve saw nobody. Where could the people have disappeared to in such a short time? News travelled fast, even if it hadn't been made public. Some workers had their own C-10s, and as Steve had come to realise, some of them had been modified, enabling them to listen to secure conversations.

"Steve, look at that monitor. Look what he's doing. He's killing thousands at a time!"

The gate cameras at DOK 1 revealed the bloodiest scenes. It was mass execution, human dismemberment on a grand scale. Bombs were exploding and splattering human parts in all directions. In those brief seconds inside the Security Centre, Quaid and Payne had sneaked in behind Steve to see the spectacle for themselves. As they looked at the flickering screen, something else began to happen. It was another war, a war inside DOK 1.

"What the hell are they doing? I am going to switch to another camera." Gossard fiddled with a small control panel, bringing up the central plaza on the viewer. People were fighting amongst people, their own kind. Somehow groups of infected had already gotten inside. How was it possible, how could they get in? Gossard fiddled with the control panel again.

"Peter, what's going on?" He asked furiously into the direct-link video monitor. Another face appeared. It was Peter's secretary.

"David, what the hell is going on over there, how did they get in?"

"They didn't, we let them in ourselves! We let them in. Why didn't we see it coming? How could we have been so stupid?" David looked away.

"What are you raving on about? Look at me when I talk to you. Tell me, man!" Gossard banged his fist on the table.

"Our bombs. It was our bombs that let them in. It was our bombs." David creased his face.

"Explain yourself, man, that's an order!" yelled Gossard.

"When our bombs exploded in the middle of those unmoving, unimaginably colossal crowds, bits of bone and splattering of blood came through the wall view-ports and hit our wall-stalkers on their faces as they looked through. It infected them, hundreds of them!"

Gossard looked at Steve in shock, before steering his view back to the monitor. "Pedro, are you getting this?"

Pedro was sweating for probably the first time in his life. "Damn right, I am."

"Where's Peter and the president?" asked Gossard.

"I don't know. They've been out for some while." The man coughed and spluttered. "I saw them ten minutes ago when Carnell gave the order to fire. I haven't seen them since."

"And the infection, is it under control?" asked Gossard.

The man paused before answering. "Oh yes, it's under control. We are under control. We are quite under control, I promise you."

"Oh, Jesus!" Gossard went white and tore himself away from the direct video link with DOK 1. The man on the screen was looking downwards, rubbing his eyes. Circular movements, once, twice, thrice before peering upwards again with ungodly blue eyes. Hair, stubby and bristly, already began to exit his once-bare flesh.

While in this new state and before the man on the screen could utter his first word, Gossard caught him in the act and off-guard. "Now you listen to me, you bloody freak of nature. We're waiting for you. If you come here, we'll wipe the ground with your ass."

The thing spoke. "You speak valiantly. Go ahead and destroy us. It is not these pathetic bodies we need. In any regard, they are inefficient, transporting devices, nothing more." The thing put

213

its finger in its nose. "Until the last human is rehabilitated, we cannot become what we must become."

Gossard twisted his face. "And what is that, a freaky side show?"

The thing spat at the camera. Out of focus blotches of phlegm ran down the lens. Gossard's presence on the screen seemed to excite him. He issued an inhuman cry, a psychotic, primitive cry, a caterwaul of the sort that sometimes wakes you in the night and leaves you wondering about the origin of species. Then he spoke.

"I don't know what a freaky side show is. The truth is, I don't give a damn. Remember, one night you'll wake up and they'll be all over you, or maybe they'd take you by surprise in what you call the Admin Building, or maybe you'll be praying to someone. As you kneel down at the altar with your pathetic beliefs, they will come down on top of you and squash you like the bug you really are. Eventually you'll surrender yourselves to us. You'll surrender to us in ecstasy. I might even surprise you and come for you myself. Surely you are going to suffer your way up to your heaven."

Gossard rammed his fist into the monitor. Smoke was accompanied by a burning smell as resistors jumped out their sockets on the printed circuit board.

"Who the hell do they think they are?" yelled Gossard.

"The new dominant species, what else?" said Steve excitedly.

Gossard exuded a dirty look before making a sharp-knuckled fist and pounding it into the other as if he needed to hear the sharp sound of flesh-on-flesh.

"How the blazes could they know about the Admin Building?" said Gossard.

"Clearly they know everything there is to know about us. Their intentions are obvious, they have wiped out DOK 1. Next, they will move on to DOK 6, wipe them out, and then come down to us with their entire army."

"That'll be in six months," said Gossard.

"Yes, that's six months we have to prepare ourselves for the inevitable. As you heard, they don't need us. They only want to convert us. We're on the endangered species list. You saw it, we are excessive baggage."

Gossard switched on the internal cameras of DOK 1 with the hope of seeing President Carnell one last time.

"Did everyone see the speed at which it takes over the human will? It's getting quicker," said a worried Quaid.

Pedro's voice surged from the other monitor. "I personally think they anticipated Carnell's intentions with a brilliant exactness. They knew he would hit them with bombs. They purposefully waited for their execution. I feel they know an awful lot about us, maybe too much. Look, Gossard, we have studied this thing from all angles. Our only defence is to defeat them any way we can. We must not allow them to enter. Hell, I'm sure I'll even have my wall-stalkers placing bets on who pops the president when he comes into view."

"I hope you're right, Pedro, I hope to God you're right."

"Another thing, my wall-stalkers tell me they are already out there again on the mire."

Gossard switched on his C-10. "Sanchez, is there any activity?"

"Yes, sir, there's a couple of hundred out there." Gossard was deep in thought.

"They're watching us, I tell you," said Quaid. "They're making sure we don't run. If we did, I'm certain they'd warn the others. We're stuck here until we can prove ourselves worthy of leaving."

"What are you ranting on about?" asked Gossard.

"It's our only chance. We have to defeat them, like Pedro said. Obviously, they won't bargain. It doesn't interest them. You see, it's not about us killing them, it's about us preventing them from entering and contaminating us."

✸ ✸ ✸

During the forthcoming days, Gossard sent a battlewagon outside to do a bit of cleanup. On the seventh morning as the armoured vehicle combed the terrain, it suddenly disappeared from view. Worried, Steve sent another team to investigate. They reported that the battlewagon had fallen into a deep hole, a metre deep. The hole wasn't there the day before.

Pedro had also warned them of similar occurrences happening around DOK 6, and that his team had already been infected by the time help arrived. Luckily, Gossard's team had escaped before the infected could reach them.

Pedro's infected remained on the horizon. The next day he contacted Gossard while Steve was in the Security Centre.

"Gossard, maybe I'm just going paranoid, but I think they're up to something."

"What is it, Pedro?"

"There's a group concentrating around the same area, about five kilometres out. I can't be sure, but it looks like they are shovelling."

"Then get a team out there to have a closer look!" exclaimed Gossard.

"We won't even get close. They have these damn holes everywhere."

"Then send out a bloody foot patrol!"

Pedro's angered face disappeared from the screen.

"Gossard," said Steve," I have to go, it's 6:00 already. Mara's waiting for me." Steve hated lying, especially when using her name as the basis for the lie. Instead of going home, he went off to his hidden alcove in the wall. The workers had done a brilliant job of hollowing it out and disguising it. The painted wooden door gave it the exact texture and appearance of the outer bricks, making it invisible to the untrained eye. As the door noiselessly swung inwards on craftsman-made hinges, an accumulating humidity had formed a thin layer of moss against the floor and up against the wall. In the two months since its construction, Steve had come occasionally to get away from reality. It was his own private piece of hell.

A rectangular peephole positioned at eye height between two false painted bricks on the outside made Steve invisible from outside eyes. It resembled a skewed crack. From the inside of his private domain, he had a full view of the exterior. Inside, he had a few personal belongings and had twice come there to read a bit with his flashlight. A strikingly well-made Windsor chair lay against the far wall under a simple bookshelf. Some dust had gathered, so Steve reached down and gently wiped the surface with his hand.

Steve needed this place of seclusion and was sure if anyone knew of its existence, they would think he was either crazy, or well on his way. Steve didn't care anymore. He had learnt not to worry about other people's opinions. All he could think about was

Mara and their three-month-along son unhurriedly growing inside her womb.

They planned to call him Ethan. Mara liked the name. She had always agreed to the choices Steve made. She said his ideas were always for the best. They were ecstatic and couldn't wait for the day when he breathed his first gulp of air.

Sitting in his chair, Steve reached over and picked up *Twenty Thousand Leagues Under the Sea*. The paper was crispy and smelt musty as he opened it for the hundredth time. Steve loved Verne's work. He'd been an admirer of his since childhood. Steve particularly had this volume stashed in there because his father had given it to him for his seventh birthday. It was his first book. However, that was over forty years ago. Since then both his parents had passed on, luckily due to normal circumstances. Steve's father had been a pilot in the army. Thirty years of gruelling military joint venture ended in a heart attack nine years ago. His mum followed him only six months later.

Steve looked back to his book and began to read. Most of it he knew by heart and would often read entire paragraphs out aloud before even getting to them. In there he could break away from reality, he felt safe, out of harm's way. In the end, Steve dozed off and fell asleep.

* * *

It was 9:15 when Steve woke with a jerk. *Twenty Thousand Leagues* had, at some stage, fallen from his hands and onto the ground. He put the book away, closed the false door with the magnetic catch, and got into the Jeep. Rapidly turning the key, Steve shot off for home.

"Your video thing was switched off—where the hell have you been?" Mara asked suspiciously as Steve stepped inside. Orson padded over and gave him a double licking.

"I contacted the Security Centre, but no one had seen you in hours. Gossard said you suddenly jumped up from your chair and disappeared to come and see me at 6:00."

Mara's suspicious look couldn't make Steve tell her the truth. No one must know of the hiding place, not even her. Even the workers that built it thought it was for storage. If one day the world was at peace, maybe Steve would consider telling her. Until such a day arrived, it had to be his and his alone.

"Sorry, honey, some workers found a crack in the wall in Sector Two. I went to plaster it up before it got out of hand."

As always, she believed him, even if his benign intentions were clean.

"Have you felt Ethan yet?" he asked.

"No, silly, he's only three months along. Have patience."

Patience was a virtue Steve didn't possess, and likewise with every passing day he, like all of the others, could think only of the advancing wall of infected moving towards Pedro in DOK 6. Even as the end of June brought no new advances in either of the encampments, it was certain the infected would arrive, and it was only a question of time before they did.

July 2034

The temperature had risen slightly as Earth's pitiful offering of summer for the first time in over a year had given temperatures above zero degrees. The exosphere was still trying to recuperate and repair itself, dispelling huge amounts of unwanted powder from the seventy high-altitude balloons a year before, but it was a major task, even for the Earth.

"As the outside temperature goes up, their walking speeds will increase. There is a possibility of them arriving at DOK 6 ahead of schedule. Some of Pedro's civilians are on their way down here in dozens of vehicles. They should be here any moment now. They prefer to watch the spectacle from a safe distance. We, of course, as good citizens, couldn't deny them that right. Besides, new faces are always welcome."

Mara smiled, taking interest in what Steve had to say as they moved into the shade of a Security Complex.

"Pedro let them go. It was their choice of destiny. Intercepted radio broadcasts revealed that some didn't make it. They knew the risks before they left two weeks ago. Speaking of which, look, here they come."

The gate swung open and swirls of desert dust began obscuring Steve's vision. *It must have been one hell of a trip*, he thought. These were vehicles and refuelling trucks of all shapes and battered sizes after the immense journey. These survivors were not deserters of doom, neither had they feigned their escape for any other reason than they, too, had families. They told Pedro before they left that if they were to die, they wanted it to be at the last DOK, just to be on the safe side, in the last refuge on Earth. As cars came to a halt, cumbersome, tired bodies began opening car doors. The children, the perplexed little souls, were not smiling. They weren't happy like the local children. They'd been worn out by the sights they had seen along the fourteen-day route. They cried as their tired legs touched DOK soil.

"Poor little things," said Mara. "Look at them." Mara smiled, walking over to one of the recent arrivals. "What's his name?"

"Gerald," said the woman, cupping a hand on his head. She was smothered in dirt and her ragged clothes were testimony of their trip through hell.

Mara moved closer. "Hello, Gerald, would you like something to eat? Are you hungry?"

Gerald didn't answer. Despondently, he lowered his face and backed away towards his mother, feeling intimidated by Mara's closeness and interest towards him. His inquisitive stare and sour face highlighted a bruise on his front temple.

"Sorry about that," said the man, admiring Mara's concern. "It's been a rough ride. This is my wife Susana, my name is George. You've already met Gerald."

They moved closer to shake hands. Gerald, noticing his parents' interest for Mara and Steve, made him lose his shyness. He ran off, disappeared into the back of the dusty Land Rover, and produced a dinosaur with one of its legs missing.

"I call him Dino," said Gerald, running it up and down excitedly on the front bonnet of the four-wheel drive. "Dino will protect us. I know he will."

Steve watched Gerald as he excitedly pushed and pulled the three-legged dinosaur over windows and the mirror. "How many didn't make it?" asked Steve, looking into George's attentive face.

"What you see is less than half of the number who left. Bastards had booby traps set up everywhere, deep holes in the ground like trapdoors. They must have known we were coming. As we left, a false-bottomed pit swallowed ten cars in one go. They waited inside like spiders. All those children—God, you should have seen it. And the screaming."

Gossard walked over to the group. "Good, I see we are making acquaintances already. Everybody, may I have your attention, please? My name is Major Gossard. We have set up temporary housing for you and your families. Our guides will show you where to go and will attend to your every need on your arrival. Feel free to stay as long as you wish. One point: Pease remember the water restrictions. Our limit is five litres per day, per house. We need you to quarantine for fourteen days."

As normality once more came upon them and the remaining cars and people disappeared towards a bed or a sleeping bag, Steve made his way to the Security Centre to run routine checks on the Light Shapers.

Rawling had seemingly read his mind. He was jotting down notes and looking at one of the monitors. "They are behaving wonderfully. I can only hope Pedro's engineer is saying the same thing I am. Look, there's DOK 6." Rawling's hand pointed to the monitor.

"What on earth?" said Steve. "Get me that image again. I think I saw something."

Rawling scuffled with a push button and the image returned.

"What are they up to?" asked Steve, moving closer and fiddling with the zoom knob.

Huddling together like herds of sheep, groups of infected, dozens of them, had gathered around a humpy area four or five kilometres outside Pedro's main gate.

Rawling began panning the image from left to right. They were shifting into something, downwards in single file before vanishing.

"There must have been fifty of them; how odd." Rawling's puzzled grimace met Steve's. "Did Pedro ever send out the foot patrols that Gossard recommended?"

"No idea," replied Steve. "I never brought up the topic again, I presumed he would have."

Rawling continued panning the landscape. "Look, there's more of them. They are grouping themselves underground."

Steve contacted Pedro and asked him to have a look from his side. "Pedro, are you watching this?"

"What's up, Steve? What are you talking about?"

"Your gate monitor, are you watching it?"

"No, why?"

"You've got activity on your Gate-A monitor."

"Steve, if there is something out there, Robinson will contact me."

"When last did you last speak to this Robinson of yours?"

"An hour ago. Wait, while I have you on viewer, I'll contact him." A pause. "Robinson, what's the situation outside Gate-A? Come in, Robinson, what's the situation on our Gate-A monitor?"

"Pedro, did you send out those foot patrols?" Pedro didn't answer. Steve added, "I think Robinson has taken a little stroll. If I were you, I'd get someone reliable in your control room right away."

Pedro's face disappeared even before Steve had the time to finish his sentence.

Pedro contacted Steve again two minutes later from his Security Centre. "Yes, I can see them now. What the blazes are they doing out there?"

"That's the same question we asked. Get your stalkers with a good view of that area to have a look through their binoculars."

Pedro's form moved forward and reached a control panel. "Wall-stalker 76, come in."

A faint response came through the speaker. "Sir."

"What's happening in Quadrant Twelve? I can see activity on the monitor. Don't tell me it's another one of those blasted holes."

Pedro was studying the image as the wall-stalker came back over the communicator. "Sir, they are digging, dozens of them. No, I don't think it's one of their holes, it seems bigger. They are going down and into whatever it is without coming out again."

"You mean they are disappearing?"

"Yes, sir."

Steve spoke up. "Pedro, we've heard every word your stalker said. We can see the same from here. Sound maximum alert!"

As Steve's words were transmitted over to California in less than a microsecond, Pedro's middle plaza began to shake and shudder like he was experiencing a ground tremor. Hearing the uproar, Pedro tore away from the monitor and vanished.

Undisturbed by his flight, Steve switched to Camera Two, now showing the ground beginning to tear and crack as rocks, dust and dirt flew into the air in every direction. Steve panned the camera to get a better picture just in time to see solid ground sucked down and pulled under. In its place, soil changed places with heads peeking up through the murk. Panicking, frantic wall-stalkers didn't know what to do, so they started firing upon the intruders as fast as they emerged from the hole. This was all well and good, but as the pile of charred human remains grew higher, it collapsed under the weight. Blood and gore were everywhere, and it was inside the walls of DOK 6.

From then on propagation was easy. All it took was one small touch, a tiny blotch, a rub, or a whiff. It took two hours for DOK 6 and its two million inhabitants to fall under the spell of the infection. People were screaming in their attempt at escape. Rawling and Steve watched until they couldn't take it anymore. Steve was sick at the sight of this ultra-modern city, defeated by medieval trickery, running and scrabbling for their lives. Rawling ran outside and vomited before collapsing in the midday sun.

"Don't you die on me, soldier!" Steve grabbed him by the scruff and whacked him across the face. "Come on, Rawling, don't you see? This is exactly what they want."

Rawling's face regained colour and his eyes met Steve's. "They were spitting at them, throwing bits of themselves towards innocent people. Poor bastards. My God, one of them even bit into his own hand and sprayed passersby with his blood. It was horrible!" Rawling was hysterical.

"Rawling, calm down!" urged Steve, reclaiming his grip on him. Ignoring his plea, Rawling vomited again and passed out.

"Quaid, I need you at the Security Centre, Rawling's fainted."

"I'm on my way. What's happened?"

Steve didn't respond with the natural enthusiasm and speed like Quaid would have expected. Instead, he looked towards Rawling's limp and quiet body lying still on the ground.

Quaid's voice reached out, firmer this time. "Steve, what's happened?"

"DOK 6. It's gone!"

"What! Shit, when did this happen? How?"

"Not two minutes ago. I haven't even had time to notify Gossard."

"How did they get in?"

Steve gave a cynical laugh. "They dug a tunnel, a stupid, simple tunnel. They walked along its interior popping their heads up in the middle of DOK 6 plaza. It must have taken months."

As Quaid listened, his car pulled up. "They are ingeniously full of surprises. Contact Gossard while I see to Rawling." He knelt down and opened a bag of medication while Steve inputted Gossard's C-10 number, thinking of the pending atomic bomb he would drop in his ear for not being here when it happened.

"Major, I think you better get down to the Security Centre."

Identifying Steve's harsh tone, Gossard's voice changed. "Why? What's up?"

"It's DOK 6. It's gone."

"WHAT! I'll be there in a second."

The news of the annihilation of DOK 6 spread through DOK 16 like the virus itself. A rapid, widespread panic took control of DOK 16 and every living human being within its walls. The more they thought about options, the more feasibility dwindled and shrivelled into dust. They were incompetent and ineffective against this malignant marauder disguised as man, or rain, or prickly rosebushes. Escape from that moment on seemed impossible, so they issued shotguns and plasma rifles to all the adult inhabitants.

Steve always believed in miracles, until one day, he knew they wouldn't happen anymore. The miracle maker wasn't here. He had finally gone home to rest, hiding where no one could find him. He had purposefully evaded the millions of calls for help.

People thought otherwise; they said he was still around. "God doesn't just disappear," they said. "How could he?"

Gossard, meanwhile, was so shocked by the incident, his only comment was, "What resources do we have left? Yes! Bricks and cement, they are resources, aren't they!"

Two workers ran off and returned minutes later with a stock list. "Two million bricks and five hundred tons of bagged cement," they reported.

"Good, it might just do it." Gossard excitedly looked around. "I want the DPF, the head wall-stalkers, Matthew, Rawling, Arthur, Quaid, and you, Steve, right now in the Admin Building!"

Ten minutes later, they were all sitting at a long conference table, staring at Gossard anxiously getting up from his chair. All eyes were fixated on him.

"This despicable incident at DOK 6 has left me with little breath. You have more than likely gathered that it also leaves us with quite a duty on our hands as we go forth representing the last of humanity. I personally consider it an honour to be here today facing you all as we sorrowfully mourn those who were once our friends. Our true worth and might at this time is resting on our shoulders. My proposal is the construction of a tower on the outskirts of our DOK city. I want it to rise until every solitary brick inside our city is used up. The tower will give us a vantage point. Our wall-stalkers will see where we cannot, and they will warn us long in advance. We only have three months, so building has to commence immediately. Steve is going to supervise the construction to the end."

Steve's vacant stare brought a smile to Gossard's reanimated face as he reached for his C-10. "Sanchez, issue the order to all workers to move all our available bricks and bags of cement to Gate-A."

Gossard handed a hand-drawn proposal of his thumb-sucked plan to Steve. An anechoic silence gripped the room as Steve glared at Gossard's simple design. Eyes tore into Steve's. Inquisitive minds hungrily searched for answers as he absorbed Gossard's intention.

While studying the simple layout, Steve reached for some paper, performed mathematical equations and stood up a short while later. "Major, it's quite an idea. I'm really impressed. Firstly, the 2-degree increase in temperature will allow the foundation to set quicker. Remember, the same rules we used in the wall must apply to the tower foundation."

Steve lifted the paper higher. "To suspend the weight of the tower, the foundation has to be twenty-five metres deep. It's a safety minimum. I have made allowance in my calculations just in case the ground does grumble and shuffle a bit. Now comes the heavy part, the tower itself. To withstand nature and Major Gossard's profound idea, the base will be twenty metres in diameter. This, gentlemen, means that with the supplies on hand, we'll reach 140 metres. It will be the perfect observation height, allowing the wall-stalkers or DPF to warn us if anything out of the normal decides to come and pay us a visit. On the inside, stairs and a ladder will enable them to reach the top or any of its forty-two levels. I will put in a surveillance window every five metres, providing a perfect view of the exterior."

As Steve spoke, every face in the room focused on him. "I would like to add one important point: Please be advised, I am a wall engineer. I've never undertaken anything even remotely similar to this, so if it does fall down, don't blame me." Laughter roared across the table, successfully reanimating the day.

Gossard stood up. "Thanks, Steve, for that bit of extra information. We have three months to construct the tower before they arrive. I am using the words 'they arrive' lightly."

Matthew handed Gossard a piece of paper. "These are the preliminary calculations based on our visual findings so far. As we are already aware, every infected on the surface of the planet knows our whereabouts."

Gossard quietly fixated on the note in front of him. "Adding the original quantity of infected with those scooped up along the way, then adding them to both DOK 1 and 6, we can expect 26 million to come knocking at our front gate by the end of October. Matthew anticipates that two million will die along the way. I'm afraid DOK 16 is it, people. It's them or us."

At the conclusion of the one-hour meeting, every brick and bag of cement was already waiting at Gate-A. If Steve had ever thought that the building of the wall involved everyone, he was mistaken. Even volunteers were re-volunteering in case their names weren't on the list. The air of a fiery confidence left him staggered in awe.

Gate operator Harris, who'd replaced Gibbons after his premature death, pressed a button. Steve stepped outside for the first time since his arrival from Tierra Colorada months ago. It felt eerie to be out again. Dispassionately strolling outside, he began marking the terrain. He was erecting the tower only five metres away from the wall. He wanted it close. An overly inclined Light Shaper would protect the tower from the rain.

On the third day, they prepared the cement. One hundred tons of one part cement, one part small stone, and two parts sand were mixed and poured on top of gigantic rocks already waiting at the base. Iron rods, like those used in the wall, ate into the sides of the inner foundation wall for extra strength. It seemed they would run out of cement before construction could begin. In five hours, the immense hole was full.

Wall-stalkers and DPF would use infrared in the tower. An auxiliary trench alongside, filled with the same cement, housed the communications cables and provided power to the plasma recharge points.

Gossard's stare broadened. "How long do we have to wait for the foundation to dry?"

"Well, Major," replied Steve, "as I mentioned previously, since Mother Nature is giving us a big helping hand, we can begin construction in two weeks."

"Two weeks? The wall only took a week."

"True, but remember, the wall foundation was only a metre deep. This tower is going to weigh hundreds of tons, and it's going to concentrate all that weight on one small point. The drying time of fourteen days is essential. We mustn't rush the process of chemical union, now mustn't we?"

Gossard never argued with Steve; he liked that in the man. The strength he portrayed with others was the squishiness he shared with Steve. Their respect was mutual.

The waiting period had begun. It was during this phase that they trained themselves. Workers made scaffolding, frameworks, trellises, stair boxes, segmented ladders, and window frames for the insides of the tower. Everything was readied according to specification. Extra infrared units were coming off the assembly line, while Matthew prepared a special C-10 allowing the tower wall-stalkers to talk to anyone within DOK, on any frequency, even allowing them to interrupt. It was a permanent hotline to anyone.

During the fourteen-day period, they were helpless in the seemingly never-ending, psychological mind-sucking eternity. The fourteen days would fortify them; they would reveal who and what they really were. On the other hand, it would also give needed time to prepare physically for what lay ahead.

August 2034

By early August, the foundation was dry. The training, to call it such, during the infinite period had been hairy, explicit, and rushed, as well as a godsend for many.

Early one morning, Steve told Gossard to put the first brick into place. "Hey, it was your idea!"

That brick, that one solitary brick, marked the first of many that day. As the enormous triple-layered exterior wall rose, workers carved steps with cement and imagination. Wooden tablets were neatly positioned on top, enabling workers to traipse on them without damaging the wet cement below.

Every five metres the steps would widen, becoming a levelled walking platform below a lookout window. For those patrolling the interior, extreme care would have to be taken, as there was no safety barrier, no balustrade to hold on to. It was an abyss, a sheer drop certain to cause death for the absent-minded or careless.

As the tower slowly made its way upwards, the Herculean task of getting the bricks up to the workers' waiting hands worsened. One of the workers developed a crude crane system which worked well until they reached twelve metres, then its inefficiency and instability became a hazard to those operating it. Next, they began using a motorised hoist. It was slow, cumbersome, and only managed to lift fifty bricks at a time. Adding to their frustrations, the motors started heating up far above normal operating temperatures. Luckily, the outer wall rope hoist was obstacle-free. It went up and down without difficulty, but the central shaft provided obstacles and often took longer. They pumped up the sloppy cement via a thick hose to anxiously waiting hands far above.

August was also the month in which Steve and Mara lost Ethan. Steve was inspecting the third level as his C-10 vibrated. "Steve, Mara's just arrived. She said when you left this morning for work, stomach cramps set in."

By the time Steve got to the hospital, Ethan was dead. Quaid said it was a vitamin deficiency and nervous spasms that had interrupted the flow of blood to the growing foetus. "Sorry, Steve, there was nothing I could have done to save him."

Mara, fast asleep on the bed, occasionally tossed and turned about in her bad-dream world. Her breathing was surreal. Steve hadn't heard anything like it before, so he moved closer and placed his ear to her mouth, listening to her torment and internal pain.

Steve sat in a chair next to her, watching her limp, tired body, divorcing his mind from his other problems. Intentionally, he bit into his lower lip. Cursing the infected that started all this in the beginning. *Let them come*, he thought. *Damn this tower.* That day, he left the building tasks in the hands of the workers.

The following day when Quaid released her, Mara didn't say a word, although Steve could see her discharging fury in her way. For two days, she never uttered a single word. Steve consoled her and gave her all the loving she deserved, but it was in vain. The next day as she climbed out of bed and walked into the kitchen, she began to cry like a baby.

Hearing this, Steve ran to her side and gave her a big hug.

"Oh darling, I'm sorry, I know you wanted Ethan as much as I did," she said, rubbing her eyes.

"Honey, it wasn't your fault, don't blame yourself. Quaid told me you were low in vitamins, your body couldn't take it anymore. Baby, when we get out of this, we'll try again, don't worry. I want to get back to a normal life just as much as you do."

Mara caressed her eyes and looked at Steve. "Honey, about tomorrow: Go and work, go and finish that tower, you mustn't just sit here. There's nothing more you can do for me here. I can't love you any more than I do." Mara sighed. "Do you want to know something? While I was lying in that awful hospital bed, I was wondering about that tower. Maybe it's not going to be enough. Maybe we need ten towers. Honey, I want you to know, whatever the circumstances are, you know when the day arrives, when that day comes, I'll be out there with you, you can bet your boots on it. It's just this waiting, knowing they're coming. We don't know when and we don't know how they plan on getting in."

"Well, we're going to have to make do with one tower, won't we? Hell, we just don't have the material for more of Gossard's illusions, even if they are good ideas," said Steve.

"I know, darling, I am just so worried about this whole damn thing. I've often thought about us filling up the Jeep and making a run for it down south."

"And if we make it, what do you suggest we do? You know they'll find us. Where do we hide? We'll need food and water. Our supplies won't last us forever. It is better to make a stand right here. If we have to die or get infected, you can bet another pair of boots we'll be together, just the two of us."

Mara took a deep breath. "I only hope we are doing the right thing, that's all. Just sitting here makes me so jittery."

"Yeah, I know. Quaid told me it was another one of the reasons for you losing Ethan."

"Well, that's bloody reassuring. Next time you try falling pregnant if you're so sure you can handle the stress I went through!"

"Sorry, darling, I shouldn't have said that." Steve bit his tongue.

"Honey, I'm the one who should be sorry, you know damn well I have faith in you and your abilities. I'll even confess, I have so much faith in you and what you do. I know and feel that with your insight and guidance out there, we'll finally rid ourselves of this oncoming threat once and for all."

❋ ❋ ❋

At dawn the next day, Steve looked out the dining room window towards the tower. Day-by-day, its progress was revealed by the augmenting, creeping shadow it made on the road at certain times of the day. At thirty-one metres, it had dwarfed his wall.

DPF had assumed duty posts on the inside, familiarizing themselves with its walkways, perils, and cold winds that rustled through its dark interior during the nocturnal hours.

At thirty-five metres, after Steve's inspection, he told the workers to stop. "We've got to let the foundation settle a bit. It must get accustomed to the weight on top."

"How long, sir?" one of them asked.

"We'll wait two days."

Bobbing his head in all directions from the seventh level, Steve began observing the immensity of his wall. The protective barrier from this altitude appeared greener. The natural brown hue of the ground somehow enhanced the plasma particles, giving them a vivid, almost leaf-green appearance. He turned away from DOK for just a moment and peered towards the far-off hills to the east. Twenty or thirty double-storey houses dwarfed by a hill revealed no signs of life. Through a pair of binoculars, he made out scattered belongings and a couple of vehicles. Much nearer, recuperating rubber trees and coffee plants had won their struggle against doom. From where Steve was, he could see Brook Bridge far in the distance, adjoining the road he had travelled along when all this started. Creosote bushes and cacti, still adamant in their private war, were clumping together in a persistent, meaningless battle. They were also ideal locations to hide behind, as some cacti reached almost a metre in width at their base. Steve made his way down, passing by three DPF.

"See you in two days, Steve."

"Don't get your hopes up. I'll be here tomorrow, I have to do foundation checks in the morning."

Foundation sinking was a common problem in new buildings, especially heavy structures like this one, and it had to be monitored every step of the way.

✻ ✻ ✻

The next morning, Steve began punching in the stress/strain information of the foundation and tower onto his C-10. Minutes later, as numbers depicting results rushed up the screen, he quickly realised the foundation would easily withstand a construction four times as heavy.

From the first brick, they measured their progress by how long it took a worker to put a brick into place after it had left the ground. This time augmented from the original ninety-four seconds to almost five minutes. It was just as five metres per day had dropped to two by the end of August. Four motors had already burnt out by the time the tower reached eighty metres, and they desperately needed bigger, stronger ones. Without the resources, the only feasible option was to weld ventilators onto the sides of each of the existing motors. The cooling time worked well, and it increased the up-time by an additional three minutes.

Temperature-sensing devices and thermostats fixed onto the sides of each motor automatically switched it off if it reached 85 degrees. Building reduced to a snail's pace made the workers start running up and down the stairs carrying bricks.

It was during one of these worker stunts of theirs that one died falling down the central shaft. Worker death was an unknown factor in DOK, and he'd been the first. As a result of this incident, in mid-September Steve stopped the building and stabilized the height at one hundred metres. Going higher was too hazardous and too exhaustive.

From the top of the tower, DOK's unobstructed wholeness anchored Steve's attention in all directions. Away from his curiosity and against the ledge to his left, somebody had planted a Bisley telescope with a bronze rotary wheel onto a cement balustrade facing the exterior. It was probably fifty years old. Undisturbed and excited at the same time, Steve bent down to have his first enigmatic view of the landscape. As he manually brought the first impression into focus, his aim met with small, random-sized groups. They moved about so sluggishly that the only indication that it was really life was a twitch or a feeble invertebrate body movement. He saw it all as he twiddled with the zoom knob. Excitedly, Steve reached into his jacket pocket and retrieved Matthew's prototype communicator. Gossard was talking to Rawling.

"It's perfect, Major. I can see everything."

"I can imagine. That's what it's for. Remember, these infected are full of surprises. It depends on what they have planned for us, Steve," said Gossard.

Steve's attention was broken off as a DPF came onto the roof, ready to begin his twelve-hour shift. Even before the tower had been completed, especially selected wall-stalkers and DPF began with these insane twelve-hour turns. They were long days or nights for anyone based there. Although it wasn't called on for the full observation teams to be present inside the walls, these scant few men, privileged enough to withstand the boredom and monotony, had been proudly offered the post as a tower guard.

On the other hand, the waiting seemed endless as a scant fifty or sixty of the infected per day were settling themselves out on the hills in random locations.

On the last day of September, a voice came surging through the communicator. It was a frantic, excited, high-pitched tone that interrupted all their C-10s. "They're here! I can see them. Oh, sweet mother of God, just look at them. The whole world is out there!" It was a tower guard from the seventeenth level. That day marked the turning point in their existence. Gossard, Rawling, and Matthew were standing on the top discussing the situation as Steve appeared. Ideas were bouncing around, trying to figure out what their next move could possibly be. They studied the infected, watched them for any behavioural changes and clues, a hint to their plan, however small. DOK had all the protection needed from above, but the main concern was what if they tried to attack from below.

Gossard placed a watch force on top of the tower to warn of any changes. Not just simple composure alterations—anything out of the ordinary. DOK had to be as devious as they were. The Light Shapers didn't protect subterranean regions.

As the late-September temperature gradually dropped, ice and snow made its appearance on the far-off mountains. Autumn had them once more in its sights.

October 2034

Autumn had settled upon DOK. The infected on their haunches kilometres away were unmoved and unconcerned by this recent magnificent seasonal change. They had been there for almost a week, and the tower watch reported nothing out of the ordinary.

Steve was awful at comprehending large numbers. That unforgettable day when Matthew told him there were over twenty million sitting outside the walls, he didn't know what to say. Matthew laughed at Steve's stupefied, null look.

Steve looked into the Bisley and observed the infected for a half an hour, gently sweeping the instrument up and down, from left to right. Some were naked. Their clothes, if they had any, were ripped.

Steve imagined them staring at him as he was staring at them. Could they see him? He jumped and dislodged his eyes from the telescope for an instant. After convincing himself of his own stupidity, he continued watching them.

Nearer nightfall, they began to light up like beacons. Feeling sick, Steve increased the magnification on the optical instrument. If the infected fed on their fears, they certainly had a lot of mouths to feed. Yet somehow, he was sure that DOK's pitiful forty thousand wouldn't satisfy the type of hunger they had in mind. Distastefully, he turned the telescope and pointed it in another direction. He watched one fighting over the spoils of food, or a mate. Maybe he was just a troublemaker, or maybe this was the way in which they had fun.

Unstoppably as Steve watched, daytime succumbed to dusk. The exterior lights came on, extending his stay. He contemplated that the clothed ones were probably from DOK 6 or DOK 1, whereas the naked ones had probably been with the pack since the beginning. They were the hardened, experienced ones.

Returning the Bisley to its resting place, Steve knew these twenty million now sitting at their doorstep had already eaten, and it certainly wasn't fear. They had fed on the innocent in their path coming down from DOK 1 and DOK 6, and DOK 16 was next. Conversion was not always their way, just as fear was not the only thing they ate.

They surrounded DOK like a modern-day Palestine, covering the hills from top to bottom, cowardly hiding themselves behind creosote bushes or cacti. They knew DOK was outnumbered. Even from their six-kilometre distance, Steve could smell their accumulated reek. Their disgusting odour invisibly breached the desert terrain, reaching the walls of DOK. Amalgamating with the smell was an ocean of glowing blue eyes that gently swayed in the approaching darkness. They provoked a fear. Steve knew they could sense it and taste it, enjoying its every drop of sweat and quickened heartbeat.

Yet, through the telescope they couldn't hide. Steve wanted to see them, unveil their ugliness to the remnants of this beautiful world. They never came closer. They never retreated. Instead, knowing the power of DOK's weaponry, they waited like rats out of harm's way. What in God's name were they waiting for?

That night, like every other since their arrival, 480 wall-stalkers were on full alert along the perimeter wall. Sixty stalkers and DPF were inside the tower. As the darkness transformed into daytime, the infected hadn't moved. They were nothing more than an unimaginable group of people, the same ugly faces, day after day.

✳ ✳ ✳

Thirteen days after their arrival, Tino exasperatingly organised a hunting party, so he was sent out as one of six on the roof of an armoured Jeep. As the Jeep shot out the opened gate towards the hillside, Steve watched it slowly disappear through his binoculars. The left-side front lens was smashed, so he turned it sideways and used it as a telescope.

Steve estimated the Jeep was two or three kilometres out when its tiny-boxed form swung and veered towards a verge and started firing at anything mobile or otherwise.

The communicators sounded. "They are just sitting there. They're not moving a muscle. They're not even trying to stop the onslaught!" exclaimed a tower guard.

"Damn, if it's this easy, we need a hundred Jeeps out there," said Gossard, feeling intimidated by their calmness.

"Sir, not even a thousand Jeeps will make a difference, there are just too many of them."

Gossard looked downwards in desperation.

The Jeep moved slowly onwards, like a grain of sand on a beach, clearing a path directly in the middle of them, moving from left to right. That was when it disappeared from sight. The tower watch gasped in horror as the Jeep's heavy metallic body fell down—vanished.

"Sir, the Jeep's fallen into one of those blasted holes."

"Why didn't anyone see them dig the damn thing? What the hell is tower watch doing up there, telling jokes?" yelled Gossard. "Get another Jeep out there immediately!"

Steve turned the monocular and tried to get a better view.

"Sanchez, talk to me, what's happening out there?" Sanchez was on tower watch.

"I can see movement—no, make that A LOT of movement. The infected are relocating themselves directly between the Jeep and us. Sir, they won't stand a chance!"

"How's that rescue Jeep coming along? I should be seeing it leave by now. What the hell is taking it so long?" yelled Gossard impatiently.

The rescue Jeep shot through the front gate seconds later in the direction of Tino's discarded vehicle. It took only a minute to reach the first of the infected. By the time the Jeep reached the vicinity of the downed Jeep, Tino and his crew were encircled by thousands of infected. They were desperately firing their plasma rifles at the onward-marching wave of infected.

The communicator vibrated, almost falling from Steve's hands. "Sir, there are just too many of them. What do you want me to do?" said Sanchez.

"What do you see?" Steve asked frantically.

"The infected are closing in on them. Ah, there they are, Tino and the others have climbed out of the hole. They've seen Hartley's Jeep."

Steve contacted Hartley. "Hartley, for God's sakes keep firing on the infected. Clear a path for Tino and the others. Someone get more Jeeps out there, now!"

From Tino's point of view, the situation wasn't jovial. His dilemma was that two plasma rifles had burnt out, thus allowing the infected to advance closer. Sanchez communicated that there were too many for Hartley's rifles alone to have any effect, so two more Jeeps, fully laden this time, shot through the gate towards Tino and Hartley. Between both of them, they expended deadly rounds in various directions in an attempt at opening up an escape route for Tino to reach Hartley, but in every direction the infected appeared out of nowhere.

"Shit, the infected seem to be crawling out of the sand!" cried Sanchez. "Where the hell are they coming from?"

As Tino concentrated his firing on the infected coming from Hartley's direction, they came from behind. A rock appeared from nowhere and hit him on the back of the head, making Tino fall to the ground like a sack. Sanchez saw what was going on and radioed down.

"Sir, I don't see Tino. I think he's been hurt. The other five are making a run for it."

By the time Steve received his transmission, he was already running up the steps of the tower. Shoving Sanchez to one side, Steve looked through the telescope and turned the zoom knob.

Tino lay on the ground in an ever-widening pool of blood, and in less than two minutes, it was all over. Infected began lancing objects of varying sizes towards the five desperate guards and driver. Steve could just make out Bill's frame before an object of immense size hit him square on the face. He fell down without option. Another two minutes passed as infected crawled or walked their way towards the seven of them, completely smothering them. Tino, Bill, and the others now formed a part of this relentless army.

"Hartley, get back here, there's nothing more we can do for them. Signal the others."

As soon as Hartley drove in alongside the other Jeep, the infected resumed sitting out there as if nothing had happened. Despite the effort, their immensity hadn't dwindled in the least. God, they had paid dearly this time. Looking once more through the telescope, Steve was sure he could see Bill standing out amongst the ranks. He thought he recognized his clothes. Then he saw Tino pull up alongside him; Steve would recognise that jacket anywhere. The other five weren't anywhere to be seen, so he returned his attention to Bill and Tino. As Bill fought with the change in his body, he didn't stand a chance. He couldn't defend himself from this microscopic menace.

At that moment, Hartley walked up to Steve. "Sorry, sir, there was nothing more I could have done."

"I know, Hartley. I saw it all. Get up on the wall and start giving orders to the stalkers. They're going need you, especially now that Tino's gone."

* * *

The last three days October the first snows began to settle. Not only did it snow, it came down with antagonism. Quaid, using the communicator's emergency channel, confirmed its infectious state.

The late October blizzard was accompanied by strong gusts of wind, bringing with it sleet and showers of hailstones. It entered with ease through the viewing portals on the wall and tower, and on the first evening, twenty-seven wall-stalkers were infected simply because of snowflakes blowing through the apertures. Protection suits were in short supply. The cameras would have to take over as DOK's guiding eye to the exterior.

DPF, alert to the situation, immediately dealt with it in the only manner possible, the way in which they had been trained. Wall-stalkers began to panic. They felt betrayed. One ended his own life by touching Gate-C. His body vaporised and disappeared as the super-heated plasma quelled his anguish.

As a wall-stalker became positive to the molecular alteration rushing through his body, numinous infected sensed it; they seemed to know. It was their glory, their fidgeting. It provoked a change, a stir, even an emotion in them. It was an achievement as their caterwauling intensified. They were waiting for the moment to advance and catch DOK off-guard at a weak moment, and it was obvious they were not in a hurry.

Maybe it would happen as DOK tended to the sick. Steve changed his thoughts and peered upwards. A patch of cloud had opened, revealing Orion's Belt easily distinguishable on the darkened nightscape. The three stars slightly out of line and out of harm's way made him wonder if anywhere else in the universe there existed problems similar to theirs. He let off a sigh as the wind strengthened. It whistled and played tricks on his mind as it childishly danced beneath the rafters, producing random, eerie melodies. Steve zipped up the front of his jacket and placed his arms around his chest in order to keep warm. Normally, he loved the sound of the wind, but not tonight.

In his jacket side pocket, Steve began toying with a spare magazine between his fingers. He'd called it his lucky Walther. It must have been there now for more than a year. But his jacket not only came with a reserve magazine; a tiny solar panel was fixed onto the back. It recharged a battery hidden on his collar that provided sufficient power to warm his pockets. Many a winter he'd welcomed it, especially in unusually cold days.

But it wasn't the coldness or the wind and rain that prevented the infected from sitting out there. Obviously, they were immune to nature's bad moods and to whatever she could throw at them. Steve, on the other hand, began to fear that their persecution would continue until there were no survivors.

At home things weren't calm either. Mara was suffering from a belated trauma that Quaid aptly called postpartum shock. After Ethan's death, she'd seemingly returned to her normal self, but as days twisted into weeks, she began a painful mourning process. Mara and Steve always wanted children. They'd tried on numerous occasions, even going to the most reputable specialists, but a viable solution to a Gotlar family seemed as clear as a legitimate government. It simply did not exist. Well, at least it was the final diagnosis. This prediction persisted until she fell pregnant those few months ago. It made them realise the possibility still existed.

Yet, despite Steve's patience and efforts, Mara was losing herself to this oblivion; and at nights, often as he opened the door, she would break down at the sight of him.

"I am sorry," she would say repeatedly.

Steve suffered with her. On the outside of their home, the expressionless faces spoke for themselves. Mounting tensions and fears spread like the icy wind. The more Anthony and Steve tried to put them back into order, the worse it seemed to get.

Twenty-five extremists formed a militant group called The Holy Givers. They stormed the front gate with plasma rifles early one morning. Taking the law into their own hands, they stole four Jeeps and a truck and drove directly towards the infected, killing anything in their way. The battle lasted minutes.

Wall-stalkers who watched the scene were convinced of the dexterity of the outsiders. "They may be slow, but their ingenuity eludes us," one said. "It's as if they anticipate our every move before we make it."

November 2034

Quaid's news came as a surprise. "There is a possibility the virus will automatically burn itself out once all the water has been contaminated."

A silence fell.

"Explain yourself," said Gossard.

"I'm not crazy. Believe me, I've considered that possibility, considered it carefully. But there are several undeniable facts: Instead of trying to communicate with us, they have converted us to be like them. It is their prime objective. And instead of us trying to think of some way to reach them, make them understand, we have killed them. Murder is always easier than judicious, reasoned action. It is the primary resource, the first reaction. And that is why there is no hope for a peaceful future, regardless of our scientific and technological advancements. We are flawed because the universe is flawed. The universe is a madhouse and we are all madmen, whether we are humans or infected."

Quaid took a deep breath. "Once there is no more room for the virus to spread and nothing more to infect, it will burn itself out and dissipate. I reached this conclusion after exhaustive observations and months of hard work; but I am afraid to say, gentlemen, it is mere hopeful speculation and my personal opinion. Call it what you want. I don't have any scientific backup for my statement, I only wish I could tell you more."

Rawling turned his head. "Then we wait, right? We wait till it's got hold of all the water molecules and one morning it won't be there."

"We could try that approach, but somehow I don't think that is what it has in mind for us."

"What are you saying, Quaid?" snapped Gossard.

"As you know, the water molecules are joined like an infinite chain, transmitting information from one molecule to the other much like a telephone wire. I am convinced this data travels at tremendous speeds, similar to that of light. That's how they know we are here. It transmits some kind of intelligence along the chain. If we ran, the water molecules would pass on the information of our whereabouts until the infected came and converted us to be one with theirs, so to speak."

Gossard's face reddened. "Quaid, have you gone mad? Where could it possibly process this kind of data?"

"Gossard, it's a living life form that's grown like an embryo. It has developed itself over the months into what it is today, a life form in a liquid state, nothing more. In addition, yes, it is probably highly intelligent. I would assume that out there in some lonely open part of an ocean, you'd find its memory bank and data processor. We could possibly locate it if we had satellites, but as we are all aware, we've been somewhat in the dark for some time. Only God knows where it is."

Quaid fiddled with notes on the desk. "There's more. Did you know the water in this condition is totally non-conductive?"

"Non-conductive, that's odd," said Gossard.

"I don't know why I didn't think of it before. Even using scales of hundreds of millions of ohms, it didn't register. It's as if I'm measuring fresh air. Water as we know it has become a super-isolator, capable of withstanding thousands of volts."

"Quaid, now I'm positive you've lost it."

"No, look: It's simple. Our bodies are principally made up of water. Of course, I'm talking about the conductive type. It is the water within these bodies that it wants. It needs to change us, reconstruct us. I feel that only once we've been reconfigured and infected, it'll leave us alone and die out."

"So what you're saying is there's no way out, no escape!" said Gossard piercingly.

"It would certainly appear that way," said Quaid.

"Then why did we even bother to construct these DOK cities? Why don't we just walk out there right now and accept defeat?"

"Because we're human. It's not our way to give up without a fight. It knows this."

"You keep on mentioning 'it,'" said Steve. "What is 'it'? Who are they?"

"Months ago I thought I knew that answer, now I don't have the foggiest idea. The more I study it, the more vague this thing becomes. The deformed molecule is so complex, it can only come from someone scientifically far more advanced than I am. Its inability to conduct electricity eludes me, but what freaks me out is how it manages to relay information along this non-conductive path. I have exhausted all my resources." Quaid's voice faded.

This was not the answer Steve sought. Was this a problem without a solution?

Suddenly Steve's C-10 vibrated. It was Sanchez from the tower. "Sir!" It was an agonizing tone.

"What's up, Sanchez?"

"They're coming."

"How many?" asked Gossard, hearing Sanchez's shuddering voice through the speaker.

"All of them. The ground, the ground is moving in every direction."

A brief silence struck the room. Gossard spoke first. "Alright, is everyone prepared?"

"Yes, sir, everyone is standing by."

Gossard got up from his chair. "Well, gentlemen, it's time. Steve, good luck out there."

Without replying, Steve walked out of the office. Outside, as cold afternoon air rushed into his face, the breeze carried a vast assortment of frantic madness emanating from the wall. Steve's C-10 was going crazy as well. Everyone was trying to speak at the same time, making it impossible to have even the simplest conversation. If people weren't in the subterranean safe bunkers, they were already on the wall or in the tower endeavouring to protect their families and future.

Suddenly, the darkening sky was lit up by a single shot emanating from the tower. The evening air in seconds had transformed into living rivulets of silvery plasma blasts. It had been the wish of every DOK citizen or able-bodied man to get this over and return to a normal life, and now after months of waiting and preparation, their chance had finally arrived.

Before long, the constant plasma gun recharging had caused the generator to blow a circuit breaker, and a maintenance team was quickly dispatched to repair it. While they waited during the six eternal minutes for the energy source to come back on line,

Anthony and a few others were impatiently detonating rocket-propelled grenades from the tower into the dense areas of infected. Matthew, like all of them, was pointing, shooting, and recharging his plasma rifle. His stomach twisted this way and that, as if it were an animal trapped inside of him. Perspiration gathered over his whole body, a symbolic film of his repressed terror. Without Steve's knowing, it would be the last time he would see him.

It all seemed so easy, the thousands against their twenty million. They moved slowly. Often, they crawled towards DOK, these once-human beings. But even at their ridiculously slow speeds, DOK had weak points. At one stage, a large group of infected advancing towards Sector Six managed to get within three hundred metres of the wall.

The hours wound down, and the statistics of the assault remained anonymous until their numbers finally began to dwindle seven hours later. It was during that time that more than two hundred plasma rifles had burnt out. Two of them had exploded. It was also during those seven hours that no one had said a word. Sometimes Steve could make out an occasional scream, or shout emitted by anxiety, but apart from those excited voices, there was only silence and the distant murmur of infected.

By five o'clock, it was over. Mara was exhausted as she switched off the plasma rifle and turned towards Steve. She didn't have to say anything. Her expression did the talking. The wall-stalkers were in the same condition, as some of them went down the ladder in the hands of others.

During the shootout, more than twenty thousand people had managed to hide in the equipped shelters behind the school and in the church interior. After the battle, they appeared on the surface one at a time. Their terrified faces transformed into a tired glee as they appeared outside and into the amethyst-blue of early morning.

Tired, Steve walked to the Security Centre and switched on the shortwave radio to see if there were any more survivors. Unhurriedly, he swept the bands and flicked switches. From longwave to shortwave, the only perceptible sounds he heard were that of random hissing and the occasional solar murmur. The Morse code had disappeared, and the radiotelegraphy had vanished. DOK 16 was alone on Earth. Even the transmissions Steve had once received in Russian had perished. The Asian-European continent was deathly silent. Inspiringly, he twiddled the dial to 702 KHz with the hope of hearing that familiar and well-trained Afrikaans accent from Pretoria. The hiss and crackle ate into his mind. Had DOK 16 really been victorious this day, or was this foul game going to continue?

Sanchez radioed from the tower. "Sir, there's nobody. It's as if they were never there to begin with. I've looked everywhere. It's as if the ground just came up and swallowed them."

Steve rushed up the stairwell after Sanchez's communication and took hold of the telescope. Sanchez was right; there was nothing, no one. In the place of infected, creosote bushes and cacti laden with their bright pinkish winter flowers beautified the land.

From his position high in the tower, Steve saw the sun before the long shadows touched the wall below. But there was more: as the rounding orb gently lifted, a sharp flickering caught Steve's attention. Turning the Bisley magnification wheel to maximum, he swivelled it towards the ominous shimmering source close to the hillside four kilometres out. It was one of their Jeeps. The glimmer must be from a window or side mirror moving in the desert wind. It blinked with a constant flicker.

Steve contacted Anthony on his communicator. "Anthony, are you still with us?"

"Of course, what's up?"

"Put together a recon team. These things couldn't have just vanished. They have to be somewhere. While your team's at it, recuperate some of those stolen vehicles, I've caught sight of one northeast of here about three or four kilometres out."

"Consider it done."

Five minutes later a recovery vehicle stormed out the front entrance with six DPF heads bobbing out of the false roof. The driver was a worker Anthony had specifically selected from an unusually tough group of nobodies.

Steve watched as it methodically made its way towards the winking Jeep. Farther and farther it went until it became nothing more than a slow-moving, insignificant boxed outline barely perceptible against the immensity of the wasteland.

Through the telescope, Steve watched it reduce speed and stop as it pulled alongside the derelict Jeep. One of the DPF jumped out and climbed into the stationary Jeep, and within seconds, it started on its homeward journey. Metres from the recovery vehicle, the Jeep suddenly disappeared from view in the same eerie manner Tino's Jeep had. Its heavy metallic form dropped like a stone down a hole. The moment it disappeared, infected began appearing from their subterranean hideouts, and in less than a minute, dozens became hundreds.

Steve was experiencing déjà vu as the crumpled Jeep only moments from salvation began exuding smoke from the engine compartment. Seconds later, it caught fire and exploded. Luckily, the DPF driver had miraculously climbed out before the Jeep blew. The remaining DPF from the roof relentlessly fired their plasma rifles towards the advancing nightmare, endeavouring to rescue their fallen comrade. The infected hid in their trapdoors the same as a spider broods on its prey. The gruesome scene was over in minutes. The driver was already covered by hungry infected, adding his name to the ever-dwindling list of human citizens. The smoke from the Jeep, a grey dissipating diagonal cloud, marked the spot where a sane man once stood.

After the conversion of their comrade, the salvage team didn't attempt more rescues. It could only think of its self-preservation. The only radio contact Steve ever had with the salvage Jeep lasted four seconds.

"Sir, the ground is covered by trapdoors. You have to look carefully to see them. They are everywhere!"

The transmission ceased and the hysterical voice was abruptly cut short by a whelp. A large rock hit him just above the ear. As the officer fought with the genetic reconstruction, one of the others vaporised him. Steve saw the entire spectacle from his vantage point a few kilometres away.

Sanchez was also watching. He lowered his optical instrument in dismay the instant the DPF was vaporised. "I knew that man," he said, stumbling.

"Shall we send out another Jeep to rescue the salvage team?"

"No. They have to make it back on their own," Steve said.

Sanchez resumed viewing through the telescope. The driver exited the vehicle with his plasma rifle, and began his own feud upon the advancing infected. Projectiles came from every direction. Steve saw the five of them ducking until another reached its target. Then shortly afterwards another one struck a worker on the face. He fell down quietly. The remaining three DPF panicked. One of them vaporised the worker and the infected DPF and jumped down to assume control of the Jeep. As he did so, he began squirming like a snake.

"What the hell!" exclaimed Sanchez.

Simultaneously, the two DPF still on the top of the Jeep began to writhe and twist their bodies.

"What the hell is happening out there?" Steve asked. As his words reached inattentive ears, the wind stirred a bit and the infected scurried back to their hiding places in wait for DOK's next move.

"You know, they kind of remind me of hermit crabs. Look how that one is climbing into his lair," Sanchez commented.

A DPF lying on the ground and still undergoing the effects of change on the other end of Sanchez's telescope suddenly disappeared from sight. Sanchez almost dropped the Bisley. "Sir, one of them has just been pulled underground."

By the time Steve had focused the apparatus onto the area, the man had completely disappeared. Steve contacted Gossard to relay the results of the salvage team, and five minutes later, Gossard stepped up onto the roof.

"What do you mean, they started contorting by themselves? How is that possible? You must've missed something!"

"It's like I told you, the three of them started twisting on their own just before they were pulled underground."

There was a silence as Gossard played with Steve's words.

"It's airborne," said Quaid as he appeared on the roof. "Sorry about that, Gossard, I didn't want to interrupt your conversation. It's autumn. There's saguaro pollen in the air." The vacuity actually surprised Quaid. He continued, "Carnegiea gigantea, the cactus. Hello, is anyone listening to what I'm saying? In case you haven't noticed, there are millions of them in full bloom." Quaid made his statement with sarcastic intention. "Each saguaro produces between three and nine flowers, each capable of spewing forth immense quantities of pollen. Need I not reiterate, all it takes is one grain, one tiny microspore to enter the nose, eyes, or mouth? Just a whiff of wind. I won't bother telling you more, the results are quite clear."

Sanchez began to sob. "God, it's in the water. It's in the air. It's in the rain. It's in the snow. It's in the plant and animal life. It's everywhere. We are doomed, you hear? Doomed!"

"Sanchez, it's just the water. Plants and animals need water to survive, just as snow is made of the stuff."

Steve placed the Bisley in its place and everyone went back to the Admin Building. As they entered the front door it began to rain, taking only scant seconds to transform itself into a vigorous cloudburst. It was undoubtedly the strongest downpour they had seen since the hurricane. The sudden shower had taken them by surprise and infected sixty wall-stalkers and two DPF officers too close to the wall. Ten minutes into the storm, seven external cameras in Sector Three became waterlogged and blurred their view in that area.

Steve dispatched a repair team in watertight suits to go and fix the problem. Each suit came with an oxygen bottle and had a communications device implanted inside the helmet to maintain constant contact with the monitor in the Security Centre. The only problem in DOK was the lack of materials used to manufacture the waterproof suits. They only had ninety, so they had to use them sparingly. Matthew had tried synthesizing the material. It was a specially adapted, elasticized cloth providing total flexibility and protection to the wearer.

The rain continued to pelt down while the working cameras revealed no movement on the outside of the city. That was until a general alarm sounded, illuminating all the C-10s at once with a fiery yellow. One of the tower guards had spotted infected prowling about in man-made shadows inside the wall close to Sector Three.

"They are behind Sector Three's Security Complex building! How the heck could they have known the cameras were faulty?" The tower guard's thundering breath rammed against the microphone.

Anthony, without wasting time, sent two DPF to Sector Three.

Steve's C-10 vibrated again. "Sir, they're climbing out of their burrows!"

They had one serious problem: It was still raining, and it proposed a danger to anyone on the wall. Anthony, who was back in the tower and in constant contact with the two DPF, was advising them of their progress. Steve heard the report through his communicator.

"Get a bloody move-on! They're close to inhabited homes!"

Anthony watched as the two DPF officers neared the intruders in amongst a rain of thrown objects. Rocks, bricks, and bottles, anything that was within reach, smashed into their body armour, penetrating their protection gear. As a result, six more DPF were dispatched to finish the job.

Steve selected the best wall-stalkers to assess the situation in Sector Three. The only way they could get near to the wall in order to shoot the advancing threat was to use the last of their protection suits. Gossard and Steve quickly nominated wall-stalkers, and between them, they zipped the men into the suits.

Ninety frenetic shooters climbed the ladders and started pacing the wall while infected thrust forward with renewed vigour after sensing DOK 16's short-sightedness. Not only was DOK outnumbered, the infected were once again uncontrollably advancing towards the city on all points of the compass.

Gossard and Steve were unprepared, having thought only of those few who had gained entrance earlier outside Sector Three. They had forgotten about the thousands that patiently waited outside for the right moment to attack. Most of the stalkers had been allocated to where the infected had entered earlier. A recently arrived wall-stalker in that area informed Steve that there was nothing out there. It was quiet. They'd been tricked, and in an absurd kind of way, Steve knew that the infected would now enter under the walls unseen and begin concentrating on the easy prey.

The only safe position was ten metres from the wall, as splashing rain had already converted more than a hundred stalkers parading too close to its base. DOK was being picked off one person at a time. As innocent stalkers and workers became positive, the DPF knew what to do. It was necessary slaughter.

But even they had human qualities. After cleaning two wall-stalkers, one of the DPF guards smashed his plasma rifle on the ground and started crying.

"I can't take this anymore!" he screamed as he unfolded his fisted hands, wrapping one over his eyes and nose. Removing his sidearm, he placed the barrel into his mouth and pulled the trigger. His pain became everyone's memory. While this was taking place, the concerned voice of a wall-stalker came through Steve's communicator. He heard the familiar sound of plasma fire in the background.

"Sir, we've got thousands of infected about to breach the walls. They are only a short way off!"

Because of their close proximity to the wall, not even the torrential rain was able to wash their stench from the air. It was a thick, unforgettable floating aroma. Steve gagged, clenching his hand over his nose, barely managing to issue orders through the communicator.

The groaning of the infected had transformed into an ululation as the first of them reached their goal, the wall. As they dug with bare hands, Anthony and Steve issued orders to the wall-stalkers; but even in the scant thirty minutes to disperse them, they couldn't be everywhere in the allotted time. DOK had gaps in its defences.

The rain continued, forming a haze, making it hard to see. Anything beyond that limit was pure imagination. Thirty minutes later, the infected began entering under the wall.

Damn rain! Why doesn't it stop? Steve thought. Maybe they'd somehow assumed control of God, as well. Whatever it was, it was a bad day to have the fight of one's life.

As the infected gained entrance into DOK, a rain of objects soared through the air towards defenceless people. Rocks of all sizes hit them wherever they could. As those injured in sporadic battles fell idly to the ground, it already marked the beginning of his or her individual painful conversion process. From every point within DOK, there were these mini-battles. Both small and large groups of individuals were tussling for what they had left.

The infected's strategy was as brilliant as it was simple. Those hiding below ground had patiently waited for the rain to arrive. They'd known the wall would be undefended during a rainstorm. Not only did they attack the stalkers and DPF they encountered, they attacked anyone in their way: women, children, dogs, cats. If it moved, something was hurled at it.

All DOK residents had plasma rifles, yet somehow the infected could distinguish between the residents of this world and the leaders. They knew. They could tell the difference. Doubling their efforts, they concentrated on infecting the leaders first, disabling DOK's line of authority.

The first to go was Rawling. Steve recognised his outline even from a distance of more than fifty metres. Everyone was helpless to assist him as they were too busy fending for themselves. Frantically walking backwards, stumbling over rubble, Rawling was shooting the advancing wave, rarely hitting the targets. Scant metres away from him, they started to chuck their missiles. Steve watched as one smashed into his foot, while another remorselessly came in contact with his face.

"Damn, did you see that?" said Arthur Payne as he and Quaid pulled up beside Steve with their plasma rifles at the ready. "Poor guy didn't stand a chance!"

"Neither do we, if we don't open fire!" said Payne.

Quaid, paying full attention to Payne's hysteria, raised his weapon to eye level and pulled the trigger. Arthur had his eye particularly interested in one group that suddenly appeared from behind a large jutting rock. They were naked and probably were the ones from Alaska or Philadelphia. It didn't matter; they were the hardened, experienced ones, and between Arthur and Quaid, they vaporised many of them.

The diminishing number of infected began picking up objects from the ground. Steve watched as one spat onto a rock and twiddled it around in his hands before chucking it with all his might, barely missing Quaid's face. Instead, it broke into pieces against the wall directly behind him. Quaid disintegrated him. As the rain of objects increased, rocks both large and small missed sometimes by millimetres. At one stage, it appeared they were winning this tiny portion of the war with the infected.

That was when Steve caught sight from the corner of his eye of a rectangular object flying towards them. Instinctively, he ducked, only to hear the sound of splintering bone and the muffled sound of pain. The brick hit Payne full on the chin, smashing his mandible. He fell down silently without alternative. Blood was gushing from his mouth and, as Steve watched, the blood began to change colour. It was losing texture, becoming anaemic. Its intense blackness had slowly turned into a bleached pinkish red.

Quaid grabbed Steve. "Look at his blood. Payne's infected! Look at the speed that thing devours him!"

As both Quaid and Steve looked down towards the crumpled body of Payne, a finger moved. It was a nervous twitch, and Steve positively thought it denoted the end of his life until another finger moved.

Quaid jumped. "Shit, he's coming around. The virus is starting to mend his body!" Quaid was frantic. "Steve, you know it has to be done, don't you? It's him or us!"

Steve stared back at Quaid as Payne began moving his head from side to side. Steve might have killed a hundred men before this, but they weren't like Payne. The killing had been done from a distance, and he had been able to think of his targets as simply the enemy. That made it impersonal, acceptable. But now, with his friend lying here on the ground, Steve could not avoid the truth, could not avoid the fact that he was looking directly into this likeable man's face while he slowly stared back at him. Looking into his open mouth full of bad teeth, an earlobe that had been pierced for a ring that wasn't there now. Steve knew himself incapable of putting this man down. Another brick of equal proportions struck the wall next to Steve, waking him from his anxious state.

Quaid came over. "Steve, you've got to do it. Consider it as a favour to him. He's no longer Arthur Payne. The real Payne died two minutes ago. Steve, he's waking! You have to do it!"

"Sorry, Quaid, I can't," Steve said firmly.

Quaid pushed Steve to one side. "Steve, he's not aware of what's going on anymore. Hell, he didn't even know what hit him. The moment he comes around his only thought will be to infect us both. This is not the man we grew fond of. He's an impostor, a fake!"

Payne coughed. A small rivulet of pink blood ran from his mouth. Quaid moved himself in front of Payne with his plasma rifle and pointed it directly at his chest. Without hesitation, he pulled the trigger.

"Sorry, old pal," said Quaid as the liquid plasma rammed against Payne's chest, instantly wrapping his body in a reddish glow. Within a second, the plasma energy changed colour from its dull red to bright orange.

As this was happening, Payne distressfully glimpsed up at Steve from within his orange cage. Steve forgave him for what he had become, and felt sorry for the man he knew and liked.

Payne, in his colourful world, wasn't sure of what was going on. Still capable of thought, fear emblazoned his face as the orange haze gained intensity. The gruesome spectacle was followed by yellowy blotches disintegrating his skeletal structure. A second later, Arthur Payne wasn't where he'd been moments before. A simple, blackened burn mark was all that remained of this wonderful man.

Steve's attentiveness was restored as another projectile hit the wall nearby. Their aim was improving, and instead of thinking of Quaid, Steve's own safety became a priority. The conflict would last only another ten seconds as a cement brick probably weighing three kilos smashed into Quaid's face, completely crushing his nose. His last moments would remain on Steve's conscience forever.

As his muscular body fell down like the brick itself, Steve was sure that if Quaid wasn't unconscious, he was dead. His crumpled, inanimate remains exuded lifelessness. Uniquely, his only contribution to those who would ever see him in this state was an unforgettable expression of total shock. Blood streamed from his mouth and twisted nose. His wide-open eyes fixated on nothing. That day, that moment, Steve was Quaid's only witness. Steve had become his priest and his family at the funeral pyre. An invisible scattering of close friends moved closer to say goodbye and pay their final respects.

Steve's momentary sadness was shattered as five more infected moved closer. Slowly bending down to pick up rocks, Steve watched as they spat onto them, twiddling them about in their hands like bread dough. Steve, now remorseless, raised his weapon long before they did and disintegrated them.

Suddenly something caught his eye, something close. It was Quaid's finger. It twitched, beckoning; Steve's attention moved toward him. Without thinking twice, he raised his still-smoking plasma rifle just as another brick smashed into the wall above his crouching head. Steve pointed the rifle towards Quaid and pulled the trigger. Like Arthur, Quaid's form fizzled and vanished in an orangey-yellow fanfare.

Alone for the first time in hours, Steve felt the wind blow across his face. A distant plasma shot snatched his attention away from the breeze and made him look towards the tower. Anthony must still be alive. He must be fighting with the infected wall-stalkers trapped inside with him. It was only a short battle before silence once more gripped the plaza. Anthony was still human, too.

Desensitised and uncompassionate, Steve returned his thoughts to his present predicament once more as a bottle smashed against the wall of the Security Centre. Following it, a half-brick went through a window to his left, abruptly ending its voyage against a monitor. Smoke appeared from the ventilation gauze, and the once-functioning coloured image faded.

In the distance, wall-stalkers and DPF were holding their hands on their heads screaming in pain. Fear-struck and scared out of his wits, Steve ran to the Jeep amongst a rain of objects and drove off. Steve's world was crumbling and he felt helpless. His only goal was to reach the house and collect the only thing of valuable he had left, and make their way to the hideout. He leapt from the Jeep like an athlete and ran towards the door. There came no reply as Steve shouted Mara's name. A tear ran down his cheek. Orson wasn't anywhere either. The doggy basket Mara had made for him and placed in the kitchen was empty. Steve searched the house and finally went into the bedroom to find her lying on the bed, holding her hand.

"Darling, what happened?" Steve gaped at Mara. Her features were firm and set, her skin a deep olive in colour. She was dressed in a black, thigh-length jumpsuit with matching boots and gloves. Her hair streamed down past the small of her back. She wore a dark shade of lipstick and had somehow painted wide black circles around both eyes. Now turning to face him directly, the dark pit of her mouth opened slightly; she seemed to be trying to smile.

"Orson went mad. He bit me for no reason. I went outside to take a look at the commotion, and that was when he suddenly jumped up and bit me on the hand for no reason." Mara began frothing at the mouth.

Damn, Orson must have encountered those infected who came in under the wall. "Was Orson wounded when he bit you?" Steve asked piercingly.

Mara was suddenly having great difficulty concentrating and waited for almost a full minute before she uttered, "His back was bleeding."

Steve looked away from the answer. The infected hadn't only destroyed his life, they had almost certainly infected his wife and eaten their dog.

Mara leapt from the bed. Her long black hair began falling out in chunks, and a tiny lump made an appearance on her forehead just above her black, now slightly bluish eyes. They ogled at Steve with an unaccustomed hunger, making her tremble at his proximity. Steve seemed to excite her as she got closer with outstretched arms.

Seeing this, he could only cringe and go hysterical. Knowing the impossibility of the situation, Steve headed towards the still-open doorway and ran for dear life. Steve ran from the house as he'd never run before and climbed into the Jeep. Slamming the door and locking it, he placed his forehead on the steering wheel and cried. He was there maybe two or three minutes before Mara's languid, still transforming body ambled out the front door down the pathway towards the Jeep. She didn't recognise him as she bent down and picked up a large rock next to the pathway. Jesus, she looked horrible. Steve tore away from the sight of her gruesome body and started the Jeep just in time to see the rock hit the road where he'd been moments before.

In Sector Seven, Steve would subjugate himself until this nonsense was over. Parking the car alongside the Security Complex, his first sensation was a null quiescence as the engine stopped. It was deathly quiet—no one, nothing, not even a wind stirred. Even the wretched rain had stopped. Stashed away in the back of the Jeep, Steve had a couple of litres of reserved water for the radiator and a bag of dog biscuits Quaid had given him for Orson.

"Full of tasty doggy vitamins," he'd said. Steve had eaten one in a vague attempt at enticing Orson to eat his food. It was the week the dog was ill. They were a bit stale, as they'd been in the Jeep for over a month, but all the same, it was a five-kilo bag and should last for some time. Steve picked up the bag with the two plastic bottles of water and made his way towards the shelter.

As the door silently opened, a cold, damp uninhabited muskiness made him rewind his thoughts to a good old home-sweet-home. Without further choice, Steve went inside, locked the door, placed the bag of dog biscuits down on the far corner beneath the bookshelf, and literally fell to the ground, and exhausted, went to sleep.

Three hours later, Steve woke to a hushing, off-tone wind hitting the peephole. Rubbing his aching back and unnourished eyes, he got up to have a look. Steve could see that the sun had lowered as an ever-lengthening shadow produced by the nearby Security Complex had draped the Jeep. Steve began to think of the cold that was due in any moment like an unwanted visitor. Soon, he'd have to huddle himself into a ball on the floor to keep warm. He walked to the chair and sat down, wondering if it would be enough.

Vulnerable and alienated, Steve began to fidget in the already lowering light and uneasily got up from the chair again to look through the viewing hole. Strips of darkening crimson cloud floated toward the horizon and disappeared over a distant hillside. As the patchy red carpet turned a murky grey, Steve knew the sun had gone and left him to fend for himself in this new nightmare world.

Steve began to tremble. Now, he had nothing to look at. He could only look toward the imaginary floor or wall, or towards where the chair was. Most of the time he would have to get up from the chair and look through his viewing hole just to make sure the world was still there. At best it offered a gloomy dullness that reminded him a bit of the natural light inside a subterranean cellar. The safe space of Steve's came equipped with its own signatory dankness that provoked his imagination still further.

As the temperature descended, Steve started imagining the small rectangular ray of sunlight trespassing onto his side of the door in the morning. But it was only 7:15. He had another eleven hours to wait. Tiny phosphorescent green dots on his watch, signifying the twelve five-minute intervals, clearly marked the time of day. Mara's father had given the watch to him just before he passed away six years ago. His name elegantly inscribed on the underside, it had been a gift from the plastics company he'd worked for twenty-five years of slavery reduced to a watch. Angrily, Steve got out of his chair and felt his way towards the door again. He'd always loved that man. He'd always been there in the good and the bad, ready to offer good advice.

Way in the distance, dozens of ambling silhouettes and shapes began to accumulate and roam in random directions. Where Steve was in Sector Seven, there was nothing. A simple Security Complex didn't contain anything of value or interest, especially this one. Hell, it wasn't even fully equipped yet. Out here, there was nothing of importance. Where could they go and what the dickens were they looking for? Maybe they were looking for him, thought Steve. He played with the idea. Was he the last survivor of this crazy world? Who did they think they were? Why were they doing this? Whatever or whomever they were, they would surely be familiar with the weakness of the human spirit. They would know Steve would eventually break and come out from his hiding place.

Steve returned his thoughts to Quaid and his infernal words. "It won't stop until all the water molecules have been infected." They jiggled about in Steve's head, then the image of Quaid returned, lying on the ground in that final deathly state.

The ground began to rumble. It didn't feel like a typical Earth tremor, it was too shallow, too abrupt. Steve readjusted his sight in time to see a distant, orange fiery tongue lapping its way upwards towards the night sky. An explosion. That was odd. What was going on out there? A dim, rectangular, shadowy cold-yellowed light danced on the wall behind him. Suddenly, without warning, DOK's protection shield fizzled away like a fluorescent light, darkening Steve's surroundings beyond the blackness he had accustomed himself to. *Oh God, someone, or something, had turned off the city's power.*

Steve helplessly felt his way to the back of his hideout while a million thoughts rattled through his brain at the same time. Infuriatingly, he brushed them to one side and sat down on his chair. He nervously put his hand into the bag of dog biscuits. He sucked and chewed a couple until only the faint taste, which, by his feeble gastronomic knowledge, resembled or better still tasted like dill, had subsided.

After his meal, he looked into the absolute darkness once more and began to think of Mara out there, all alone. Where was she? Was she all right? Bitterly, he looked down at his watch again. Only an hour had passed since sunset. What am I going to do with my time? Steve jittered, thinking about Mara's dad. He'd loved that man more than he had loved his own father. Steve remembered that her father had accompanied them to Steve's dad's funeral, holding on to his hand with this big-brother attitude. Truth was, it was a different kind of love. Steve's dad never had time for him. He'd always hushed him to one side when he needed fatherly closeness.

"Go and ask your mother," he would say, or "Can't you see I am busy!" or just simply, "I haven't got a bloody clue, why don't you go speak to your school teacher?" In spite of all that, Steve missed him very much. Steve thought of what he would do and say if he were here with him now. Would they be laughing about their numerous stupidities of the past?

Steve wondered if his father would at least give him a hug and say, "I'm sorry for being such a rotten sod all these years." Maybe Steve was just being too hard on him. After all, a part of him was diluted into Steve's soul. He was still his dad, always would be. It didn't matter what he'd done, or who he was. These were things no one could change. Steve didn't care. He would hug him with a love he'd never shown. Steve would hug him until there were no more tears left, until the water in his body had been all used up.

Steve trembled again, running his hand up and down the arm of the chair. It had been made right there in DOK. One of the workers had slapped it together for him during the weeks they sat twiddling their thumbs in April. One morning, Steve found it lying idly next to the Jeep, so he brought it into his hiding place the same day. It was a wiry-framed, lathe-turned chair. The worker who'd made it turned out to be the brother of Ted, the man he'd helped in the protection shelter before the hurricane struck.

Disengaging Ted and better days, Steve returned to the floor and put his head on his knees, thinking about everything and nothing at the same time. He'd also noticed the green dots on his watch had begun to fade, and by the time ten o'clock came, his teeth began to chatter. Steve became irritated at himself for not being able to stop it. He started telling himself that everything would be all right in the end, and that Mara wasn't really infected. Steve also tried convincing himself that he was just a victim of some nightmarish prank. He rubbed his eyes with the intention of wiping away the misery, opening them again, then everything would be as it was before. But, as Steve walked once more to the door and peeked outside with a dose of renewed inspiration, the protection barrier was still off, and the uncontrollable fire maliciously continued lapping at the night sky. Steve cursed loudly, reached into his jacket pocket and took out his Kodak grasp lantern. Steve started thinking of it providing heat, but there again these were only light-emitting diodes; they never produced heat, only light. It enabled the charge stored in the rotary worm mechanism capacitor to last for hours. The quality of silvery light it produced left much to be desired, but at least he wouldn't be totally in the dark.

To keep himself warm, Steve traipsed around in small circles and flapped his hands on his side. By 1:00, the fire had engulfed the Administration Building, so he began forcing his attention to the moonless exterior. People shapes were definitely moving about out there. A sound or a scrape occasionally intimidated his imagination. Sometimes they even came close to the door.

At 4:00, one of the people shapes trudged directly in front of his hideout. A slow, faceless shadow bobbed its head maybe a metre from his eyes. Steve silently jumped back in fright. Steve's adrenaline level and pulse rate raced and he thought, *Hell, if he'd seen me, he would've warned the others*. The dragging, followed by a rancid pong, made Steve gag. Had he seen the light from the lantern?

Steve trampled lightly back to his chair, feeling helpless, and grabbed two handfuls of dog biscuits. He had to rest. Tomorrow he would sneak outside and find a blanket and more water. In the darkness, Steve could only stare at the view hole. Time moved so bloody slow. Truth was, it didn't seem to move at all. Steve was alive, with an urgent need of an impossible sleep. He scrambled around more, jiggling himself on the chair with his hands on his lap. But flapping hands was often not enough, so he frequently leapt from the chair in order to keep himself warm.

These abrupt attacks of annoyance Steve blamed on the thought of Mara walking past without him knowing. Although Steve wouldn't see her in the darkness, he thought of her constantly, and wondered what he would do when he did see her. Would he shout her name? Would he open the false door? Leap outside and grab her, looking into those oh-so-dark eyes, or would he feel the warmth of her body against his? It was these emotional thoughts in the end that helped him fall asleep.

The first night Steve didn't dream. Rather, his inauguration spawned a nightmare enhanced by the outlandish occurrences of that day. Before he eventually curled up on the floor next to the chair, he swept up some of the accumulated dust into a pile with one of his books and used it as a pillow. Finally, sleep came quickly.

Thundering whammy! They'd discovered where Steve was hiding. Look at that queue, longer than the horizon itself. As they pushed open the door and waffled in, inspired by an instinctive abdominal groan, Steve knocked them unconscious with a rock he'd taken from the foundation remains. Outside they were jumping up and down like a fallacious Xhosa tribe reciting ancient hymns, spiritual hoo-hah, and ecclesiastical gibberish in an attempt to convert him.

Suddenly, a brick hit him in the face. That was when Steve woke with severe lumbar pains and extreme cold. The phantom queue of infected had provoked a deep inner fear in him. Not only did he fear what they were and what they could infect him with, he detested them. Steve got up from the floor with difficulty and focused his eyes into the distance, praying he didn't see the horrendous queue he'd imagined moments before. There was nothing. *Thank God, I must be awake.*

At first light of the forthcoming day, Steve sneaked outside to go to his private toilet ten metres away from the door. But as the day wound into the next and the next, Steve found himself using it less. He watched them, waited for them to disappear, so he could go. Sometimes he waited hours. Once Steve had to go inside his hideout. On the fifth day, the last day of November, his dog biscuits ran out. As he placed the last crumbs into his mouth, he accompanied them with the last sips of water.

December 2034

Not a solitary cloud roamed the night sky. Steve was cold and lonely and, as usual, patiently waiting in the incessant ebony of darkness. Provocative images, ideas, and perturbing thoughts churned like speed-reading. Mentally repressed, Steve found himself immersed in a ridiculous conversation with himself about the existence of miracles and where they could have possibly originated from.

"Miracles, hah. Where was this miracle maker when I needed him? Where was he when billions needed him? If he was really around, he would've done something a long time ago." Steve felt silly hearing him talk out loud to himself. He started feeling more like a prisoner in his own death cell awaiting a sentence where the God he was talking about was to be the judge.

Steve had been stuck there for a week and it seemed longer, he wasn't sure anymore. He vaguely remembered the shadows of seven suns slowly rising on the wall adjacent to the door, but there again it could've easily been eight. Hunger pains had crept in that morning, such spasms Steve had never known anything like it. He was suffering; yet, purposefully he had restricted himself to this way of life for his own benefit, not forgetting the benefits of those still in their normal state on the outside, probably doing the same as he was. If, indeed, any still existed in their normal state.

Fear welled up in him as the pressure increased inside his skull. It was a hideously potent fear, a biological terror that had made him what he was today. But he couldn't afford to lose his wits now. If he began to run blindly in circles, screaming and throwing punches at the empty air, the infected would know where he was.

Steve's peephole on the door was a view to a world he'd once enjoyed. He frequently looked through it, dreaming, imagining, and watching them casually walking out there, spaced like desert grass. It was never the same face, never the same emotionless body that roamed the bare terrain, although he could have sworn he'd seen a few of them more than once. Steve abruptly jerked himself backwards, pushing himself away from the door and clenched his stomach. Oh, the pain. Steve bit into his lip and gripped his abdomen. He knew if he went out there, they would infect him. Where he was, he was safe. *What's the point in being safe? I don't have any food or water*, he thought.

Water, yeah, the human body can survive two to three months on water alone. His head drooped, thinking. Our supplies are probably infected by now. It left him with no alternative. He had to sit this thing out. He had to survive, however long it took. Snapping out of his world of pain and still holding his stomach, Steve peered at his books on the shelf. There are books, yes books, *Twenty Thousand Leagues Under the Sea*. Without hesitation, Steve yanked it out and ripped out two pages from somewhere in the middle. Tearing one of them in two, he stuffed the half page into his mouth and churned it about. It tasted awful. It tasted musty and vaguely moist. Barely capable of mastication, Steve chewed with a dry mouth until the mustiness had vanished and all the moisture had been absorbed by his hungry tongue. Somehow, he managed to swallow. Steve did the same with another ten pages until at least the awful pain in his stomach began receiving a bit of work.

Over the next two days, Steve had eaten all seven of his books from either thirst or hunger. He read it, relived it, and looked at it one last time before stuffing it into his mouth. Melancholic and bookless, he sat down in his chair and began to scratch his head for the umpteenth time. *Damn it, I can run faster than they can*, he thought. *Why don't I get up and run to the Jeep and get away from this wretched place?*

His thoughts returned to Mara. Mara wasn't fundamentally herself anymore. She had already gone. Only her physical shell remained, and yet even that had changed. Either God had somehow taken her soul home to his bosom while leaving her body to roam, inhabited by the entity into which she had evolved, or he had abandoned her. If that was the case, he would abandon all of them.

I trust in the mercy of Christ, because I have nothing else to live for. I believe, because who I once confided in had left my side forever. Therefore, if I believe, I must conform to my faith and save as many as I can. Steve began laughing at his own stupidity. Why would he knowingly save those who are trying to destroy him? Maybe it was because they had what he wanted. The thought of trying to reason with them flashed through his mind. Would they listen? He turned away from the peephole and let out a faint sniggering, knowing he was the jackpot, the undeniable pointy thorn wreaking havoc in their sides.

On the tenth day, an infected stopped directly in front of the viewing hole and sniffed the air. Steve trembled, panicking at the sight of him not one metre away from his curious, blinking eye. Was he the same one who stopped outside the door the other night? He was a truly disgusting example. Steve looked into his prosecuting eyes, while the breathing gurgle it made, almost a snore, made the hairs on Steve's arms stand up. Creaking bone joints played dull hollow tunes, and his proximity made Steve gag in revulsion as his body odour crept into the viewing port. Immobilised and silent, Steve studied him.

Truth was, he didn't want to go outside, not because of them or the infection they had. God forgive him, he would be too afraid of facing what Mara had become, what she was. It had been ten days, ten eternally long days without her. Steve tried to imagine her with facial hairs and blue eyes. Instead, horrendous mental images sprouted from the soupy depths of his invention. It made him tremble. His hands longed to hold her, to play with her. They knew her every part. Steve imagined her staring at him with that wonderful loving glare she'd always possessed. He thought of the times they'd joked and held hands while laughing about the peculiarities of others. The games and the love they shared. There was just so much he could think of. He wanted to petition the Holy Mother to intercede with her Son to take Mara from the suffering of this world. If he couldn't come, then Steve would have to somehow do it himself; free her of this torment and liberate her from what she had become.

Time was the all-important factor now. Steve was surely weakening, he could feel it. The disinclination and slowness of it all, the sorrow, and the pains that got stronger every time Steve thought about them. There had to be more people out there. There must be survivors somewhere.

That was, of course, until that same afternoon, from the confines of his sanctuary, he heard a gunshot. He was dozing when the sharp noise suddenly made him jump up from his dusty corner. Maybe we'd won after all, Steve quickly regaining a dull perception and running to the door. Maybe we'd somehow found a weak point in the infected and started to hammer them back. Steve found an urge to go out and help; but as his eye reached the peephole, his apprehension was awarded with the sight of a handful of weakened and hopelessly outnumbered survivors armed with rifles. Somehow, they'd made their way close to Sector Seven.

His impulse to shout, "Get back, sit it out like me," never left his dry lips. Steve could only stare, agape. Haphazardly, the survivors ran about firing their weapons, often missing their targets. It continued until there was no one left. It was as it was before; ravaging infected ransacking the entire area like sniffer dogs. Steve could feel his body weakening without food. Yet, not only was his body disintegrating due to lack of nutrition, his lack of anything to stimulate his mind began affecting his judgment. He recited the alphabet repeatedly, and once he counted to a thousand. Steve was beginning to forget, not only average things, he forgot the name of the town they lived in before coming here. It infuriated him as he sat in the corner for more than half an hour scratching his head, racking his brain.

✳ ✳ ✳

Early the next morning, Steve began to think of the bottled water reserves hidden in the subterranean storage site deep beneath the church. There was tinned food there as well. What if I disguised myself, maybe I could try to walk like them. Would I make it to the storage centre without them seeing me?

Excited, Steve placed his eye close to the door and analysed them from this new perspective. He was looking for a gap, but it seemed that they had some vague idea as to where he was hiding, as no gap came. Wave after wave they passed him. It was during this wait that Steve practised their walk by pacing up and down the short aisle with the same contorted face. He even ripped his clothes, simulating theirs. The imitation of their gurgle was the hardest. To achieve it, Steve had to place his tongue almost to the back of his throat to get the desired effect.

Infuriated, he imagined them breaking down the doors, dozens of them brandishing rocks like sledgehammers. Steve watched as they entered the subterranean storage area, ransacking and smashing everything in sight. His horror continued, as the last of the water reserves seeped into the waiting, hungry, dry sandy floor as invisible lapping tongues pulled it towards a new trajectory, probably an underground cavern filled with infected water far below. Then what about the agua-genies, what would've become of them? Undoubtedly destroyed, like their water reserves, Steve was sure of it. He only wanted one drop, needed one drop. Steve didn't care if it was infected, he just wanted to have that neutral, refreshing taste on his lips again. Steve stopped himself mid-sentence. What in God's name was he saying?

Thinking only of the water and the wonderful effect it would have had, his life began churning about before his eyes. I am but the mere shadow of the man I once was. In a blink of an eye, my life did a U-turn. Transforming from the successful engineer I once was, into this vile environment into which I have been nominated. I have been reduced to the last man on this planet, tiptoeing for my life in a hidden hole, deep within my own creation, hiding from the reason why it had been constructed in the first place.

That evening a vertical crack started making an appearance on his top lip. It felt like a surgeon's cut, and it hurt like crazy.

✳ ✳ ✳

By the time of the twelfth morning, his stomach pains had gotten worse and his lip began to bleed. He started to panic. *Why me?* he thought, *Why? Maybe they were normal people out there after all. Was I hallucinating? Maybe they were just trying to find me, rescue me.* Steve had this awful urge to suddenly go outside again and run up to one, so he stood up with forgotten agility, walked to the door and stared through the peephole.

As before, some of them were naked. They were hitting one another, kicking one another, spitting at one another. Damn, these couldn't be normal people, Steve said to himself, moving away from the peephole. They just couldn't be.

Later that afternoon, a severe headache crept in, so for the rest of the day Steve sat in his corner and massaged himself on the neck. His headaches had gradually gotten worse over the last few days, and he'd often blamed them on his dehydration as well as lack of nutrition. His confirmation of this was seeing Mara's deteriorated condition before he left her to come to his hiding place. Steve missed her like hell and just wanted them to be together again. She would nurture Steve back to health, he knew she would. He needed to smell her close to him, feel her warmth. He had to end whatever she'd become, whatever she'd turned into before she became one of THEM.

In a fit of rage, Steve kicked his Windsor chair and watched it fall into pieces. Dust flew upwards as legs, supports and splinters clinked to the floor. Resinous glue came adrift from the joints and formed transparent globules that disappeared into the dirt.

Keenly, he picked up a leg, wondering why he hadn't thought of it before, and started to gnaw it. The thing tasted waxy, and he was sure it contained little or no vitamins to help his headache or present physical condition. Steve chomped into it and slowly narrowed it down until large splinters managed to form tiny beads of spit in his mouth. It was because of this peculiar new intake of nutrition that a strangely painful dry diarrhoea established itself, adding one more problem to his health list. His excrement, reduced to a half hard, half liquefied, dull orange mess, was coming out in lessening amounts, and he had found them extremely distasteful. Steve was without options—his body needed water. He started to smell himself and looked away, feeling ashamed of what he had become. His muscles, now hardening lumps, began to hurt, and his flabby chin had disappeared, leaving an empty, expressionless, hollowed area.

This immoral life was by far the hardest part of his existence. Keeping his sanity, especially without the essential vitamins he needed, was mere confirmation that without them, his brain would eventually wither and die along with the rest of him.

Later that night, he switched on his torch and looked towards the peephole. He peered at its insignificant off-squared form. It was during one of these jaded moments that he moved his eyesight to the heavens and looked at bright, pointy things. Focusing his mind, he realised something was missing. For more than a week, the blanket of green hazy fuzz that had completely covered the city, offering him security, wasn't there. Instead, the transformed, shifting night air was filled and illuminated by a silvered transparency emanating from a bright yellow balloon high up in the sky.

Vague illuminated shapes were still wandering outside. Some looked familiar when their mysterious semblances ventured close to the door. Steve began to think where he had seen them before, but even these simple thoughts only made his eternal headache intensify. He would often jerk himself away from the door, thinking that they would see him if he made any sudden movements, but often found himself uncaringly smiling at them as they passed by.

Against the nightly horizon to the left of Steve's vision, a plain-looking building crept from the silvered surroundings. It was a security something. Hey, what is that? Someone had parked a big car alongside it. Suddenly, an owl hooted close to his refuge. Its frustrating hooting came from directly on top of his door. Was it telling them where I was? Frustratingly, Steve banged the remains of his Windsor chair against the wall and scared it away. It screeched in fear, and Steve watched its feathered form flutter to a less occupied area.

Every now and then, Steve saw Gossard walk past. He would never forget that face. Once he paused in front of his observation hole, sensing Steve watching him. He sniffed the air like a hound, calling Steve's name in his wolflike manner. Oh shit, how Steve's stomach hurt. Clenching loudly, he ripped out a trouser pocket and shoved it into his mouth. He was trying to reanimate his will to live, but it offered nothing.

* * *

As the fifteenth day began cold and cloudless, Steve watched the sun delicately stretch itself above the horizon, excreting a rectangular smudge of heat on his face. He lapped its life-giving qualities into his void, diminishing frame, alleviating patches of cold, numb facial skin in circular patterns. Enthusiastically, Steve shared the tiny geometric shape with other parts of his body. His only salvation was his patience, but his patience was dying along with the rest of him. It was the hope of seeing Mara that had kept him alive all this time. If it wasn't soon, it would be his rotting corpse that would tell them where he was. He shouldn't even be here now, he should be in another place, a better place, a place where it rains all the time, or where the sun brushes their bodies and caresses the two of them.

* * *

On the sixteenth day after his morning bath of sunshine, Steve saw Mara walk in front of his observation hole. He thought he heard her ostensibly calling his name. He almost fell over his feet as he focused his eyes on her.

"Stephen, where are you?" she said. Her lips didn't move. Neither was she looking in Steve's direction, but the words, those sweet words departing her mouth still managed to excite him in a forgotten way. Was he dreaming? Rubbing his eyes, he looked at her, barely recognising her. He had to look twice just to make sure it was her. Were those the same clothes she had on the last time he saw her?

Steve called to her, but there were no words. His lips, cracked and bleeding, barely squeaked her name. *Mara*, he thought. But she didn't look back. She continued walking around in search of him, purportedly calling Steve's name. Steve thought, *I must give up. Let there be an end to this, a privacy, an obscure nook for me.* Steve just wanted to be forgotten, even by God, so with the last of his efforts and strength, he opened the wall entrance and staggered to the ground, crawling up behind her.

As Steve grabbed her ankle, she looked down without either reconciliation or recognition towards the ankle aggressor and scratched him on the neck. A thin rivulet of red trickled onto his jacket and ran down the sleeve. As some of it dripped onto the ground, it had already acquired a pinkish colour. A tremendous pain made Steve lift both his hands towards his head and scream. Mara, seeing this, gurgled with joy and released a wolflike cry.

Before Steve began to lose consciousness, he noticed for the first time that there were two types of them. One was walking over to come and enjoy the spoils of what lay on the ground, while the other came running towards him. *Is he coming to my rescue?* Steve wondered.

* * *

Meanwhile, far above the Earth and out of harm's way, a couple of complicated zoom lenses whirred themselves off after watching the results at DOK 16 through an infrared telescope.

An inquisitive eye looked below for confirmation and depressed a touch panel as his hand placed a file back into a black briefcase. Equally black words adorned the front cover. They read, "Category two: Sapiens ready for occupation."

Dear Reader,
If you enjoyed this book, please tell your friends,
and write a review on GoodReads.com and Amazon.
Thank you, Michael